5 STAR

A *Willie Mitchell Banks* Novel

MICHAEL HENRY

5 Star
A *Willie Mitchell Banks* Novel
Copyright © 2019 Michael Henry
All rights reserved
ISBN-13: 9781093110951

Author Photography: T.G.McCary
Cover Design & Formatting: Laura Shinn Designs
http://laurashinn.yolasite.com

Other books by this author:
Three Bad Years (2010)
At Random (2010)
The Ride Along (with William Henry – 2011)
D.O.G.s: *The Secret History* (with William Henry – 2011)
Atmosphere of Violence (with William Henry – 2012)
The Election (2013)
Finding Ishmael (2014)
Murder in The Grove (2015)
Delbert Gets Tall (2016)

For more on the author, visit http://michaelhenryauthor.com

REVIEWS

MURDER IN THE GROVE was a great novel, but Mike's newest, 5 STAR, may be his best. It's a great murder mystery with an interesting football element.
—Archie Manning, Ole Miss and New Orleans Saints quarterback

5 STAR is packed with fast-paced excitement and an intriguing plot involving drugs, sex, and college football recruiting. I highly recommend.
—Richard F. "Dickie" Scruggs, legendary American trial lawyer.

Could not put 5 STAR down. Love the Willie Mitchell Banks character. Oxford settings add to the excitement. Mike Henry can really write!
—The Hon. Trent Lott, former MS Senator and U.S. Senate Majority Leader.

CHAPTER ONE

"Do the best you can to play the hand you've been dealt," I said to Jimmy Gray a decade ago in the weeks following the death of his youngest son. Beau was a bright, engaging 18-year-old who bled to death, alone in the woods, after being shot in the stomach when his deer rifle slid from the fence Beau was climbing. The rifle could just as easily have fallen without going off, or discharged in another direction, but it didn't.

My advice to Jimmy sounds shallow and cavalier now as I look back, given my own experience, and especially considering what I have done and what I have become. But at the time I said it, I was trying to convince Jimmy to stop drinking and grieving himself into an early death.

Jimmy said, "Easier said than done, Willie Mitchell," when I gave him the glib advice. He was right. Six months ago, the unthinkable happened to Susan and me. I tried to play the hand I was dealt for a while, but you'll see for yourself that I chose to go in a different direction—a very different direction. I'm not sure how this thing is going to work out over time. I convinced myself at the time it was the right thing to do. I have had many second thoughts.

Well-meaning friends told me after Susan's death, just like they told Jimmy after Beau's death, to place my trust in God. He has a bigger plan.

I'm pretty sure that's not true.

I've never believed the cosmos works like that. Epidemics, deaths, wars, and disasters are not carefully planned and carried out by the Prime Mover.

He doesn't pick winners and losers among the almost eight billion of us on this planet. He doesn't choose sides in a conflict based on who prays the hardest. He endows us with free will, and its flip side, which is "you're on your own." I believe He's a big picture Guy, Who caused the singularity to implode, explode, then spew matter, antimatter, dark matter, energy, dark energy, and primordial gases in every direction. To further confuse us, He not only caused the universe to expand, *but to expand at an ever-increasing rate.*

He set in motion the elements that came together to form the carbon-based life that ultimately resulted in our being here on Earth, a large rock comprised primarily of iron, oxygen, silicon, and magnesium. He designed our rock to have a molten core and to spin at approximately 1,000 miles per hour at the surface. To keep us from being flung off our rock into space, He added gravity. As a precaution, He shrouded our rock with pulsating magnetic fields to protect us from our sun constantly bombarding us with lethal gamma rays.

All quite miraculous, don't you agree? And not something that came together by chance. He had a design. Same with human DNA. How can anyone seriously argue that the human genome, the complete set of nucleic acid sequences, just came together somehow, defying the laws of entropy.

Still, there is no satisfying answer to the question: Why do bad things happen to good people? I've concluded they just do. It's not kismet, fate, karma, destiny, or anything else that implies intentionality.

Bad things have happened to me, and I am sure they have happened to you. Perhaps we didn't deserve these tragedies, but like the bumper sticker indelicately explains: *Shit Happens.*

I'm going to tell you what happened to Susan, the only woman I ever loved, and to El Ray, another bright, wonderful eighteen-year-old youngster robbed of his promising future. Beau Gray, Susan, and El Ray did not deserve their fate, but that doesn't matter. Stuff happens for no reason, and it happens to innocent people. You feel tremendous sorrow, but there it is.

All these events took place within the last six months. For me, it started with Susan's sister calling last June to say Mr. Woodfork probably wouldn't make it through the night.

Susan and I left Oxford within the hour.

Her mother had died six months earlier when a brain aneurysm silently exploded as she sipped her morning coffee at her kitchen table in their home in Mansfield, Louisiana. There had been no warning—no dizziness, headaches, or symptoms of any sort. Mrs. Woodfork was going over her plans for the day with her husband. Seconds later, she was unconscious on the floor. And after a moment or two, she was dead.

"Now it's Daddy's turn to go," Susan said, sniffling and dabbing her eyes, as I drove her Lexus toward Louisiana.

"He's had a good life," I said softly.

Even though what I said was true, it was a mindless banality I'd heard hundreds of times at wakes, and as effective an analgesic as my hackneyed trope, "play the hand you've been dealt." But in fairness, what else is there to say to a daughter mourning the imminent death of the father she loved so dearly?

"Until Mother died," Susan said.

Susan's mother's funeral in January was formal—no eulogies, just a brief message of hope from the Episcopal priest. Susan and her only sibling, Joan, had told the priest that was how their mother wanted it, and he obliged. For me, the most disturbing part of the stay in Mansfield for Susan's mother's funeral was watching Mr. Woodfork go through the visitation and church service. His mumbled responses to well-wishers as Susan and I flanked him in the receiving line were unintelligible at times. He went into shock when his wife died at his feet on the kitchen floor, and never came out of it.

We stayed for three days in Mansfield after Mrs. Woodfork's funeral, trying to help Susan's father cope. Susan's sister, Joan, who lived only an hour away in Shreveport, assured us she would check on Mr. Woodfork every day, in person or by phone.

Mr. Woodfork's decline continued uninterrupted. Grief consumed him. He ate little and would leave the house only to visit his doctors, in spite of his daughters' pleading. The pills he took had no impact on his attitude or well-being; he continued to lose weight. Near the end, his insidious, grief-induced lethargy infected his mental status. He was confused and defeated.

"I'm ready to go," he told Susan and me during our last visit.

And so he did, according to Joan, who called us again that mild June evening as we exited I-20 to head south on I-49 towards Mansfield.

"I should have been there," Susan said to her sister, then cried as she listened to Joan for another ten minutes.

Shoulders shaking, Susan turned toward the passenger window. I put my hand on her shoulder, patting, rubbing gently. There was nothing to say.

"It's okay," she said after a while. "Daddy died at home in his own bed, and Joan said he wasn't in any pain."

"He didn't care about living after your Mother went."

"It's the way I want to go—in my sleep in my bed."

"Not any time soon, please," I said and smoothed her hair.

"Daddy was the last man standing. Now all our parents are gone."

"No one gets out of here alive."

"Right," she said. "Now it's just you and me."

"And Jake, and Scott."

"And Donna. We should make it a point after this to see them more."

"Jake comes to see us when he can. We can't improve on that as long as he's doing what he's doing. Scott and Donna we can try to see more."

"I wish Scott and Donna would start a family."

"When they're ready," I said. "Better now?"

She nodded and patted my hand as we left I-49 and drove into the relentless darkness of rural northwest Louisiana, heading west on the winding two-lane to bury her father.

CHAPTER TWO

Mr. Woodfork's funeral seemed less painful for Susan and Joan than their Mother's. With no surviving parent for them to worry about during and after the service, their Father's death was cathartic in its finality. The ritual was quiet and orderly, just like Mr. Woodfork.

We stayed for several days after the interment to start the legal processes required to unwind his life and distribute his assets to Susan and Joan. We met with the Woodfork family lawyer to probate the will and notify insurance companies and state and federal bureaucracies. Susan and Joan took several long morning walks—therapy walks. Susan told me they alternated crying and laughing—feeling the stress begin to leave them as they put in their miles.

Driving home to Oxford, Susan was subdued, pensive, so I left her to her thoughts. I channel surfed on SiriusXM, keeping the volume low to accommodate her occasional naps. She slept through the transition from I-20 to I-55, during which I studied her face. She was still a classic beauty, in spite of a few lines and small wrinkles, some of which I knew I was responsible for. We had gone through a very rough patch eight years earlier, separating for three of those, when we were in our mid-fifties. I was unhappy with career choices I had made and was drinking way too much, an easy touch for a local woman with whom I got involved after Susan left. To say my sordid dalliance with Mary Margaret Anderson ended badly is a gross understatement.

Susan admitted she had her own issues at the time, obsessively examining her self-worth and wondering what to do with the years she had left. Her three-year absence was a search for "meaning." At times she would substitute "fulfillment," an equally vacuous term. A hallmark of the human condition, I believe, is the chronic inability of our species to be satisfied.

When Susan came home, I said I would try to be a better man.

"Just be yourself," is what she told me, and I said I'd do my best.

A little over an hour from Oxford on the drive home, Susan said she needed to stop.

"No problem," I said. "We're in no rush."

"Sign says Varner exit has a BP and an Exxon."

"Slim pickings," I said. "You sure you want to get off here? I don't think we've ever taken this exit."

"I have to."

I eased Susan's Lexus into the I-55 exit lane and up a hill to a stop sign. The sign said the BP station was a tenth of a mile south. The Exxon was closer, but as we neared it, I saw weathered sawhorses blocking access to the Exxon parking lot, where two feral dogs stared hungrily at us as I drove slowly by. Other than the BP station a hundred yards or so in front of us, there were no other buildings or businesses on the road. Nothing to see but oaks and pines in every direction.

"Let's hope the BP has a decent bathroom," I said as I drove slowly toward the BP. "Might as well get gas while we're here."

"I just hope it's open," Susan said.

I pulled off the road and stopped next to the gas pump. There were no other cars at the pumps or parked in front of the store. As I punched the "engine off" button, I spied the store clerk inside at the checkout counter.

"There are signs of life in the store," I said.

"Thank goodness," Susan said as she hustled out of the car.

I stood by the pump and watched Susan stop inside the glass door and speak briefly to the clerk. The clerk pointed and Susan nodded as she walked toward the back of the store. I swiped my Visa and entered our zip code. When the screen gave me permission, I began pumping fuel. I searched for the trigger to hold the nozzle open, but it had been removed—probably an indication of the owner's assessment of the character of his clientele.

I watched the money numbers spin, a blur compared to the gallon count. The store was clean outside and the pumps relatively new. The inside appeared updated as well. The clerk glanced at me. He was young—either Indian or Pakistani—most likely the owner or son of the owner. I wondered how he could make a go of it in this isolated spot in North Mississippi, serving only the interstate traffic and the sparse population living in the surrounding woods.

I felt the warm summer wind change directions, delivering a strong whiff of the gasoline I was pumping. I turned my head to avoid it and saw an older model, dark green Ford Expedition leaving the interstate exit lane and heading our way. I watched it move slowly past the shuttered Exxon. As it neared the BP, the Expedition was barely moving, its occupants no doubt giving the isolated store the once-over before pulling in, like Susan and I had.

The Expedition came to a stop on the other side of my pump. It was gigantic, at least ten years old. Its long-neglected finish was dull and dusty, worn off in a couple of places on the hood.

I switched hands on the nozzle, and glanced inside the Ford. The driver was a woman, with a dark tan or perhaps Hispanic ancestry. I heard the heavy Expedition passenger door shut and glanced up to watch a young man as he walked toward the store, hands in the pockets of his faded red windbreaker. I caught a glimpse of his face, enough to tell he was a light-skinned black man with an unruly Afro and loose-fitting, torn jeans. White tendrils of denim thread dragged the concrete behind his flip-flops.

I turned back to the woman driver. She was staring intently, following her passenger.

I glanced at my pump readout. Thirty-five dollars and change. I watched the passenger stop at the entrance, look back at the woman driver and wink.

I felt the hair on the back of my neck bristle. Windbreaker?

I took my hand off the nozzle trigger and hurried to open the Lexus passenger door. I reached under the seat and pulled my .38 caliber Chief's Special revolver. Not much of a weapon, but it would have to do.

I heard two loud gunshots inside the store, then two more. I bent over and ran toward the store, pointing my .38 at the front door.

I was almost there when the passenger burst out of the store firing his semi-automatic pistol at me.

They told me later I got off two rounds.

CHAPTER THREE

Susan died inside the BP, four days after she had buried her Father, 185 days after she buried her Mother. The Tallabusha County coroner said Susan's death was instantaneous—the .45 caliber bullet had shattered her heart.

In the months after Susan's death, each day in the condo seemed to last an eternity. On one of those bleak, endless afternoons, I grabbed my weathered copy of Joseph Heller's *Catch 22*. I searched for and found a passage that intrigued me the first time I read it in college.

Heller's protagonist, Captain Yossarian, was a bombadier in the U. S. Army air corps in World War II. He would lie in his bunk when he wasn't on a dangerous bombing run over Italy, eyes glued to the second hand on his watch. Convinced that each bombing run would end in his death, he wanted every moment of his life last as long as possible. Focusing on the plodding arc of the second hand made time pass very slowly for Yossarian.

Unlike Yossarian, I wanted time to pass at the speed of light.

Five long months or so after Susan's death, I parked my truck in one of the spots marked VISITORS on the loop in front of the Lyceum, Ole Miss's elegant Greek Revival administration building. I walked through misting rain to the shelter of the east side portico, briefly scanning the massive white columns and the front wall of the building in another futile effort to find the infamous bullet holes from the 1962 Meredith riot.

They say the pock marks were intentionally left unrepaired as a reminder of Ole Miss's part in the violent struggle resulting from the federal government's push to integrate public institutions in the Deep South. But I've never been able to find the holes, confirming again my belief that stories of Mississippi's troubled racial past are part apocryphal, part factual. These days, the distinction doesn't really matter. Everyone wants to believe the worst about Mississippi.

I brushed drops of moisture from my navy blue blazer, straightened my red knit tie and entered the front doors. It was the first time I had set foot inside the historic building since Susan and I moved to Oxford full-time over two years earlier.

I gently fingered the scar that began at my hairline in the center of my forehead, a souvenir of our stop at the BP. Even five months later, it remained painful to touch. "A kind of phantom pain," my doctor and friend in Sunshine, Nathan Clement, told me.

The Tallabusha Hospital E.R. doc who treated my BP wound the evening Susan and I were shot went on about how lucky I was. Said the bullet ripped the skin off but fortunately ricocheted off my thick skull, causing a lot of bleeding and immediate unconsciousness, but no permanent damage. I had studied the crime scene photos for many hours. A huge puddle of blood marked the spot on the BP's concrete pad where I face planted after being shot.

The youthful murderer must have thought he had blown off the top of my head, his conclusion buttressed by the bloody deluge from my forehead. So, the young E.R. doc was right. I was fortunate to survive. Susan was not so lucky.

I paused on the rich blue carpet covering the Lyceum's ten-foot-wide central hallway. The hall ran the length of the building, like a formal, enclosed dogtrot, to matching doors on the west side, which were protected under an identical portico. I read the brass plaque in the wall detailing the construction history of the building, the central part built in 1848 and identical wings added in 1903, forty years after the Lyceum was used as a hospital in the Civil War. I studied the facsimile of the building in relief on the plaque, admiring the symmetry and logic of the design.

The empty hallway was silent, evoking in me the same hushed reverence I feel when I enter an empty church. If ghosts exist, there are bound to be some living in the Lyceum, including the spirits of two men murdered in the Grove on the east side of the Lyceum the night of the James Meredith riots, September 30, 1962. One was a local juke box repairman, purportedly in the Grove to experience the excitement, felled by a stray bullet. The other, a reporter for a French newspaper, was assassinated, shot in the back at close enough range to leave powder burns on his shirt.

I remembered a particularly stark black and white photograph in Ed Meek's Meredith photo collection, taken by Ed in 1962 when he was an intrepid reporter for the Ole Miss newspaper covering the riot. It portrayed the mound of long guns on the Lyceum basement floor confiscated by the four hundred U.S. Marshals who ringed the Lyceum that September night. The marshals had been ordered not to defend themselves or fire their weapons. They were easy targets for the violent non-students, non-locals who surrounded them, angry white men from all over the South who had assembled that night in the Grove to fight the federal government's integration order.

I walked through an opening off the Lyceum's central hallway leading to the reception desk.

"I have an appointment with the Chancellor," I told the receptionist, an attractive black woman who could not have been more than nineteen. "Willie Mitchell Banks. Eleven o'clock."

She moved her cursor, studied the screen a moment, and entered something into her keyboard.

"I've let them know you're here, Mr. Banks. Please have a seat."

"Are you a student?" I asked her as I took a seat.

"Yes, sir."

"Where are you from?"

"Tupelo," she said.

"I moved here a couple of years ago from Sunshine."

She nodded, but I could tell she had no idea where Sunshine was.

"It's in the Delta. Yaloquena County."

"Yes, sir," she said, breaking off our momentary eye contact.

A well-dressed young white man with a buzz cut stepped out of the door marked "Office of the Chancellor" and walked toward me, extending his hand.

"Mr. Banks? I'm James Braswell, the Chancellor's assistant. Good seeing you this morning. Follow me, please."

I followed James through a narrow hallway into the Chancellor's office.

"Good morning, Mr. Banks," the Chancellor said, walking around her desk to greet me. "I'm Clare O'Donald."

"My pleasure, Chancellor O'Donald. We met briefly in a receiving line at an alumni function shortly after your installation. But, I don't expect you to remember. You met hundreds of people that night."

"Oh, I'm sure we did," she said, gesturing for me to take a seat and returning to her chair. "Frankly, my first few months here were a blur. I've met so many nice people. Everyone has been very cordial and welcoming. It's certainly true what they say about hospitality in the Deep South."

"Charlottesville is also below the Mason-Dixon line."

"Virginia's rapidly diminishing cordiality is nothing like Mississippi's hospitality, Mr. Banks. With millions of U.S. government employees living or working in Fairfax, Arlington, and the counties west of D.C., Mr. Jefferson's Commonwealth is now more like the Northeast than the Mid-South. Take my word for it."

"So I've heard. How do you like Oxford and the University so far?"

"I love it," she whispered dramatically. "During the hiring process, I was impressed with the educational opportunities here at Ole Miss. Not what I was expecting when I was first contacted, I assure you. The Honors Program is one of the finest in the country. Very active and supportive alumni organizations. It's hard for me to believe I've been here almost two years."

From articles online at HottyToddy.com, I knew Clare O'Donald was mid-fifties, unmarried and no children. She was a fleshy endomorph with a warm smile and welcoming eyes, obviously not a fan of exercise. *Matronly* was the unfortunate description that came to mind—not unattractive, but hard to picture as a sexual being. *Portly* was the equivalent adjective for overweight men of a certain age, a designation I would confer only on my worst enemies.

The media pieces said Clare O'Donald was a New Hampshire native and a Dartmouth graduate, with a post-graduate master's degree in history from Emory, and a PhD from UVA. She converted her dissertation on the 17th Century royalist Sir William Berkeley, the longest serving governor of Colonial Virginia, into a well-received non-fiction book entitled *Sir William Berkeley and the Cavaliers*. The book endeared her to the UVA extended family because the school's official mascot was the Cavalier, a mounted swordsman sporting a feathered three-cornered hat like the Three Musketeers. Moreover, it was no doubt enlightening for the citizens of Charlottesville to read about a noted Virginian not named Thomas Jefferson.

The Chancellor accepted a tenure-track teaching post in the UVA history department and began moving up the ladder. She was a popular teacher and eventually was awarded a full professorship. After publishing two more books about the mid-Atlantic colonies in the seventeenth century, she moved into UVA administration as Dean of Students, then Provost for six years until she was recruited by Ole Miss to become the first female Chancellor in the history of Mississippi's flagship university.

Not everyone was happy about her selection, including my pal Jimmy Gray, who began referring to her immediately as "the Chancellorette, Aunt Bee." Consequently, every time I read about the new Chancellor or saw her photograph, I was reminded of former Broadway actress Frances Bavier's Aunt Bee, her hair in a bun, puttering around her dining table fussing at Andy and Opie in her high-pitched voice.

Oxford was no longer a sleepy, pastoral village dominated by the politics and economics of the university. In 2000, when star quarterback Eli Manning stepped on campus as a freshman, he jump-started population and economic growth in Oxford and Lafayette County. The expansion and prosperity that began with Eli increased every year. Ole Miss graduates from all over the South were retiring, selling their businesses and practices, and moving to Oxford at an increasing pace, causing property values to skyrocket and construction projects to blossom in every direction. Oxford was bursting at the seams, with city and county officials fighting a losing battle to update and expand the streets and infrastructure to accommodate the boom.

The influx of well-heeled, generally conservative Baby Boomers also altered the political landscape of Oxford, putting a strain on the city's long-standing town and gown relationship. As in most institutions of higher learning, the professors and administrators at Ole Miss continued to be reliably liberal, secure in their tenure-protected cocoon. Jimmy Gray referred to them as "UFOs," short for University Fuck-Offs, but only in the vault-like privacy of our conversations, because he wanted the UFOs' business for our bank.

From my brief review of some of her pre-Ole Miss writings and her official pronouncements since being named Chancellor, I felt fairly certain that Clare O'Donald was no exception. But, as in most conclusions I reach about someone based on what I read in newspapers and online, I knew I might be mistaken.

"There's no 'i' in Clare," I said. "Like the county in Ireland."

"Very good, Mr. Banks. My father's ancestral county. And my mother's family was County Cork."

I nodded, wondering when she was going to tell me why she had summoned me to the Lyceum. I didn't have to wait long.

"Well, let's get to it, shall we?" she said.

Chapter Four

"Lisa Sanders and I have become friends. She asked me to tell you she sends her regards. She speaks very highly of you."

Lisa Richardson Bailey Sanders and I had barely survived the final murderous rampage of Lisa's grandfather, the late Buddy Richardson, a couple of years earlier. Lisa seemed to me as different from the Chancellor as any woman could possibly be. I wondered how they had become friends.

"Lisa is one tough woman," I said. "Haven't seen her in a while."

"Lisa and I are in the same book club at St. John's. She's very intelligent and analytical—an auto-didact, no less. We have coffee together occasionally after the meeting."

"Her grandfather Buddy Richardson was a shrewd operator, a very bad man. Do you know Buddy's history?"

"Yes. Lisa told me about his tenure on the White Citizens' Council and other sordid details. I know what part you played in bringing him to justice."

"A hot hypodermic needle brought him to justice."

"Yes, but your investigation caused his criminal enterprises to unravel, according to Lisa. She said you're a man of unswerving character and strength. Said you saved her life."

"Nice to hear," I said, laughing. "But I'm not sure about that. We were rescued at the same time by some friends in law enforcement."

"She said you were very courageous."

I shrugged and asked her to give Lisa my regards.

"I'd like to hire you, "Mr. Banks. "Lisa says you're independent and strong-willed. I'm not pleased with the outside lawyers representing the University, and our in-house counsel, Mr. Pratt, owes primary allegiance to the University. I want someone to look after me, not my employer."

I had been the elected District Attorney in Yaloquena County for six terms. No one "hired" me to do my job in those twenty-four years—they voted for me. Since stepping down and moving to Oxford a couple of years earlier, I had not practiced law. I was still licensed and in good standing with the Mississippi Bar Association, but I had neither the need or desire to practice law of any kind—especially after Susan's death.

"I don't really practice law," I said to the Chancellor. "And there are personal reasons why it would be difficult for me...."

"I am very sorry for the loss of your wife," she said. "I followed the story in the newspapers and online. The university's in-house attorney, Mr. Pratt, said it would be unlikely you would take on legal work of any kind."

"I'd say Lawrence is right on the money."

"Have there been no arrests in your wife's case?"

"No," I said, thinking it was a good time to bid the Chancellor *adieu.*

"I beg you to consider making an exception," she said. "The University has its lawyers, in-house and outside attorneys. I like Mr. Pratt, but I want you to represent *my* interests, personally and as Chancellor, in the state and federal investigations surrounding the death of Elston Raymond. I also want you to counsel me during the NCAA examination of our football program. They began unofficially nosing around the University after El Ray gave us his verbal commitment at the close of his junior year. Their investigative efforts accelerated after his death ten days ago."

I wasn't expecting her request and didn't know quite how to respond. Aunt Bee thought highly of my courage and character, both of which I had seriously questioned since Susan's death. My forehead scar began to throb as I wondered whether I still had the concentration or confidence to take on the Chancellor's representation.

"You are aware of the death of our young recruit Elston Raymond?"

"I am."

"We have been inundated here at the Lyceum and all over campus with detectives and agents from local and state law enforcement agencies. And the NCAA has a contingent camping out in the athletic department. As you might expect, the NCAA people have a definite opinion about race relations in Mississippi. And in fairness, Ole Miss has a well-known history of racial unrest on campus."

"If you mean the Meredith riots, I'm certain you're aware, Chancellor, that angry and violent acts took place in Arkansas, Louisiana, Alabama, and Georgia in response to the school desegregation orders of the federal courts."

"I know all about the cycle of resistance all over the South following *Brown versus Board of Education*, Mr. Banks. However, Mississippi in general and Ole Miss in particular seem to have been unable to put the stigma of racial intolerance behind them. The other southern states have been allowed by the gods of public opinion to atone for their sins, but not Mississippi."

"On that we agree, Chancellor. Louisiana is now Mardi Gras, Cajun cooking. Georgia is Atlanta, the business capital of the South. Alabama is Nick Saban and championship football. But when my wife and I travelled, and we told new acquaintances we were from Mississippi, we could almost see them shudder. You say Mississippi, and people think only of one thing: lynchings."

"And I believe that to be so unfair to the state and Ole Miss."

"No doubt," I said, surprised at her comment. "Has the SEC been supportive of us thus far in the NCAA investigation?"

She shook her head.

"When the first NCAA investigators showed up here after El Ray committed to us, the SEC powers-that-be met with me a day later in this office, saying all the right things. They spent the rest of their time in Oxford with the NCAA's head of enforcement, an unpleasant sort named Jeffrey Blanchard, and his *apparatchiks*. The SEC people left the following day."

"Have you talked to them since?"

"Briefly. They seem to be avoiding me. I think the SEC management was here long enough to make sure there were no allegations against Alabama, and once they were told that, they lost interest in our investigation. They've hurt us more than helped."

"Well," I said, "SEC headquarters are in Birmingham."

"Seems incestuous to me, but I'm no sports expert."

"Maybe not, Chancellor, but I think you have them pegged."

"I've been told the NCAA has interviewed some of our other recruits who chose to go elsewhere, and have discussed giving immunity to these eighteen-year-olds in exchange for damaging testimony against us. I'm not sure what immunity means in the context of a sports organization, but to offer immunity to recruits who signed with our competitors in the SEC, including the agriculture school southeast of here, whose name I refuse to utter because of their deranged hatred for Ole Miss, is inviting false testimony against us."

"The NCAA has no shame," I said. "They've ruined many careers."

"I do wish you would take my case. I believe a man of your integrity and experience might be the very person to set the record straight by proving that Mr. Raymond's murder had no connection to us. In order to represent me adequately, Mr. Banks, you're going to have to find out why El Ray was killed and who did it."

"I hope your premise is correct, that his murder was not related to his recruitment." I paused. "But what if it turns out that they were connected, or that he was killed because of his race?"

"Well," the Chancellor said, "you and I will cross those bridges if and when we come to them." She paused. "Several attorneys whose opinions I trust have told me you were the best District Attorney in the state, and a very effective courtroom litigant. I do hope you will represent me."

I lowered my head, then stood to leave. Before I could say thanks for the kind words, but no thanks to the job offer, Aunt Bee beat me to the punch.

"It would help me, your alma mater, and your state," she said in an authoritative tone like Mrs. Breda, my favorite elementary school teacher.

"I'll think about it," was all I could muster. "But I'd like to know the real reason why you think you need your own personal attorney. Lawrence Pratt is a smart guy, and honest. I don't know anything about the outside firms hired to represent the school with the NCAA."

The Chancellor hesitated a moment.

"Are you familiar with the litigation arising out of the Rolling Stone article about the so-called 'rape' that took place in a fraternity house at UVA?"

"Yes. Turned out to be a totally made-up story."

"It was. But before it was proven to be fiction, a colleague of mine at UVA was abandoned, or thrown under the bus, which I think is the term in vogue these days, by the school administration. The school's in-house attorney and the big private firm in Richmond were supposed to be looking out for my friend's interests. She was ultimately vindicated and prevailed in litigation for money damages against the school, but the stain on her reputation and harm done to her education career is irreparable."

"That's a very good answer to my question."

"And I have been a good steward of my resources, Mr. Banks. I assure you I can afford your services."

"I'm certain you can, Chancellor O'Donald."

"Lawrence Pratt refers to me as 'Chancellor O'Donald' when we work together on university matters. I'd rather my personal attorney call me Clare."

"All right, then, Clare. And I'm Willie Mitchell." I paused. "Let me think about this and I'll give you an answer shortly."

I walked out of the Lyceum and paused a moment under the portico, still digesting Aunt Bee's words. The misting rain had turned into a steady drizzle, and dark rainclouds in the southern sky promised more to come.

CHAPTER FIVE

"You got to do it," Jimmy Gray said to me in Susan's condo on University Avenue in Oxford.

"I asked for a day or two to consider it." I paused and pointed to his chair. "Susan used to worry when you sat in that chair."

Jimmy Gray was wedged into a Queen Anne-styled chair, his bulk constituting the ultimate test of how well the stuffed arms were constructed. Susan bought the condo and furnished it in the last year of our three-year separation. We used it as a weekend getaway in the five years we remained in Sunshine after getting back together, especially for home football games. It had been our home since we moved to Oxford full-time two years ago.

"You want me to sit somewhere else?"

"Nah," I said. "You can wallow in it all you want. I don't care."

"I think I'm stuck anyway," he said, wiggling his big frame and moving the chair with him. "By the way, I got the new title from DMV on Susan's Lexus. It's now in Ina's name and I'll keep the title at the bank so Ruby can't pledge it as collateral and end up losing the damn thing for Ina."

"Thanks," I said, thinking about Ina, who started working for my parents as a housekeeper then stayed on to work for Susan and me for over twenty years. "That's something I'll never understand. John worked hard right up until he died, and Ina's still working. Honest, devout churchgoers, good as gold—but they produced some of the most worthless kids in town. Always in trouble...."

"Ruby swears she's clean and sober and is going to help Ina."

"She's told me that twice before. Ruby's probably going to help herself to Ina's car and whatever money Ina's saved."

"Ina doesn't drive, so somebody's got to drive her. Ruby's the only one that's stepped up. I don't know what else to do."

"I know. I'm just thinking out loud. Thanks for handling that."

"You get your thirty-eight back from the Sheriff's office?"

"No. They're keeping it as evidence until all this is over."

"You'll never see that pistol again. Anyway, you mark my words on this NCAA thing and El Ray, bet you my last dollar there ain't going to be anything connecting his death to Ole Miss football. It's something else got him killed."

"I hope you're right. I don't have a lot of faith in the evenhandedness of the NCAA."

"That's an understatement. You notice the big schools that generate a lot of money and have a lot of clout—the NCAA leaves them alone. They go after the little guys, just like the IRS."

"But the IRS doesn't leak like the NCAA," I said.

"Amen. Back to this lawyer thing, Lawrence Pratt is a nice enough guy," Jimmy said. "Plenty smart. But he ain't no fighter. He's an office lawyer, just like the silk-stocking firms the University has hired. Ain't none of them courtroom lawyers. They'll do a bunch of posturing and run up big bills, then they'll talk the school into settling and take whatever suspension or sanctions the gangsters at the NCAA want. The A.D. told me they hired 'em because they've represented a lot of schools in NCAA investigations."

"How about a toddy?" I said.

"It's about time you asked."

With no small amount of effort, Jimmy separated himself from the stuffed chair. I watched the three-hundred-and-twelve-pounder step lightly into the kitchen. Jimmy had blown past *portly* many pounds ago. He and I grew up together in Sunshine, a small Mississippi Delta town, county seat of Yaloquena County. Jimmy effects a dumbass, country-boy demeanor, but he's the smartest, shrewdest, and funniest man I have ever known. Our late fathers were good friends. They founded Sunshine Bank and together owned the majority of the outstanding stock. Since Jimmy took over as Chairman and C.E.O., he had grown the bank from a hundred million in assets to over a half-billion. His management had drawn the attention of bigger financial institutions with large agricultural lending departments, particularly one bank headquartered in Birmingham and another in Nashville. During the most recent period of regional bank consolidation, Jimmy had fought off buyouts and takeover offers. Like our fathers before us, the two of us together owned well over fifty percent of the stock.

We had been through a lot together, including the death of his high-school senior son, Beau, in a hunting accident; Jimmy's descent into grief-driven alcohol abuse; Susan's three-year sabbatical and the Mary Margaret fiasco; my last election three years ago; and now Susan's murder.

While I was trying cases as District Attorney for Yaloquena County, Jimmy was growing our bank. About the time Susan and I moved permanently to Oxford, Jimmy opened an Oxford branch of Sunshine Bank, just off the Square on Jackson. The branch was doing well, and gave Jimmy an excuse to spend more time in Oxford. I pulled for Ole Miss, but nothing like Jimmy. He was a diehard fan of all Ole Miss sports.

"Here you go," Jimmy said and handed me a Ketel One and tonic. "And I propose a toast to Ole Miss finally hiring a lawyer with some guts."

"I'm not sure I can work up the interest or the energy. Do I still have the confidence for the fight? Hell, I let Sheriff Burr bully me into staying out of Susan's investigation. Came back here with my tail between my legs and been sitting on my ass ever since."

"Enough of that crap, Willie Mitchell. Six months of mourning is enough. You need somethiing else to think about, and this El Ray case is just the thing. You're the best lawyer I know. You can turn that situation around with Sheriff Burr, too. You've stayed out of it and they ain't come up with shit. Take Aunt Bee's case for Ole Miss. Do it for our much-maligned state. Hell, do it for me."

"Not six months. About five-and-a-half since the murder. And you sound just like Aunt Bee, telling me to do it for the school and the state. That's exactly what she said."

"Hiring you is the first thing she's done I agree with," Jimmy said, clinking his glass to mine.

CHAPTER SIX

I followed the Oxford Police Department receptionist down the narrow wood-paneled hallway. She stopped outside an open door, gestured for me to enter, and left me with OPD Chief of Detectives, David Burke, who was much younger than I expected.

Burke was on his cell phone, listening. He smiled and pointed to a chair. I studied the wall behind him—a law degree from University of Mississippi School of Law signed May 17, 2010; an Ole Miss undergraduate diploma earned in 2007; a photo of him, I assumed, as a Lafayette County High School quarterback wearing jersey number ten, throwing a pass while in the grasp of two opposing team linemen; plaques and certificates from law enforcement seminars and academies; and a large poster depicting one of Monet's many impressionist renderings of a lily pond.

Burke held up one finger for my benefit, then did a "hurry up" gesture directed to the caller.

"Just keep me posted," he said and hung up.

"David Burke," he said, standing up and extending his hand across his desk.

"Willie Mitchell Banks," I said.

Burke was tall, maybe 6'3", and appeared to be in good shape. I figured him for 32 or 33, which is how old he would be if he went to Ole Miss right after Lafayette High then on to law school to finish in 2010. He was a handsome guy, with brown hair and light blue eyes that lit up when he smiled. No wedding ring or family photos in the office.

"Yes, sir, Mr. Banks. I know exactly who you are. You spoke at one of my classes in law school. Criminal procedure. I'm very glad to finally meet you."

"Well, thank you. And even though I'm probably three decades older than you, please call me Willie Mitchell." I pointed vaguely at the wall behind him. "I have to say I'm not accustomed to such a pedigree. I'm impressed."

"Don't be," he said, glancing at his law degree behind him. "They give out law degrees these days to anyone who pays the tuition and shows up for class on a semi-regular basis. It's scary to think some of the dumbasses in my class are actually practicing law, getting paid to give people advice or go to court and represent them."

"Law profession hasn't done a very good job of policing itself."

"So, you're wondering why a lawyer would be working as an OPD detective, I guess?"

I shrugged. "You're about to tell me."

"I passed the bar in the summer of 2010 and went to work for a firm in Jackson. Insurance defense work, mostly. I hated it. I handled a few criminal cases, part of the firm's deal with the bar association to fulfill their *pro bono publico* obligations."

"That's how you got interested in law enforcement?"

"Kind of. What I really liked was the investigation part. Much more than the courtroom stuff. Some of the police reports I read in those cases were pathetic, so I went behind the Jackson detectives, re-interviewed witnesses, discovered better witnesses, better evidence. The cops didn't like it, but I didn't care. Plus, the gumshoe work got me out of the office. I hate sitting inside." He paused a moment. "Chief Daniels says you're representing the University in the El Ray murder investigation."

"I'm representing the Chancellor personally, not the school. She's asked me to look after her interests in all the investigations, NCAA, state, local."

"She spoke to the Chief yesterday and asked us to cooperate. He told me to give you the run of the case. He thinks a lot of you, says you'll be a big help."

"Nice to hear."

"And I'm very sorry about what happened to your wife. Have they made any headway over there?"

"Not much."

"Tallabusha Sheriff's office leaves a lot to be desired. I've worked with them a few times when some of their outstanding citizens come to Oxford and break in a few cars or sling some dope. Got a good bit of gang affiliation over there, just like in the Delta. Gangster Disciples and Vice Lords mainly. We're trying keep them from making inroads in Oxford and Lafayette County."

"Lee Jones did a good job of keeping them out of Yaloquena County."

"I know Sheriff Jones. He's sharp. But Tallabusha S.O. is a bunch of stupid good-ole-boys and political hires. Lazy as hell, too."

"Lee Jones and I are good friends. Worked with him just about every day when I was D.A. in Sunshine. Has MBI been helping you?"

"The state guys were here for a week, long enough for their director and regional director to figure out that El Ray's death was a high-profile case that was not going to be solved quickly. They said call them if OPD needed help on anything in particular. I don't blame them. Everyone in law enforcement is long on cases, but short on money and personnel. FBI said their resources were available to us as needed, but we haven't called them back."

Sunshine was a couple of hours southwest of Cedar Grove, so I heard complaints about the incompetence and dishonesty in the Tallabusha courthouse when I was D.A. in Yaloquena County. I talked to Sheriff Burr and his detectives almost every day after Susan's funeral, giving them all the information I could remember. Sheriff Burr humored me for about a month when I did follow-up with their detectives to check on the investigation, but after a while, he made it pretty clear he wanted me to stop "interfering with the case," to use his exact words. It made sense to my addled brain at the time because I was the only living witness to the double homicide, and a victim to boot. You don't want your key witness investigating, talking to other witnesses.

"Knowing how they operate over there," Detective Burke said, "you need to keep pressure on them. I'll be glad to make a call for you to a detective friend. He's the only one at Tallabusha S.O. with enough sense to come in out of a shower of crap. Straight shooter, too, which is more than I can say for the other deputies I've encountered in Cedar Grove."

"What's his name?"

"Ronnie Tyler. He's about my age."

"I've dealt primarily with the Sheriff."

"I wouldn't take anything Sheriff Burr says at face value. Lots of things bubbling under the surface in that courthouse. None of 'em good."

"Don't call your friend Tyler yet, but I might take you up on it. You mind if I spend some time this afternoon reading over your files on El Ray?"

"I'd welcome your input," he said, pushing a foot-high stack of files across his desk to deposit in front of me.

"And rather than you telling me stuff, I'd like to look at the reports, crime scene photos and lab results and then get with you to go over everything. It would be nice if we could go out to the crime scene at some point."

"I can take you to where we found the body, and the place where he left his car the night he disappeared, but we really don't know where he was killed."

"The body was dumped?"

"In a ravine out in the county. Bow hunters came across him Wednesday before last. We've got an empty office you can use to look at the files."

"Desk and a chair is all I need. And I won't remove or copy anything from the files. I'll just look and make notes."

"Perfect," David said.

"Before I get into the case, one thing I was wondering is how OPD is involved if the murder happened out in the county."

"That's a good question. I'll tell you what's happening."

"Okay."

"There's pretty strong indications from city hall and county administration that there's going to be a move shortly to consolidate the city and county government into a unified governing body. There's supposed to be a lot of support for it, and the mayor and county supervisors have begun unofficially merging departments to see how it will work. Testing it out. I'm an OPD detective, but I've been sworn in as a deputy sheriff, too, and we work major felonies that occur out in the county—murders, armed robberies."

"Hard to believe something so sensible would be taking place in Mississippi."

"Well," he said grinning, "Oxford is not exactly Mississippi. Politics here are real different from anywhere else in the state."

"So I've learned."

"Follow me," he said.

My phone buzzed in my pocket as I followed David and his files into a small office featuring a gray metal desk and a wooden chair that had seen better days.

"I'm next door if you need anything," David said and closed the door behind him.

I looked at my phone. Youngest son Scott had left me a two-word text: "Call me."

"That was fast," Scott said moments later.

"What's up?"

"Do you know where Jake is?"

"No. Last time I talked to him was at the house in Sunshine after the funeral. He never tells us…, uh, me, what he's doing."

"Me either, but we usually talk every other month or so when he's back in D.C. after an assignment."

"Maybe he's out of the country."

"I don't think so. I asked Patrick Dunwoody in DOJ to check on him for me. He got back to me last night. He said Jake took a leave of absence after Mother's funeral and left D.C. Hasn't been back since."

"Let me make a call later today," I said. "I'll get back to you as soon as I know something."

I checked my phone and made certain I still had David Dunne's cell number. I wasn't sure I had it because every time my iPhone updates I lose a contact or two.

I placed my phone on the desk and opened the first El Ray file.

CHAPTER SEVEN

The file I pulled contained the autopsy report, which led off with census-type data about the corpse. Elston Raymond was a light-skinned African-American male, 18 years of age, a resident of Natchez, Mississippi. He measured 6'6" and weighed 255 pounds. Date of death was estimated as November 3, based on the amount of decomposition and insect infestation.

Cause of death was listed as "open pneumothorax."

I studied the front and back outlines of a human body printed at the bottom of the first page. There was only one wound—a single puncture indicated by a small black dot on the anterior of the outlined body a few inches below his right armpit. No other open wounds were described.

I put the autopsy report to the side and pulled the thick folder containing prints of photographs of the fully-clothed dead body *in situ,* taken by the crime scene photographer at the ravine, and shots of the nude body before and during the autopsy, which was conducted by a forensic pathologist associated with the Mississippi Crime Lab in Pearl, MS, Dr. Joseph Martinez. The pathologist signed the report above the signature of the Lafayette County Coroner.

I knew from 24 years of trying murder cases that an open pneumothorax in a homicide victim was usually the result of a gunshot or stab wound that penetrates the chest wall and allows air from outside the body to enter the pleural cavity through the wound when the victim takes a breath. The air gets trapped, puts pressure on and eventually collapses the lung, which compresses the heart and reduces blood flow and oxygen to the heart and other vital organs. The victim's heart struggles and beats faster, causing him to have an increasingly difficult time breathing. In short, El Ray died from suffocation cause by the small puncture wound under his left arm. The photos of El Ray's wound showed very little dried blood around the opening, which is not unusual in an open pneumothorax.

There were no lab results yet in the files, so I made a note on a yellow legal pad, the first entry under "Do List." I wrote: "1. Check on toxicology results." There would be urine and blood samples, and swabs of other parts of the body to be tested.

There were photos of an older model Toyota Camry on the edge of a gravel parking lot in front of a ramshackle wooden building with neon beer signs in the window and a rusted, faded sign that proclaimed "Sammy's Place" next to a vintage Pabst Blue Ribbon logo. Other photographs showed the Toyota being winched onto a tow truck with cops and deputies standing by.

I checked my phone. 4:30. I had been immersed in the file for two-and-one-half hours, but it seemed like minutes. For the first time since Susan's death, time had flown by. It was a welcome relief from my afternoons at the condo since June, where, like Yossarian, I watched the clock move glacially, thinking about our fatal bathroom stop at the BP.

"How about a beer?" Detective Burke said, popping his head in my temporary office. "We can talk about the case."

"All right," I said after a moment.

"Upstairs deck at City Grocery? I'll be there in ten minutes."

"You don't think it might be too chilly?"

"Maybe, but it means there won't be anyone else there. No ears other than ours."

"Okay, but I'll need to put on some warmer clothes."

"I knew you'd think of that. Everyone tells me you're really smart," David said grinning.

I chuckled, feeling a spark of something familiar. For a moment I felt like my old self for the first time in many months. But it soon passed.

CHAPTER EIGHT

It was cold, but tolerable on the City Grocery second-story balcony on the south side of the Oxford Square overlooking the historic Lafayette courthouse. I had picked up a Heineken at the bar and claimed a small table outside. I watched scores of women, including pretty college-aged sorority girls and their good-looking moms, populating the sidewalks around the Square, moving in and out of the clothing and gift shops. Most of the stores already featured Christmas-type decorations and displays, because after all, there were only 39 more shopping days left.

Detective Burke stepped out onto the deck, placed his own Heineken bottle on the table and took a seat.

"You got good taste in beer," I said, raising my bottle to clink lightly against his.

"I always come back to it," he said. "It's nice you live close to the Square."

"Best thing about the condo. Midway between the Square and Grove. Where do you live?"

"In a sixties-style ranch on five acres off Highway 7 south. About ten minutes from the OPD station."

"Alone?"

"Most of the time." He smiled. "You a football fan?"

"Pretty much have to be living here. But I haven't been to the stadium this year."

"Given what happened...,"

"Yeah," I said. "Not really into it this season. May never be again."

"So, what did you think about the case?"

"Before I forget, do you know if they collected vitreous at the autopsy? There aren't any toxicology reports in the file yet."

"I'm sure they did," he said. "I'll double check."

"I saw a couple of statements in file, one from the bartender at Sammy's Place and another from a patron. They both said El Ray was not inside the bar that Saturday evening. They don't know how or when his car was parked there that night, but they're certain he never set foot inside. If he was drinking, vitreous is the most reliable means of checking blood alcohol content post mortem, especially here, where there are three to four days between the murder and the discovery of the body."

"The pathologist said there wasn't much decomp because the weather was pretty cool in the interval."

"But there's still possible contamination of the BAC from natural fermentation in the gut. Anyway, you didn't find much in the ravine?"

"Naw. Heavy rain on Tuesday before last wiped out any real chance for that. People around here say a good bit of water comes down that ravine after a big rain, so we don't think El Ray's body is necessarily in the same spot he was dumped. We just don't know."

"Rushing water would destroy most forensic clues," I said.

"In the pictures he was wedged up against a beech root on the side of the creek. We don't know if the water left him there or his killer. I think the water."

"Crime lab has his clothes?"

"Yes. I'm hoping the water didn't dilute or destroy any DNA evidence in his underwear or pants."

"I wouldn't count on that. You think he was with someone?"

"He was eighteen, a football superstar, and on the road to fame and fortune. It was Saturday night. What do you think?"

"Worth checking for sure."

"You see the autopsy photos?"

"I did. Tiny little hole under his right arm. What's your thinking on the murder weapon?"

"That's one of the many unanswered questions in this case. It's a puncture wound, but the coroner said he didn't think it was a knife. Said the wound appeared to be cylindrical. You see the lipstick?"

"No."

"It's hard to see on the photos. It was on his skin, right below the belt line, above his pubic hair. I say it's lipstick. That's what it looks like to me. Dr. Martinez cut out a small skin section and sent it to the crime lab."

"Not even ravine water will get that stuff off."

"If it is, at least we'll know he was with someone that night. Might help explain what he was doing."

"Maybe. Autopsy said he was 6'6" and 255."

"Did you notice his hands in the autopsy photos? Huge. And speed to burn. He was going to be a franchise player, like Cam

Newton at Auburn or Vince Young when he was at Texas. Reggie told me El Ray was helping recruit for Ole Miss, bringing a lot of four-star and five-star players from all over the South with him to Oxford. Ole Miss coaches were talking SEC title and a shot at the College Football Playoff."

"That's what they call the BCS championship now?"

"Yep. Since 2015. Four team single-elimination."

"You were quarterback at Lafayette High. I saw on your wall."

"Pretty average player, in retrospect. But, it was fun times."

"All the girls want to date the quarterback." I paused. "I never played. Basketball was my sport. I was a walk-on and played in a few games when we were either way ahead or hopelessly behind. I busted my ankle really badly in a practice scrimmage late in the season, and it never got back to normal. Had to play heavily taped, even after the season ended. They didn't make me an offer, and we parted ways. Seems like a century ago."

"You must have been good."

"I was all right, but college basketball was changing. If I had come along a few years later, I couldn't have made the freshman team, even though I was taller back then."

David looked at me, trying to make sense of what I said.

"And black."

He put the back of his hand against his mouth to keep from spewing beer. He swallowed, then laughed.

"I wasn't sure...."

"Half the time I'm full of crap, so you have to be careful."

"Well, good. I deal with unpleasant stuff and idiots all day, including my fellow officers, so any witticism is welcome. Was SEC basketball integrated when you were a freshman?"

"Sure. That began in the late sixties, then picked up steam through the seventies. By the time I finished law school in the spring of 1980, most SEC teams were almost all black. These days, there are only a few white basketball players in the SEC who aren't from eastern Europe."

"You're right."

"And you know why? Because the blacks are much better athletes. Stronger, taller, faster, more driven. They're better shooters now, too."

"Same in SEC football," David said. "Only white players left are in the offensive line, at quarterback, and kickers. For the same reasons."

"Some of these black athletes are almost superhuman in what they can do. I see the plays they make, and shake my head at how they do it. But the refs don't call walking any more. I guess that helps."

"Have you seen any of El Ray's highlights?"

I shook my head.

"Well, you need to treat yourself. Google 'El Ray highlight reel' and spend fifteen minutes watching. He can throw the ball flat-footed seventy yards. He blows past defenders when he runs even though he looks like he's just gliding along effortlessly, like a gazelle. And at St. Mary's they played him both ways, linebacker on defense. He tackles and wraps up like Butkus or Mike Singletary in their prime."

"Shame he died," I said.

"Shame someone killed him, you mean."

"Be interesting to see what the penile swabs come back with."

"Yeah. I'm sure he had lots of opportunities. You know he was up here on what the NCAA refers to as an "unauthorized" visit. There was no home game, no other recruits on campus. I can't find anyone to place him anywhere on campus or in town."

"Who was his main recruiter?"

"Reggie Barnes. Friend of mine. He was a great receiver for us when I was in school. Fast and strong, hard to bring down. Reggie's been recruiting El Ray for Ole Miss since the seventh grade. He's really torn up about his death. They were close, almost like brothers. Reggie watched him grow up. And signing him was a real boost for Reggie's career in college football coaching."

"When can we go out to Sammy's Place and the ravine?"

"How about tomorrow afternoon? We can go to the ravine then catch Sammy's on the way back. Sammy won't be thrilled to see us."

"Why do you say that?" I asked.

"Sammy Kerry likes to fly under the radar. His customers don't want notoriety, either. He's got some hard-core regulars from Lafayette and Tallabusha that go there to drink and absorb the toxic negativity you feel when you walk in the door."

"Sammy's parking lot was El Ray's final destination."

"But no one in the bar says they saw him that night. Including Sammy. You read the statements we took. Sammy says El Ray's been in there several times before, but not the night he was killed. Sammy says he can't control who leaves a car in his parking lot."

"If that's true, maybe he was meeting someone," I said. "Kind of an inconvenient place to meet."

"Unless you don't want to be seen. It's out in the boondocks and there's only one light on the front of the building and it doesn't throw much light on the parking lot."

"I bet Sammy knows more than he's telling."

"Maybe, but he's old school, a rawboned, tough son-of-a-bitch. Sammy doesn't like anybody, especially law enforcement. And since November third, he and his regulars have been questioned by those assholes from the NCAA, the state police, and me and several other OPD detectives. Tomorrow will be the sixth time I've been in his place in the last two weeks."

"It'll be Friday. Maybe they've got a happy hour."

"Not likely," David laughed. "Ain't many happy folks out there at Sammy's Place."

CHAPTER NINE

I spent Friday morning watching El Ray's highlights online. David had not overstated his abilities. He was a natural, possessing an uncanny ability to make big plays, most of them without much help. In one defensive highlight, El Ray stood up a stocky Vicksburg High fullback, ripped the football from the runner's arms, and ran the other way eighty yards for a touchdown. Other than the running back he stripped, no other Vicksburg player came close to touching him.

El Ray's sixty-and seventy-yard running touchdowns from scrimmage were routine plays on the highlight tapes, as were long passes he threw to his receivers. His arm was a rifle. His high school receivers were not always up to the task—the reels featured a number of his perfect touchdown darts bouncing off his receivers' chests. Even so, it was easy to see how valuable he would be throwing to college and pro receivers.

Had he lived, El Ray would have become a very rich man. And he was apparently smart enough to be able to keep it. David told me the previous night on the City Grocery deck that Ole Miss recruiter Reggie Barnes went on and on about El Ray's intellect and character. He made straight A's at St. Mary's, his Catholic high school; made a 28 on his ACT; had already taken a number of AP courses at St. Mary's to allow him to take a lighter load his freshman year; was president of his school's honor society; was active in civic projects in Natchez, using his local celebrity to influence kids who adored him; reared by a straight-laced, hardworking mother; and, finally, had a spotless record, having never given his mother or local authorities a bit of trouble.

"You know what Reggie told me about him?" David asked me. "He said El Ray is like a unicorn—so perfect and rare that most recruiters believe kids like him don't really exist."

The next afternoon, promptly at 4:00 pm, I received a text from David that he was in the driveway behind the condo. I grabbed my coat and looked over at Jimmy Gray, stuffed once again into Susan's Queen Anne armchair.

"If Detective Burke says you can't go, that's it. I didn't tell him you wanted to tag along on this field trip, so it's up to him."

"I've met David a bunch of times," Jimmy said. "Ran into him at functions when I was meeting and greeting everyone I could right before we opened the doors on the Jackson branch. He ain't going to mind."

We walked out my back door, through my garage and onto the condo's concrete common driveway. Jimmy stayed in the garage as I walked to the heavily-tinted driver's window and gestured for David to roll it down.

"I hate to spring this on you, and if it's a problem, I understand." I pointed to the mass of flesh in my garage. "My buddy Jimmy Gray wants to come with us."

"I know Jimmy Gray," David said. "Sure. He can come. Jimmy bought me a drink the last time I saw him. He's a character."

I waved for Jimmy to come on. He walked quickly to his bright red Cadillac Escalade parked on the driveway, opened the passenger side door and grabbed a stainless steel case. I knew what was in it.

"Howdy, David," Jimmy said as he maneuvered his big frame into the back seat of David's black Tahoe.

"Good to see you, Jimmy," David said, reaching back to shake hands. "What you got in the case?"

"Pimento cheese sandwiches and Fritos," I said.

"Let me show you," Jimmy said.

He rolled the combination numbers just so, then pushed the latches on each side of the handle. The case popped open to reveal Jimmy's pride and joy, a .50 caliber titanium gold Desert Eagle semi-automatic pistol with a six-inch barrel and JG etched in gold onto the custom finished black aluminum grip.

"Holy shit," David said. "Can I see that? I've never held a Desert Eagle."

Jimmy lifted the four-and-a-half pound semi-automatic and handed it to David, who tested its heft and balance, then sighted it in on the condo door.

"Don't fire," I said. "It'll go all the way through the condo."

"Beautiful," David said, giving it back. "When do you use it?"

"Whenever I'm on special assignment with dick nose here."

David laughed. "So, you're on Willie Mitchell's staff?"

"So to speak."

"He's actually a pretty good p.i.," I said. "And an excellent dancer. Real light on his feet for a big fellow. Grills a mean steak, too."

"I'm not expecting trouble today," David said, "but glad to know we have plenty of firepower if we do."

"Exactly what I was thinking," Jimmy said. "You never know."

We headed west on Highway Six toward I-55. Before we crossed the county line, we turned south onto a two-lane county road and drove for twenty minutes, during which time Jimmy told one story after another. I had heard every one ten times. But David hadn't, so he laughed along with Jimmy, who always laughs loudest at his own jokes and stories. In spite of myself, I laughed right along with them.

"Ravine's up here a little ways. Crime scene tape should still be visible from the road."

There was virtually no shoulder, so David pulled his Tahoe over, but half of it took up part of the westbound travel lane. He turned on his law enforcement emergency flashers, which blinked blue and white inside the Tahoe's front grill and rear window.

The three of us walked no more than twenty feet, then ducked under the bright yellow crime scene tape, through pine trees and brush to the edge of the ravine, which was much deeper than I expected.

"Must be twenty feet from the edge down to the bottom," I said.

"There's the beech root where El Ray ended up," David said. "You saw it on the photo. We think the water moved him there from a little further north, but we really don't know. With the volume of water that came through here the Tuesday after he was killed, there wasn't much at the scene for us to examine."

"That's assuming the body was dumped here Saturday night the third or early in the morning of the following Sunday," I said.

"That's what we think happened. In the early morning hours. We checked the side of the road for tire tracks but the rain took care of that, too, if any ever existed. Not much traffic on this road."

"How far to Sammy's Place?" Jimmy Gray asked.

"Down this road another couple of miles, right inside the Lafayette County line," David said. "In fact, Sammy claims if he steps out his back door he's in Tallabusha County. Back when Tallabusha was a dry county, it was a good location for those folks to buy beer and liquor. Those days are long gone."

"So are most of Sammy's customers, I bet," Jimmy said. "This whole area's depopulated, like most of rural Mississippi."

"Like most of rural America," I said.

"Yeah, but not as bad as the Delta. Let's go get us a cold one at Sammy's," Jimmy said, "unless you want to crawl down in that creek bottom to check things out."

"Well, you're not going down there, that's for sure," I said. "We'd have to get a tow truck to get you out."

"Funny, shit head."

David chuckled. "There's not much to see down there, anyway. We had the crime scene techs comb every inch of the ravine sides and the bottom for about five hundred feet north and south. They didn't find anything. If any physical evidence was there it's long gone now, and even if we found something, all that dirt and water would have destroyed any evidentiary value it might have had."

"Is Sammy's a juke joint, a dive, or a club?" Jimmy asked.

"Is there a difference?" David asked before I could caution him not to.

"Big difference," Jimmy said. "Historically in Northwest Mississippi, which includes the Delta, our old stomping grounds, a juke joint has only black customers; a dive, also known as a honky-tonk, is usually frequented by rednecks and white trash; and a club serves all races."

"That true?" David asked me.

"I don't know," I said. "First time I've ever heard it."

"Sure it's true," Jimmy said. "I've got the empirical evidence to prove it."

"And that would be?" I asked.

"When I was drinking real heavy, I was a frequent patron of all three."

"Good to know," David said as we neared his Tahoe. "This has probably been a waste of time for you guys."

"Not really," I said. "I know one thing now, whoever carried El Ray from the road to that creek is strong."

"Possibly more than one person," Jimmy said.

"That's what I'm thinking," David said.

CHAPTER TEN

"Tell me more about your dealings with the NCAA investigators" I said to David. "Or the state police detectives."

"NCAA investigators were in Oxford within twenty-four hours of the discovery of the body. They had already been notified of El Ray's disappearance."

"Who called them after he went missing?" I asked.

"They wouldn't say, but I think Mr. Raymond, the father."

"They've been sniffing around ever since El Ray announced last spring he was committing to Ole Miss," Jimmy said. "They don't like us, and they figured whoever signed him had to put up big money. NCAA's probably pissed he didn't sign with Alabama or Ohio State."

"Reggie Barnes says there was no money involved," David said. "He said they followed the rules to a tee because they knew we'd be looked at if Reggie closed the deal. I believe him. He had a lot riding on El Ray."

"Where did you have El Ray's Toyota towed?" I asked.

"Non-stop from Sammy's to the state crime lab in Pearl. I figured what we might find in his car would give us our best possibility at figuring out what happened to him. I looked through the window, saw a half-dozen or so empty beer cans on the floor. They looked fresh."

"Good thinking to send it directly to Pearl," I said.

David rounded a curve and slowed to pull onto Sammy's gravel parking lot. I counted ten vehicles, nine of them worn out pickup trucks, all parked facing the dilapidated building. Sammy's Place was sorely in need of a paint job and a new roof. Shingles curled in a half-dozen spots, as did one of the boards on the small wooden porch protecting the entrance.

"Surely they have valet parking," Jimmy said.

"Where was El Ray's Toyota?" I asked.

"Over there under that black walnut tree," David said, pointing.

Jimmy Gray answered his cell phone in the back seat and indicated he'd be with us in a minute. David and I walked over to the hard-packed dirt just off the gravel and under the walnut. I studied the ground, littered with old, flattened beer cans, wrappers, and inedible native black walnuts, each one as hard as the gravel rocks in the parking lot.

"I picked up every piece of litter, glass, or can that looked relatively fresh, put each one in a Ziploc and sent them all to the crime lab. I don't know if they can do anything with them." He paused, then pointed south to a small road sign. "There's the Lafayette-Tallabusha line."

"I doubt there's much light over here after dark," I said.

"Very little. I came out here after dark one night last week. It's almost pitch black under this tree. If he was meeting someone here he didn't want to be seen."

"Or the person he was meeting didn't...," I said. "The Toyota looked to be in pretty good condition in the photos."

"It was, for a 2005 model. Exterior was clean, no major dents. Inside was kind of messy, and the front passenger seat was sprung, wouldn't come vertical all the way. I looked under the hood, and the engine was fairly clean, well-maintained."

"And the keys were in the pocket of his jeans."

"Right. Along with his wallet, which contained seventy dollars, driver's license, Social Security card, picture of his mom, nothing of consequence. Crime lab tech called to tell me when they got inside the Toyota they found his iPhone on the passenger seat under a jacket big enough to fit him, so we're assuming it was his."

"Anything on his phone that might help?"

"It's being processed by the crime lab tech. He's documenting El Ray's calls on a spread sheet, going back a couple of months before death. Said he would be emailing it to me Monday. I spoke to him Wednesday and he said nothing stood out, that the last call was to his mother around six p.m. the night he died."

"That doesn't make sense. If he was meeting someone out here he'd be making and receiving calls."

"Reggie said he had another phone, a burner."

"Why would he have a burner?" I asked.

"Nothing sinister. Reggie says lots of recruiters use burners for same reason drug dealers do—anonymity. He says they give burners to their key prospects when it gets crunch time, close to signing."

"So they can talk as much as they want without violating any NCAA rules. Did Reggie use burners? Did he give El Ray a burner?"

"He says no and no. Says El Ray had his own burners. And Coach Goodson has a strict rule against any of his coaches using burners, so Reggie never called him on his burner. Dialed his regular cell. The Assistant Athletic Director in charge of compliance keeps an eye out to make sure the coaches comply, picking up their phones without notice and checking calls."

"Let's go give our regards to the proprietor," I said.

It had been dreary weather all day. No rain, but heavily overcast. We were losing daylight as David and I left the black walnut tree and crunched our way across the gravel. I couldn't see Jimmy Gray in David's Tahoe because of the dark tint on its windows, but I assumed he was still on the phone in the back seat. We walked up two wooden steps to the small porch and into Sammy's. It was dark in the bar. We stood at the door to let our eyes adjust. Every head turned to check us out, and what little conversation there was among the patrons ended.

"No problem, folks," the tough-looking man behind the bar boomed. "It's the fuzz from Oxford, the San Francisco of the South."

David led the way to the bar. Sammy Kerry appeared to be in his late fifties. He sported a short, white crew cut and a couple of days of white stubble beneath piercing light blue eyes. He was about my size, 6'1" or 6'2", and lean but strong-looking, long arms and oversized hands and fingers, big knuckles that could do some damage. I assumed Sammy was one of the many rednecks in north Mississippi descended from the "borderers," Scots who lived along and north of Hadrian's Wall in England. They were too tough for the Romans, who gave up trying to conquer them and settled on building a wall the entire width of England to keep them out of the Empire. Some of Sammy's forebears probably made their way to Ulster in Northern Ireland. Their Scots-Irish progeny eventually emigrated to the U.S., trickled through Appalachia fighting Native Americans and eventually settled in Tennessee and Northern Mississippi. I doubted Sammy could confirm his provenance one way or the other.

"Those leftists running your town lettin' your homeless shit on the sidewalk around the Square yet, Burke?" Sammy said, loud enough for his loyal patrons to hear. "They leavin' needles for kids to step on?"

"Not yet, Sammy," Burke said after the snickers behind us subsided.

"Well, it's coming, I guarantee you." He eyed me, then pointed a crooked finger at David. "What'll it be for you and your buddy here, Burke? More questions or will you actually spend some money for a change?"

David checked the time on his phone. "I'm officially off duty, Sammy. I'll have a Heineken for me and one for my friend here."

"We only serve domestic," Sammy sneered.

"Then how about a longneck Bud?"

"Same for me," I said.

Sammy turned around and pulled two bottles from the old-fashioned metal cooler resembling a chest freezer. I looked around to gauge the clientele—a dozen or so men in work clothes or worse, and two women. One of the women sat alone at the end of the bar nursing a cocktail of some kind. She seemed to be well beyond the legal limit. She could have been thirty-five or sixty, hard to tell. Stringy, straight, gray-blonde hair, a ruddy drinker's complexion and skinny as a rail—a female barfly right out of a Charles Bukowski short story.

Jimmy Gray made his entrance and stood inside the door, bigger than life, grinning and surveying the crowd like he owned the place. "Howdy, gentlemen," he said to no one in particular, then spied the skinny woman at the end of the bar and walked right to her. "Eloise," he said in a loud voice, "how the hell are you?" Jimmy gestured for Sammy. "A Michelob for me and another round for the lady."

"That's Jimmy playing private eye," I said to David, *sotto voce.*

"Why are you really here?" Sammy asked David after he served Jimmy.

"This is Willie Mitchell Banks," David said.

"You were the D.A. over in Yaloquena for the longest time," Sammy said. "I knew I recognized you when you walked in. Used to see you on TV. You the one got after old Buddy Richardson, brought him down."

I extended my hand. Sammy hesitated a moment before shaking it.

"You weren't the D.A. who handled the Postlewaite case over in the Delta, were you?"

"That was Coachitto County, on the river. I didn't prosecute it but I know the case pretty well because the D.A. over there who handled the first trial consulted with me at least a dozen times before he tried it. Bad case."

"Is that the appliance store massacre," David asked, "where the owner, his wife and two employees were all put in a back room and murdered?"

"That's it," Sammy said. "Goddamned criminals who done it should have been hanged right away. Now they're going to get out after doing twelve years, looks like. Quite the system you got, Mr. D.A."

"I read something about it a few months ago," David said, "but I can't remember exactly what the current status is."

"The Mississippi Supreme Court has granted a new trial to the shooter," I said, "because of ineffective assistance of counsel and because one of the co-defendants in prison recanted his original testimony. The same lawyer originally represented all three of the defendants, then withdrew from representing the defendant named Marbury when the other two claimed Marbury did the shooting on his own. The lawyer then negotiated a plea and thirty years for the two who claimed that they didn't know the shooter was going to kill Mr. and Mrs. Postlewaite and the two employees they herded into the back. They said the shooter was just supposed to tie them up."

"The shooter is getting a new trial," Sammy said loud enough for all his customers to hear, "and his two accomplices are probably going to get their convictions overturned because the same lawyer represented both of them, some kind of conflict of interest bullshit. Now they've made up a bunch of shit about things they claim he told them."

"Like I said, it's a bad case," I said.

"And I heard that some of the evidence has been lost, and a couple of witnesses have died, and the new nigger D.A. they got over there says he might not be able to re-try them."

"I read his comments in the Memphis paper," I said, "and it's true what he said, that he's got real problems getting a conviction again of all three. It has nothing to do with the fact that the District Attorney is black."

"They all should have been hanged the day after the killings and we'd have been done with it. Coachitto is mostly black now, seventy percent or so, and even if the new D.A. tries it, those people ain't going to convict them three bastards for killing a bunch of white people that half the niggers in the county owed money to on their stoves, refrigerators, and TV's."

David looked over, waiting for me to respond.

"Postlewaite wasn't my case," I said. "But now I'm representing a client interested in what happened to Elston Raymond," I said.

I hated to admit that Sammy's preferred method to handle the three Postlewaite killers was something that crossed my mind when I read the article about the Supreme Court ordering new trials. Jury trials in the Delta were hard enough to win when the evidence and testimony was fresh, much less fourteen years after the murders. Pity for murder victims wanes each year that passes after the crime, while sympathy for defendants imprisoned for many years increases each year. I had seen all the Postlewaite photos, many so gruesome the first trial judge kept them away from the jury. The physical evidence against the three defendants was overwhelming—there was no question of their guilt. Sammy's remedy, instant death for the shooter and his two accomplices, would have been closer to justice than what was happening now.

In my early years as a prosecutor, I would have argued with Sammy, defending the criminal justice system. Not any more. My oldest son Jake would agree with Sammy on the immediate need to dispatch the killers. It pained me to admit it, but intellectually, I was moving closer to their side.

"I figured you guys didn't just drop in. I told you everything I know about the night the Raymond kid went missing," Sammy said to David, irritated. "He didn't come in here that night. I didn't know his car was outside until I closed up about two a.m. and got in my truck."

"Had he been in here before?" I asked.

"Yeah. A few times. Alone, like I told the detective here."

"Did you know who he was?" I asked.

"I didn't until one of the fellows told me after his first visit."

"Why do you think he decided to drive all the way out here?"

"Why don't you ask your partner next to you? I told him I have no idea." Sammy surveyed his audience and raised the volume. "This is a public establishment. I don't ask people why they come in here. I assume they come to drink. It ain't like the old days, when I could serve who I wanted. Now I follow the U.S. Supreme Court saying I can't discriminate, so I serve everyone—niggers of all colors, shapes, and sizes, Jews, sand niggers, Catholics, wetbacks, sodomites, carpet munchers—anyone who comes in with money and shows me an i.d. I treat all of those no-good bastards just like my regular customers. Better, maybe."

Sammy sneered, playing to his admiring customers. He wanted us to believe he was joking, but I knew he wasn't. His sinister, threatening nature came through loud and clear. He was one of those guys itching to get into it at the slightest provocation, like a few of my contemporaries in college. I knew frat guys my age who would get tanked up and go out to bars in the county on Saturday night intending to get into a fight with perfect strangers over nothing.

"The customer who identified El Ray for you," I said, "is he here tonight?"

"No," Sammy said. "I already gave his name to Burke."

"I talked to him," David said. "He's a logger, big football fan. But he didn't know why El Ray picked Sammy's place. He didn't see him with anyone."

"Anything else?" Sammy said.

"I don't guess," I said. "Pleasure meeting you, Sammy. Let's go, David."

Burke looked over at Jimmy, but I nudged the detective toward the door before he said anything. We walked outside and waited in the Tahoe for Jimmy. Ten minutes later, Jimmy opened the saloon door, laughing loudly, waving indiscriminately over his shoulder to the patrons inside.

"How's Eloise?" I asked Jimmy as David pulled onto the highway.

"Drunk. She used to live in Sunshine, was a bank customer. She divorced old man Fite's boy, Walt, who's been busy the last few years running the bulk plant in the ground. He's a drunk, too. Eloise says she lives with her mother in Tallabusha now, just a few miles over the county line."

"You acted like you were good friends," David said laughing.

"I just knew her enough to speak to her. She used to be good-looking, with a nice figure, but now she looks like she's been rode hard and put up wet. We talked about people she knew in town, kind of reminiscing."

"She lives with her mother?" David said. "Her mother must be ninety."

"Naw," Jimmy said. "Eloise is only about forty, I'd say."

"I'm waiting," I said. "Let's have it."

"Eloise wasn't here the Saturday night El Ray died. Had to take her mother to the hospital."

"And," I said.

"But she was here twice before when El Ray came in. Said he was hard not to notice. She claimed he did the same thing both times. Sat at the bar and had a beer, kept checking his phone.

Eloise said she went outside to get another pack of cigarettes out of her car and saw a good-looking blonde girl driving a big, black SUV pull into the parking lot. She didn't know what kind. But El Ray came out of the bar and got in the car with her. Eloise got a good look at the woman under the dome light."

"She say who it was?" I asked.

"She had never seen her before. Said she was to be too old to be a college girl. Eloise said the blonde was all dolled up."

"Damn," David said. "That's great information."

"You have any idea who it might be?" I asked.

"Not sure," David said, "but I'll make a few calls tomorrow, see what I can dig up."

"Who were you on the phone with for so long?" I asked Jimmy.

"Banker friend in Nashville. We've been playing phone tag."

"I'm impressed with your investigative chops, Jimmy," David said.

"Don't encourage him," I said, making David laugh. "I'm just glad he didn't walk in Sammy's with the Desert Eagle in his hand."

"Just one of my skills as a full service banker," Jimmy said. "And by the way, regardless of what Sammy said about his enlightened policy on who he serves, that place is definitely a honky-tonk."

CHAPTER ELEVEN

My do list was growing.

Saturday morning, I spent time in my office in the condo organizing and adding to my do-list, including making a note to interview Reggie Barnes and head coach Carl Goodson. I also wrote: Question the Raymonds in Natchez; get Jimmy Gray to quiz alums in his Ole Miss network to pick up any rumors on who was "working" with Reggie Barnes to entice El Ray to sign; get crime lab toxicology results, check on analysis of Toyota contents, phone analysis; report to Aunt Bee; check with DB on identity of blonde in dark SUV; contact NCAA investigators; and research NCAA recruiting rules.

David Burke emailed me to say the crime lab would be sending results no later than Wednesday. The Ole Miss coaches were with the team playing Vanderbilt in Nashville. Natchez was a two-day round trip. So, I focused on what I could do at home in Oxford. I spent two hours online studying the pharisaical NCAA rules governing the amount of contact universities were permitted to have with their football recruits. Given the complexity of the regulations, it's a wonder recruiters don't commit rule violations every day. Maybe they do.

The rules establish how many authorized visits a recruit may make to a school; when they can be exercised; when recruiters may see or contact prospects in person, on the phone, or texting; different rules for head coaches; rules on unauthorized visits; quiet periods where no contact was permitted; strict guidelines for permissible benefits such as housing, meals, school paraphernalia, and transportation; and prohibitions against alumni providing anything of value, and I do mean *anything*.

I reviewed one case where an alum gave a ride to a star recruit from his hotel to the football stadium during an authorized campus visit, and the NCAA ruled it an impermissible benefit resulting in a minor recruiting violation against the school. In another, an alum allowed a recruit to hunt one time on the alum's land, for which the school was cited and the alum barred from any contact with the school for a year, including banning his attendance from all sports contests. Perhaps because the NCAA realized it had no jurisdiction over the alum in question, it required the university to enforce the ban. In other words, the university had to make sure the alum did not come to a football game and hide among the 75,000 attendees. I was surprised the NCAA had not suggested the university use a home-confinement ankle monitor on the alums who had the audacity to give the kid a ride or allow a recruit to hunt on his property.

But the saddest disciplinary cases involved student-athletes who the NCAA ruled were recipients of impermissible gifts and benefits. Some of these eighteen-year-olds were stripped of their scholarships and banished from intercollegiate athletics *forever,* a draconian punishment depriving some of them of their only means of lifting themselves out of poverty and enjoying a better life.

"Such dictatorial bullshit," I muttered that morning as I reviewed the NCAA enforcement cases.

Under the NCAA rules and according to Detective Burke, the weekend of November 3 was an unauthorized visit by El Ray. Burke said he wasn't aware of any evidence that El Ray came to Oxford or the campus. In a written statement, Reggie Barnes said the same thing. I made a note to double check with Reggie on how often he kept in touch with El Ray. He would know more than anyone at Ole Miss about El Ray's whereabouts at any given time.

I turned on the television to clear my head of the arcana of college football recruiting and channel surfed, watching Game Day at Ohio State for ten minutes, then switching to the SEC network just in time to hear a former SEC lineman, now paid analyst, discuss the impact of El Ray's death on the future of Ole Miss football. Without citing any evidence, he warned of dire consequences to the program, suggesting that rumors indicated big money had changed hands to induce the five-star recruit from Natchez to sign with the Oxford school. He added that his "sources" told him that the NCAA investigators were all over Ole Miss football, turning over every rock to expose what he called the "dark underbelly" of college recruiting at "second tier SEC schools" like Ole Miss.

"Bama is so good they don't have to cheat anymore," I muttered to the television and turned it off.

I Googled "El Ray's death," read scores of newspaper and sports e-magazine articles, clicked on and watched regional and national newscasts of his disappearance and death.

I fell asleep reading the weekend Wall Street Journal and woke up mid-afternoon. Martha and Jimmy Gray were staying at their Oxford home for the weekend, and Jimmy had asked me to come over and watch football, have a few cocktails, and grill a steak with them.

I sent him a text saying I'd be there as soon as I showered and dressed. I wasn't really interested in watching football or drinking, but anything to get me out of the condo, the land where time stood still.

It was painfully empty without Susan around.

CHAPTER TWELVE

Sunday seemed to last a week. I woke up about six. I jogged slowly for less than a mile, then walked through campus, north to Price Street and North Lamar, through the Square and back to the condo. I fussed at myself for neglecting my conditioning and health since Susan died. But, unlike previous self-reprimands, this time I didn't resolve to get back in shape. I was content to let myself go to seed, a sentiment I had never before experienced. *Portly* might be just around the corner.

No church for me. I had not been inside one since Susan's funeral. Not sure I'd ever go back.

I piddled until noon, then drove to Oxford Country Club with thoughts of joining Jimmy Gray and the Sunday Geezer Group for a one p.m. tee time. I hit a dozen practice balls, but my interest in playing ebbed with each shot. Tiger Woody, Sheriff, Radar, BB, Eddro, Potato Head, Boo, Dr. Brainer, Tee-L, Ooslee, Hulk, Captain Kenny Wayne, and Duck were complaining about the lack of talent on the Ole Miss football team or the hapless coaching, two subjects I had no interest in discussing. I decided to leave the practice tee before Jimmy Gray arrived, because I knew he'd talk me into playing, even if I didn't want to.

I picked up a few essentials at Kroger and returned to the condo. I lay on the couch, half-reading a collection of H.L. Mencken essays, and half-watching "What On Earth?" on the science channel, where scientists try to figure out satellite images of strange-looking phenomena on Planet Earth.

I dozed for an hour or so. The remainder of my Sunday was not nearly as exciting, but I made it through, got in bed early and dreamed that Sheriff Burr and his shiftless detectives at Tallabusha Sheriff's Office had closed the investigation into Susan's murder because they were "too busy" with other cases to devote any more time on it.

I woke up angry at Sheriff Burr, then realized it was a dream—a dream that revealed feelings I had suppressed for months about the inadequacies of the Tallabusha investigation. I was mad at myself, too, for following the Sheriff's instruction to stay away from the investigation. Don't know what I was thinking. Apparently I wasn't in my right mind at the time. I showered, dressed, and was in my truck by 7:00 a.m. on my way to Cedar Grove for an unannounced visit with Sheriff Burr.

Like most Mississippi small town county seats, the courthouse was in the center of "downtown" Cedar Grove. Nearby one-story brick buildings that formerly housed mercantile establishments were vacant or had been converted to law offices and government program centers. Grocery, clothing, and hardware stores had moved to new buildings on the "bypass" that ringed the town, leaving the downtown bereft of shoppers and pedestrians but rich in empty diagonal parking spaces. I pulled into one on the street next to the courthouse.

The sign on the first floor exterior door said "Do Not Enter. Deputy Sheriffs Only. Use Main Entrance On West Side." I entered anyway, surprising a deputy in plain clothes just inside the door. He appeared to be about forty, with dark hair and an olive complexion, about my height and weight. There was a pale, crescent scar hugging the orbital bone around his left eye.

"Sir, you'll have to enter the main entrance of the courthouse and go through security," he said in a courteous manner.

"I'm Willie Mitchell Banks, used to be D.A. in Yaloquena."

"Oh, yes sir, Mr. Banks," he said and extended his hand. "I'm Detective Ronnie Tyler."

"I'm actually living in Oxford now."

"Yes, sir, I know. I spoke to David Burke this weekend. He's a friend of mine, says he's working with you on the El Ray killing."

"He mentioned you to me," I said, trying to make up for not recognizing Ronnie's name. "Said you were a good hand over here."

"Pretty low bar," Ronnie said quietly, leaning in. "What can I do for you?"

"I want to talk to Sheriff Burr."

"He expecting you?"

"No. I just drove over hoping to see him about my wife's case."

"It's Monday, so he might be a little late getting in today." He pointed to a row of three wooden chairs with padded seats. "You have a seat and let me give him a call."

I took a seat and Detective Tyler disappeared around a corner. There was little activity in the office. Several uniformed deputies walked by and nodded. I heard an occasional staticky radio squawk from around the hallway corner. In five minutes, Ronnie returned.

"He'll be here in fifteen minutes," he said. "Asked if you could wait. I told him you would."

I gestured to Ronnie and patted the seat next to me. He sat down.

"You know of any developments?" I asked quietly.

"No, sir," he said. "I'm not working the case. For the first month or so there was a lot going on, but leads kind of dried up, or so I was told."

"David says you're the best detective in the office."

"Well, thanks, but the two major felony detectives working it will do a decent job. They pulled in a couple of narcotic officers to help, because almost every violent crime that takes place in Tallabusha County is drug-related in one way or another." He paused. "I'm really sorry about your loss, Mr. Banks. The Sheriff will be able to give you up to date details that I'm not in on. Wish I could be of more help."

"I understand."

"Sheriff asked me to let you wait in his office. We've got felony arraignment and some bond hearings in court this morning so a few of our outstanding citizens will be coming through the outside door and parading right past here. They'll be shackled but no need for you to be exposed to them. Their personal hygiene often leaves something to be desired."

Ronnie led me into the Sheriff's office, where I sat in a more comfortable chair in front of the Sheriff's desk. He grabbed a newspaper from the Sheriff's leather chair and gave it to me.

"This morning's Jackson Clarion-Ledger. Memphis paper will be delivered later." He shook my hand. "Nice meeting you. Let me know if I can help you in any way," he said and left.

I looked at the headlines. One announced that today was the 55th anniversary of the ambush murder of Julius Vernon, an NAACP organizer, in Tallabusha County in 1963. Being in the political heart of Tallabusha, ground zero of the 55-year-old homicide, I read the CL's account of the sordid details, most of which I already knew. I was eight years old in Sunshine when it happened, only a couple of hours from where Vernon was killed under a bridge about five miles from downtown Cedar Grove. I knew nothing about the murder until I was in college.

The Vernon murder, the Philadelphia Three ambush, and the Emmett Till tragedies were heinous, evil deeds. Everyone I know in Mississippi is ashamed and sorry they happened, but I don't know what the newspaper expects us to do about it 55 years later. The editors don't have any suggestions, but apparently feel a civic obligation to pick at the scab of racial hatred and remind everyone how bad it all was back in the day. It was worse than bad, but it's history. The facts are immutable. There's nothing we can do to change them or to make up for what was done.

Sheriff William Burr filled the doorway. A big man, the Sheriff was about six feet and thick, with broad shoulders and a barrel chest. Wiry, white hairs climbed like ivy above the open collar of his uniform shirt, their progress halted uniformly at his shave line. Tuffs of white hair whorled on his big, bare forearms. He hung his beige Stetson cowboy hat on the antlers of a trophy buck on the wall behind his desk and smoothed his thin white hair.

I stood and shook his large right hand, which squeezed mine in a death grip that went beyond firm and into intimidation, letting me know he was the alpha male in the room.

"This is a pleasant surprise," Sheriff Burr said, displaying his well-practiced political grin. "Always good to see you."

"Yes, sir," I said, "just wanting to get a status report."

"Wish I had something significant to tell you, but things are about like they were the last time we talked. We put out a lot of money to informants in the first couple of months. That's usually how this kind of thing breaks open. We got a sizable underworld of drug users and dealers, men and women of every race and color, in their twenties and thirties, living out in the county, mostly south of town in the woods, getting government checks. Don't none of 'em work. They get their checks or deposits around the first of the month, and parlay the cash into drugs, which they use themselves or sell to raise more cash. Some of 'em trade drugs for sex. They're always getting' high or screwin', or both. Whites, blacks, Mexicans, race don't seem to matter with them. Lost souls, ain't never going to amount to anything. Some of 'em ain't going to live very long, either."

"I'm willing to put up some reward money, or supplement your informant fund," I said. "If that would help."

"I put out enough money already to flush out anyone with information. Thing is, my detectives have worked with the descriptions you gave us of the driver, the shooter, and the vehicle. They say there ain't a male-female team like that working in our county. We'd know about 'em if it was."

"So you think they weren't from around here?"

"That's what we're thinking. Interstate's right there by the BP station. They get off, do their deal, get back on. In ninety minutes they're into Tennessee or Arkansas. Lot of that going on in this country—more than people realize."

I thought Sheriff Burr's opinion was uninformed. No, that's not strong enough. I actually thought it was stupid. The couple in the Expedition were not interstate gangsters. They were from the area, if not Tallabusha County, one of the adjoining rural counties. But, I kept my opinion to myself.

"Have you worked with surrounding counties on identifying...?"

"Oh, yeah. Communicated with Sheriff Departments all over north Mississippi. None of them's come up with anything."

We sat in silence a moment.

"Look, Mr. D.A.," Sheriff Burr said. "We're pretty sure this is just a random murder. These two pulled off I-55 intending to rob this isolated BP station, and you and your wife were just in the wrong place at the wrong time. And you know from your own experience that's the hardest kind of case to break, because there ain't no motive. Nothing to connect the victims with the killers. It's just bad luck on y'all's part."

For a moment I thought about letting Sheriff Burr know I was very unhappy with his investigation, but decided against it because it would do no good. I was in his courthouse, his power center where he controlled everything and everybody, including the judges. Sheriff Burr was the quintessential old-fashioned Mississippi Sheriff, long the most powerful political force in each county. Rural county sheriffs could deliver or withhold votes for the other county officials. He was the biggest employer of all the county officials. Moreover, he alone decided who was arrested or got a get out of jail free card.

"By the way," Sheriff Burr said with a big grin, "I hear you and your banker friend Jimmy Gray patronized one of Tallabusha's fine public houses."

"Sammy's Place?" I said.

"Yes siree, Bob! That Sammy is a real character. What did you think of his establishment? Real nice, ain't it?"

"Nice is not the word I would use to describe it, Sheriff. Unique, maybe." I paused. "I was told Sammy's Place is in Lafayette County."

"It is. Not spittin' distance from the line. But Sammy lives and votes in Tallabusha, so we talk. Up in those hills along the county line, they's more   joints and honky-tonks like Sammy's. Don't know how they make it. Most of their customers have died or moved away. Ain't hardly nobody lives out in the woods any more. They all want to move to the big cities."

"That's where the jobs are, Sheriff. Same thing all over the Delta. Not many young people."

"Damned shame is what it is," he said as he stood and moved around to my side of the desk, ready for me to leave.

"Thanks for your time, Sheriff," I said. "Let me know if I can do anything to help with the investigation."

I smiled, shook the Sheriff's hand, and walked back into the hallway where I had spoken to Deputy Ronnie Tyler. Sheriff Burr wasn't making idle chit-chat about Sammy's. He was letting me know in a subtle way that his finger was on the pulse of his county, that anything I did in Tallabusha would get back to him. I wasn't surprised because I had dealt with rural sheriffs for thirty years. They all had deputies, political supporters, and stringers feeding them intelligence on any interloper asking questions about anything.

I felt good about the encounter even though it was a waste of time. My mind was working, and I had the wherewithal to consider standing up to Sheriff Burr but decided in the blink of an eye it wasn't a good strategy. Not sure I was entirely back on my game, but I was in much better shape than when I let him talk me into staying away from his investigation in the first month after Susan's murder.

I didn't sit down in the hallway because the outside door I had entered earlier, the one I was not supposed to use, opened to admit a half-dozen men, five black, one white, clad in orange jump suits, their wrists cuffed to a waist restraint, feet shackled. I had seen hundreds of these parades when I was the Yaloquena D.A.

I stood back. They shuffled past me, faces downcast. I glanced at each prisoner for a moment, wondering what crimes he committed. As the white inmate stepped through the outside door and walked past me, something about him seemed familiar. His face was pale, sort of an unhealthy gray, and was turned slightly away from me. His dark hair was long and greasy.

I hadn't gotten a good look at his face, but for some reason was positive I knew him from somewhere. Maybe I had prosecuted him in the past.

I kept my distance, but followed the prisoners and the two deputies escorting them. They stopped in the hallway to wait for the elevator to the courtroom on the second floor. I moved to get a better look.

As I stared at the white prisoner, he turned to look at me. It was the first time I had seen his face full on. His eye contact and body language sent an unmistakable message to me: don't approach, don't acknowledge.

I watched him enter the elevator. I walked up the stairs and into the main courtroom. I sat in the last bench and watched as the two deputies and court bailiff escorted the six prisoners into the jury box, where they sat and waited for the judge to enter.

I tried to be subtle, but it was difficult for me to keep my eyes off the pale white man seated in the jury box. He never turned to look at me again, but no matter. Even though he was shackled, pale, and dirty, I recognized the prisoner's walk, how he held himself, how he tilted his head when listening. After all, he lived with Susan and me for eighteen years, then some weekends and summers when he was in college and law school. I read to him in my lap, I taught him to tie his shoes, and to say yes ma'am and no ma'am, yes sir and no sir, whenever he spoke to an adult. I played basketball, baseball, and golf with him, fished and hunted with him back in the day when I did those things.

I knew exactly who the prisoner was.

He was my oldest son, Jacob Pinckney "Jake" Banks.

CHAPTER THIRTEEN

To say I was in shock seeing Jake in the Tallabusha courtroom jury box with the other defendants is an understatement.

Jake was 35-years-old, my height, 6'2", but slimmer than 175 pounds, what he weighed throughout his twenties and early thirties. He looked and moved like me, unlike his younger brother Scott, who was willowy and graceful like his late mother, and a few inches shorter. Jake had dark brown hair and blue eyes like his old man, strong-looking in a wiry sort of way. Scott was blonde with hazel eyes like Susan. In athletics, Jake moved like a lion, Scott like a gazelle.

Jake finished at my alma mater, Ole Miss law school in Oxford, in 2008 and went to work immediately as an Assistant United States Attorney for the Southern District of Mississippi in Jackson. He was a great young prosecutor, in spite of growing misgivings about the politics of the Department of Justice. It was in Jackson that he met FBI Special Agent Kitty Douglas, who first worked with him in Jackson on the prosecution of Adolfo Galvan Zegarra a.k.a. "El Moro," a Caucasian-looking, bilingual Mexican drug smuggler who murdered Yaloquena Deputy Sheriff Travis Ware, a friend of mine.

Jake had girlfriends in high school and college, but I had never seen him fall for a woman like he fell for Kitty.

After the El Moro prosecution ended, Kitty was transferred to the New Orleans FBI office to assist in the investigation of Los Cuervos, an Hispanic gang smuggling weapons in and out of the port of New Orleans after Hurricane Katrina. Jake finessed a move to the U.S. Attorney's office for the Eastern District of Louisiana in New Orleans to be with her. As the FBI closed in on them, the Los Cuervos gang targeted Kitty, violently raping and cutting her to within an inch of her life in her Faubourg-Marigny apartment north of the French Quarter. She never fully recovered from the damage to her lungs and internal organs, and died two years later at our home in Yaloquena County.

The FBI failed to locate Kitty's assailants but Jake did. At least I'm pretty sure he did. He took a leave of absence from the DOJ after the assault on Kitty and ultimately found the two men and killed them. Yes, you read that right. Jake didn't turn the two murderous gangsters over to the FBI or the New Orleans Police Department. He delivered the justice they deserved in a more efficient manner.

Jake never admitted this to his mother and me, but I know in my heart it's true. Susan never asked about what happened to the two Los Cuervos members. After Kitty died, I brought up the subject with Jake on a ride to check on our duck camp in rural Yaloquena County. It was just the two of us. He said he wasn't sure of all the particulars but was glad they were dead. Said it turned out they had been involved in a number of ritual killings of innocent women. It was something in the way Jake said it— something only a parent would notice. I remember being emotionally torn at the time, half-glad, half-horrified, that Jake took the law into his own hands. Neither Jake nor I ever discussed it again.

It was shortly after our trip to the duck camp that Jake told me he was leaving DOJ for good and "going in another direction." I knew he had been talking to David Dunne, the purported FBI agent who worked with us on the El Moro case, and I figured Jake was going to work with him, doing something outside the scope of the legal system.

That was six years ago. Jake virtually disappeared from our family. He did communicate by phone and text occasionally, but his in-person visits with Susan and me were rare. Because Scott was in D.C., Jake had more contact with his younger brother, who would tell us Jake was fine, but little else. Jake never shared details of his missions with me, but I knew he was involved in lethal and dangerous work in the United States and overseas. His supervisor, David Dunne, occasionally called me in the first few years to assure me that Jake was in good health and continuing to fight the good fight. Dunne also told me that Jake had become his most valuable operative.

Dunne's last call was over two years ago. He implied that his "organization" was in its final stages, but Jake was staying on to work "with" the government, which I took to mean Jake was not working "for" the government. The clandestine nature of Jake's activities bothered me, but it really got next to Susan. I knew she worried about Jake every day, but she rarely brought it up for discussion.

As I sat in the back of the courtroom watching Jake and waiting for the judge, I examined my conscience about Jake becoming a mercenary of sorts. Even though David Dunne was guarded in our discussions, I assumed that Jake was dispensing extrajudicial lethal sanctions to those malefactors for whom imprisonment was simply not a symmetrical response to their crimes. Not knowing details of what he was doing, I imagined the worst. As his father, I was more worried about Jake getting killed than I was concerned about the righteousness of his activities.

I had a long career working within the criminal justice system, but my respect for its effectiveness and fairness had waned considerably through the years, especially in my last term as District Attorney. In my rural county, it was more difficult each year to convince jurors to return a guilty verdict, even for those guilty of heinous crimes. And when I convinced the jury to vote guilty as charged, upholding the verdict on appeal had become equally challenging because of the poor quality and political nature of judges on appellate benches. In highly-publicized cases in big cities across the country, I am amazed when a jury returns a unanimous guilty verdict, because distrust of law enforcement and prosecutors has become endemic in urban jurisdictions.

Nidal Hasan, a military psychiatrist who murdered thirteen and wounded thirty at Fort Hood in 2009 while screaming "Allahu Akbar," was finally found guilty and sentenced to death in 2013, but is still pursuing appeals ten years after the murders. Though there were hundreds of witnesses who saw him do it, although he was wounded at the scene, and although there is no question of his guilt and his intent to kill as many American soldiers and civilians as possible, Hasan is in prison being cared for at taxpayer expense. He is represented by a lawyer who has told the media he intends to continue appealing Hasan's case for decades.

That's not the way a justice system should respond to such a horrific crime. Hasan's case, Kitty's murder, and many other miscarriages of justice made Jake turn away from the system. He didn't ask for my opinion or my permission. It was Jake's decision, not mine. I took comfort in knowing Jake had a strong moral compass and would always be a force for good, and left it at that. But still I wondered that day in the back of the Tallabusha court-room how the hell he ended up in an orange jump suit, handcuffed and shackled, awaiting arraignment. Jake was no criminal.

The bailiff walked in and ordered everyone to stand. The judge trailed him and climbed the steps to his bench while the assistant district attorney and a young woman indigent defender followed and took their places.

"What do we have today, Mr. Procell?" the judge asked the prosecutor.

"Six felony arraignments, your honor, and a bail hearing for the one defendant who has not had a bond set."

"Very well," the judge said and looked over at his clerk. "Call the first arraignment."

I tried to be as innocuous as possible on the back row, but it wasn't easy because I was the only person in the courtroom behind the rail. The indigent defender stood with each African-American defendant and entered a not guilty plea. The judge gave her ten days to file what motions she deemed appropriate for her clients.

"Call the last case," the judge ordered his clerk.

"State of Mississippi versus James Agee," the clerk said.

Jake shuffled through the jury box gate to stand before the judge's bench. The indigent defender whispered to him and Jake nodded. The judge opened the charging document.

"James Agee, you are charged with simple possession of a schedule two drug, namely, cocaine, and possession with intent to distribute methamphetamine, another schedule two drug, both felonies. How do you plead?

"James Agee" looked over at his public defender.

"Mr. Agee pleads not guilty to both charges, your honor," she said.

"Is there some reason why bail hasn't been set?" the judge asked, looking over his glasses at the prosecutor and defense attorney.

"He was just arrested late last night, your honor," the assistant d.a. said.

"Any objection to the setting of bail as set forth in the schedule?"

"No, your honor," both attorneys said.

"Very well. Bail is hereby set on the first count at $5,000 and the second at $10,000, cash or bond. Anything else this morning?"

The lawyers demurred, the judge banged the gavel, and two deputies ushered the defendants out of the courtroom.

The entire time he was in the courtroom, Jake never once looked at me. I walked out of the courtroom and down the stairs to the first floor. I caught a glimpse through a glass door of Jake standing at a counter in the Sheriff's office with the woman indigent defender. A man in a short-sleeved white shirt and glasses joined them, spreading documents on the counter in front of Jake. I figured he was a bondsman. A deputy removed Jake's handcuffs and Jake signed the documents where the bondsman indicated.

I left the courthouse and positioned my truck in one of the many vacant diagonal spaces where I could see the main entrance door. I also had a view of the side door of the courthouse I had entered earlier, the one reserved for deputies. I checked my phone for messages and emails, and settled in for a long wait. Bonding out and releasing a prisoner typically took a couple of hours because the prisoner was the only participant in the process who was in a hurry to complete it.

Ninety minutes later, Jake walked out of the main entrance in his street clothes, nasty-looking jeans, a tattered long-sleeved shirt, boots, a faded baseball cap and wrap-a-round dark sunglasses. He stood on the steps for a moment, looking at traffic around the courthouse square, tapping the envelope he held against his palm. He appeared to look right at my truck, but I couldn't be sure.

I watched an older model black Camaro park in one of the spaces in front of the courthouse steps. Jake walked down the steps toward it. The windows were darker than Detective Burke's Tahoe; so dark it was impossible for me to see who was inside.

As Jake approached the passenger door, he dropped the envelope. He bent low to pick it up next to the Camaro, looked directly at me and briefly held his thumb to his ear and little finger to his mouth and pointed at me. He stood, opened the Camaro door and hopped in. I watched the car back out and pull slowly away. Because of my position, I could not see its license number, but I took a picture of the Camaro with my phone.

I waited for a few minutes before I started my truck and headed back to Oxford. Driving home, I knew one thing for sure. I didn't know when or how, but Jake was going to call me.

Chapter Fourteen

On the drive back to Oxford, I went over everything I had seen and heard in the Tallabusha courthouse that morning. I considered everything Jake did, from the look that said "you don't know me" to his gesture to indicate he would call me. I was pretty sure Jake, a.k.a. James Agee, was doing something I should have been doing all along, pulling out all stops to find out who killed Susan and the BP clerk, and tried to kill me. His work was undercover, that much was clear. It was the only reasonable explanation for his appearance and behavior. Like Jake's decision six years ago to avenge Kitty Douglas's death and work outside the system, it both exhilarated and troubled me.

I was proud of Jake for trying to find out who killed his mother. He had the skills and intelligence to do it. But I was worried about Jake's safety and the lengths to which he was prepared to go in his pursuit of the killers. He had allowed himself to be arrested in possession of drugs I knew he didn't use. My mind raced with thoughts of what else he was willing to do in his Mother's name.

I was also embarrassed at what little I had done over the previous five months but sit on my hands and brood in self-pity. Seeing Jake jolted me out of my preoccupation with *my* loss. I resolved on the drive from the Tallabusha courthouse to Oxford to get off my ass and do something, to revert to what I was as D.A. in Yaloquena County, an avenger of blood for the victims of lethal violence. Only this time, the victim was Susan.

I grabbed a quick bite at home and made it to my appointment at 1:00 p.m. in the Ole Miss football offices in the Manning Center on the south side of the football stadium. Walking from the parking lot, my mind was racing about Jake and finding out details about what he was doing. I regretted taking on the Chancellor's case and wondered if I could gracefully exit. I should have been helping Jake instead of trying to find out who killed El Ray.

An athletic-looking student worker, Elise, ushered me into an empty office and said she would tell Coach Barnes I was there. I tried to put Jake out of my mind. I studied my notes, trying to focus on what I was going to ask Reggie Barnes. Just minutes later, Reggie Barnes walked in followed closely by his boss, Ole Miss head coach Carl Goodson, both wearing navy blue coaching shorts and red knit shirts with the distinctive cursive logo, *Ole Miss.*

The contrast in body language was telling.

Reggie Barnes was like a whipped dog—eyes downcast, submissive, beaten down. He was tall and rangy like the star wide receiver he was at Ole Miss over a decade ago. His skin was a golden brown, his head shaved on the sides and back to match his naturally bald scalp on top. Physically, he seemed to be in good shape; emotionally, he appeared severely depressed.

Carl Goodson was combative. I could see it in his eyes. I knew from his bio on the Ole Miss football web site he was forty-three. He was an All-American defensive end at Alabama and spent two years with the Green Bay Packers before a crippling knee injury on a snowy field in Cleveland put him on the sidelines permanently. Goodson took a job the next year as linebacker coach in Gainesville for the University of Florida, then became a defensive line coach at the University of Michigan, where he produced several all-Big Ten linemen and developed a reputation for being an intelligent, no-nonsense, hard-nosed defensive coach who could teach a player how to hit and tackle. He was hired by UCLA to be its defensive coordinator, and became a coaching star in the huge Southern California media market. Goodson was mentioned as a potential candidate for every head coaching job that became available at big name football colleges across the country. After four successful years at UCLA, he accepted the offer of Ole Miss to be its head coach, putting him back in the SEC Western Division where he started as a player.

Jimmy Gray had told me Coach Goodson was making $5 million as the first black head football coach at Ole Miss, and was turning the football program around. He also told me that everyone in college football was surprised he took the Ole Miss job, because he could have gone anywhere. Jimmy said Goodson's slogan, which was plastered everywhere in the locker room, was "Defense Wins Titles!"

Coach Goodson, according to Jimmy, was supposed to be a religious man who never cursed. But the way he glared at me that afternoon, I did not get the feeling he was about to break out in a rendition of "Kumbaya" and extend his arms for a warm embrace. His dark eyes matched his very black skin. His hair was natural and cut short, his cheekbones high. His formidable forehead and jaw were large and square, and his upper body very muscular. Though Carl Goodson had not played football in almost twenty years, he looked as though he could still deliver a crushing tackle.

"You're not talking to him without me," he said, gesturing toward Reggie.

"Is that all right with you?" I asked Reggie, knowing it was rhetorical.

"Sure," he said quietly.

"I'm Willie Mitchell Banks. I live here in town and I've been hired by the Chancellor to be her attorney in this matter."

"You working with Lawrence Pratt?" Coach Goodson asked.

"I'm not associated with University counsel. My client felt that she needed an independent set of eyes looking out for her interests, but Mr. Pratt and I certainly are working toward the same goal."

"Which is what?" Goodson said.

"To see that justice is done," I said.

Reggie seemed oblivious, but the head coach almost scoffed at my meaningless powder puff of a non-answer. I didn't know why he was so hostile, so I decided to do what I think is always best in such situations—I confronted it head on.

"You don't seem very pleased to be here with Reggie," I said. "You are welcome to stay, but if you have other things to do...."

"I'm not leaving, so ask your questions."

"Reggie needs to answer, Coach Goodson, not you. If you want to add something to what he says, that's fine. But I need to hear from him first and if you don't want to go along with that, I suggest we call the Chancellor right now and clear this up so I can get on with my work."

He gestured dismissively and grunted, which I took as permission to proceed.

"Did you know El Ray was coming to Oxford the weekend he disappeared" I asked Reggie.

"No, sir, I didn't. It wasn't an authorized visit, and he didn't call me. So, there was no way I would have known he was coming."

"How often did you talk to him?"

"As much as I could under the NCAA rules. I been knowing him since he was thirteen, when I watched him play a junior high game in Vicksburg. He was a man among boys at that age."

"When is the last time you saw or talked to him?"

"He came up for his official visit with other recruits in late October for the Auburn game. That's the last time I actually saw him.

I talked to him on the phone on the Thursday before he disappeared. I tried to stay in touch with him as much as I could."

"How did he seem that Thursday?"

"You know, just the same he always was. Real friendly, nice and polite. Excited about finishing up his high school requirements in December. He planned on enrolling for spring semester so he could be at our spring camp."

"Did you call him that time or he call you?"

"He texted me first then called me on his cell. Coach has access to all our phones, and we have to bring them to our compliance administrator every two weeks to let him check our call records."

"Do you have a separate personal phone?"

"No. I just use the phone the university provides. I had another phone but cancelled it a year ago because it was just too confusing going back and forth between phones. Coach said we could use our university phones for personal calls."

I asked him a number of softball questions about his duties as an assistant coach and recruiter to get a feel for him and how he did his job. He explained how he went about communicating with his prospects. Coach Goodson let me know through loud sighs and occasional grunts he thought I was wasting his time and Reggie's.

"You know he had his own car?" I asked, provoking a raised eyebrow from Coach Goodson.

"He got that sometime over the summer. I guess his Mother helped him buy it. He never said. He said the car ran good, just not much to look at. A Toyota. At least ten years old."

"We didn't buy it for him if that's what you're suggesting," Goodson said.

I nodded and paused. "Just a few more questions, Reggie," I said. "Do you know of anyone who might have wanted to hurt El Ray for any reason?"

"No. No, I didn't. El Ray was a sweet kid. He wasn't cocky and arrogant like a lot of the kids I deal with. He was respectful and...,"

Reggie's voice cracked and he grew quiet. I watched him for a moment. Tears filled his eyes.

"Rags and El Ray were tight," Coach Goodson said without rancor for a change. "The kid was a five-star, something we don't get a shot at here very often. We have to develop our three-star talent into four-and five-stars after we get them on campus. Everyone in the country wanted El Ray. He could have gone anywhere but he picked Ole Miss because of his relationship with

Rags. It was like he was his big brother. It's a damn shame what happened to him and I hope you all can get to the bottom of it."

"Rags is what they call you?" I asked.

"That's what El Ray started calling me when he was a sophomore at St. Mary's, 'Coach Rags.' He said it was because he liked the way I dressed, you know, as in 'nice rags, man' and now everyone around here calls me that."

It was the first time Reggie had smiled.

"Did he have any friends on campus or anyone in Oxford he hung with?" I asked. "Any girls?"

"Naw, Mr. Banks. The girls loved him, but he didn't have anyone special. He had his pick, believe me. Ain't nothing the girls wouldn't do to be with him, even just to hang out. He had charisma, you know. Like a movie star. I never saw him be anything but nice to the girls he met and to other recruits."

Reggie hung his head. I watched a tear drop to the floor. Reggie sat up, sniffed deeply and wiped his eyes.

"We through?" Coach Goodson asked. "He's going on the road for a few days in Louisiana, so you better ask now. This time of year recruiting gets real intense. Lots of traveling."

"If I have more questions I'll work around Reggie's schedule, Coach," I said and stood to leave. "Appreciate y'all's time this afternoon."

Walking toward my truck, I checked my phone. No call from Jake.

CHAPTER FIFTEEN

I spent the rest of the afternoon online, reading newspaper stories about Reggie Barnes and Ole Miss football. I called Aunt Bee to give her a brief progress report and a recap of the meeting with the coaches. The conversation was brief because I had not made much progress. I told her the meeting with the coaches was predictably uneventful, except for Rags being so emotionally distraught over El Ray's death. She said the athletic director had mentioned how close the two were. I told her I was probably going to drive to Natchez Thursday to meet with El Ray's parents and mentioned that the toxicology reports were due at OPD by Wednesday.

By five o'clock I was beat. The knock on my front door was not welcome. No one who knew me ever came to the front door. I peeked out the window and saw a white man in a dark suit with salt and pepper hair, wire rim glasses, and a briefcase. He looked like a lawyer, probably in his mid-forties.

"Can I help you?" I asked when I opened the front door.

"I'm Jeffrey Blanchard with the NCAA. Do you have time to talk?"

"A few minutes," I said reluctantly. "Come on in."

We sat in the front room of the condo. Unlike Jimmy Gray, Mr. Blanchard had no problem fitting between the arms of the stuffed Queen Anne chair. He handed me his business card, which gave his office address in Indianapolis and his title, Chief Investigator.

"Does Chief mean you're in charge of all the other NCAA investigators?"

"In my department, yes. College football."

"You look like an attorney."

"That may be because I am."

"Where did you go to law school?" I asked.

"Georgetown. I took a job with the FTC right out of school, stayed three years, then was an associate at a couple of firms in D.C. I went in-house with the association about ten years ago."

"Must be interesting work."

"Very much so."

Michael Henry

"What can I do for you?"

"I spoke to Chancellor O'Donald briefly thirty minutes ago to ask a few questions and she said she wanted Mr. Pratt and you to be present before she answered."

"That's good. I'm representing her individually."

"Why would she hire her own attorney?" he asked in an abrasive tone. "She doesn't have confidence in Mr. Pratt?"

I looked at him for a moment, to see if I had misread him.

"Or maybe she's got something to hide," he said.

I read him right. Georgetown Law School inside the beltway, a federal agency, and D.C. firms until about ten years ago when he left for the NCAA. I suspected he left private practice at the firms because he wasn't on track to make partner at either one. Enough time inside the Beltway Babylon to develop the attitude that lawyers in rural America, especially the South, were rubes. *Chief Investigator.* An inflated sense of power added to the mix. Definitely an asshole.

"Now, Mr. Blanchard, you're a lawyer. You know I can't discuss that with you," I said smiling. "Anything else?"

"We have reason to believe that a large amount of money changed hands to entice Mr. Raymond to commit to Ole Miss," he said.

I didn't respond, staring a hole right between his lawyer eyes.

"What does your client know about that?"

"I think we're done here, Mr. Blanchard," I said and stood.

Blanchard sat in the Queen Anne for a moment, then grabbed his briefcase and followed me to the front door, which I opened for him.

"Nice meeting you, Mr. Chief Investigator Blanchard."

"We're going to interview your client, Mr. Banks, with you or without you. There can be severe repercussions for schools that choose not to cooperate."

"Call my secretary to set it up," I said, neglecting to tell him I didn't have one. "And, oh yeah, really nice job you guys at the NCAA did exposing that basketball shoe payola scheme involving Adidas and those college assistant coaches. There was some big money involved."

Blanchard studied me a moment, taking my measure. He was trying to figure out if I knew the Adidas scandal was uncovered solely by the FBI and U.S. Attorney's office in the Southern District of New York, not by the NCAA. The vaunted NCAA enforcement team found out about basketball shoe companies funneling millions of dollars to college players at the same time the general public did.

"And I'm so happy you guys punished the University of North Carolina for its fifteen-year phony college course scam to keep their athletes academically eligible," I added to twist the knife.

"We have no jurisdiction over the academic content of member university's courses," Blanchard said, "which I would not expect you to know with your rural district attorney background."

"Oh," I said. "Sorry. I thought you gave them a pass because March Madness provides 85% of the NCAA's gross revenue and the Tar Heels are in the Final Four or Elite Eight just about every year."

Blanchard's cheeks reddened. He pointed his bony index finger at me.

"You watch your step, Mr. Banks. You're out of your league."

"Good meeting you, too," I said and closed the door.

I called Detective David Burke.

"You busy?" I asked.

"What's up?"

"Mr. Blanchard with the NCAA just paid me a visit."

"Real piece of work, isn't he?" David said.

"I've got some ice-cold Heineken in my refrigerator over here. You care to have one with me? They're free."

"Be there in thirty," he said.

I Googled NCAA Chief Investigator Jeffrey Blanchard and compared his credentials listed on the NCAA website under "About Us" to what he told me. All consistent. I clicked on a link to an interview of Blanchard by one of the jabbering goofballs at ESPN. Blanchard said all the right things, came off as very professional. Smart and ambitious, too. That's the thing about television or online interviews—they don't always reflect the true nature of the guest, especially if the host lobs softballs, as in the ESPN interview I watched. Not a single question about the NCAA's giving a pass to flagship and revenue-generating college football and basketball programs and hammering lesser universities that are easy targets.

I smiled as I recalled the late, great UNLV Runnin' Rebels basketball coach, Jerry Tarkanian, who was always at war with NCAA's selective enforcement. "The NCAA is so mad at Kentucky," Tark the Shark said, "they're going to give Cleveland State another year of probation."

My phone buzzed with a text from David. I opened my back door and punched the garage opener, gesturing for the detective to pull in. Since Ina was now in possession of Susan's Lexus, there was only my truck in our two-car garage, a depressing daily reminder of her absence.

We sat down with two Heinekens.

"Why would the NCAA send its Chief Investigator down here?" I asked David. "If they think Ole Miss paid El Ray to sign with Ole Miss, their star witness is dead."

"You met Blanchard," David said. "You think he's interested in being fair and impartial in looking into this? Or do you think he's planning to leverage this high-profile investigation to give him the inside track on being named NCAA President next year? Big pay increase, lots more power."

"Oh? I pick number two. I didn't know the current guy is leaving."

"Yep," Burke said. "Already announced."

"Bad time for Ole Miss to be in the NCAA crosshairs." I paused. "You have any inkling that somebody paid El Ray?"

"You talking about the university or the coaches?" David asked.

"No. That wouldn't happen. I'm talking about well-heeled alumni."

"I'm not saying that didn't happen, but I haven't heard anything during this investigation to suggest that."

"All right. Tell me about our blonde. Did you find out anything?"

"Her name's Reese Conklin."

"She's the one picked up El Ray at Sammy's, the blonde Eloise saw?"

"Yes."

"Did you ask her about the night he went missing?"

"Yep. She picked up El Ray at Sammy's that night, too."

"How do you know?"

"Because she told me she did."

CHAPTER SIXTEEN

"How did you know to ask this Conklin woman if she was the blonde that Eloise saw that night?"

"It's a long story."

"Hold on," I said and hopped up to get us two more Heinekens.

Kind of nice to have a sense of purpose again, even after a long day that started in the Tallabusha courthouse. It felt good to be mentally engaged in something besides grief. My brain had succeeded in compartmentalizing, setting aside worrying about Jake in order to get a good feel for Reggie Barnes and Coach Goodson at our meeting. And I had the mental acuity to go toe-to-toe with the arrogant NCAA Chief Investigator Jeffrey Blanchard and put him on the defensive. My brain was making a comeback.

"Hey, David," I called out from the kitchen. "Do me a favor and don't congratulate Jimmy Gray because his interrogation of Eloise at Sammy's Place led you to Reese Conklin."

"Why not?"

"Because I'll never hear the end of it," I said and handed David a beer. "Just kidding. Jimmy is actually a pretty good detective. He knows people and how to talk to them, no matter their station in life."

David smiled and took a pull on his fresh Heineken.

"I'm ready for the long story," I said, making a mental note to forget about firing Aunt Bee as a client. I was finding my way back into the zone, and beginning to relish solving both murders, El Ray's and Susan's. I felt useful and driven for a change. Not so focused on myself; not feeling as guilty. Maybe the antidepressant was finally kicking in. Or maybe the Heineken.

"I met her one night in a bar on the Square," David said. "We hit it off right away. She was by herself when I walked in. We made eye contact. She seemed receptive so I introduced myself and asked if I could buy her a drink. She said no, that she would buy me one. I sat next to her and we talked. And drank. She was lively. Smart, too."

"What does she look like?"

"She's kind of short, 5'4", maybe. A stunning figure, showing just enough cleavage that night. You know who Brittany Spears is?"

"I'm not that old, David."

"That's kind of who she looks like, but sort of classier. She's thirty-five or so. And sexy? Oh, shit. You know how some women, even if they're not beautiful, but plenty attractive, exude sexuality. It's hard to explain."

"I know exactly what you're talking about," I said. "It's something in the way they are—it's not put on. Pheromones maybe. You can't talk to them without thinking about it."

"Yeah. Well, you understand. Reese was just like that. Except she was sexy *and* beautiful. I mean, what a body. So that night, after a few drinks, we went to my house. She followed me in her car."

"The black SUV?"

"No. She was driving a Mercedes then. She didn't get the Range Rover she drives now until about a year ago."

"We're getting to the good part now?"

"I'm not going into the exact details but it was an hour of intense sex. I mean, *in-tense*. She knew what she liked to do, and what she wanted done to her. She was very frank about it. It was unique—in my experience, anyway."

"She stayed over?"

"No. She got dressed and left right after. I asked for her phone number, but she said she wanted mine instead. That she'd be in touch."

"Is this the part where you say you felt used? Violated?"

"No," he said, chuckling. "I felt great. I wanted to see her again. Not giving me her number was her way of controlling the dynamic, when and if we got together again. She knew I was an OPD detective and could find out what I wanted to about her, but I went along with her game. She told me only her first name that night. We talked about me, my background, history, but not much about her. It didn't bother me at the time. Looking back on it, I can see now that it was all part of her needing to be in charge. She had to control the relationship, if there was going to be one."

"I guess there are worse things. She call you?"

"A week later. I had just about given up on the idea and out of the blue she calls right after I got off work. We meet at a place she said was hers, a condo over in Grand Oaks, you know, by the country club."

"One of the ones north of number five?"

"Part of the same complex. Her place was across the street. I checked it out later. It's in her name, according to the tax assessor. And it was pretty much the same deal as at my place, except we weren't drinking. Maybe ninety minutes going at it full speed, then she's getting cleaned up and dressed. So, I did the same. She tells me to push in the door lock when I leave."

"No discussion of a return bout?"

"I knew better. But at least I had her cell number in my phone. Next day I did a reverse search on the number, got her last name and address and started looking into who she was. Ran her through DMV. The Mercedes was in her name, too. I did a social media check, but she's not on Facebook or Twitter. Does have an email address, though, which is linked to her husband's original business domain."

"Which is?"

"The domain name is still Conklin Restaurants. Her husband started his fast food empire in the late sixties with McDonald's franchises all over north Mississippi, Louisiana, and Arkansas, but sold them all as a package and plowed that money into Pizza Huts, Sonics, and later into Chipotles."

"Sounds like a smart businessman."

"That's an understatement. Richard Conklin was way ahead of the curve in fast food franchises. He was smart enough to get in early on the newest trends. Then ten years ago he started his own concept, Conklin's, which is a soup, salad, and sandwich place. He's got a significant presence in every major southern city now. He owns over a hundred Conklin's that he built and operates himself, and is expanding into Texas in a big way."

"I've heard a good bit about him but never met him," I said. "He lives on a big spread in Tallabusha County. Jimmy Gray tried to get some of his banking business for our Sunshine Bank but couldn't get even a small slice."

"He's a recluse. Shuns publicity. Apparently all he does is work."

"Must spend some time with his hot young wife."

"You would think so, but who knows. After being on the job a few years, even in this little town, nothing I learn about people surprises me anymore.

"How many more times did you see her?" I asked.

"Once. And afterwards she said she couldn't see me anymore. I tried to find out why and she wouldn't say. I didn't like it but I didn't get a vote, so I never called her again. For about a month I hoped she would call, but she never did. I guess it was all about her control thing."

"Reese is Mrs. Conklin number two, I take it?"

"No. But they've only been married five years or so. He's kind of an odd duck, or so they say. I've never met him. I think he's right at seventy or seventy-one. He was a lifelong bachelor, born entrepreneur. He's worth no telling how many hundreds of millions."

"Gotta admire that. And landed him a trophy wife half his age."

"Right. She was married before. Some guy from Greenville. That's where she's from. She told me he wanted kids and she didn't. After five years they split. She was single a couple of years then married Conklin."

"She say what kind of relationship they have?"

"If you mean does he know about his wife picking up guys in bars? I don't know. She and I never talked about her personal life or about him. Most everything I learned about her I dug up on my own."

"How long ago was your involvement with her?"

"Two years. Little more, maybe. It was in the summer. So, it'd be two years and four or five months."

"Have you run into her since your last time?"

"I pass her on the highway or street and wave, but I hadn't talked to her until I called about El Ray this weekend."

"We need to get a court order to get access to her phone records," I said.

"I already started on the paperwork. I'll get a judge to sign a subpoena to her carrier tomorrow. I'm sure she wouldn't give it to us voluntarily. Her control thing, you know."

"She make a habit of picking up high school seniors?"

"I don't know. But she likes college athletes. I talked to some of the detectives at the station this weekend and a few of them knew about her. Said Mrs. Conklin liked football and basketball players, all races, all sizes. She's good-looking, has plenty of money and time on her hands. Plus they're kids, so she calls all the shots—satisfies her need to dominate."

"Well, maybe that's just her way of making our players feel welcome."

David laughed out loud.

"Funny. Her husband Richard Conklin is by far the biggest donor to Ole Miss athletics. Tens of millions. Anything they ask for."

"Jeez," I said. "I've been here full time for two years and I never heard that Richard Conklin was a big Ole Miss donor."

"Just to the Athletic Department. His gifts are conditioned on the school not disclosing that he's the donor. Turns down any attempt to put him in the Alumni Hall of Fame or shine a spotlight on him in any way. They wanted to name the new practice field after him but he said no."

"Any possibility that Conklin used his young wife to slip a few hundred thousand to El Ray or his parents?"

"It's something we need to look at. His Conklin's stores probably generate a ton of cash. Anything's possible."

"So, Reese admits she was with El Ray the night he went missing?"

"Very matter of fact about it. Said he had called her about getting together while he was driving from Natchez to Oxford. She said okay, she'd meet him in the parking lot at Sammy's. Same routine they had done several times before."

"Why Sammy's Place?" I asked.

"Exactly the question I asked her. She said it's less than ten miles from her husband's camp and it's so far out in the boonies no one would see them. She said El Ray was paranoid about being seen."

"How'd they meet the first time?"

"On one of his authorized visits. They met at some recruiting function in one of the student bars on the Square on a home game weekend in September. Anyway, the Saturday night he went missing, she said she rang him about eleven o'clock and he told her he was already under the walnut tree at Sammy's. He got into her Range Rover and left his car there under the tree, right where we found it. Took him to her husband's hunting camp, had their fun, then dropped him back off at his car maybe an hour-and-a-half or two hours later. She must have called his burner number because her number didn't show up on the log of El Ray's phone the lab tech prepared."

"We'll probably never locate El Ray's burner," I said. "But we can identify his burner number by process of elimination using Reese's records. At least that gives us a time line. We add two hours or so to get the time she dropped him off at Sammy's. That is, if Mrs. Conklin is telling the truth."

"I'm pretty sure she is," David said. "She never lied to me about anything when we got together. She just didn't give out a lot of information. I guess you could call it lying by omission."

"Did you ask her about the lipstick on El Ray's groin?"

"Sure did. She didn't miss a beat. Said that lipstick was hers, unless he was with someone else after her that night."

"Good to know," I said, shaking my head.

CHAPTER SEVENTEEN

I met Jimmy Gray Tuesday morning at the new breakfast place, First Watch, in the shopping center between the sprawling new Baptist Hospital and the old Baptist Hospital facility on South Lamar.

I filled him in on the details of my busy Monday—everything except seeing Jake. Until I found out exactly what Jake was up to, I wasn't telling anyone, including Jimmy and Jake's younger brother Scott.

"Don't Coach Goodson have a big head?" Jimmy said after I recounted my meeting with Reggie Barnes and his head coach, Carl Goodson. "I'd hate for him to head butt me with that noggin of his. I think it's bigger than Coach Orgeron's."

"Maybe," I said, picturing LSU's Cajun coach. "Sheriff Burr's got a decent-sized dome, too. Not sure how much gray matter is in it."

"Yeah, but he's a shrewd one, they say. He's wrong about the couple in the Expedition. They're local for sure," Jimmy said. "The interstate robberies I read about are pulled off by real pros, like Robert DeNiro's crew in *"Heat."* From what you've told me about those two at the Varner exit, they don't sound like professionals. More like home-grown Mississippi dumbasses. Pros don't knock over a low-volume operation like the BP, and they don't commit a store invasion in flip-flops."

"I agree with you on that. What did you find out from your Ole Miss alumni network? Anybody slip El Ray or his people money to sign?"

"I talked to some die-hards who follow those subscription sites. There's a couple of sites exclusively about Ole Miss sports, mostly football. A lot of what's posted is wishful thinking or bullshit, but my buddies in that loop tell me there's never been a suggestion of money changing hands. They all credit Reggie with bringing the kid along, building a strong relationship with the mother, getting El Ray committed early on to Ole Miss. I called on a couple of well-heeled guys who know everything there is to know about the program, and they said no money was paid. Main reason, they said, was they knew the NCAA was going to be looking at any school that signed him. Plus, they all know the NCAA's got a hard-on when it comes to Ole Miss. We're easy pickins'."

"What do you know about Richard Conklin?"

"Why?"

I told him what David Burke had said about Conklin and his randy wife, her connection with El Ray.

"Jeez," Jimmy said after listening intensely. "That's some serious scoop."

"You think Conklin paid El Ray to sign with Ole Miss?"

"A few hundred thousand is nothing to Conklin, but I doubt it. Conklin makes that much in his Conklin's empire during his lunch hour. But he's not a typical Ole Miss supporter. Never comes to the football games. Doesn't suck up to the coaches or players. When I was calling on him he told me he prefers watching the game on his big screen television at home. You ever met him?"

"I'm not sure I've ever seen him," I said.

"He's a little roly-poly guy, like he's had more than his share of chicken and dumplings. And soft. He's not big-boned and rangy like me."

I almost choked on my scrambled eggs, making Jimmy chuckle quietly.

"I'm down to 310," he said, "but that's as low as I can go without affecting my performance."

"At what?"

"You'll have to ask Martha," Jimmy said. "I like to keep some things private."

"Since when?" I said. "You don't keep anything secret."

"That ain't true. All my detective work for you—they could torture me and I wouldn't give up the goods. Like what I got out of Eloise at Sammy's that's blowing the El Ray case wide open."

"You did good with her," I said, smiling. "Burke was impressed."

Jimmy Gray and I were closer than most brothers. Sitting there sipping my coffee, I thought for a moment about changing my mind and letting him in on my encounter with Jake the day before. But I decided not to. It was the only thing I had ever kept from him. Jimmy watched Jake grow up. But what Jake was doing in Tallabusha was dangerous. I couldn't help him yet, but I could keep my mouth shut. I would tell Jimmy at the right time, but not that morning at the First Watch breakfast table.

"Back to Conklin," Jimmy said, "It'd be easy for him to funnel a bunch of cash to El Ray through Miss Hot Pants, but what's an eighteen-year-old kid going to do with a wheelbarrow full of hundred dollar bills?"

"Payoffs like that usually go to a parent or to somebody close to the family who claims they're looking out for the kid," I said.

"Yep, the parents, or family preacher or lawyer, or somebody acting as the boy's shade tree agent, who's going to drag more than the usual ten or fifteen percent. Maybe Reese's honey pot was part of the inducement."

"Maybe," I said, "maybe not. Burke says the word is she's spreading her love among a lot of the University's football and basketball players."

"And it wouldn't make sense to pay the kid a ton of money to sign with the school then have him rubbed out because he's diddling the old man's wife. He's a real savvy businessman, and if she's notorious about being generous with her favors, Conklin's bound to know about it. Maybe they have an understanding."

"David talked to Conklin's secretary yesterday afternoon. She said Mr. Conklin was on the road at some of his locations in Dallas and Fort Worth this week. She's going to set up a time for us to question him at Conklin's office Monday."

"Well, be prepared because what everyone says is right, he's a cagey old bastard," Jimmy said. "When I was courting him for our bank, I met with him three or four times. Always at his office. And out of the fifteen minutes of his time he gave me, ten of 'em he was on the phone. His secretary put every call through to him like I wasn't even there. Tell you something else." Jimmy leaned toward me. "Far as I can tell, he ain't got any friends. I can't name a one. He's all about work. And don't be surprised if he goes off on some tangent, talking nonsense in the middle of your questioning. You know, like Les Miles in a post-game interview. Or Ted Turner."

"I'm driving down to Natchez tomorrow night," I said. "Meeting with El Ray's parents on Thursday. Driving back Friday."

"You need me to go with you? Dig up some more clues on the case?"

"Not really," I said.

"Good. Because I'm going to be in Nashville Thursday and Friday on bank business."

"What kind of business?"

"Corresponding bank stuff, boring details that you have no interest in."

Jimmy gave the waiter his Sunshine Bank credit card, explaining to me that we had discussed bank business, albeit briefly, so the breakfast meeting between Jimmy, the CEO and largest stockholder, and me, the bank's second largest stockholder, was definitely a tax-deductible business expense.

A text popped up on my phone from Detective David Burke.

"Call me re crime lab test results. Got them a day early."

CHAPTER EIGHTEEN

I sent a text to Detective Burke saying I was on my way. There was little traffic. In ten minutes, I pulled into the Oxford Police headquarters. It's nice living in a small town.

"Any smoking gun?" I asked David as I sat down in his office.

"There's nothing of consequence in the Toyota," he said. "The crime lab tech pulled El Ray's calls from his cell phone he left on the seat. No calls on Saturday except his mom."

"So, he was on his burner," I said. "That's the one we need."

"And you're right, we'll probably never find it. There's a call he made to Reggie Barnes on the Thursday before he disappeared. It confirms what Reggie told you yesterday about his last contact with El Ray. About a twenty minute call."

"Nothing from Reese?"

"No. Not on his regular cell. Reese gave me the number she had for him. The number wasn't his personal phone, so it had to be his burner. She said that's the only number she ever called him on. Outgoing calls on her phone to him on Saturday confirm what she told me about Saturday night. Her last call with him was at 10:47 pm, which would have been right before she picked him up at Sammy's."

"Anything on the jacket he left on the seat?" I asked.

"Just his DNA, his hair. No trace of anyone else. Beer cans had only his DNA and prints. They found plenty of El Ray's prints in the car, as you'd expect, and only two from unknown sources, but they don't match anyone in the state system."

"Probably friends of his who rode with him in Natchez."

"So," David said, "he leaves his regular phone and his jacket in the Toyota, gets into Reese's Range Rover. After a couple of hours she drops him off at his car sometime after midnight, but he doesn't drive away in it."

"He left with someone else."

"Right," David said. "He rode off with his killer. There's no sign of a struggle in the Toyota. No blood, nothing torn up, everything the way you'd expect a kid would keep his vehicle. I figure someone was waiting for him at Sammy's Place. Someone who knew him, I'm guessing. They might have called his burner to set it up."

"Yes," I said, "he wouldn't have gotten in a car with someone he didn't know and trust. He was a smart kid."

"I need to get some of my fellow officers to ask around to find out everyone he knew or hung out with in Oxford."

"It's possible he encountered someone in the parking lot leaving the bar, someone who didn't care for people like him. They had words, maybe, and one thing led to another."

"That's a whole different scenario," David said. "If it was a stranger who confronted him in Sammy's parking lot, say a redneck and his buddies who had a snootful and didn't like blacks patronizing his honky-tonk. It'd have to be a pretty good-sized man to take on El Ray."

"Or a drunk redneck with a screwdriver and maybe three or four drunk friends," I said.

"Reese said she didn't see anyone in the parking lot, but she was only there a minute. Let him out at his car and she left. And the people I canvassed who were there that night didn't say anything about a fight in the parking lot."

"Do you have the names of everyone at Sammy's Place that night?"

"I have a list, but I got it from Sammy. If he knows more about that night than he's telling, he might have left some names off on purpose."

"That's a follow-up you ought to handle personally," I said. "And I'd question everyone on the list you have and ask them to name everyone who was in Sammy's that Saturday night. That might produce a more accurate list than just relying on Sammy."

"All right," David said. "I'll work on those two lists, one for everyone in Oxford and the University who El Ray knew or hung out with, another for a more reliable survey of everyone in the bar that night."

"Sheriff Burr seemed to be tight with Sammy," I said. "Maybe Sammy confided in him, telling him who was there that night," I said.

"If he did, the Sheriff's not going to tell us about it," David said. "He doesn't share information with us over here. I can call Deputy Ronnie Tyler and see if he can figure out how to draw that information out of Burr without making a big deal out of it. Tyler's sharp."

"I met him yesterday morning," I said. "He's the one called Sheriff Burr for me to make sure he was coming in. How'd he get that scar on his eye?"

"I don't know. Tyler should have been working on Susan's case from the beginning. I don't know why Burr didn't have him on it."

"Lots of things should have been done differently on Susan's case," I said. "I should have camped out over there."

"I imagine you were in pretty bad shape for a while."

I shrugged.

"The crime lab did say the smear on the patch of skin above El Ray's pubic area removed in the autopsy was consistent with lipstick, but that's all they could say. They said there wasn't enough to identify the brand."

"So much for the crime lab results helping us," I said.

"Well, there was this. Their analysis of El Ray's vitreous humor was positive for alcohol and for methamphetamines."

I leaned back in my chair.

"Well, you're a good poker player, Detective Burke. You saved the best for last. What was his BAC?"

"Point zero eight."

"Legally drunk for an eighteen-year-old in Mississippi," I said.

"Four times the legal amount for someone under twenty-one."

"Damn," I said. "This is going to be a letdown for everyone. El Ray was supposed to be a model athlete and student."

"He was a senior and his high school career was over. I'd cut him some slack on the alcohol. That's not a big deal."

"Might be to his parents. The methamphetamine certainly will be. I hate for that to go public."

"I'm keeping it under wraps for now, but it's going to be out there at some point. This kind of thing gets around in a hurry."

"I know. Did you have any indication from your investigation that he was drinking up here in Oxford or using meth or any other drugs?"

"Not until I got this," David said.

"You ever know of Reese Conklin using crystal meth?"

"Alcohol was the only drug she ever did in my presence. She told me she didn't do other kinds of drugs. Meth stays in the system up to six days, so El Ray could have done it in Natchez before he drove up."

"That's possible. But he might well have gotten it from Reese."

"Or somebody else up here."

"Right. Something we need to ask her—away from her husband. They need to be interviewed separately."

"His secretary said Reese was with Conklin on the road. I'll firm up a time for both of them Monday."

"I'm headed to Natchez tomorrow afternoon," I said. "I'm meeting with El Ray's folks Thursday."

"You want me to go with you?"

"You got enough to do here. It'd be a waste of your time."

"All right. That makes sense."

"Unless you want to be the one to break it to Mr. and Mrs. Raymond that their son was high on alcohol and meth when he died."

"Uh, I'd just as soon let you handle that," David said. "I'm the one called Mrs. Raymond to tell her as soon as we found El Ray's body."

"How'd she handle it?"

"Like you'd expect, but after a few minutes she said she already knew in her heart. Said when he didn't answer his phone Sunday morning she was certain something bad had happened."

"You talk to Mr. Raymond?"

"No. They're divorced. Reggie says the mother is nice, but his father drinks and is hard to deal with. Reggie said El Ray and his mom were sold on Ole Miss from the get go, back when he was in junior high. The old man kept hinting about LSU, Mississippi State, and Alabama, even Notre Dame. He talked to Reggie about the big money he heard other players had gotten from colleges for signing. Reggie said when the father talked to him, he danced around it, never coming right out and asking for money from Ole Miss. Reggie told me he never took the bait, never said anything negative about other schools, always played it straight."

"Better the parents find out from us about the BAC and the meth."

"It's a shame they have to know at all," David said.

"Like you say, it's going to come out sooner or later. And it may have something to do with his death. I don't want the parents picking up the Jackson paper and reading about alcohol and drugs in his system."

I left David and drove home, thinking about how many times in the twenty-four years I was District Attorney I had to share heartbreaking news with parents about their children. I don't know the number, but it was a lot. There's no easy way to do it. Beating around the bush doesn't help soften the blow. It only stretches it out, heightening the fear and anxiety. Best to say it up front, get it over with for them and me.

I didn't have to tell the Raymonds their only son was dead. Because of Detective Burke's call, they had known that for two weeks. All I had to do was tell them about the crime lab toxicology results, something that will taint their memory of their dead son forever. Learning of his death no doubt broke their hearts. My news was going to make them angry.

Chapter Nineteen

I left the condo for Natchez a little after noon on Wednesday. My phone conversation with Mrs. Raymond was brief. She agreed to meet with me at her home in Natchez and said she would let her ex-husband know. She wasn't sure he would show up.

"Depends on his mood," she said matter-of-factly. "And how much he drinks tonight."

As soon as I got onto I-55 at Batesville, I called Robbie Cedars, head of the Mississippi Forensics Lab in Pearl to talk to him about the El Ray evidence analysis. I had worked with Robbie on scores of cases when I was District Attorney and considered him a friend.

The call to Robbie was the first of several I planned to make on the four-and-a-half hour drive. There would be little cell service when I turned off the interstate onto the Natchez Trace just north of Jackson at Ridgeland, so I had to make the calls in the first two hours of the trip. The phone conversations made the time pass faster and kept my mind from obsessing about Jake.

It had been two days since I had seen Jake in the Tallabusha courthouse, and still no phone call.

I got through to Robbie on my first try.

"Great to hear from you, Willie Mitchell. I miss working with you."

"I know you're staying busy, Robbie. I read about your cases in the Jackson paper."

"Yeah," he said. "And it's the same story it's always been. We've got a great new facility but the legislature won't give us enough money to keep it properly staffed. We can't be as efficient as I'd like to be."

"Sorry you have to deal with those idiots."

"Aw, I knew the job was dangerous when I took it," he said laughing. "David Burke told me to expect a call from you. He said you were representing the University Chancellor in the El Ray investigation and helping him figure out what happened."

"That's right. I went over your analysis of the evidence and had a couple of questions if you have time."

"Always time for you, Willie Mitchell."

"Anything more you can tell me about the methamphetamine in El Ray's vitreous? Can you tell if it's crystal meth or powder, or how he took it?"

"Not really. The autopsy report didn't indicate any needle marks on the body, so he most likely snorted it if it was powder or smoked it if it was crystallized. No pipe or paraphernalia in his Toyota. No signs of any drug use in the vehicle either. Just the empty beer cans. Only his prints on the cans, by the way. We can analyze the precise chemical makeup of the meth, but that doesn't tell us if it's powder or crystal. The chemistry is only useful if we have meth to compare it to. Burke said there wasn't a comparison sample."

"Right," I said. "I've done a little research online about the combination of alcohol and meth, its effect on behavior."

"That's a little outside of our work here, but common sense would say the alcohol reduces inhibitions and the meth amps up the suspect's normal behavior. Some studies show meth reducing inhibitions, too."

"Makes some users more aggressive, more confrontational, from what I read online in papers by behavioral scientists. Bad combination for an eighteen-year-old."

"No kidding," Robbie said. "A big, strong eighteen-year-old to boot. Does Detective Burke have any idea where he got it?"

"Nothing solid," I said. "Did you read the autopsy report where Dr. Martinez described the puncture wound as cylindrical? What do you make of that? Ever come across anything similar?"

"Oh, yeah. Plenty of times. Martinez report indicated it wasn't a knife, in his opinion. I looked at the photos. Hole was too big for an ice pick. Sometimes you can barely see those, especially if the blood has been washed away. Burke said the body was probably inundated with fast moving water for hours in the creek where they found him. No water in his lungs, so he was already dead from the lung puncture when the body was dumped into the ravine."

"That's right," I said.

"We've had cases where the fatal puncture wounds to the chest causing a pneumothorax were caused by a variety of objects. Lots of tools like screwdrivers, drills, nails, even pencils. All it takes to pop a lung is something with a pointed end stuck through the ribs with plenty of force."

"But in those cases you were sent the weapon, right?"

"Yes. Collected at the crime scene. If there's nothing submitted, nothing much we can do with the coroner's description of the hole, even if he takes measurements. Anyone's guess would be good as mine." He paused. "Did you know that in World War II mortality studies, death from pneumothorax accounted for about ten percent of chest injury fatalities."

"No," I said, "surprised it's that low."

"It was twenty-five percent in World War I."

"You got nothing from the penile and pubic swabs?" I said.

"Nothing a prosecutor could use. I checked everything they sent us in that regard, but it was pretty clear the water adulterated those samples. Just traces of semen from the swab inside the penis. Martinez found no foreign pubic hair and our tests didn't show any vaginal fluid on what was submitted."

"Rainwater probably took care of both of those."

"And the change in grooming habits of females these days," Robbie said. "Slick surfaces, you know. No hair to trap male discharge, and nothing to capture the assailant's pubic hair."

"Unintended consequences," I said.

"All helping the criminal," Robbie said.

"In this case it was to corroborate what a witness told Burke about El Ray's activities right before he disappeared, not for a prosecution."

"If he had sex before he was killed, there's nothing submitted to us so far to corroborate that."

We ended the call reminiscing with war stories from our past collaborations. Robbie was a real professional, a stickler for procedure and detail. And just as important, he was impeccably honest and had a stiff spine—courage enough to stand up to any prosecutor or defense attorney pressuring him to shade a finding.

I channel surfed on the FM channel trying to get something local instead of what my XM Sirius subscription had to offer. I gave up after listening to two Mississippi stations airing some sort of unintelligible urban glossolalia promoted as rap or hip-hop. I listened to about half of one song and thirty seconds of another and failed to understand a single word in either. Showing my age, I guess.

I had sent an earlier text to schedule a call with Chancellor O'Donald for two o'clock. I called her exactly at two. I got her voice mail and left a message. Moments later, she called.

"Excellent timing, Willie Mitchell," she said.

"Yes, ma'am. This can wait if you're busy."

"No, indeed. I was on the line with Jeffrey Blanchard from the NCAA. I told him I would not schedule an appointment with him until you and Mr. Pratt were available. The Athletic Director wants to attend, too."

"I'll be back in Oxford early Friday afternoon, so anytime after two is fine with me."

"I'll check with Mr. Pratt and we'll shoot for three o'clock. I normally have an aversion to Friday afternoon meetings," Aunt Bee said. "They're always unproductive because I find participants have usually checked out mentally for the weekend."

"Monday is fine, too."

"Not for the demanding Mr. Blanchard, I'm afraid. He's insistent on meeting this week."

"Okay. I'll be in your office at three unless I hear otherwise from you."

"Good. And by the way, Mr. Blanchard felt it necessary to remind me that he is the *Chief* investigator for NCAA college football."

"Kind of insecure, isn't he."

"Yes, but we do have to humor him to the extent we can, because he does have quite a bit of enforcement power, enough to cause our school serious problems."

"Even if there's nothing there," I said. "Just the official announcement of an investigation into Ole Miss's football program will be a sanction in itself. I've seen publicity about ongoing NCAA investigations affecting other programs. Recruiters from competing schools warn prospects to beware of signing with the school under investigation, because 'the NCAA's going to give them the death penalty.' It's pretty effective to keep a seventeen or eighteen-year-old prospect from signing with the school under the NCAA microscope."

"There's been no formal announcement yet by the NCAA," she said, though my athletic director tells me someone is leaking it because the collegiate sports rumor mills are swirling with speculation surrounding our recruitment of El Ray."

"I'm sure that's right," I said and proceeded to tell her about the crime lab results, saving the toxicology findings for last.

"Oh, dear," she said. "That's unfortunate. Do we know how he might have obtained the methamphetamines?"

"Not yet. I'm going to try to explore that down here after I meet with the parents."

"Be as diplomatic as possible. We don't need the Raymonds taking out their anger on the school."

"I'll do my best," I said. "And Chancellor, please keep the crime lab results between you and me for now. Don't even tell Lawrence Pratt."

"All right, Willie Mitchell. Mum's the word."

I was only a few minutes from the Natchez Trace exit and used them to call the Oak Hill Inn, the bed and breakfast I had booked for Wednesday and Thursday night. Susan and I had stayed at Oak Hill several times over the past few years and gotten to know the owners, Doug and Donald, well enough to consider them friends. Both of them made a day trip to Sunshine for Susan's funeral. I vaguely recall speaking to them at our house in Sunshine after her burial in the old Banks family cemetery in a corner of the cotton land my parents left me, but I was so out of it I wasn't coherent. My head wound was pounding at the time and I'm pretty sure I was still in shock.

Doug answered my call and assured me my room was ready and they were looking forward to seeing me. In short order I left I-55 and pulled onto the Natchez Trace Highway, where the federally-enforced speed limit of fifty-five was strictly monitored. The Trace is shorter in mileage than the four-lane route, but I arrive in Natchez in about the same time because of the reduced speed.

I cheated a bit and set my cruise on fifty-eight, turned off the radio to enjoy the majesty of the towering oaks and pines lining the entire route. The Trace followed the trail of pioneers from Nashville to Natchez, where they either boarded a paddle-wheeler to New Orleans or took the ferry across the Mississippi to the El Camino Real. This equally historic trail meandered across Louisiana to Texas for settlers to take up Stephen F. Austin on his offer of free land in Texas for pilgrims seeking a new way of life.

I thought back to the last time Susan and I made this drive. She wanted to see Staunton Hall, Monmouth, Dunleith, and Longwood again. I agreed to go as long as I could play golf at Beau Pre just south of town while she toured. It was the third time we stayed at Oak Hill Inn, and the third time we were treated to their elegant multi-course breakfast featuring sweet potato pecan waffles, creole eggs, and the finest crème brulee French toast in the country, all served in the original 1835 breakfast room under its magnificent 1850's Waterford crystal gasolier. I was sure Oak Hill would be still be world class, as usual, but also certain I wouldn't enjoy it as much as I did with Susan.

Before I checked in I went to see two people in Natchez I knew and trusted, though I had not spoken to them in decades. One was Julian Sawyer, El Ray's football coach at St. Mary's and Tommy Joe White, who owned the biggest sporting goods store in town. Both were friends and contemporaries of mine at Ole Miss. I had called them the day before. I pulled into Tommy Joe's big store on Highway 84 between the Mississippi River Bridge and the turnoff to Baton Rouge. Both men were waiting for me in Tommy Joe's office.

I talked to them for an hour about El Ray. They knew him well and confirmed everything Reggie Barnes and everyone else said about El Ray. He was the best high school football player each of them had ever seen and were saddened by his death. Coach Sawyer teared up talking about him. They said he was a good student and a role model for other kids. I asked gingerly about alcohol and drugs, and both insisted he was clean as a whistle, never in trouble of any kind. Full of personality, but down to earth, they said.

Both men admired Mrs. Raymond, but neither could abide her ex-husband. They warned me to be on my toes if I talked to him, because if he was drinking, he was liable to go off at the slightest perceived provocation.

"And don't believe a word he says," Coach Sawyer said. "He'd rather climb a tree and tell a lie than stay on the ground and speak the truth."

"He's bitter as hell," Tommy Joe said, "because he was counting on El Ray to be his ticket to fame and fortune."

I felt I had to tell them about the toxicology results, and made them promise they wouldn't say anything about it until it hit the papers or they heard it on the street. Neither could believe it, saying if there wasn't a mistake in the testing, El Ray must have been tricked into taking it.

I turned onto Homochitto Street off Highway 84 and meandered past antebellum mansions Dunleith and Twin Oaks to Oak Hill on Rankin Street, where I greeted Doug and Donald and enjoyed several cocktails, conversation, and the surprisingly mild weather on their veranda. Though it wasn't part of the stay, Donald fixed me a delicious ham and pimento cheese sandwich and I turned in early.

I was in bed by nine-thirty, reading Bill Bryson's *The Road to Little Dribbling* for the fourth or fifth time, when my cell buzzed. I didn't recognize the number, which had a North Mississippi prefix.

"Hello," I said after waiting a moment to see if it was a marketing call.

"It's me," Jake said quietly.

"I got a million questions," I said.

"I'm sure you do. Can you meet me tonight about 2:30?"

"No. I'm in Natchez. I'll be back in Oxford Friday. Can you talk then?"

"No," he said. "I'll call you again in a few days."

"Whoa," I said, "hold on. You have to tell me what you're doing."

"I can't now. Sorry. And it's important you don't call this number. I'll try to call this weekend."

Jake ended the call. I stared at my phone and whispered.

"What have you gotten yourself into, son?"

CHAPTER TWENTY

I left Oak Hill and drove north on M.L.K, checking the house numbers like I did in the old days before GPS guidance or Google Maps. I found Mrs. Raymond's house on the east side of the street about a mile from downtown, a small, white frame house with dark green shutters, set back from the street. The neighborhood was clean. The houses, including Laura Raymond's, were neat and well-kept. I parked my truck on her concrete drive and checked my watch. Ten a.m. I was right on time.

Laura Raymond opened the door. She was tall, about 5'8", and trim in her light blue nurse's scrubs. She was light-skinned like her son and pretty, with short hair and a pleasant smile, which disappeared as soon as we sat down in matching stuffed chairs in her small front room. She picked up her remote off a lamp table and turned off her television.

"Would you like some coffee, Mr. Banks?" she asked.

"No, thanks, Mrs. Raymond. I had plenty at Oak Hill this morning."

"That's a lovely place," she said. "Doug and Donald are wonderful."

"My wife and I stayed there several times over the past few years."

"Did she drive down with you?"

"No. She died about six months ago."

"Oh, I'm sorry."

"She was murdered," I said. "Like your son El Ray."

Mrs. Raymond's brave face melted. She began to cry. I waited, giving her
plenty of time. She dabbed her eyes with a Kleenex and after a moment, looked up at me, blinking.

"I've had a hard time with this," she said.

"It doesn't get easier with time," I said, "but the pain becomes less intense. I wish I could give you some advice that would help you through it, but I don't know of any. And I suspect losing a child is much worse than what I've endured."

"I don't know, Mr. Banks," she said, lowering her head and pressing the Kleenex against her nose. "I just don't know."

"Your son was an outstanding young man."

She nodded. "You said on the phone you're representing Ole Miss."

"Not the University, just the Chancellor, Clare O'Donald, who asked me to give you her deepest condolences."

"But you're a district attorney you said?"

"I was, but no longer. As part of my representation of the Chancellor, I'm assisting the Oxford Police Department in investigating your son's death. That's why I'm here to talk to you."

"I see. I spoke to Elston's father about meeting this morning, but don't know if he is going to show up or not. We shouldn't wait for him."

"All right. First I'd like to ask you a few background questions, if you don't mind."

She told me that she was born in Natchez, got a nursing degree from Alcorn University, and married Sam Raymond when she was twenty-two and five months pregnant with Sam's child, Elston. Sam was older, and had been a friend of Laura's late parents. He had a good job with the City of Natchez, and was kind to her when she broke up with her boyfriend from Alcorn, and "one thing led to another." She took a nursing job with Regional Hospital in town after her son's birth, and was still employed there eighteen years later. She said Sam had kept his job with the city all these years as a building inspector not because he was proficient at construction, but because he could deliver a lot of votes at election time.

"After Elston was born, Sam changed. He said I was paying too much attention to the baby. He started drinking during the week, something he never did before we married. I took it as long as I could until he started threatening to hurt me and the baby, and that's when I got a lawyer. He disappeared from our lives until Elston began getting noticed in the fifth grade for his athletic ability. Then Sam started coming around again—not for me, but for bragging rights for Elston."

I asked her about the recruiting wars for El Ray, and she said he always planned on going to Ole Miss because he loved Coach Reggie Barnes.

"I think he looked up to Reggie like a father figure or a big brother. Reggie was a kind person, and he was so good to Elston."

"Did any coaches or recruiters ever offer any money?"

"Not when I was around," she said, "but those people showed up at every event. They all wanted a piece of Elston. At first he enjoyed the attention but after a while he got tired of them hassling him. He told me Ole Miss was where he was going, and told them, too. But that didn't stop them."

"His car...."

She hopped up. "I've been waiting for someone to ask me about that," she said over her shoulder as she disappeared down a narrow hallway.

She returned with two envelopes and pulled bank statements out of each, handing them to me as she talked.

"Everybody around here was saying some recruiter gave Elston a bunch of money and he used it to buy that Toyota, which is a joke because that car is a 2005 model and had 150,000 miles on it when he bought it from Mr. Hicks's secretary. Mr. Hicks is the CPA that does my taxes and he's always been good to Elston, paying him to mow his grass starting when Elston was ten. Mr. Hicks taught Elston about saving money, paying his bills, the things nobody else teaches fatherless kids these days. He's always helped me stay financially sound, too. I don't make any big purchases without talking to Mr.Hicks."

The first statement was a savings account with a balance of $3,546. The second was a checking account with $780 in it. Both accounts were in the name of Laura Raymond, custodian for Elston Raymond.

"My name is on those accounts because he was a minor when he opened them. He opened the savings account when he was eleven, and put the money he made from mowing lawns, washing cars, babysitting when he got older, and all kind of odd jobs. He paid Mr. Hick's secretary $2,500 cash for that Toyota last summer. You can look on those statements and see when he transferred the money from his savings to his checking account. I can show you the cancelled check."

I looked at the statements, asked for permission to make a note of the bank name, account number, and balance.

"He liked to work, and he liked to save his money. If he earned twenty dollars he would keep five and put the rest in his savings account. He was tight as a tick. He didn't get that from his daddy. Money burns a hole in Sam's pockets. He makes a good salary with benefits but he spends it faster than he makes it. Always been like that."

I asked about El Ray's social life. She said Elston had lots of friends, including girls, but never went with one in particular. She said she let him drink a little beer at home, but never when he was out in public. She said he was never involved in drugs or anything illegal. She said he wanted to be a pro football player and a doctor.

I told her about the autopsy report, but she already knew about the pneumothorax that killed him. Laura had been involved in numerous pneumothorax and hemothorax procedures as a nurse. She said she didn't understand how that could happen to Elston, how someone could get that close to him and stab him under the arm. I said we were trying to find out.

"Did they ever find your wife's killer?" she asked.

"Not yet," I said, "but I will."

"You find Elston's killer, too. I want answers. I want to know who killed my boy and why."

"What I'm going to tell you next is not good news, Mrs. Raymond. The toxicology screen came back positive for alcohol and methamphetamine."

"That's not right," she said raising her voice. "There was some mistake in taking his blood or urine."

"This was based on his vitreous. I checked and the chain of custody is intact, so everything seems in order."

"What level was the alcohol?"

"Point zero eight."

"Oh, Jesus."

"There were empty beer cans in his car with his fingerprints on them." I paused to let that sink in. "All young men his age drink beer."

"I knew he did. But the methamphetamine, he wouldn't have done that. It's just not possible."

"There wasn't any evidence of drug use in the car, nothing to indicate it was his drugs." I paused. "We do know he was with a woman right before he disappeared. She says she dropped him off at his car after midnight Saturday, and we believe her."

"Who was she? A student?"

"No, ma'am. She was in her mid-thirties. I can't give you her name right now until we know more, when we're further along in the investigation."

"Oh, my God. She's almost my age. I didn't even know he was going to Oxford that weekend," she said. "It wasn't like him to keep something like that from me. Now you're telling me he had a woman up there? I bet she gave him the dope."

"We're looking into that."

"If she did I want you to arrest her."

There was a loud knock on the door. She stood and peeked out of the front window.

"It's him," she said, shaking her head and opening the front door.

Sam Raymond stepped inside. He was tall, at least 6'4", about 190 to 200 pounds, with very dark skin mottled with several days growth of white stubble. I stood and extended my hand. He glared at it with angry brown eyes, not offering his. He smelled of alcohol and stale cigarette smoke. I shrugged and returned to my chair.

"What's this about?" he growled.

"Sit down, Sam," his ex-wife said. "Try to be civil."

"I'm sittin'," he said after plopping down on the well-worn couch.

I went through the same introductory comments I had with Mrs. Raymond. He stared at me as I spoke, not responding, but displaying angry, aggressive body language. I could sense Laura was embarrassed. When I asked him if he knew of anyone offering El Ray money, he finally spoke.

"You don't know much about how things work, do you?" he said.

"Coach Barnes said he warned your son about people offering money, that it was against the rules, and...."

"Oh, he said that? You ask me Barnes is full of shit. Lots of people offered money."

"To El Ray or you?" I asked.

"I already talked to the NCAA. They getting to the bottom of it. You here to try to cover up whatever Ole Miss and Reggie done to get him to sign?"

"That's not true, Sam," Mrs. Raymond said. "Can't you behave like a normal person for a change. This man's trying to help us find out what happened to Elston. He said Elston's body fluids came back that he was drinking and was using methamphetamines before he was killed."

"We don't know when he took the drug," I said as nicely as possible.

Sam Raymond stood up and shook his fist at me.

"You makin' up shit on my boy. Better get your ass going before I bust your head wide open."

"You leave now," Laura said to her ex, standing and pointing to the door. "Before I call the police."

He gave me a long, nasty look and stormed out, slamming the door.

"I'm sorry," Mrs. Raymond said, tears filling her eyes again. "I don't think I can answer any more questions. My shift starts at eleven."

"Thanks for seeing me," I said and walked to the door.

"I don't know anything that would help you find out who did it. Elston was never in trouble, never arrested, and never hung out with those kids who do drugs. He was a good boy. He never told me anything about any woman in Oxford. I just don't understand about the methamphetamines in his system. He was never involved with that stuff here."

"At some point it's going to come out, Mrs. Raymond, and I thought it best you hear it from me."

"Thank you," she said. "I'm sorry about Elston's father's behavior."

I left Mrs. Raymond's for the Natchez Police Department. On my way, I passed my favorite palimpsest of all time, an ancient Coca Cola sign peeking out from behind the huge Wilson-Holder Drug Store sign on Rankin Street painted on the antique brick side wall of the drug store building. I noticed it on our first trip to Natchez and had admired it ever since.

I spent the rest of the day Thursday talking to police detectives and deputy sheriffs who had been called by Detective Burke to let them know who I was and what I was investigating. It turned out to be unproductive, because every officer I spoke to said the same thing. El Ray had never come up on their radar for any kind of illegal or rowdy behavior. The city's chief narcotics officer said he gets information daily on which kids in town are selling, buying, or doing drugs. Said it comes from informants and from other kids. He was emphatic that El Ray's name never came up, that he was clean as a whistle.

"Believe me," the narcotics detective said, "these kids know who's slinging drugs and who's using them among their crowd. And not a one of them has ever mentioned his name."

I turned in early after saying my thanks and goodbye to Doug and Donald, explaining I was going to get on the road before seven to return to Oxford, so I was going to miss breakfast.

I didn't sleep well, worrying about Jake and thinking about what a good kid El Ray was, and how his death was such a tragedy.

I showered, dressed, and walked out the Oak Hill back door Friday morning at 5:45, heading to Oxford for another unpleasant encounter with the Honorable Jeffrey Blanchard, *Chief* investigator for the all-powerful and grossly unprincipled NCAA.

When I pulled onto I-55 an hour later, I got a call from Detective David Burke in Oxford.

"Where are you?" he asked.

"On my way back to Oxford."

"I thought so. I'm at your condo. OPD got a call a few minutes ago from one of your neighbors. Said your garage door was open. Dispatcher called me and I drove over. Your back door was wide open, too."

"I locked it when I left. Garage door was closed, too."

"I figure you've had a break-in."

"Damn," I said. "Would you look inside?"

"I did. Everything's in order. Can't see any damage anywhere. Who knew you were out of town?"

"Handful of folks. You had a lot of burglaries lately?"

"Nothing out of the ordinary. Condos are usually targeted when the University's out of session. College students are out for Thanksgiving. Could be juveniles just out for a cheap chithrill."

"I'll be back before noon. Can you lock it up?"

"Will do. Check the place out for missing stuff when you get back here."

I didn't keep money in the condo, and I had divided Susan's jewelry, giving the family pieces to her sister, Joan, and the rest to Scott's wife Donna. Even if nothing was taken, it was unsettling that someone could get in so easily. Irritated, I drove a little faster.

CHAPTER TWENTY-ONE

I pulled into Newk's parking lot on University a little after eleven a.m., grabbed a pre-made Cobb salad from its to-go counter on the side of the building, and drove home. I did a quick walk through, upstairs and downstairs and couldn't find anything disturbed, much less missing. In Yaloquena, when I was D.A., burglars stole guns, electronics, and jewelry, usually in that order. My two televisions were intact, there was no jewelry to be stolen, and my long guns were still in my house in Sunshine. Since Sheriff Burr's office had my .38 revolver, the only other pistol I kept in the condo was my 1911 Springfield .45 caliber semi-automatic my father had given me as an office warming present when I opened my law office in Sunshine right out of law school.

I walked into my office, plopped behind my desk and opened the top drawer on the right side.

The Springfield was gone. In its place, my burglar left a battered .25 caliber Raven automatic, the prototype "Saturday night special." There was an empty hole in the bottom of its grip where its small magazine was supposed to be. I didn't touch the Raven. I called David Burke again.

"You are kidding me," he said when I told him about the pistol swap. "Is someone playing a joke on you?"

"Jimmy Gray's the only person who knows where I kept the Springfield, and he wouldn't touch a Raven automatic."

"So, if it's not a joke...," he paused.

"I don't know what this means," I said, "but it's not a joke."

"Just leave it and I'll pick it up to check it for prints. You want me to dust inside your place?"

"No. It makes too big a mess. Just the Raven."

After David bagged the gun and left, I spent a couple of hours taking the time to check every drawer and cabinet more thoroughly. The thief hadn't taken anything else, nor had he done any damage. I had an odd feeling I couldn't shake, but I was pretty sure I'd never find out who broke into my place or why they left the Raven.

I showed up at the Lyceum a few minutes before three and checked in with the student receptionist. Jeffrey Blanchard arrived a moment after me. I didn't offer my hand, merely nodded to acknowledge him. He reciprocated with the smugness I had come to expect from him.

James Braswell, Aunt Bee's *aide de camp*, greeted us and led us into the Chancellor's office. The Chancellor stood when we entered; as did Lawrence Pratt, the University's in-house counsel; Athletic Director Robert Flowers; and Coach Carl Goodson, all of whom had apparently participated in a pre-meeting with Aunt Bee. Everyone exchanged niceties and handshakes, then took seats in a semi-circle around Aunt Bee's large and uncluttered desk.

In his early forties, A.D. Flowers was the youngest person in the room. He was nice-looking, with a square jaw and a shaved head. He wore a dark sport coat, gray slacks, and a rep tie in Ole Miss's red and blue. Flowers and his head football coach were grim, as was lawyer Pratt. Lawrence was mid-fifties, slightly-built, and all-business.

"Thank you all for attending, which I know can be difficult on a Friday afternoon. I don't think anyone needs an introduction, so let's start by hearing from Mr. Blanchard on what information he would like to discover from us. Mr. Blanchard?"

"Thank you, Chancellor O'Donald. The National Collegiate Athletic Association takes very seriously our obligation to the young men who are recruited to play intercollegiate athletics at our member institutions, and...."

I tuned out, not wanting to hear Blanchard's self-aggrandizing preamble about the NCAA in advance of his explanation of the real reason he wanted the meeting, but Coach Goodson didn't cut the arrogant jerk any slack.

"Why don't you just tell us what you want from us?" Goodson interrupted, jarring Blanchard, the Athletic Director, and the University counsel flanking him. "I got things to do."

"I think what Coach Goodson means," A.D. Flowers said, "is we're all extremely distressed about what happened to Elston Raymond, but no one in this room was aware that he was in Lafayette County on an unauthorized visit. His tragic death has shaken all of us, but it has nothing to do with Ole Miss."

"My assistant coach Reggie Barnes was like a big brother to El Ray," Coach Goodson said. "He's torn up about what happened, but he didn't know the boy was anywhere near Oxford that weekend. I don't even know why you're here looking into it. His death had nothing to do with our football program."

"I think Mr. Flowers has expressed what we all feel, Mr. Blanchard," the Chancellor said.

"Fair enough," Blanchard said. "I'll tell you why the NCAA is here. After young Mr. Raymond committed to your school in the summer before his senior year in high school, we received a complaint from another institution in your conference that there was a significant financial inducement paid to him or someone on his behalf."

"Which school?" A.D. Flowers asked.

"I'm not at liberty to say."

"If it was Mississippi State, they have a bottomless hatred for our school, exacerbated by their former head coach," Flowers said.

"I'm sure Mr. Blanchard would not rely on a complaint by an archrival recruiting the same prospect as Ole Miss," I said, "because the motive of such a rival is obvious, especially when the prospect commits to Ole Miss. You wouldn't rely on something so inherently tainted, would you, Mr. Blanchard?"

"We verify or dismiss a charge by investigating," Blanchard said. "That's how we proceed."

"It's selective enforcement," Coach Goodson said. "It's because the NCAA wants to punish Ole Miss for its racial history, which no one in this room wants to talk about, a history which no one on my team is responsible for."

"Like how the Special Counsel in Washington works," I said. "They target an individual then try to find a crime to pin on him or her. It's also the way the Spanish Inquisition, the Salem Witch trials, and Stalin's purges were conducted."

It was fun ganging up on Jeffrey Blanchard.

"We are also investigating whether bigotry had something to do with Mr. Raymond's death," Blanchard said. "One of our long term goals in Indianapolis is reparative justice for our African-American student athletes."

"That's a bunch of crap," Coach Goodson said. "You think because it's Ole Miss there's race involved. Well, eighty percent of my team is black and the only reparations they're interested in is playing at the next level where they can get paid. You want to elevate my players? Change the rules so they can earn a little money. College football is a multi-billion dollar industry. Every-one makes money off college football except the players. And that includes you. Half of my coaching staff is black. 60,000 people, mostly white, show up on Saturdays and pay big money to watch us play. They don't seem racist to me."

"Like the Romans watching the Gladiators," Blanchard said.

"That's offensive, Mr. Blanchard," the Chancellor said. "Gladiators were slaves, but they were allowed to keep the money and gifts they received from grateful bettors, whose purses the gladiators's victories fattened. You should do some research before you choose your metaphors."

"Way to go, Aunt Bee!" I thought, and watched Coach Goodson stand up to face Blanchard.

"I know a lot more about racism than anyone in this room," he said to Blanchard, "including you people at the NCAA. I coached in bigger programs at Michigan and UCLA, and I can tell you for a fact that people in Mississippi are no more racist than people in Ann Arbor or Los Angeles. Maybe less so."

A.D. Flowers touched his head football coach on the arm, and Coach Goodson sat down.

"I spoke with Elston Raymond's father yesterday," I said, "and he told me that he had called the NCAA after his son's death. Did he speak to you?"

"I'm not permitted to answer questions about an ongoing inquiry."

"If he told you that there was money paid by Ole Miss or anyone else, I'd suggest you talk to him in person before you go any further. He is not a credible witness, nor is he without prejudice against Ole Miss."

"We have talked to Mr. Raymond in person since his son died," Blanchard said. "And he made a number of allegations. He said, among other things, that Ole Miss offered El Ray more money to sign than other schools."

"That is not true," A.D. Flowers said.

"If we discover evidence that it is, and we find a history of such payments, we will impose severe penalties on your school, including perhaps the forfeiture of previous games in which improperly paid athletes participated."

After Blanchard's threat, the meeting continued for another twenty minutes. Everyone on Ole Miss's side was too angry to engage with Blanchard except Aunt Bee, who rose to the occasion. She countered each threat Blanchard made with a pleasant rejoinder, defusing the vitriol he was spewing.

The only takeaway for me was the NCAA was convinced Ole Miss or someone on its behalf had paid money to ensure El Ray's attendance and that somehow it led to his death. Nothing any of us said to Blanchard made a bit of difference. His investigators were on campus to stay, and it was inevitable that sports media would continue to speculate in print and on television why the NCAA was investigating El Ray's commitment to Ole Miss, and how it might have led to his murder. That kind of speculation on national sports talk shows and college football blogs would do as much damage to the University and its football program as a loss of scholarships, a bowl ban, or forfeiture of previous wins. Everyone in the room, including Blanchard, knew that a well-publicized NCAA investigation, even if groundless, was a severe sanction in and of itself.

Aunt Bee and I were the only ones in the meeting who knew the results of El Ray's toxicology report. I was not about to share it with Jeffrey Blanchard. I would let the Coach Goodson, A.D. Flowers, and lawyer Pratt know in due course, but I wanted to keep the NCAA in the dark as long as possible. No good could come of Blanchard knowing.

I left the meeting proud that Aunt Bee didn't mention the toxicology results. I was also firmly convinced that regardless of what the truth turned out to be, the El Ray inquiry was not going to end well for Ole Miss or anyone else involved.

CHAPTER TWENTY-TWO

My cell phone buzzed in my pocket as I returned to the condo after the meeting with Blanchard. I smiled when I saw "Walton" pop up on my screen.

"Yo," I said to my former Assistant D.A. and current District Attorney for Yaloquena County, Walton Donaldson. "This is a nice surprise."

"Maybe not," Walton said, "you got time to talk?"

"Sure, Walton. What's up?"

"Bad news on the Pickett habeas petition in federal court."

"I've been expecting it," I said.

Brent Pickett was a month past his sixteenth birthday in 2005 when he showed up at the Dilworth home in northern Yaloquena County and shot to death Russell Dilworth's seventy-five-year-old mother and his ten-year-old son for absolutely no reason. At the time of the murders, Russell Dilworth had been working in a soybean field three miles away and his wife and daughter were in town at the grocery store. Pickett was not on drugs, nor was he intent on robbing the Dilworths. He told his court-appointed psychiatrist that he had noticed the isolated home while riding in the back seat of his parents' car as they drove to Greenville one Sunday afternoon when he was fifteen, and decided he would return after he got his driver's license and kill whoever lived in the house, "just to know what it feels like to kill someone."

I tried Pickett as an adult and convicted him of the murders, in spite of the defense psychiatrist testifying that Pickett's temporal lobe was undeveloped, as shown on a PET scan of his brain, and therefore unable to appreciate that his actions were wrong. I countered the testimony with my own expert psychiatric witness, who testified that Pickett was the "purest sociopath" he had ever encountered, and that Positron Emission Tomography analysis of the human brain was highly controversial, bordering on junk science. He said the majority of professionals who studied PET scans in connection with teen violence thought the scans were unreliable and added nothing to the understanding of how the developing human brain worked.

Pickett was sixteen at the time of the murders. The U.S. Supreme Court had made it clear in earlier cases that no juvenile who committed a murder was eligible for the death penalty, no matter how heinous the homicide. Judge Zelda Williams sentenced Pickett to two life terms, with no eligibility for probation, parole, or reduction of sentence for any reason. She also made the two life sentences run consecutively so that Pickett would have to complete serving his life sentence for the grandmother's death before he began serving his life sentence for the ten-year-old's murder.

In 2016, eleven years after Pickett's senseless murders, the U.S. Supreme Court decided *Montgomery vs Louisiana,* in which they made retroactive their ruling in *Miller vs* Alabama, which held that no juvenile can be sentenced to life without parole no matter how vicious and cold-hearted the killing, ruling that such punishment was "cruel and unusual."

Walton and I had discussed the *Montgomery* decision and knew the day was coming when some court would issue an order directing that Pickett be considered for parole, in spite of his original sentencing.

"Well," Walton said, recalling our talk, "that day has come."

"You need me to do anything?"

"Nope. Russell and his wife just left here. They couldn't understand how a case decided in 2016 could change a sentence that was legal when it was imposed in 2005. I gave them the law school answer, but...."

"I agree with the Dilworths," I said. "There's nothing fair about this."

"There's not, but nothing I can do about it. Pickett will come up for parole within the year, I'm betting."

"It's why people don't think much of our system these days," I said. "There's nothing more cruel and unusual than the two murders he committed. Pickett's revised punishment doesn't fit his crime."

We talked for a few more minutes. I was thankful I no longer had to explain such a miscarriage of justice to innocent victims like the Dilworths.

I pulled a frozen lasagna casserole I had bought at the grocery store the previous week and put it in the oven, then cobbled together a salad out of lettuce that had begun to turn brown, a shriveled cucumber, and wrinkled cherry tomatoes. I topped it with bottled ranch dressing that had exceeded its "best used by" date by two months.

I ate watching ten minutes of depressing national news about a government shutdown, then the last half of an *Ancient Aliens* episode.

With the burglary of the condo, the meeting in Aunt Bee's office, and the call from Walton about the Pickett case, it had been a particularly bad day. I set aside *The Road to Little Dribbling* and pulled up the complete works of Arthur Conan Doyle on my Kindle for the umpteenth time. I got in bed and clicked on *A Study In Scarlet* and let Sherlock Holmes and Dr. Watson entertain me until I drifted off.

I was deep in REM sleep when my cell phone woke me up.

"Hello," I croaked.

"Dad," the caller said, "it's Jake."

CHAPTER TWENTY-THREE

"Where are you?" I said.

"In my beater on the way to Sardis Lake."

"Why are you going there this time of night?"

"To meet with you."

I scrambled out of bed and into my clothes. Within a couple of minutes, I was in my truck backing out of my garage. I didn't need any coffee. The adrenaline rush that kicked in with Jake's call had me amped. I headed west on Highway 6 and turned onto the two-lane on the north side of the highway heading toward Sardis Lake, the largest lake in Mississippi.

FDR authorized the Sardis dam construction project for flood control during his second term. I had spent time on the lake drinking beer with Jimmy Gray in his pontoon boat, and had been mightily impressed with the massive dam that held back the Little Tallahatchie River.

That's where I was headed to meet Jake—the center of the three-mile dam. He told me that there were lights on the dam for half a mile at the north and south sides, but the center of the dam was pitch black on a dark night like this one. He told me to make sure no one was following me and to cut off my headlights when I reached the dam.

I followed Jake's instructions and slowed considerably when I passed the lighted part of the dam on its south end. Creeping through the darkness, I squinted, making sure I kept my truck on the paved surface. After a few moments I saw a headlight blink on and off quickly—Jake's signal—and continued to poke along toward the center of the dam.

I stopped my F-150 front bumper two feet from the front bumper of the small truck against which Jake was leaning, waiting for me. I stepped out and hugged my oldest boy in the narrow space between the two vehicles.

"I'm really glad to see you, Jake."

"You, too. I guess you've got a few questions. Before you start, I'm keeping my eye on the south end of the dam, you keep yours on the north end. If you see headlights, we get back in our trucks and leave."

"Okay," I said. "How long have you been living in Tallabusha County?"

"Since the funeral. I didn't go back to D.C. when I left Sunshine after the services. I drove to Memphis, traded my Four-Runner for this truck and some cash, then drove it to Cedar Grove. I looked at ads in the local newspaper for rental property out in the county and found a furnished house trailer owned by a little old lady who told me on the phone she had just lost her tenant. She had not been out to check on the trailer since her husband died a year ago. I found the trailer, made sure it was livable and the utilities were working, drove back to town and rented it from the lady for a hundred and fifty dollars a month. It's perfect for me."

"Perfect for what?"

"Living in the woods until I find the two people who killed Mom."

"Maybe you can explain to me just how James Agee being arrested and arraigned on drug charges would fit into such an investigation."

"You remember Billy Gillmon, the computer and government systems genius working for what used to be David Dunne's group?"

"Yes. Last time I talked to Dunne he told me y'all's domestic operations group was going out of business."

"It did," Jake said. "But Gillmon stayed on with some government shadow organization, doing the same thing he was doing for us. He's become my handler, more or less. He created James Agee, giving me a social security number, driver's license, passport, everything, including a criminal record and a B.O.P. history. Gillmon funnels my pay through a network of dummy government agencies. He's a genius. Still looks the same, like an unassuming small town CPA."

"B.O.P.?"

"Bureau of Prisons. James Agee did time at a couple of federal lows. All drug related offenses."

I nodded. I knew "lows" meant low-security prisons. I looked out into the inky blackness of the lake, no horizon to distinguish the water from the sky. It was all so strange, so far removed from what I had done all my life. I had lived a public existence. My whereabouts was always known, and my cases, my face, and my comments were in the local and regional papers and television stations on a regular basis. Now, here I was, at a clandestine meeting in the center of a three-mile dam in total darkness at two in the morning, talking to my oldest son, who was living off the grid under an assumed name, on the hunt for Susan's killers.

"The fictional life Gillmon built for me is a work of art," Jake said.

"Why go undercover in Tallabusha County? How can you be sure the killers are from around here?"

"While I was in Sunshine for Mom's funeral, I learned as much as I could from you about how things went down at the BP. I spent time out at the Varner exit, studying the secondary highways *vis-a-vis* the station's location. You told me what you remembered about the woman driver, the shooter, how he was dressed, how the two of them acted. You described the vehicle in detail. I asked Dunne to get Gillmon to scour the FBI systems to pull up profiles of interstate gangsters operating all over the country, and I studied those profiles.

"The two who you described don't fit in to the typical mold of highway robbers, which are almost always just two men, close to the same age, operating far away from their home base. And interstate armed robbers do recon; they case their targets. They know the time of day when the store is going to have the most money. There's no way professionals would target that BP. There would never be enough money in the BP till to justify even the small risk they would be taking. People traveling pay for gasoline with credit cards. The BP's remoteness actually works against it being chosen by pros. Not enough interstate traffic to blend into, and not nearly enough crossroads and exchanges between Jackson and Memphis for the getaway."

"If you're right, have you come up with any information to corroborate your assumptions?"

"Not yet, but it's a long process," Jake said. "I've been living rough out in Tallabusha now over five months, and the locals have taken me in as one of their own. You ought to see how these people live day to day."

"I can imagine."

"I don't think so. I couldn't. Sex and drugs every day—no forethought, no long-term plans. They wake up, do what they have to in order to make it for the day, and that's it. When they wake up the following day, it starts all over. Stealing, screwing for drugs or money, selling the drugs they buy to some other sucker dumber than they are for more money than they paid."

"And you?"

"When in Rome...."

"Damn, Jake. I hate that you...."

"It's what it takes. I never sought these people out. I stayed to myself the first month, just observing. I noticed that almost all these low-lifes visited the same country store several times a day. It's got a hand-painted sign out front that says "Kip's Korner" that looks like it was drawn by a ten-year old. Kip's is at a crossroads way out in the woods. Sells gas and cigarettes and beer; has a fried food counter for chicken and potato wedges; and has a few wobbly metal and plastic tables and chairs. One nasty unisex bathroom. The parking lot is a drug and sex bazaar, lots of transactions and hooking up for money or dope."

"Sheriff Burr's deputies have any kind of presence?"

"No. They stop in the store for coffee and snacks, but they don't roust anyone. The Sheriff has to know what's going on out here. I guess he's made a political decision to leave these people alone."

"Are you one of 'these people' now?"

"I guess I am for as long as it takes," Jake said, chuckling. "The way I got inside this community, it started with this girl I met at Kip's one day. I had seen her in there a few times before she spoke to me. She said she was twenty, and looked it. A natural blonde, not bad looking. Said her name was April Wolff. "Like the animal with an extra f," she said. She asked me who I was. I was coy, but she came back to my trailer with me. We still hang out together from time to time. She knows all the players out here. She introduced me around, told me about Q-Man."

"I hope you, uh...."

"I always protect myself. Especially in the hellholes I've worked in the last six years. Always have my gun handy, too." He paused. "You know, Willie Mitchell, this April girl, she grew up in this bizarre world out here. Lived here all her life. Never been outside of Mississippi. Her mother was born in Cedar Grove, got into drugs in the Tallabusha woods when she was in her thirties and lived day-to-day trading sex for drugs or money with these nasty redneck and black dopers. Gave birth to April at age thirty-eight, then died of an overdose when April was ten. April never knew who her father was.

"So, this April is uneducated, but she's intelligent and has a better moral compass than you'd expect for someone who's grown up like she has. She moved in with her mother's sister after her mother died, and the sister's sorry live-in boyfriend started sexually abusing her right away. He left with April's aunt for North Dakota when the shale play started up there, and April hasn't heard from them since. She lives in their old run down trailer, pays her monthly expenses from welfare benefits, eats on food stamps, and picks up cash from the drugs she buys and re-sells.

"The thing is, this life is all she's ever known, which is the real tragedy. From spending time and listening to her, she still has a sense of right and wrong. I don't know how, but she does. Someone ought to rescue her."

I could barely make out Jake's face in the darkness as we stood there. He leaned against his small truck. I rested against my F-150. I remember thinking how odd it was to be talking to my oldest son about his involvement with drugs, sex, and guns in Tallabusha County.

"Maybe someone will recognize the same qualities in her and get her out of this mess. Tell me how you got arrested."

"It was just bad luck. I was with a couple of those guys who were arraigned with me and they got pulled over. I had a little coke and meth on me. No gun that day, thank God. But the drug charges are no big deal. I didn't get arrested. James Agee did. Gillmon would never let it be linked to me. And getting busted enhances my credibility with my worthless peers."

"What about getting fingerprinted?"

"Gillmon's fixed it so that my fingerprints come up James Agee in the national crime databases."

"How much drugs do you have to use?"

"Not much. Just enough to pull off the image of a dead-ender on the run from a murky past riddled with a couple of stints in the federal pen for drug possession and distribution." He paused. "I only use drugs when I'm around the dumbasses who live in this hell on earth, and they all know coke is my drug of choice. Not physically addictive like meth, which I rarely do, and only if I'm with one of these losers I need to ingratiate myself with, like Q-Man."

"Who is he?"

"He says he's Quintavius Jackson, and goes by Q-Man, but that's not his real name. Everyone's got a nickname out in these woods. Q-Man has everyone calling me 'A.G.' Mr. Gillmon ran the name Quintavius Jackson through every database imaginable and came up empty. Q-Man is the person who picked me up at the courthouse in Cedar Grove the day you saw me."

"Where's he from?"

"He says he's from somewhere in the Delta, but he's been out in these woods the past five years, since he got out of Parchman."

"What did he go in for?"

"Some kind of serious drug offense. That's all I know because he doesn't like to talk about his life before he settled in Tallabusha County. He never mentions his time inside. Even if he did, from listening to guys I've worked with the last few years, I know enough about federal prison life to talk about time behind bars. Besides, Q-Man never did any federal time."

"Why did you pick Q-Man to buddy up with?"

"He's the Vito Corleone of these woods. These dead-enders kowtow to him, treat him like their leader, which I guess he is. He settles disputes among these drug heads, using force if he has to. It's a real tribal thing, like he's the chief. Not much goes on in the Tallabusha drug underworld that he doesn't control or at least know about. He's the best possible source for me to find out who did the BP attack."

"But you can't bring it up."

"No. I've got to wait until it comes up organically, and hope I'm there when it does. Q-Man has native intelligence, shrewd—a real criminal. He tells me he likes hanging with me because I'm not brain-dead like the rest of his confederates. I'm riding with him to the Tallabusha Job Center today. He says it's to meet with a couple of his people. You ought to tour that place. Observe your tax dollars at work."

"I've been to the job center near Sunshine. Where is this one?"

"It's west of Cedar Grove, almost to Chee Chee Lake. It's the only federal job center one I've ever been in, but it's the biggest boondoggle you've ever seen. The government pays these eighteen-to twenty-five-year-old men and women to stay there and learn a trade, but all they do is lie around all day smoking weed and screwing."

"Depressing," I said. "The government can't do anything right."

Jake punched the button on his cheap digital watch and held it to his face to check the time. In the watch's dim light, I saw the toll his recent life had taken on him. His face was gaunt, his cheeks hollowed out.

"I've got to go," Jake said. "I'm pressing my luck staying out here this long."

"Wait a minute," I said. "You can't keep doing this without communicating with me. Now that I know what's going on, I'll be worried night and day about you getting into something that you can't handle."

"I'll call or text every three or four days, but you cannot call me. That's a rule, and it's important."

I felt the need to say something profound, something moving, but the best I could come up with was lame.

"I admire you for doing what you're doing, son, but you might be wasting your time. Those two who killed your Mother may not be from around here. And the way you look, I can tell it's taking a lot out of you."

"You might be right," he said, "but my gut tells me the woman and the shooter are locals. I've learned to trust my instincts in finding bad guys."

"All right, but you be careful. And anything you need me to do you call me. No matter what it is. You have to promise."

"Will do. You replace your revolver the Sheriff took into evidence?"

I said no, and told him about the burglar exchanging my Springfield for a banged-up Raven .25 that looked worse than his truck.

"That's strange," he said. "Get you a .45 caliber Glock. They're reliable and easy to use. You don't have to clean them every time you use them. A Glock doesn't need first class maintenance." He paused. "How's your seizure situation?"

"Haven't had one since I got shot in the head. Maybe it cured me." I pointed to his vehicle. "Fine truck you got there," I said.

"Runs good," he said. "It's an old Nissan. And it's a manual shift on the floor. These idiots I'm hanging out with can't steal it because none of them can operate a clutch."

"Well," I said, "you got that going for you."

Chapter Twenty-Four

Back in the condo, I was too wired to sleep. I went online and Googled "interstate highway robberies" and read abstracts of studies on crime, especially robberies. I found a study of Georgia crime reports where the authors confirmed the conclusion of previous researchers in academia that an increase in the number of interstate exits in a particular county results in a commensurate increase in the number of robberies in the county. I read different explanations of the "pattern theory of crime," which I had never heard of in my twenty-four years in the trenches trying criminal cases. After a couple of hours of searching, I could not find anything that unequivocally substantiated what Jake had told me, that interstate robbery offenders were usually two men about the same age who lived far from the crime scenes.

But, what Jake said made a lot of sense. I recalled a team of two brothers, the Beringers, who terrorized convenience stores located on interstate exchanges in the South in the early 2000's. When they were finally arrested, the Beringer brothers were charged with two dozen robberies ranging from Texas to Florida. Details of their crimes after their indictments showed how well-organized the brothers were, even using a scouting checklist when studying a prospective store to victimize. Their escape routes were mapped out in advance, with the goal being to get back on the nearby interstate and cross an adjoining state line as soon as possible without speeding excessively. I did a search for "Beringer Brothers Robberies" and found links to a number of newspaper stories about their *modus operandi* and arrest. At one of their sentencing hearings, the oldest of the brothers told the judge, "The last thing we wanted to do was have to shoot somebody, Your Honor. Me and my brother are stick-up men, not killers."

That comment made me think about the sequence of events at the BP. Sitting at my desk, with the sky transitioning from dark to light outside, I closed my eyes and pictured the shooter in the red windbreaker in my mind's eye, the way he winked at the woman driver, and the brief amount of time between his entering the store and the gunshots. Looking back on that moment, I realized the shooter seemed more like a killer than a robber.

And as a team, the woman driving the Expedition and the shooter at the BP did not strike me as organized. The more I thought about Jake's theory that the couple was local, the more I became convinced he was correct. They were not interstate gangsters. But I wasn't entirely sold on Jake's opinion that the two were Tallabusha residents. They could have easily been from one of the adjacent counties. On the other hand, Jake had a lot more experience chasing bad guys. When I was District Attorney, I interacted with criminals only after they were arrested.

I got back into bed as the sun began to rise, slept for a few hours and called Jimmy Gray. He was at the Oxford branch bank, unusual for a Saturday morning. I invited him to drive with me back to Sammy's Place and the ravine where El Ray's body was found. He asked if I could wait until noon, which I did. When we pulled onto the gravel parking lot, I was surprised at how dilapidated the building was. Daylight was not a friend to the aesthetic appeal of Sammy's Place. That Saturday morning, it had the look of a recently abandoned structure. The gravel parking lot was filthy, littered with trash, flattened beer cans, and thousands of cigarette butts.

"Damn," Jimmy said. "This place really is a dump."

We drove on to the ravine. Someone had removed the crime scene tape where El Ray's corpse was found by bow hunters. As Jimmy and I stared down at the protruding beech root on which El Ray's body had been anchored, I had hoped that something about it would inspire an original thought that would help solve the crime. But all the visit produced in me was sadness at the loss of such a promising young man. What a waste.

Driving back to Oxford, I asked Jimmy Gray what he was working on at the bank on a Saturday morning.

"Just odds and ends," he said. "Still dealing with our correspondent bank in Nashville on some housekeeping issues we talked about when I was up there day before yesterday. I'll tell you this, they're a strong institution with a capital base that can withstand any stress test the bank auditors want to use to gauge its solvency in case of a downturn."

"How do we stand up under the same type of analysis?"

"Sunshine Bank is much smaller, but I think our capital position and loan quality is stronger than the Nashville Bank, and that's saying something. With some of the idiotic Dodd-Frank requirements being eased by this latest Congress, we're about the most stable bank in Mississippi, not counting the big regional institutions."

"What's our stock worth now?"

"It's value as of our last quarter is so high, it's possible I may achieve one of my lifelong dreams."

"Which is what?"

"In about twenty years, when people see me tottering on the streets of Oxford, drunk as a skunk, I want those people pointing at me and saying: 'There goes old man Jimmy Gray. Money ruined him'."

I laughed harder than I had in quite a while.

"That's a lofty goal," I said, still chuckling. "It's good to set your aspirations high."

"I been checking on your Mr. Conklin this past week. Nothing new to report. For a man who's lived in this area all his life, nobody knows much about him."

"David Burke and I are interviewing him and his wife Monday."

"You need me to come along?"

"I think it would be best if you sit this one out. You may want to call on him again to try to get some of his banking business."

"No chance of that," Jimmy said, "but it would be awkward."

"I'm just spitballing here," I said, "but I've been thinking about who would have come up with the idea of Reese Conklin meeting El Ray at Sammy's Place. It had to be her. It'd be unlikely that El Ray would have picked out Sammy's as a meeting spot."

"Agreed. He's not from here. He wouldn't know about Sammy's unless someone told him about it or took him there. There's a lot of places just as secluded and a lot closer to town. Hell, there's places in town."

"So, how would she have known about Sammy's Place?," I said. "Sammy's seems a little déclassé for a rich blonde who drives a Range Rover. And she's from Greenville, not Tallabusha County."

"But she's lived with Conklin for five years in Tallabusha County," Jimmy said. "That's long enough to know the lay of the land over here."

"She's got a condo in Oxford and frequents local bars, according to David," I said.

"Maybe Conklin drove her by Sammy's some time."

"You said he never goes anywhere."

"That's true. He doesn't."

"Let's go at it from another direction. Sammy or somebody in the bar must be close to Sheriff Burr because the Sheriff knew we had been at Sammy's Place Friday night a week ago. This past Monday morning Burr made a point of letting me know he was aware we were in Sammy's the Friday night before."

"You think Reese has some connection with Sammy or the Sheriff?"

"I don't know, but I'm going to ask her Monday. Her husband, too."

We rode in silence the final five minutes of our drive back to Oxford, which was very uncharacteristic of Jimmy Gray.

"You doing any better with Susan's death now?" he asked me.

"I'd have to say yes," I said, glancing over at the big man. "Getting busy on this El Ray case and being more proactive in the search for Susan's killers has helped get me out of my funk. You were right."

"I knew I was. It helps to stay busy," he said, his voice catching slightly, something only his wife Martha or I would notice. "The thing I hate the most is Doc Nathan said it probably took forty-five minutes for Beau to die. Alone in the woods, in the middle of nowhere. Forty-five minutes of terror for my baby boy. No one around to help."

He wiped his eyes with the back of his big right paw.

"Sometimes at night, when I put my head on the pillow, I close my eyes and ask God to take good care of Beau."

There was nothing for me to say that would help. "I know you do," was all I could get past the lump in my throat.

"Then I ask the Good Lord to turn back time, and let me be the one climbing over that fence instead of Beau when that rifle falls and goes off." He paused and sniffed. "I swear, Willie Mitchell, I wish it could have been me."

CHAPTER TWENTY-FIVE

I rode shotgun in Detective Burke's black Tahoe on the drive Monday morning to Richard Conklin's office on the bypass around Cedar Grove. I asked David how Reese knew about Sammy's Place. He thought for a minute.

"I don't know. I was stupid not to ask her when she was telling me all about her relationship with El Ray. I remember she said her husband's hunting camp was only about ten miles from Sammy's Place. I guess she could have driven past it at times, but it's not on the way to Oxford from either the camp or their home."

"You know how to get to their home?"

"I've driven past it before."

I looked over at him.

"Before I hooked up with her, if that's what you're thinking. I've never been in it, but it's supposed to be the nicest house in Tallabusha County."

David caught me smiling.

"I know that's not saying much, but it's supposed to be huge."

We turned off Highway Six onto the Cedar Grove bypass. We passed a Walmart and a shopping center anchored by Penney's and a Big Star Grocery & Market. A couple of strip centers were next, populated with convenience stores and gas pumps, paycheck loan stores, discount cigarette shops, Mexican restaurants, and fast food outlets.

"Conklin's place is just up ahead on the right," David said.

He slowed the Tahoe as we passed the Conklin office building. "Conklin Enterprises" stood out in bold, red letters above the main entrance. "Conklin's Headquarters" was below Conklin Enterprises in smaller, blue letters. Expansive parking lots surrounding the building.

"You ever been in a Conklin's?" Detective Burke said.

"Nope. I'm surprised there's not one in Oxford."

"Not enough population. Lots of his stores are in malls and shopping centers in high traffic, suburban settings, like Cool Springs outside Nashville. They'll have more traffic past the store in two hours than they would in a week in a town like Oxford."

We walked into the building. The reception area was decorated in Mississippi State maroon and white, which surprised me. While David spoke quietly to the receptionist, I glanced at the college football schedule posters on the paneled wall, counting a dozen regional university and junior colleges represented.

We followed her down a paneled hallway plastered with football photographs on each wall, and into Mr. Conklin's office, sporting Ole Miss red carpet and Ole Miss blue window treatments.

Conklin continued his phone conversation and pointed at chairs across from his desk. We sat down; he kept talking. I scanned the office walls and credenza and noticed there was not a single photograph of Conklin and his wife anywhere. Conklin held up his right index finger, and abruptly ended the call, saying to his caller "you tell the Governor hello for me when you see him."

Richard Conklin's scalp was pink, bordered by close-cut white hair on the sides and back of his round head—Charlie Brown-type round. He was a short, pudgy man with a pasty face and inquisitive eyes. His mouth was a horizontal gash with lips that did not curl on the ends, giving the effect of a grimace rather than a smile. Atop his desk was nothing but an office-style phone, a red and blue felt desk pad, one nineteen-cent Bic ballpoint pen, and a plain white five-by-seven-inch note pad.

He stood to shake our hands and said "What do you want to know?"

"I'm a detective with…"

"I know you're Detective David Burke with OPD and this other fellow is Willie Mitchell Banks, former district attorney for Yaloquena County," Conklin said, gesturing to me. "And I know you're here to ask me about the Raymond boy, El Ray, who died over in your county about three weeks ago."

"That's right, Mr. Conklin," David said. "The NCAA…."

"They're on campus I hear, trying to stir up trouble. They wouldn't have batted an eye if one of Alabama or Georgia's recruits went missing on a weekend trip. But anything that goes on at Ole Miss, and they send in the troops, just like they did in '62."

"Were you there the night of the Meredith riots?" I asked.

"No. I was in high school then, about fifteen. I had a weekend job fixing flats at a local truck stop, worked every Saturday and Sunday the entire time I was at Cedar Grove High. Tell you the truth, I guess I heard about it later but it didn't make much of an impression on me. Earning money was what I was about, same as now."

"I noticed you have State colors in your reception area," I said.

"Got lots of folks around here who are Mississippi State fans. I got a business degree from Ole Miss, worked every afternoon and weekend running a gas station and deli on the northwest corner of University and Lamar. Back then there was a station on each corner of that intersection. I'm an Ole Miss fan, but I don't advertise it. Bad for business."

"We understand you're a donor to Ole Miss athletics," David said.

"Seven figure donations," I added.

"I'm a donor."

"Has the university or its coaches ever involved you in recruiting?" I asked Conklin.

"I have no interest in that. Don't really care to spend time with high school boys they're trying to sign. The coaches either. I haven't been on campus but a couple of times since I graduated. I don't mind giving the money, but I don't have time to hang out in Oxford."

His desk phone buzzed. Conklin picked it up and started talking, continuing non-stop for ten minutes as if we were not in his office. He hung up and didn't miss a beat.

"I'm worth a good bit of money. Earned every nickel of it. All I've ever done is work. I know it sounds strange to you, but I enjoy putting in twelve-to fifteen-hour days running my operation. I don't go out to eat or go on vacation. I've got no children, no family. I don't believe churches and charities do much good. I've got to give my money to somebody. When I die Ole Miss will get a big chunk of it, mainly because I don't want the government to get it."

"And Mrs. Conklin?" David asked.

"We got a pre-nup. If I die while we're married, she gets twenty million in my will, plus the house. If she leaves me while I'm alive, she gets two million and the will gets changed. I travel a good bit setting up new stores, so I don't see Reese much, but I let her know when I want to be with her. She traveled with me last week to Texas. I know you look at me and wonder why I've got a beautiful young wife who's on her own most of the time. Truth is, I like having her around when I'm not working, which is not often. But she's always there when I wake up at home. Gets me my coffee and cooks my breakfast. I don't put many demands on her."

The phone buzzed again. Conklin answered and listened for a minute.

"Let me call you right back," he said to the caller.

"Look, fellows. I'm busy. I didn't put up any money for El Ray, either directly or indirectly. Don't know anything about what happened to him. You go ask my wife. She's waiting for you two at the house."

He stood up, walked around the desk and opened his office door.

"Call me if you have any more questions, but I got to get to work. I'm building out a couple of new stores in Texas and the general contractors are giving me fits."

David and I walked out. He didn't offer his hand and neither did we. We got into the Tahoe and headed for the Conklin home to interview Reese.

"What did you think of Richard Conklin?" David asked.

"I think the man likes to work."

CHAPTER TWENTY-SIX

"That was a good open-ended question you asked him," I said.
"Which one?"

"After he told us he didn't get involved in recruiting and then described his work habits, you asked 'And Mrs. Conklin?'. It wasn't clear why you were asking him about her, but he ran with it, telling about their pre-nup and about their relationship. The question made him open up a little."

"I didn't really think about it like that."

"Even better. Instincts make the difference between a mediocre investigator and a good one like you. Same with trial lawyers. I've been in trials with lawyers who ask questions but don't really listen to the witness's answer. It's got to be more of a conversation than an interrogation if you want information."

"Interesting," David said. "Thanks."

"What do you want to get out of Reese Conklin?"

"Whether she was involved in recruiting El Ray; what she saw when she dropped him off at Sammy's; how he got the meth in his system. You?"

"What she thinks about you."

David chuckled and pointed to a huge house on the west side of the county road. "Maison Conklin."

"Big place for two people."

David turned into the circular brick drive and stopped at the front door. I saw the black Range Rover in the garage. David knocked and Mrs. Conklin opened the front door immediately.

"I saw you drive up," she said with a bright smile. "Y'all come in."

Reese Conklin was a knockout. About 5'4", shoulder-length blonde hair, and a figure like an hourglass. David was right—she did favor Britney Spears. Extremely sexy, she wore skin-tight black jeans and a close-fitting gray cashmere sweater with plenty of cleavage bulging out from its vee-neck.

"I'm Willie Mitchell Banks," I said, shaking her hand in the foyer.

"I've heard a lot about you, Willie Mitchell. Seen you on television."

"Not lately, thank goodness. And you know...," I said gesturing to David, but she interrupted me and hugged him.

"I certainly do know Detective David Burke," she said. "We met a few years ago. You did tell Willie Mitchell about us, didn't you David?"

"I had to," David said, "but I hope...."

"Sure you did," she said. "It would have been odd if you hadn't. How did your meeting with Richard go?"

"Fine," David said. "It was the first time either of us had met him."

"That's not surprising. Unless you're a contractor or business associate building out a Conklin's location, he doesn't have much time for you."

"He's an interesting man," I said.

"With a one-track mind," Reese said. "I admire his ambition, his drive. He's really sweet to me, but building out and operating his stores is the only thing that truly interests him."

David and I paused. Neither of us felt comfortable asking about the Conklins' physical relationship—a reservation she obviously didn't share. She led us into her living room.

"I know people think it's very odd, our marriage, but neither Richard nor I care much about what people think. I have needs, and Richard understands. When we met he was very up front about it. He wants companionship when he's not on the road or working around the clock on a new store opening. That's really all he wants. I do care deeply for him, and he loves me."

"How is his health?" I asked, sitting down.

"He's borderline diabetic, but is good about what he eats and taking his medicine. I don't nag him." She faux-slapped her knee. "How rude of me. May I get either of you coffee or a soft drink?"

"Coffee is good for me," I said, "if it's not too much trouble."

"None at all. We've got a Keurig in the kitchen. Anything in it?"

I said no, and David said he'd have water. We both stared at Reese sashaying out of the living room toward the kitchen. It would have been impossible to ignore her behind.

"Man-oh-man," I whispered to David.

"See what I mean?" he said quietly.

Reese returned in five minutes with a silver tray, on which sat two black coffees in fine china, and water and ice in what looked like a Baccarat tumbler, with its distinctive vertical lines.

"Baccarat?" I asked, pointing to the glass.

"I'm impressed, Willie Mitchell," she said. "Not many folks around here would recognize it."

"My mother had a set of four. In fact, they're still in a china cabinet in our family home in Sunshine."

Reese turned to David. "How can I be of help to y'all?"

"I told Willie Mitchell what you indicated to me about you and El Ray the night he disappeared."

She nodded unabashedly, seemingly eager to help.

"When did you and El Ray meet?" I asked.

"It was sometime in early September on a home game weekend. The coaches had a gathering for recruits Friday night on the Square that included a few alums. I was introduced to El Ray, and thought he was so cute and shy. I gave him my phone number discreetly, and asked him to call me after the game. He called the next night, and I picked him up at his hotel about one a.m. We went to my condo and I got him back to his hotel about 2:30." She turned to David. "The same condo you visited."

"How many more times did you see him?" I asked.

"Three or four. He had his own car and would drive up by himself. He would call me when he got close and I would pick him up at Sammy's and take him to Richard's camp, which he never uses, in case you're wondering. He hasn't been out there in years."

"Why Sammy's?" David asked.

"He wanted someplace remote, didn't want anyone knowing about his meeting me, especially his coaches. I had driven by Sammy's many times on the back road to the hunting camp. El Ray isn't the first person I've arranged to meet out there."

"Have you ever met Sammy Kerry?" I asked.

"Yes. He's a gross old man. I met him four or five years ago in the courthouse when I was called for jury duty. He came up to me in the hall and said he could get me out of jury duty if I wanted. Stared at my chest the whole time."

I thought about passing on to her the advice I had given to women over the years who voiced the same complaint: "If you show it, men will look." But I kept my mouth shut. Since I was older than Sammy, I didn't want to come off as just another lecherous old guy.

"Did he get you out of jury duty?" I asked.

"He did. After we talked he disappeared into the hall leading to the Sheriff's office. I didn't see him again, but after a while the deputy clerk lady came out into the hallway where we were all waiting and whispered to me that I was excused and could leave."

"Did you ever take El Ray anywhere but your condo and the hunting camp?" David asked.

"The condo just that once, the rest at the camp."

"Did he drink when he was with you?" I asked.

"Beer. He liked beer. In fact, he drank beer on the drive from Natchez when we would hook up. I think it helped his shyness."

"The NCAA is looking into El Ray's recruitment by Ole Miss," I said.

"I read that online. I hope they don't contact me."

"We're not going to tell them about you," I said. "You can rely on that. We don't owe them any favors or cooperation. Would anyone else know about you and El Ray?"

"Thank you for keeping me out of it. I don't think anyone knows, unless he told someone. And he was so secretive, I don't think he would have."

"Did you have anything to do with recruiting him?" David asked.

"No. He told me at that alumni supper on the Square when we first met he was going to Ole Miss because of Coach Barnes. They were close."

"Ever give him any money?"

She hesitated. "Will this get me in trouble?"

"Not with us," I said.

"I got the impression he didn't like spending his own money. So, I paid for his gas and food the times he drove himself up. He never stayed at a hotel or anything. And I know at least twice he drove right back to Natchez afterwards."

"How much money are we talking about?" David asked.

"A hundred dollars each time."

"What about the last time, when he went missing?" I asked.

"I got a hundred dollar bill out of my purse, but he laughed and said for me to keep it, that he didn't need it."

"Did you ask him why he didn't need the money?" David asked.

"No. I think he was a little tipsy. I don't know how much he had to drink before I picked him up at Sammy's, but he was feeling no pain. Then he had three or four more at the camp."

"When you dropped him off that last night," I asked, "what can you tell me about the parking lot? Was anyone out there?"

"Nobody," she said. "I'm sure of that. Unless someone was hiding or sitting in a car where we couldn't see them. When I would bring him back to his car at Sammy's, if there was anyone outside he would ask me to drive past and wait until he was certain there was no one in the parking lot."

"When was the first time you became aware something had happened to El Ray?" David asked.

"When I saw it on the news. I'm not sure what day it was. At first they said he was missing, then a few days later it was on the news that some hunters had found his body. It upset me. He seemed like a nice boy. Not stuck up or anything like some of them."

"Did you ever use drugs of any kind with him?" I asked.

"Never," she said. "It never even came up. Alcohol is the only drug I'm interested in doing. You can ask David."

"Far as I know," David said, a little embarrassed.

"The toxicology tests done on El Ray after his death showed positive for methamphetamine," I said.

"No way," she said. "He didn't do it in front of me. Just beer."

"Did you see any signs of it when you picked him up that night?"

"No. He just seemed a little tipsy, like I said. Other than that, he seemed perfectly normal to me."

"Do you know Sheriff Burr?" I asked.

"I have met him at a couple of local functions my husband has asked me to attend so he doesn't have to. Just small talk. I don't know anything about the man except that he's the Sheriff. He always asks me to tell Richard hello. Richard is one of his big political donors, I think."

I gave David an "anything else we need to ask?" look. He shook his head.

We thanked Reese for answering our questions and stood to leave. She said she was glad to help and to call her if we had more questions.

Driving out of the circular drive, David asked me what I thought.

"It was interesting hearing her talk about Sammy Kerry getting her out of jury duty."

"Yep," David nodded. "It shows he's got connections with someone in the courthouse. More than likely it's Sheriff Burr. It would explain how the High Sheriff knew about us patronizing his honky-tonk two Friday's ago."

"Each of those $100 gifts she made to El Ray is an NCAA violation."

"I'm not going to share that information with that asshole Blanchard."

"What gifts?" I said, smiling. "Reese is not ashamed of picking up young guys," I said. "She acted like she was telling us a recipe for pumpkin bread."

"She never talked about her personal life or her marriage when I was with her. Kept it off limits," David said. "You surprised by anything else she said?"

"No," I said, "but after meeting her, I do have this to say. I'm sorry El Ray is dead, but it does make me feel better knowing that he died a satisfied young man."

CHAPTER TWENTY-SEVEN

David dropped me off at home around noon. I sat at my desk and made notes of the Conklin interviews, then went over my entire file on the El Ray investigation. I was out of ideas, so I put on my running stuff and headed west on University, hoping my subconscious mind had been collating and analyzing the El Ray information I had collected. It had done that for me many times when I was District Attorney.

It was chilly and overcast that Monday afternoon in late November. I started out at a pretty good pace to generate some internal heat. After a mile I was in a comfortable rhythm—not as fast as I used to run, but good enough considering my less than optimal physical conditioning.

I was headed south past the football stadium. As I neared the Manning Center, I thought about Reggie Barnes. Coach Goodson said he was sending him to Louisiana last week to recruit. I wondered if he was back.

"Is Coach Barnes in?" I asked the young man in dark blue sweats sitting behind the reception desk guarding the entrance to the coaches' offices.

"Let me check," he said and picked up the phone on the desk.

"He's at home today," the young man said. "Sick."

"Are you a graduate assistant?" I asked.

"Yes, sir."

"How'd Coach Barnes do in Louisiana?" I asked.

"I haven't talked to him," he said.

"Could you give me his cell number?"

"Not allowed to do that," he said, looking at my outdated running gear.

"My name is Willie Mitchell Banks. I'm a lawyer here in town. I met with Coach Goodson and Coach Barnes last week, and I'm doing some follow up with Reggie. Would you ask Coach Goodson if it's all right to give it to me?"

He nodded and disappeared down the hallway. Moments later, Coach Goodson came out. He wasn't smiling.

"Reggie's under the weather today," he said. "I sent him home. What do you need him for?"

"Just some routine follow-up, Coach. Nothing important." I paused. "I thought your comments in the Chancellor's office last week hit the nail on the head."

"I just said what was on my mind." Coach Goodson looked at me a moment, apparently deciding if I was trustworthy. "Give me your cell and I'll text you his contact information."

I wrote my cell number down on the Ole Miss powder blue Post-it Note the young man plopped on the counter with a ballpoint.

"Thanks, Coach," I said and resumed my run.

When I got home I checked my phone. Coach Goodson had come through. Pleased that I had passed the Head Coach's loyalty test, I showered and dressed, then called Reggie's cell number. A woman answered.

"Is this Coach Reggie Barnes phone?" I asked.

"Yes, it is," she said. "I'm his wife."

"Mrs. Barnes, this is Willie Mitchell Banks. I'm a local lawyer representing the Chancellor in the investigations surrounding the death of El Ray. Coach Goodson gave me your husband's contact information. I'd like to swing by and talk to him today if that's all right."

"Reggie's mentioned you. He's in bed right now. Can this wait until he's feeling better? Maybe later in the week?"

"I wish it could, but I've got some information about El Ray that he needs to know. I won't keep him but a few minutes, but I need to tell him in person." There was silence on her end for a moment. "All right, Mr. Banks. When did you want to come?"

"Right now if that's okay. It's important."

What I meant, but did not say, was this: it was important that I talk to Reggie by himself, with no one else around, especially Coach Goodson.

I was in my truck driving north toward Oxford Commons on Highway 7 within five minutes of Mrs. Barnes's telling me to come on. I exited and drove east past the Oxford Commons Cinema and the new commercial structures that had popped up contemporaneous with the construction and opening of the new Oxford High School. I followed my phone's instructions and turned south into the last residential area before reaching the school. I parked in the Barnes's driveway after the pleasant-sounding female hidden in my phone announced that I had arrived at my destination.

The house was new, very similar to all the new houses on the street, some of which were still under construction. The Barnes's small front yard was sodded, but the grass squares were dormant. Torn cardboard boxes were stacked on the brown turf next to the concrete drive, and landscaping plants in black plastic pots were scattered in front of the house, waiting to be planted.

"Come in, Mr. Banks" Mrs. Barnes said after opening the door and extending her free hand. "I'm Lana Barnes."

She was a pretty woman, about Reggie's age, *café au lait* skin. She carried an infant on her hip, and a young boy looked up at me with bright eyes from behind his mother's leg.

"Looks like y'all are still settling in to your new house," I said.

"Everything's a mess," she said. "There's been so much going on."

"I'm sure. I won't keep Reggie long."

"This is Marietta," she said, nodding to the baby, "and this young man behind me is Reggie, Jr." I tried to shake Reggie Jr's hand but he slunk further behind his mother. "Come out here and speak to Mr. Banks, Reggie."

"That's all right, Mrs. Barnes. It's natural to be shy around a stranger."

Reggie Jr. dashed off into another room. He returned in a moment holding his father's hand.

"You two sit in the living room," she said. "I'll take the kids to the kitchen so you can talk."

Coach Reggie dragged himself to the couch and sat down. He tossed a note pad and a vintage gold Cross pen on the coffee table.

"Sorry you're not feeling well," I said as I sat. "I hope you did some good in Louisiana last week."

Reggie looked at me, puzzled.

"At our meeting last week. Coach Goodson said you were heading there to recruit for several days."

"Oh, yeah," Reggie said and shrugged.

"Look, Reggie, there's just a more few things I wanted to discuss with you. Coach Goodson sent me your contact information."

He took a deep breath and sat up straighter.

"We got El Ray's toxicology screens back from the crime lab. At the time of his death, El Ray had a good bit of alcohol in his system."

"That's no big deal," he said. "Just about all of our recruits sneak a few beers. Not much we can do about it. I never saw him take a drink."

"He also tested positive for methamphetamines."

"That's not true," he said forcefully. "El Ray never did drugs. If he had, I'd have known about it. He's lived under a media microscope the last two years."

"I'm afraid it is. You have any idea where he might have gotten it?"

He shook his head. "That's just some mistake. Those tests are wrong."

"I drove to Natchez last week, met with his mother."

"You meet his sorry excuse for a father?"

"Briefly. He wasn't real pleased to see me. He'd been drinking."

"As usual," Reggie said. "I never talked to him when he wasn't."

"He claims he's got information on money that programs paid or offered to El Ray to sign."

"That's all bullshit. El Ray would have told me. I warned him all along about people trying to buy him, what a mistake it would be to take any money. He had a good head on his shoulders. What people offer him now is peanuts compared to what he would make when he went pro if he kept his nose clean."

"You know if his father took money from anyone?"

"It wouldn't surprise me, but El Ray knew his dad was no good. He didn't take advice from that drunk. El Ray took better care of his money than his old man did."

"Mr. Raymond ever ask you for money?"

"He hinted at it, but I told him if he took money it was going to get out and it would harm his son, get him into trouble. He said other programs were talking real money, but I don't know if it was true. He was always drunk. Couldn't believe anything he said."

I watched Reggie lean over to grab his note pad and pen. He scribbled something with his left hand, underlined it, and put the pen down.

"Do you know a woman named Reese Conklin?"

Reggie thought a moment. "Who is she?"

"She's a pretty blonde in her mid-thirties, married to a rich alum, lives in Tallabusha County but has a place in Oxford. Drives a black Range Rover. You ever come across her?"

"I don't know. I meet so many people. What's she got to do with El Ray?"

"Not sure," I said. "I just wanted to see if you had ever met her."

"I could have," he said quietly. "I just don't know."

I asked Reggie a few more questions, thanked him and left. Back in my truck, I thought about Reggie's demeanor. He never seemed feverish, coughed or sniffed while we talked. He might well be sick, but not in the conventional sense. Reggie appeared depressed, a debilitating, very real "sickness," one with which I had become very familiar in the weeks and months immediately following Susan's murder. Winston Churchill called it "the black dog," and struggled against it all his life, self-medicating with brandy at breakfast and strong drink the rest of every day. Reggie was fighting his own "black dog," and until I found out what happened to El Ray, why he was killed, I didn't think Reggie was going to get any better.

CHAPTER TWENTY-EIGHT

"How'd it go with Reggie?" Detective Burke asked me.

"About like I expected," I said, handing him a cold Heineken him and sitting down across from him in the condo. "He said the meth finding had to be wrong, some kind of lab error. I told him about Mr. Raymond's claims about money being offered, and he said neither he nor anyone on Ole Miss's behalf ever gave or promised to give money to El Ray. I asked him if he knew who Reese Conklin was and he said no."

"What kind of illness does Reggie have?"

"No one has said, but I think he's just depressed. I believe the psychological trauma of El Ray's death has brought him down."

"I think you're right about that. He's always been upbeat, full of energy as long as I've known him. I've never seen him like this."

"He tell you anything of significance before I got involved?"

"No," David said, shaking his head. "But I do have some news."

I waited a moment. This wasn't the first time Detective Burke kept me in suspense. "Are you going to make me guess?"

"Just making sure I've got your attention," he said grinning. "After we got back from the Conklin interviews, I drove out to Sammy's Place. Passed by several times to make sure no one was around, drove a half-mile south, then went off road on an old logging trail and drove through the woods to a spot across the road from Sammy's."

"Not in your Tahoe, I hope."

"Naw. OPD has a four-wheel drive jeep with open sides and a camo paint job. We bought it with a DOJ grant last year."

"What did you do in the woods?"

"I backed the Jeep up to a huge red oak tree, climbed up about thirty feet off the ground, and placed a trail camera pointed at Sammy's front door and parking lot. Ever used one?"

"A trail camera? No. I know people who set them up to scout deer."

"That's the only thing I've used it for until today. I'm going after bigger game with it now. Sammy Kerry hates us and anyone else who works for any branch of government. I think he knows more than he's told us, but he's not going to share it with us unless he has to. It may be a waste of time but I want to see who comes and goes out there."

"Was it hard to set up?"

"Climbing the tree was the toughest thing. It's a Bushnell camera, really top of the line. A trail camera is just a self-contained digital camera with plenty of power and data storage. It's activated by movement. I looked online at the specs for the Bushnell. It has night capabilities using infrared flash, which is invisible to people."

"Any way Sammy or his customers can see it?"

"No way. I placed it at the outer parameters of its detection zone. And it's relatively tiny. I figured I'd give it several days then go out and get it, check what it picks up, recharge it and put it back up."

"You have any idea who owns the property?"

"No. I find it's easier to get forgiveness than permission."

My phone buzzed in my pocket. It was Jake's number.

"This is Jimmy Gray," I lied, walking to my office. "He was supposed to ask me something about bank business. I won't be but a second."

I closed my door and answered.

"Jake," I said quietly. "Everything all right?"

"I got something I want to give you. I'm hoping you can get it analyzed on the QT. Can you meet me tonight?"

"Sure. When and where?"

"Coming from Oxford, about a mile into Tallabusha County, there's a road that goes north off Highway 6. It's County Road 402. Locals call it Deer Creek Road. I'll be there about ten o'clock."

"Where?"

"There's an old logging road I'll back into and wait. I'll see you when you drive past, then catch up with you and blink my lights. You let me pass and I'll take you to an old farmhouse about a mile and a half off the road. Nobody lives there, and the gate is chained, but not locked."

"I'll turn on 402 right at ten," I said.

Chapter Twenty-Nine

Burke finished his beer and left. It was a few minutes to seven. I would have to leave about 9:30 to make the CR 402 turnoff at ten. I wondered what I was going to do for the next two-and-one-half hours other than pace.

I put on my running stuff and headed out faster than normal, knowing from experience that a little exercise would calm my jitters. I ran through the darkened campus for twenty minutes, stopped to walk for about ten minutes, fussing at myself for getting so out of shape. I alternated jogging and walking back to the condo. I showered, dressed, and ate a sandwich while reading the Wall Street Journal online.

At ten o'clock, I turned off the highway onto CR 402. There were no houses or structures of any kind for the first mile, just curves and hills. Dormant kudzu draped from the tops of telephone poles and their supporting guy wires, creating small pyramids lining the dark country road.

Headlights blinked in my rearview mirror, and I slowed to watch Jake zip around me in his little Nissan truck and lead the way. Five minutes later, the truck slowed, then turned abruptly into a privet-shrouded driveway that I would have never seen if not for Jake's turning into it. Fifty feet off the road, Jake stopped, jumped out of his truck and removed the chain from the fence post. I followed him through the gate and waited for him to re-chain it.

Jake switched to his parking lights, and I followed suit. I stayed close to him down a steep hill. We slowed in tandem and crossed a small levee that skirted a pond. At the top of the next hill, Jake stopped next to an old country house and cut off his engine and parking lights.

"Are we going inside?" I whispered.

"No. We can sit on the porch."

Jake turned on a flashlight no larger than my little finger. He led me up rickety wooden steps and briefly scanned the porch with his light to reveal two wooden steel cable spools that had been turned on their sides.

"Have a seat."

"Kind of creepy out here," I said. "You don't know who owns this?"

"Whoever it is, they never come out here. My first visit was during the daytime. I walked over the place and checked out the old farm house. There's no electric lines running to the building. You can look through those window panes and tell no one has lived here for decades."

"I'll take your word for it. What did you want to give me?"

"Two things. I have them in a Ziploc bag. One is a beer can, the other is a roach. Q-Man and I drank beer and smoked a couple of joints in my trailer last night. There should be good prints on the can and plenty of DNA on the roach, which is in a small plastic sandwich bag inside the bigger Ziploc. You think you can get these analyzed? Q-Man did time in Parchman, so he's definitely in the state system. I want to find out his real name and his criminal history."

"I believe I can get Robbie Cedars to do it off the books for me at the crime lab. He still owes me a favor or two. I'll overnight them to him, unless you want me to drive to Pearl."

"No need. Chain of custody's not important for this. Overnight is good. Can you ask him to do it as soon as he gets it?"

"I believe so. I'll call him before I send it."

I shuddered as a cold wind swept through the porch.

"It's pretty out here in the daytime," Jake said. "Really peaceful, too."

"In contrast to your surroundings the last six years?"

"Sometimes."

"I'd really like for you to tell me where you've been and what you've done. Now that Susan is gone, you don't have to be so secretive. I know some of it was necessary because you didn't want her to worry."

"That was part of it," he said. "But the truth is, I didn't want either one of you to know, because I knew both of you would disapprove. And, Dunne made us swear an oath to keep our mouths shut under penalty of dismissal." He paused a moment. "Or worse."

"Meaning what?"

"He never said. Based on the type of operations we conducted, we all assumed if we broke the silence we'd be...."

"Silenced?"

"No, but we knew it would be bad. Talking out of school could have easily led to a botched mission and teammates killed. Thank God we never found out what the ultimate punishment was."

"What countries did you work in?"

"Every hell hole you can think of. At least half the time we were abroad in the Middle East, Africa, the former Soviet Union, Southeast Asia."

"The other half was domestic?"

"Pretty much," Jake said. "I spent a lot of time in the Pacific Northwest and along both sides of the southern border with Mexico, all the way from Brownsville and Matamoros to Mexicali and Tijuana. There were a lot of things Border Patrol couldn't do, so they called us in."

"You mean things like operate in Mexico."

"Lots of bad dudes try to get into the U.S. through the Mexican border, and I'm not talking about just Mexicans or Central Americans. Like Dunne used to say, we don't kill anyone that doesn't need killing to save American lives."

"And only if there's no alternative?"

Jake chuckled. "The people we go after cannot be rehabilitated. You put some of the *jihadis* and killers we deal with in prison, all you're going to end up with is more *jihadis* and killers. Right now in the U.S., our state and federal prisons are the principal source of Islamic radicalism and home-grown terrorists. I mean, they're behind bars, what do they have to lose?"

"Yeah. Some of the men I sent away to Parchman come back home a lot more dangerous than when they went in."

"And your justice system does a piss-poor job of dealing with them."

"Yes, it does."

"Your justice system..." It was Jake's way of confirming the irrevocability of the choice he had made. He had no interest in being brought back into conventional law enforcement. He seemed dead set on staying in the life he had chosen, and not rejoining mine.

"The system didn't start out like that," I said.

"That's the way it's ended up. Even if we find out who killed Mom and tried to kill you, no matter how strong the evidence, they're not going to be convicted in Tallabusha County. You ought to hear these dumbasses I've been hanging with the last five months talk about the Sheriff and the District Attorney over here.

They say Sheriff Burr's on the take and the D.A. is a babbling idiot."

"Maybe so," I said.

"Every meth head or crack addict out in these woods has a story to tell about the Sheriff or one of his deputies. And even if they're arrested, somehow their case never goes to trial. The rest of the people must not care, because they keep electing them.

"Even if one of the cases got to a jury, these Tallabusha people are so stupid they'd never convict. If some criminal actually gets found guilty, the Courts of Appeal overturn the verdict on some trumped-up technical or constitutional argument, or the D.A. mishandled it somehow."

I told Jake the saga of the appliance store massacre in the Delta, how the Mississippi Supreme Court ordered a new trial twelve years after the fact, and related the latest on the Pickett disaster, the sociopathic sixteen-year-old who murdered strangers, a grandmother and child, just for the adventure.

"Fat chance Walton has of rounding up the witnesses from murders in that appliance store over a decade ago."

"The shooter will end up pleading out and get sentenced to a few additional years and then he'll be out," I said, "fifteen years or so after murdering four people."

"That's a damned shame. Just like what happened with El Moro," Jake said. "If it hadn't been for Dunne, you and I would be dead and El Moro would have gone scot free. You came close to cashing in your chips."

"No doubt about that."

"Speaking of El Moro's trial, how's your left leg and your eye?"

"As slow as I run these days, my leg doesn't give me much trouble. I'm still wearing a contact in my left eye, and I see out of it good enough. I've become more right-eye dominant, though, to compensate for the weakness in the other. I can really tell it when I putt."

"You been playing much?" Jake asked.

"Nah," I said. "Not since the BP. Haven't been doing much of anything. I do have this case that's keeping me busy. I'm representing the Chancellor in the NCAA investigation and the murder case involving this five-star recruit who was killed on an unauthorized weekend visit up here. Killed out in the woods south of the highway in Tallabusha, probably not far from here."

"I heard about it. 'El Ray' Raymond from Natchez."

"How'd you hear?"

"I saw it on the front page of that weekly shopper that passes for a newspaper out of Cedar Grove. I swear the people putting that paper out are illiterate."

"It's a tough case, but I don't think the murder had anything to do with the school. Something personal, I believe."

"You buy that Glock I mentioned to you?"

"Not yet."

"You don't have a gun in your condo in Oxford?"

"No."

"Did you forget about someone breaking in and stealing your Springfield? What if they come at you in the dead of night? This time they might not leave you a Raven to mess with your head. They might mean business. You gonna use karate on them?"

"I'll borrow one of Jimmy's until I get the Glock .45."

"How's he doing?" Jake asked.

"Same as always. He's got the bank humming."

"I wish I could talk to him. I sure miss him. He ever get over Beau?"

"You don't get over the death of a son, Jake. He's learned to live with it."

"I can see that."

"I want you to call me if you get in trouble. I'm serious."

"What for? You going to get Sheriff Burr to arrest them? Fat chance."

"No. I'll help you do whatever is necessary."

"You mean help me kill the people who killed Mom?"

"You can't take them on by yourself."

"Yes, I can. But that's beside the point. Are you telling me you're willing to abandon all you've stood for all your life and cross the Rubicon with me? Because you have to be willing to give up everything you've worked for, everything you've accomplished. To most people, I'm on the dark side. And once you're there, you can never go back."

"I'm sixty-three, Jake, and already done just about everything I wanted to. The people who murdered Susan are not going to be arrested. If I can't help you take out the people who killed her, then I'm not much of a man."

"Even if you wanted to, Willie Mitchell, you're not in good enough physical shape to do what I do. And when's the last time you shot a pistol? I'm certain you've never shot *at* anyone. Believe me, it's very different. You've got to suspend your humanity and become a predator. And once you do, you're no longer part of polite society."

"I understand all that, but I can't let you do this alone. Look, it might not come to this, but if it does, I want to be your wing man. Just speaking hypothetically, what would I need to do for you to consider it?"

"First thing, you have to buy that Glock and get good with it. That means doing a lot of shooting, and practicing changing magazines, over and over, until you can do it in the kind of darkness we're sitting in out here. You have to learn to shoot on the move well enough to get center mass groupings over and over. You've got to be proficient at shooting from five to twenty-five yards, standing, kneeling, and prone."

"I can do all that."

"And your physical conditioning—are you still running?"

"Just a little."

"You've got to get to where you can run five miles at better than an eight-and-a-half minute pace. Do some sprints, too. Build your strength. You don't need to do weights, just do pullups, situps, and pushups. Work on strikes, punching, slapping, and kicking a heavy bag. When's the last time you were in a fight?"

"College," I said.

"People I go up against aren't drunk, and they don't take prisoners. You need to get you a sparring partner, preferably an ex-military guy. Get him to teach you how to put someone on the ground. It's not with your fists."

"I need to make some notes," I said. "You got any paper to write on?"

I sat in my truck and pulled a Sunshine Bank ballpoint from the console. Jake reached into his Nissan, walked to my door, and gave me two sheets of letter-sized paper and the Ziploc containing Q-Man's beer can and the remains of a joint.

"Shine your light in here, Jake, and go back over what you said."

Jake dictated and I jotted words to remember the homework Jake wanted me to do with the Glock and my conditioning.

"Okay," I said. "I'll begin tomorrow."

"After you overnight the evidence to the crime lab."

"Right."

"Follow me out. I'll call in a few days."

CHAPTER THIRTY

I woke up the next morning embarrassed about what I had said to Jake. It wasn't the conditioning or developing the shooting and fighting skills that concerned me. It was my brave declaration that I wanted to be there to help him when and if he found Susan's killers. I rolled out of bed and stared at the mirror. Who was I kidding? I was no tough guy, much less an armed avenger. I fought criminals and helped victims by using my intellect and my words, not my fists or a gun. Like Jake said, I had never shot at another human. I even gave up deer hunting when I realized I no longer wanted to kill such beautiful animals. I have no problem with hunters harvesting deer. It's necessary to keep the herd healthy and strong. But someone else can do it, not me.

I dressed in my running gear and drank a cup of coffee reading the dreadful Jackson paper online. After overcoming the lassitude my six months of inactivity had produced, I set my watch and took off. For the first five minutes, my body was begging me to quit. But then muscle memory from times past kicked in. Three miles was my goal, and I made it, though it wasn't pretty. I checked my watch. I had pushed the pace, but it was still slow.

Cleaned up and back at my desk, I called Detective Burke and asked him if he knew any trainers. I explained I not only wanted aerobic conditioning, I also needed strength and agility work. I mentioned I needed to hone my shooting skills, too.

"You trying out for the Senior Olympics?" he asked, laughing. "What's that event where they do cross country skiing and shoot rifles?"

"The biathlon, smart ass. I just need to get in shape, and the break-in reminded me how vulnerable I am. The burglar who left the Raven automatic could have just as easily broken in the condo when I was upstairs sleeping and taken me out. Plus, in twenty-four years as D.A. I sent a lot of people to Parchman and other penitentiaries. They let some out every year, and some of them may still hold grudges."

"You need to talk to the Brass brothers," David said.

"Never heard of them."

"They're ex-military, ex-FBI. Early fifties or so, but they're still muscled-up and tough as nails. They operate a training business called Brass Tactical out on Highway 6 just west of town. We send some of our rookie cops out there to learn how to manhandle drunk students on the Square without hurting them. They've got a nice outdoor shooting facility where they can run you through shooting drills. They're on contract with the state to conduct periodic special forces-type training for Mississippi State Troopers."

"You know 'em well enough to call them and refer me for training?"

"I do. I know the older one, Darwin, best. I'll call him and tell him about you, what you need done."

"And send me a text after you talk to him with their contact info."

"All right, but the Brass brothers are going to turn you into a badass, Willie Mitchell. I just hope you're mature enough to handle your new powers."

"Just make the call, Burke."

"Ten-four," he said laughing.

I called Robbie Cedars at the crime lab and asked him if he could analyze the beer can and the roach off the books for me and run his results through the state systems. He said he'd be glad to, and gave me the crime lab street address for ground deliveries. I drove to the UPS store less than a mile away and placed the Ziploc into a padded envelope, then a hard-sided box, and paid for next day delivery. I wasn't worried about the roach, but I didn't want the can getting crushed.

Back at the condo, I called Shooter's Paradise, a gun store located out of the city limits on Highway 7. I had passed it many times but never gone in. The clerk said they had plenty of Glocks on hand, and I said I'd be right out. I was there in fifteen minutes.

I settled on the Glock 30 Gen 4 .45 caliber automatic with the black matte finish, two extra ten round magazines, three boxes of ammo, and a Glock carrying case. I showed the young clerk dressed in camo my drivers license and filled out the background check form. He said it would only take a few minutes to run the check. Fifteen minutes and $650 later, I left Shooter's Paradise with my new .45 caliber Glock and accoutrements.

I got comfortable handling the Glock, dry-firing it a dozen times at my desk in the condo. I struggled with loading the magazines because the new springs were so tight. The Glock had a good feel to it, lighter than my recently departed Smithfield, but substantial enough.

I spent an hour online reading the comments of Glock owners about my new automatic, learning the pros and cons of handling and cleaning it. I put the gun in its case and placed it on the steps to take up later. I had decided my office desk drawer was too far from my upstairs bedroom to do me any good if my burglar returned.

Back at my desk, I re-read my barely legible notes from Jake's conditioning suggestions the night before. After some grumbling, I tossed the two pages to the edge of the desk, causing both to flutter and drop on the floor. When I bent to pick them up, I noticed for the first time that the two pages I had made notes on were the back sides of Xeroxed flyers of the "Have You Seen This Woman?" type usually found thumb-tacked to notice boards at post offices or police stations, or on telephone poles at street corners. I studied the black and white image of the woman on the flyer. Though the copy was of poor quality, there was something familiar about her. I was pretty sure I had seen her somewhere.

The flyer said the woman's name was Lynda Gianelli Guthrie. There was a phone number with the North Mississippi prefix, 662, for "anyone knowing the whereabouts of Lynda Guthrie" to call. I Googled her name with "missing person Mississippi" and found a much clearer color photograph of Lynda.

I stared at the photograph.

The hair on the back of my neck bristled and goose bumps appeared on my arms. The woman on my monitor was younger and prettier than she was when I had seen her. In the photograph, Lynda Guthrie wore makeup, had her hair fixed, and smiled pleasantly. The day I saw Lynda, she looked much worse for wear, but I was sure she was the woman I had seen driving the dark green Ford Expedition at the Varner exit.

The missing person, Lynda Gianelli Guthrie, drove Susan's killer to the BP in June, and waited while he killed her.

CHAPTER THIRTY-ONE

My finger was unsteady as I entered the number on my cell phone. The call went to voice mail.

"Mrs. Gianelli," I said. "My name is Willie Mitchell Banks. I'm an attorney in Oxford. I happened upon a flyer with Linda Gianelli Guthrie's photograph and this number. I am not certain, but I may have some information on your missing daughter. I would like to discuss it with you. Please call me at...."

Ten minutes later, I answered my cell.

"Is this Mr. Banks?" the woman caller said in a tremulous voice.

"This is he, Mrs. Gianelli."

"Were you the D.A. in Yaloquena County who used to be on the news?"

"Yes, ma'am."

"You have some information on my daughter?"

"I think so, Mrs. Gianelli. I believe I saw Lynda back in June at a gas station off I-55. At the Varner exit in Tallabusha County."

"What was she doing?"

"She was driving a dark green, older SUV and pulled up next to me."

"Was it a Ford Expedition?"

"Yes, ma'am."

The sound she made is hard to describe. It was as if she began to cry and scream at the same time. I waited for her to say something. It seemed like a very long wait. Mrs. Gianelli was obviously very fragile, and I did not want to upset or mislead her. It was 2:30 in the afternoon. The community of Grundy was on the outskirts of Tunica, about an hour and a half away. Anything else I told her needed to be in person.

"Mr. Banks?" she said in a weak voice.

"I know this is very stressful for you, Mrs. Gianelli, and I think it would be best if we talked about this face-to-face. This is not the sort of thing that should be discussed over the phone."

There was silence on the other end.

"I'm only an hour and a half away. I could be there by four if you can see me." I waited a moment. "Mrs. Gianelli?"

"Are you telling me the truth?" she said hesitantly. "Because if...."

"I think I saw her, but I'm not positive. I don't want to upset you."

She cleared her throat.

"All right," she said, "if you're who you say you are."

"I'll bring some identification. You might recognize me from television news stories a few years back."

Ten minutes later I was in my F-150 on Highway 6 heading west to I-55. An hour later, I exited onto I-69 and drove west to its intersection with U.S. Highway 61, "the Blues Highway," which runs north and south 1,400 miles from New Orleans to Minnesota, hugging the serpentine curves of the Mississippi River.

I drove south on U.S. 61, past Tunica's giant casino hotels rising from former cotton and soybean fields on the banks of the river. I slowed to look out over the huge Harrah's parking lot, now a concrete wasteland with weeds two feet tall sprouting from the cracks between the slabs. Harrah's Casino Tunica had prospered in the 1990's and early 2000's, with its huge casino, golf course, RV park, and three hotels on 2200 acres on the banks of the Mississippi. In its boom days, Tunica was the third highest grossing gambling venue in the U.S. behind Las Vegas and Atlantic City. Harrah's Tunica closed in 2013.

In Tunica's boom times, casinos employed over 12,000 workers. I read online that number had dwindled to 4,000 now. In the early years, Tunica drew a torrent of gamblers from Memphis and West Memphis. Tennesseans, Arkansans, and North Mississippians who could least afford to gamble converged on Tunica to be seduced by the glamor of huge gambling halls where drinks were complimentary and night and day were indistinguishable. It was profitable for the casinos and an economic disaster for the patrons, who gambled away money previously destined for mortgages, rent and car payments, and groceries.

Heading south to Grundy, on either side of Highway 61, there were paycheck cashing and lending stores, pawn shops, flea markets, and used car lots—the flotsam and jetsam of remora-like businesses that follow casinos to profit on the misfortunes of the gaming underclass.

I took a right off the highway onto a county road, and neared the address Mrs. Gianelli had given me. I parked in her driveway behind an old Buick LeSabre, a model I believe General Motors stopped making around 2005. The house was a small, brick veneer ranch situated lower than the county road, which guaranteed near-flooding events in times of high water, evidenced by the stack of brown-stained sandbags leaning against the front wall of the house.

Mrs. Gianelli answered my knock almost immediately. I held out my drivers license but she waved it away. She was short and stocky, with wiry salt-and-pepper hair, heavy-lidded eyes, and no makeup.

"I recognize you from the television, Mr. Banks. Please come in and have a seat. Would you like some water or coffee?"

"No, thank you," I said and sat down on a sagging, threadbare couch in her small front room. "Thank you for seeing me, Mrs. Gianelli,"

"I'm sorry I got upset on the phone, Mr. Banks. It's just that...."
She dabbed her eyes with the crumbled Kleenex she palmed.

"I know. Let me show you this flyer."

I had made a copy of one of my two flyers and gave it to her. She looked at it and took a deep breath.

"One of my brothers drives a truck for a poultry plant southeast of here, and he helped put out these flyers. He put them in stores along highways and county roads as far south as Jackson. Where did you get this one?"

"In a store off of I-55," I lied. "How long has Lynda been missing?"

"Soon be a year. She left her home the week before last Christmas. Drove away in their Expedition one afternoon. Her husband and their two children were shopping at the Walmart in Senatobia, buying something they could give to their mother for Christmas. When they got home, she was gone."

"Is it possible she was taken by someone?"

"I think that would have made it easier on us. She left a note to her husband, saying she couldn't handle it anymore, and was leaving because the children would be better off without her. Took some clothes and makeup and one suitcase, drove away in the Expedition and vanished."

I wondered how a mother of two could be so cruel and selfish.

"Have you had any leads on where she might have gone or any responses to the flyers?"

"The Tunica County Sheriff sent word to other sheriffs, the State Troopers, and the FBI. The Sheriff and Deputy Tyler worked on it for a while, but after a month of hearing nothing, they kind of let it slide. My brother kept putting out these flyers from time to time. I've had a few calls, but mostly from crazy people or crooks. Some of them asked me to send them money and they would come here and tell me where they saw Lynda."

"Scam artists," I said. "Let me tell you where I saw the woman."

I described the BP station location at the Varner exit in rural Tallabusha County, how the Expedition pulled up to the other side of the pump I was using. I described the woman driver.

"I'm pretty sure it was your daughter."

"Did the Expedition have places on the hood where the finish had worn off?"

"Yes," I said. "But the woman I saw had skin darker than in Lynda's photograph."

"She always loved to tan. Her father and I are both half-Italian, and Lynda inherited her father's beautiful golden skin. When she was a girl she would lie out in the sun as soon as it was warm enough. I would fuss at her about skin cancer but she didn't care."

"It was last June when my wife was killed. The weather was warm."

"Lynda would have been darker in June. Was this woman you saw with anyone?"

"Yes," I said. "A young black man in a red windbreaker and flip flops. He got out and went in the store."

"Did you talk to Lynda or this boy?"

"No, ma'am," I said and told her exactly what happened next.

Mrs. Gianelli hung her head and began weeping. There was nothing I could say that would console her. She cried for ten minutes.

"I am so sorry about your wife, Mr. Banks. I feel so ashamed."

"It's not your fault, Mrs. Gianelli. You're not to blame."

"I raised her as best I could. Her father ran off with some woman he worked with in the casino when Lynda was fifteen. Didn't say goodbye, kiss my foot, or anything."

"He worked in the casino?"

"When the Splash Casino opened, Elbert was in one of the first dealer training classes they had. He had worked before that at the John Deere dealership as a mechanic, and he thought dealing cards would be an easier way to make a living. It was only the three of us. I couldn't have any more children after Lynda. Everything was going good. I stayed home and raised Lynda, but then Elbert started staying later, working the night shift, drinking more when he wasn't working. Finally, he just took off with some woman he worked with. That was twenty years ago. I haven't heard from him since. It broke Lynda's heart, too."

"I'm sorry, Mrs. Gianelli."

"What is it about me, Mr. Banks, that people just up and leave me?"

"I'm sure it's not you," I said, though I knew nothing about Mrs. Gianelli. "These things just happen to people. Do you mind if I ask you a few more questions?"

"Okay, but do you know if Lynda is still in Tallabusha County?"

"No, ma'am. I'm not from there, and I only saw her that one day."

"It was the drugs, I'm sure," she said. "Started after her daddy ran off. Lynda began hanging out with a bad crowd, staying out late, smelling like smoke and alcohol when she came in. I begged her to stop, but she was fifteen going on twenty, taller and stronger than me, and had a mind of her own. I guessed I failed her."

"You did your best, I'm sure."

"Her husband Tim Guthrie is not the smartest man, but he works hard, and loves his two boys, Jed and James."

"How old are they now?"

"Jed is eight, James six. Tim went ahead and got a divorce and full custody. He's moving on with his life and the boys are adjusting. He lets me see them any time I want."

"That's good, Mrs. Gianelli."

"What should I do now?" she asked. "I don't know anyone in Tallabusha County to ask for help."

"I know Sheriff Burr and Deputy Tyler. I've worked with their office on investigating my wife's death. I'm going to tell them what I've found out and ask them to get their deputies to be on the lookout for Lynda and the Expedition."

"Oh, thank you, Mr. Banks. I'm so sorry for what happened to your wife. Lynda was never violent, and I hope she didn't know what that young man was going to do in that store. It's just so awful."

"You're probably right." I paused. "It's important you understand that I don't know if Lynda and this man were living in Tallabusha County at the time of the shooting. They might have come from another county."

"Like I said, it's the drugs, Mr. Banks. Her husband and our priest had to do an intervention two years ago. She got treatment at the local health unit, and we thought she was better. Tim told me she got back on them two months before she left."

"Did Tim say what kind of drugs?"

"He told me it was uppers of some kind. Meth, maybe he said."

"If I think of anything else to ask, do you mind if I call you?"

"No, please do. And you'll let me know what the Sheriff says?"

"I will," I said and stood to leave.

"She's been in Tallabusha County before. Her father's parents, she called them Paw-Paw and Mee-Maw, she would go stay with them for weeks at a time on their farm about ten miles outside of Cedar Grove. I never went much, but Lynda loved it down there in those woods. When her grandparents passed, Lynda told me at the funeral that when she stayed with Paw-Paw and Mee-Maw on their farm, it was the happiest time of her life."

CHAPTER THIRTY-TWO

I was waiting in the Cedar Grove courthouse when Sheriff Burr walked in with Deputy Ronnie Tyler. Burr pursed his lips when he saw me, then put on his politician smile.

"Good morning, Willie Mitchell. What can we do for you this morning?" the Sheriff said.

I held out the Lynda Gianelli Guthrie flyer.

"This is the woman who drove the shooter to the BP," I said. "There's a better photograph of her online."

Deputy Tyler took the flyer from me.

"The Sheriff put me in charge of the investigation when we first got contacted about this missing woman a year or so ago. These flyers used to be all over North Mississippi. I haven't seen one in a while. Where'd you get this one?"

"A store on I-55," I lied again. "I called the number on the flyer and drove to Grundy. Spoke to the mother and went over details of her daughter's disappearance."

"Let's step in my office," Sheriff Burr said, taking the flyer from Tyler and leading the way.

"What Mrs. Gianelli told me in Grundy confirms my belief that the woman driver and shooter were local," I said. "She said Lynda spent a good bit of time with her paternal grandparents, the Gianellis, who lived on a farm about ten miles south of Cedar Grove."

"I knew 'em, the Gianellis," Burr said. "Nice old couple. Voted for me in every election. But I didn't know anything about their granddaughter."

"No reason you would, Sheriff," I said.

"Did you look into this Gianelli connection, Ronnie?" Burr asked.

"We did, Sheriff, but old man Gianelli and his wife died at least ten years ago. Their farm's been owned by Billy Nugent ever since. He bought it from the Gianelli's estate, I believe."

"Which Nugent is that?" the Sheriff asked.

"That's old Booger Nugent's boy. He works offshore in the Gulf, two weeks on, two weeks off. When I caught up with him last winter I asked him about Lynda Gianelli Guthrie, showed him the flyer. He said he had never seen the woman, that she hadn't come around his place, leastwise not when he was there."

"Mrs. Gianelli described Lynda's Expedition as older, dark green," I said, "with a few places on the hood where the finish was coming off, exactly like the one I saw at the BP that day in June. And she said Lynda's skin got darker in the summer."

"Well," the Sheriff said, "this is good news."

"Sure is," Deputy Tyler said, "we never connected the woman on the flyer with your shooting."

"No reason you would," I said, making sure they knew I wasn't blaming them for not locating Lynda. "She disappeared in December, the week before Christmas, and the shooting was six months later."

"This gives us something we can work with," Sheriff Burr said. "Ronnie, I want you to get with Albert and Wilson, share this new information with them, and the three of you make another stab at locating this Lynda woman."

"We'll do it, Sheriff," Tyler said and turned to me. "But I don't want you to get your hopes up, Mr. Banks. This is a small county, and our deputies see just about the whole population over the course of a few months, what with regular patrols out in the county and in town."

"That don't matter. Let's get on this right away" the Sheriff said to Tyler. "I want you to get the word out to every shift." Burr turned to me. "If this woman's still in this county, we'll find her, Willie Mitchell."

"That's all I can ask," I said in my mendicant mode, sucking up in hopes of getting a real effort out of them. "That Expedition is fairly distinctive, too."

"If they didn't ditch it after the shooting," Tyler said, leading me out of the Sheriff's private office and into the hallway where I first saw Jake.

"I'll light a fire under every deputy, Mr. Banks," Tyler assured me quietly. "Give my best to Detective Burke."

I left the courthouse encouraged, but not banking on the Sheriff's office finding her. The woman had been gone from Grundy for almost a year, and I knew that she had been in Tallabusha County that day in June, but only on that day. Lynda and the shooter may have fled the state after the murder.

If Lynda Gianelli Guthrie and her shooter friend were not living in Tallabusha County, Jake may have sacrificed his physical well-being and wasted six months of his life.

I left the courthouse, frustrated that I couldn't call Jake. Riding through Cedar Grove's decimated downtown, I came up with Plan B.

I Googled the Cedar Grove Democrat Examiner, praying it was still in business. I drove to the address on my phone and parked in front of a low-slung, stand-alone building that looked more like a natural gas utility's office. The front façade was glass and there were people inside, so I was in luck.

"Good morning," I said to the tiny octogenarian behind the counter. "I hope you can help me."

"Help you with what?" the lady said in a surprisingly sharp tone.

"Do you have archives of your paper?" I asked.

"Sure do. Every week going back fifty-eight years," she said proudly.

"Are you the owner?" I asked.

"My late husband and I bought it in 1960 and ran it together until he passed away five years ago. Now it's just me and the two people working for me full time."

"Times are tough for the newspaper business," I said.

"We still make it, but just barely," warming to me a bit. "Getting harder and harder. Now, what years are you interested in?"

"Just this year. I'd like to look at June and July issues."

She beckoned me to follow with an arthritic right index finger, and led me to a dusty room in the back. She gestured for me to sit down while she reached into a stack of newspapers on a shelf, shuffled through it, pulled out four papers and put them on the table in front of me.

"This year's papers haven't been bound yet. Here's the June issues."

I thanked her and began looking at the classifieds, beginning with the first week in June. I found what I was looking for in week three, a small advertisement for a trailer out in the county for $150 per month. I checked the last of the four papers and saw the ad was no longer there, probably because Jake had rented it.

I thanked the lady, bought that week's edition on the way out of the office to help the cause of small town journalism, and called the number on the ad when I was back in my truck. The lady who answered sounded as old, but more genteel than the owner of the paper. When she told me the trailer had been rented already, I said I was sorry to bother her, that the newspaper I had been checking for rentals was published in June.

"But just in case it comes available again in the future, can you tell me the address so I can take a look at it?" I said. "I won't bother your tenant."

I entered the rural address of the trailer on my phone and drove for fifteen minutes. As I neared the location, I had second thoughts. Jake made me promise I wouldn't call him, and driving to his trailer was not exactly keeping in the spirit of his request. I picked up speed as I approached and drove quickly past, glancing at the trailer to make sure there was no vehicle there.

I turned around a half-mile away, and drove back to the trailer, this time slowly enough to do some recon. The small, rusty trailer was at least one hundred feet from the road, partially hidden from view by trees and dense undergrowth. I understood why the trailer was ideal for Jake. Unless a passerby was looking for it, the trailer was not noticeable from the road.

I didn't want to push my luck. I started for Oxford and after a few minutes, realized I was headed south instead of north or east. I turned around and consulted my phone, typed in my Oxford address, and started out again. There was an intersection I didn't recognize coming up, so I slowed down. As I got closer, I read the crudely lettered sign on the store building on a corner of the intersection: Kip's Korner.

I lingered for a few seconds at the intersection to watch the store. There were three trucks in the gravel parking lot.

When I realized the small black truck might be Jake's Nissan, I took off.

CHAPTER THIRTY-THREE

On my way back to Oxford, I got a call from James Braswell, part of Aunt Bee's palace guard. He was talking so quietly I couldn't make out what he was saying.

"Can you talk louder, James?" I said. "I can barely hear you."

"Let me call you back," he said.

Moments later, I picked up again. Braswell's voice was much stronger.

"I couldn't talk normally because I didn't want them to hear me."

"Who?" I asked.

"The NCAA investigator Jeffrey Blanchard is here waiting to see the Chancellor. Mr. Raymond from Natchez is with him. The Chancellor said she wouldn't meet until you could participate. Can you come now?"

"I'm on Highway 6 headed to Oxford. I'll be at the Lyceum in twenty minutes. Ask her not to see them until I'm there."

I picked up speed and wondered what Sam Raymond was doing. I called Mrs. Raymond to ask if she knew. She said I was lucky to catch her, that she was about to go on duty at the hospital. I told Laura that her ex was in the Chancellor's office.

"Oh, dear Lord," she said, "what is that fool up to now?"

I told her I was on my way and would try to minimize the damage, but I knew if he was with Blanchard, nothing good could come of it for Ole Miss or Laura Raymond. I walked into the Lyceum. James Braswell, relieved, led the three of us in to the Chancellor's office.

Sam Raymond and Blanchard sat across from Chancellor O'Donald. I pulled a chair to the side of her desk to provide a physical demarcation. I was on Aunt Bee's side, not theirs.

"Mr. Raymond, all of us at the University are truly sorry for your loss," she said. "What did you wish to discuss this morning?"

"I will cut to the chase, Chancellor. Mr. Raymond has advised us that his son received a substantial amount of cash from your University...."

"Which the Chancellor denies any knowledge of," I said, directing my comment to Sam Raymond, not to Blanchard. "Who gave your son the money, Mr. Raymond?"

"Mr. Raymond has provided that information to us," Jeffrey Blanchard said, "and the details will be provided to the University and you, Mr. Banks, in due course."

"Are you acting as Mr. Raymond's attorney?" I asked Blanchard.

"Of course not. I'm speaking for NCAA enforcement."

"Then let Mr. Raymond answer the question. I didn't ask you."

Blanchard placed his hand lightly on Raymond's forearm.

"He is our witness, Mr. Banks."

"Did you ask your witness what other schools gave him or El Ray money? He told me in Natchez that several other programs were waving around big sums to sign."

"We've looked into those other allegations," Blanchard said. "But we don't find them to be credible."

"How can you consider Mr. Raymond's claim against Ole Miss credible but not his claim against the other schools?"

"Because El Ray committed to Ole Miss," Blanchard said. "He turned down those other schools who allegedly tried to give him money."

"What is the purpose of this urgent meeting?" I said, irritated at the simplicity and logic in Blanchard's comment, just the type of easy linkage a lazy sports reporter would emphasize.

"Mr. Raymond has asked the NCAA to let you know that he intends to file suit against Ole Miss for allowing the death of his son to occur on your watch."

"He was up here on an unauthorized visit," I said. "No one from the University knew he was here."

"Mr. Raymond says that's not true. He says Coach Reggie Barnes knew. His son would still be alive if he hadn't committed to Ole Miss."

The Chancellor looked at me.

"I have met with Coach Barnes on multiple occasions and he adamantly denies that he knew El Ray was in or around Oxford that weekend," I said. "And you don't have a witness to rebut what Coach Barnes says."

"Yes, we do," Blanchard said. "We have Mr. Raymond. We believe him."

"What El Ray told his father is hearsay," I said.

"NCAA investigations are not bound by the hearsay rule or any other rules of evidence for court procedures. We are not a judicial body."

"Apparently you're not bound by any sense of due process, either," I said. "And since you're practicing law without a license on Mr. Raymond's behalf, you might mention to him that Mrs. Raymond, as legal custodian of El Ray since he was a toddler, is the proper party to bring a suit for damages on behalf of El Ray's estate, not Mr. Raymond."

"We are giving you notice as a courtesy, Mr. Banks," Blanchard said.

"There is nothing courteous about you or your organization, Mr. Blanchard," I said. "The Chancellor has nothing further to discuss with you. You and your client may now leave the Chancellor's office."

Blanchard stood and gestured to Sam Raymond. They left, but not before I caught the odor of stale whiskey and cigarettes emanating from El Ray's father, generating in me a momentary wave of sadness that such a fine young man as El Ray had to endure his sorry reprobate of a father.

"That was certainly confrontational, Mr. Banks," she said when we were alone. "I hope we haven't worsened our position with the NCAA."

"Not possible, Clare. Blanchard's got it in for Ole Miss and nothing we say or do is going to stop them from doing their worst."

"Dear me," she said.

"And remember, I'm representing you, Clare, not the University. I'm making sure none of this impacts you personally."

"Well, good, Willie Mitchell. Keep it up."

I shook Clare's hand and left. James Braswell gave me a wink and a thumbs up when I walked past him.

CHAPTER THIRTY-FOUR

I wasn't home from the Lyceum for very long when my cell buzzed.

"This Willie Mitchell Banks?" the caller asked.

"Yes."

"This is Darwin Brass. David Burke says you're tired of being a pussy."

"I may be, but Detective Burke didn't say that. He worships me."

"He also said you're an asshole."

"Did he tell you I made up my mind a long time ago that I would only be friends with other assholes, and that I've succeeded beyond my wildest expectations?"

"In that case, I think we'll get along just fine, Willie Mitchell. Why don't you come out to our place right now and let me show you around."

I needed something to take the edge off after my conversation with Sheriff Burr and Ronnie Tyler and my confrontation with the NCAA's conniving Jeffrey Blanchard and Sam Raymond in Aunt Bee's office.

"Tell me how to get there," I said.

"Put on your workout gear and bring your weapon," Brass said and gave me directions to his facility about five miles east of the city limits in the woods off of Highway 6 to Tupelo.

In twenty minutes I turned north off the highway onto a county road and drove another five miles or so to the entrance to Brass Tactical. I parked on the asphalt parking lot adjacent to a large metal building and walked inside. Behind the counter was a man with a neatly trimmed beard, about six-one, and built like an SEC linebacker. He wore a tight-fitting black shirt. Tattoos peeked from his shirt's neckline and long sleeves.

"You Darwin Brass?" I asked.

"Who wants to know?" he snarled, then grinned and extended his hand.

"Willie Mitchell Banks."

"I had heard of you before David called me. You used to be somebody."

I laughed out loud. "I still am, just not on the TV news anymore."

"Follow me," he said, coming around the counter and leading me outside to a four-wheeler. "I'll show you the outdoor shooting range, our running trail with workout stations every half-mile, then we'll hit the gym."

Ninety minutes later, I was whipped. Darwin put me through a much tougher workout than I was expecting, I guess to test my mettle. I ran three miles on the trail through the woods to warm up, which was much tougher than running on the even surfaces of sidewalks and streets in Oxford. I ran up hills and down, dodging tree roots surfacing from the shiny packed dirt, and ducking to avoid limbs. Darwin was waiting at the finish with his stopwatch.

"Not bad," he said, "but you can do a lot better."

"I used to be in shape," I said, breathing heavily.

We went indoors and Darwin gave me a sheet with blank spaces next to the list of exercises, which included pushups, situps, pullups, "burpees," and a dozen others. He filled in seven blanks with the number of each of the drills he expected me to do.

"What's a burpee?" I asked.

"Squat thrust to you old-timers."

He watched me complete six of the seven calisthenics, and chuckled as I struggled to do a third of the pullups he expected from me.

"Damn," I said. "I'm weak."

"Too much sitting on your ass behind a desk, Willie Mitchell. It's beginning to drizzle outside, so let's do your shooting inside."

As he walked me through the gym to the door to the indoor shooting range, I asked him why there was no one else working out.

"I've got a class that starts at three, then one at five. I do individual sessions in the mornings. I wanted you here in between so you wouldn't make a complete fool of yourself."

"And?"

"You're in way better condition than most guys starting out. You work with me every day for a couple of weeks, and you'll see a big difference."

Inside the range, he watched me load the Glock and do stationary shots at paper targets five, ten, and twenty yards away. I changed and reloaded magazines in between.

"You're comfortable with the gun," he said, "so that's good. We'll work on your accuracy and speed of firing. We'll go to the outside range to work on shooting from different positions, including running. There's a situation course in the woods where we'll put you through drills shooting or holding fire depending on what you think the situation calls for."

"Okay. I'd like you to teach me how to fight, too."

"You are definitely set on becoming a badass," he said with a grin.

Back at the condo, I cleaned up, feeling soreness creeping into every muscle I had neglected for the last six months, which was most of them. I called David Burke and Jimmy Gray and asked them to come by about five that afternoon so I could bring them up to date on what I had uncovered. Jimmy said he was already in town, working at the Sunshine Bank Jackson Street branch.

Jimmy Gray showed up at the condo a little early, Detective Burke a bit after five. I opened three Heinekens and began by filling them in on the morning conference in the Chancellor's office.

"NCAA ought to stand for National Corrupt Athletic Association," Jimmy Gray said, "because that's what they are—crooked as a barrel of snakes."

"I hope you get to meet Jeffrey Blanchard," David said to Jimmy. "He'll confirm your worst suspicions about the NCAA's enforcement arm."

"I bet they paid Sam Raymond's expenses to get him up here," Jimmy said. "I wouldn't be surprised if they set up a news conference for him."

"Blanchard is devious," I said, "but he's not stupid. He's not going to put his star witness before the public unless he controls the situation. Sam Raymond is a powder keg."

"It's been three weeks to the day that El Ray's body was found in the ravine," David said, "and I don't feel like I'm any closer to solving that murder."

"Just keep digging," I said. "Any results on your trail camera?"

"I went over there about noon today. The camera's only been up there two days, but I wanted to make sure it was working right. There wasn't much on it because Sammy's is closed on Monday nights and that place is so remote there's very little to record most of the day. Sammy didn't have much business last night. One thing I picked up that surprised me was seeing Ronnie Tyler pull into Sammy's about one-thirty yesterday afternoon. Sammy's doesn't open during the week until two o'clock. Tyler knocks, and seconds later the door opens. Ronnie goes in, carrying a bag of some kind, stays about fifteen minutes, then comes out with the bag, gets into his vehicle, and leaves."

"What car was he in?" I asked.

"His detective's car. It's an unmarked sedan, a Chrysler I think."

"Maybe he stopped in to get a pop," Jimmy said.

"I don't know for sure, but that's not likely," David said. "Sammy's is out of the way, and a pretty good drive from the Sheriff's office."

"Sammy's is probably a good place to get information on what's going on crime-wise in Tallabusha County," I said. "Sheriff Burr knew we had been to Sammy's Friday night before last, and Reese said Sammy spoke to someone in the Sheriff's office, she thinks, to get her off jury duty."

"Anyway, I put the trail camera back on the tree," Detective Burke said. "I'll check it again in a few days."

"I've had a development on Susan's case," I said.

I told them about my coming across the Lynda Gianelli flyer at a convenience store on I-55, continuing the lie to keep secret Jake's presence in Tallabusha. I showed them a copy of the flyer without my notes on the back, then led them into my office to let them view on my desktop monitor the photo of Lynda I found on the internet. I said I was certain the Lynda on the flyer was the driver of the Expedition. I let them know what Mrs. Gianelli told me about Lynda and her love for her grandparents' farm in rural Tallabusha County.

"Well, in my book that just about confirms that she and the shooter were local," Jimmy Gray said.

"Ronnie Tyler told me this morning he headed up the search for her last winter when they first got the notification from Tunica," I said. "The Sheriff told him to get back on it with this new information."

"Ronnie will be thorough," Burke said. "Do you want me to ask him what he was doing out at Sammy's yesterday?"

"No. Let's keep some separation between the investigations, just in case," I said. "Whatever the purpose of his stop at Sammy's, it had nothing to do with Susan's case, and it's highly unlikely that it was relevant to El Ray's murder."

Burke got a call and had to leave. Jimmy Gray helped himself to another Heineken.

"It's possible that Lynda Gianelli and the shooter are long gone from Tallabusha," I said.

"Maybe," Jimmy said. "Maybe not. What store was it you picked up that flyer?"

"That Marathon C-store right at I-55. It was thumb-tacked to a community bulletin board near the entrance."

Jimmy took a long pull on his beer.

"Right, Willie Mitchell," he said. "I've been in that store many times." He paused. "You remember it was me uncovered the information about the blonde in the black SUV picking up El Ray at Sammy's. I got it by sweet-talking the lovely barfly Eloise, kick-started your whole investigation."

"I know that. It was good detective work."

"Then maybe one day you'll tell me where you really got that flyer."

CHAPTER THIRTY-FIVE

I woke up the next morning stressed out by an awful dream. I was back in Sunshine. It was late in the afternoon and Susan and I were hightailing it in my truck to the Yaloquena County Courthouse. It was the last day of qualifying for my District Attorney reelection, and my candidate paperwork had to be filed with the Circuit Clerk of Court by five p.m.

"We'll never make it," Susan said calmly.

"Yes, we will," I said as I fishtailed around a corner in downtown Sunshine, stomping the accelerator as the courthouse came into view.

My truck screeched to a halt and straddled the sidewalk at the main entrance. I vaulted up the courthouse steps just as the custodian was locking the door. I yelled and pointed to my paperwork, begging him to let me in, but he acted as though he couldn't understand me.

Finally, the custodian relented and opened the door. I raced down the hallway to the Circuit Clerk's office and dashed inside just as the institutional-looking wall clock struck five.

I thrust the papers into the Clerk's hands. She glanced at the bottom of the first page and pointed to a blank signature line.

"You didn't get it notarized, Willie Mitchell."

"You're a notary. Just put your stamp on it."

"Office policy is we cannot notarize candidates' signatures," she said smiling, and pointed to the huge, round clock. "Besides, you're too late."

She threw my papers back at me and hustled me out the door, where my opponent, former indigent defender Eleanor Bernstein and her campaign manager, the Reverend Bobby Sanders, stood laughing and pointing at me.

Susan appeared at the end of the long hallway and walked slowly toward me. She was smiling, too, motioning for me to join her. As I drew closer to her, disconsolate over failing to file on time, I noticed her face began to blur, making her unrecognizable.

"It's for the best," the blurred figure said as I slumped against the wall and slid down to sit on the hard tile floor. "Eleanor was going to win anyway."

My disappointment morphed into rage. I hopped to my feet and began running toward Bobby Sanders, intent on beating him to a pulp.

That's when I woke up and realized it was a dream. Feeling a wave of relief, I checked the time and rolled out of bed.

"Anxiety dream," I muttered on the way to the bathroom.

At eight-thirty, I called Robbie Cedars's direct line at the crime lab.

"Any results yet?" I asked him.

"Haven't received the package yet," he said.

"It was supposed to be there yesterday before noon."

"It didn't make it. And I just checked our after-hours deliveries. It's not in there, either."

"I'll get back with you when I find out what's going on," I said, hung up and took off for the UPS office.

There were two people ahead of me in line. The only person behind the counter was the office manager with whom I had left the package almost forty-eight hours earlier. I waited for what seemed like forever.

"This package was not received yesterday or this morning," I said, handing her my receipt. "I sent it next day guaranteed."

"Sorry," she said as she entered the tracking number on her computer and read the response. "Looks like it never made it to Jackson, which would be the first stop on its way to Pearl. Let me check something else."

I was angry at myself for depending upon a commercial shipper. I should have driven the roach and the beer can to the crime lab myself.

"It looks like they have it in Kentucky at the dead-letter repository," she said. "The notes indicate the package did not have a label."

"I saw you put the label on," I said. "That's crazy."

"Sometimes the labels have a sticky edge that gets caught on another package and ripped off. At least we've located it."

"Can you get them to overnight it to Pearl today?"

"Be glad to do that for you. The address is in the system. But I have to call and talk to someone in Kentucky. They're changing shifts now, so it'll be an hour or so before I can reach a live person."

"This package is really important," I said. "It's critical evidence in a murder investigation."

She reacted as if I had said it was an invitation to a birthday party the following month. I took a deep breath, reminding myself that it wasn't her fault. She probably dealt with errant deliveries every day.

The manager gave me her card with her office and cell numbers.

"Call me late this afternoon," she said, "I'll have an update by then."

I drove back to the condo and dressed for my workout. I did three miles, clocking my best time since I began my new training. Back at the condo, in a space I had cleared in my office, I did the calisthenic and strength exercises Darwin Brass had given me, then drove to Brass Tactical for my shooting drills.

"When can we begin the fighting instructions?" I asked Darwin after we finished shooting.

"Tomorrow," he said. "We'll substitute close combat work for shooting. Your gun work is to the point where I think you can hold your own. We'll start working on situation shooting at our make-believe village day after tomorrow."

"Okay," I said.

"Before we start the fight training, I want you to think about something, and maybe go online and check out some sites I'll give you."

"All right."

"The first rule is to forget about the fighting you've seen on television and in movies, and forget about boxing or martial arts matches. That kind of fighting is only for professionals who train for it daily. I'm going to teach you the kind of fighting you'll need in whatever real world you're imagining you'll need it. It's 'kill or be killed' fighting, the kind that takes place in bars or street confrontations. You won't learn jabs or reverse karate kicks or anything fancy from me. I'm going to equip you for real fights, where you'll use your knees, elbows, teeth, and any kind of brick or rock or piece of wood or steel that's handy. It ain't pretty, and one other thing. I ain't gonna teach you to hit with your fists. For a non-professional, you hit someone in the head with your fist, you're just as likely to break your hand as hurt your opponent." He paused. "See you tomorrow."

On my way out, Darwin jotted down a couple of websites for me to look at before our next session.

I showered and dressed at home, then called the UPS store manager in the early afternoon. She said she had spoke to someone in Kentucky, who assigned it an incident number, and was waiting for the person to call her back. I urged her not to rely on a call back, but to call Kentucky again. She said she would.

Susan had always encouraged me to suppress my sense of urgency. She said other people I dealt with didn't have it. She pointed out that my expecting them to share my need for rapid feedback or results was a constant source of stress for me. I knew she was right, but re-wiring my expectations at my age was just about impossible. My desire for timely and thorough follow-through from others was the main reason I was terrible at delegating work, which could have been why I stayed a small-town district attorney for virtually my entire legal career. My sense of urgency was a cruel taskmaster. It was deeply encoded in my DNA. I came into the world with it, and without Susan around to counsel me, it would never go away, regardless of my "retirement."

On the other hand, my sense of urgency was one of the reasons I was a good lawyer and prosecutor. I never let anything slide, no matter how inconsequential. Most lawyers I encountered, even big city attorneys with reputations for excellence, didn't have it. Consequently, I was a good trial lawyer, picking up on nuances during a trial because of obsessive preparation that I insisted on doing myself.

I made a mental note to call the UPS store again at three p.m., then turned my attention to my most pressing need—contacting Jake without blowing his cover. I had an idea that involved Jimmy Gray and a burner phone, so I called him to find out if he had carried out his latest investigative assignment.

Chapter Thirty-Six

I stopped by Walmart on my way to meet Jimmy Gray and was surprised to see how many makes of "pre-paid," a.k.a. "burner" phones were available. I spent $95 cash for a Korean-made flip phone and three hundred minutes on the tracfone network, using the North Mississippi area code of 662.

It was my first step, albeit a baby step, in working off the grid.

I made my first official call on the burner to check on Jimmy Gray's status. He didn't answer, and I didn't leave him a message. Thirty minutes later, I stopped in the parking lot of a finance company disguised as a furniture and appliance store on Highway 6 near the turn off to Cedar Grove and waited. In ten minutes, Jimmy pulled in and stopped behind me in his old farm and hunting truck, a blue-and-gray Chevy Silverado, which I think was a 2004 model. I jumped in the passenger seat, placing my Glock in its case on the floor at my feet.

"Why didn't you answer my call?" I asked.

"You didn't call me."

I picked up his phone from the console and pointed to the odd 662 number on his list of recent calls.

"Here it is," I said, holding the phone for him to see. "It's my burner."

"Why do you need a burner phone?" he asked. "How was I to know it was you? And what's this secret mission we're on?"

"We're going to leave a message for Jake."

"As in your Jake?"

"Yes."

"Holy shit!" Jimmy said, slapping the dash. "We're big time, now! Tell me everything that's going on."

"First, tell me what you found out about Ronnie Tyler."

"I went to see my counterpart at First Bank of Tallabusha in their main office in Cedar Grove. I think it's the biggest building in that one-horse town."

"Is that the Friedman fellow?"

"Yep. Russell Friedman. His daddy founded the bank about the time your your dad and mine got the state charter for Sunshine

Bank. The Friedmans used to be Jewish, but old Mr. Isaac converted to the Methodist church when he started the bank. I think his 'come to Jesus' moment was more about gathering assets than saving his soul. But I give the Friedmans credit for sticking around when the boll weevil chased just about all the Jewish merchants and businessmen out of the Delta and North Mississippi.

"Turns out Russell's main loan officer, Shannon Allgood, has a daughter who was married to Ronnie Tyler for about three years. Russell told me all the scoop on the marriage but made me swear I didn't get it from him."

"My lips are sealed. What'd he say?"

"He said Mrs. Allgood's daughter was a sweet little thing, but made a major mistake marrying Tyler, who was a Cedar Grove city cop at the time. Russell said Tyler was a real jealous type, with a bad temper. The fourth time the girl showed up with bruises and scrapes, Mrs. Allgood moved her back home and hired the best divorce lawyer in Cedar Grove."

"Best divorce lawyer in Cedar Grove?"

"Yeah, I know. Damning with faint praise. They ain't but three or four lawyers total in Cedar Grove to this day."

"They got divorced, I take it?"

"Yep, and the girl moved to Tupelo, worked in a bank and found her a decent husband. Mrs. Allgood told Russell her daughter never comes home to Cedar Grove because she's still afraid of Deputy Tyler."

"Damn," I said. "That's a little different story about Tyler than I got from David Burke."

"Now this was probably ten years ago," Jimmy said. "Maybe Deputy Tyler's matured."

"How many wife beaters you know change their ways?"

"You got a point. Now, tell me about what's going on with Jake."

"All right, but you've got to swear you'll never mention this to a soul, including Martha."

"She don't really listen to much I say any more anyway," Jimmy said.

"Before I forget, when I saw Jake he asked me how you were, asked if you ever managed to put Beau's death behind you."

"When he was a kid," Jimmy said, waxing nostalgic, "Beau worshipped Jake. Scott was Beau's best friend, but Beau thought Jake hung the moon. Super athlete, really cool guy without trying to be, and always nice to Beau." Jimmy paused a moment. "It's going to be great seeing Jake again."

I told Jimmy about my watching "James Agee" being arraigned at the courthouse on drug charges ten days earlier; the meetings on Sardis dam and at the abandoned farm house off CR 402; the failed delivery of the roach and beer can to the crime lab; and making notes on the back of the flyer Jake pulled out of his truck.

"I knew you didn't get that Lynda Gianelli flyer from the Marathon station. I've seen that community board a half-dozen times this past year, and she never was on it. Besides, I could tell you were lying."

"How? What was the tell?"

"I've known you your whole damned life," Jimmy said. "I don't need a tell. I can sense it. And by the way, for a lawyer, you ain't a very good liar."

"I take that as a compliment."

"Now tell me exactly what we're going to do when we get to Jake's trailer."

After explaining how I found the trailer through the classifieds in the local paper, I outlined what I wanted to do.

"All right," Jimmy said. "I brought my Desert Eagle just in case."

"I'm pretty sure you won't need it."

"You ain't leaving your new Glock on the floorboard when I drop you off, are you?" Jimmy said. "You taking it with you through the woods, right?"

"Sure am."

"Then I'm getting the big boy out, too. What was it David Dunne used to say? Wasn't it 'you never know'?"

"That's right."

"Well, I'm getting my Desert Eagle ready because, you never know."

I pulled my Glock out of its case and with it, the Eleanor Bernstein push card from her campaign against me. The card was part of the sampling of paraphernalia from my last election for Yaloquena District Attorney that I kept in a cardboard file box in my closet. The card was vertically oriented, three-and-a-half inches wide and seven inches tall. At the top was a photograph of Eleanor, outfitted in her typical dark blue business suit. Below the photo, the caption read: Eleanor Bernstein for District Attorney—She's One Of Us. It was a thinly-veiled reminder to seventy-five percent of the electorate that she was African American, too, as if her photograph weren't enough of a reminder. It was a Reverend Bobby Sanders special. He viewed everything as racial, no matter the issue.

And the sad thing was, Eleanor would have beaten me handily if it weren't for a smear campaign against her in the last week— one that I had nothing to do with. Ironically, I never served a day as D.A. in the new term I won in that election.

As we neared the trailer, I wrote on Eleanor's card below her photo: "Sorry I missed you. Appreciate your consideration. If any questions, please call...," writing my burner number. It was what I wrote on every political push card I left in a voter's door when no one was home. It was a win-win for the homeowner and me. The voters really didn't want to talk to me, but were impressed that I came to their house to solicit their vote. For me, it saved a lot of time, allowing me to avoid time-wasting small talk and move on to the next household.

Jake was the only person in Tallabusha County who would understand the Eleanor Bernstein card and my written message. If the card were seen by anyone other than Jake, they would assume it was left by some politician of whom they had never heard for an election of which they were not aware. Jake would know that I left it and no one else.

Jimmy Gray drove his Silverado past Jake's trailer without slowing. I glanced through the brush at the front of the trailer.

"His truck's not there," I said, "just like I expected."

In a quarter of a mile, in the apex of a sharp curve, he checked his rear view mirror and the road ahead, and abruptly pulled over. I jumped out with my Glock and the campaign card. I scampered into the woods while Jimmy continued down the road.

It was near dusk as I quietly made my way through the woods to Jake's trailer. I stepped into the clearing and tapped on the trailer window closest to me. No response. I walked quickly to the door, stuck the campaign card between the doorknob and the jamb, the way I had done it thousands of times before in my election campaigns. I made sure the card was secure, turned and walked quickly into the woods, returning to the road at the same place Jimmy had dropped me off. I had waited for no more than sixty seconds when the Silverado came around the curve heading my way.

Jimmy slowed to a crawl. I opened the door and jumped into the passenger seat. As soon as I closed my door, Jimmy picked up speed and drove us away from the scene.

"Everything go all right?" he asked.

"Perfectly. Jake'll call when he can. It'll probably be late."

I placed the Glock back in its case, noticing a tremor in my hands. I took several deep breaths, hoping my adrenaline rush would subside.

"This is more exciting than banking," Jimmy said.

"Not as lucrative."

"Like George Peppard always said on 'The A Team' at the end when he puffed on that cigar?" Jimmy said. "I love it when a plan comes together."

"We'll see," I said as we headed back to Oxford.

Chapter Thirty-Seven

When Jake called me on my brand new burner at 1:30 a.m., I was in that gray area—not in deep sleep, but not fully awake, either. I had not been able to fall asleep. I knew Jake would call sometime during the night, and I was on edge waiting for it.

"Yo," I said into the flip phone.

"You'll never guess who campaigned out here yesterday and left a push card in my door," Jake said. "That was good thinking."

"I'm trying. Covert activity is new for me."

"Seems like you have the instincts for it. I see you've gotten a burner. Another smart move." He paused. "Did you get the results from the crime lab?"

"I screwed up, son," I said. "Instead of driving the beer can and roach down to Pearl like I knew I should have, I took the lazy man's approach and sent it by UPS for next day delivery."

"Don't tell me it's lost."

"No. Just delayed. Should get to the lab sometime today. It ended up in Kentucky."

"Figures. Is that why you left the card?"

"No. I've got other news. You know the two flyers you gave me to write on out at that farm on 402?"

"That was the only paper I had in my truck. Q-Man left them in there."

"When?"

"Earlier that day. I didn't pay much attention to them. What about the flyers?"

"It was so dark out at that farm I didn't know they were flyers until the next day when I noticed the woman's picture on the flip side of my notes. Lynda Gianelli Guthrie is not just some runaway."

"The woman on the flyer? Who is she?"

"She's the woman who drove the shooter to the BP."

Jake was silent for a few seconds.

"Are you sure?"

"The first time I looked at her picture on the flyer, I knew I had seen the woman somewhere. When I pulled up a better photograph online, I was almost positive she was the driver that day. Then I went to see her mother in Grundy and she told me Lynda left in her dark green Expedition with the finish worn off in some places on the hood. That confirmed it for me. It's her, Jake. Lynda Gianelli drove the shooter to the BP."

"No chance this is your imagination?"

"You tell me. Her mother told me Lynda always said the happiest times in her life were with her Paw-Paw and Mee-Maw Gianelli on their farm in Tallabusha County. Sheriff Burr said he knew the old couple when they lived out there about ten miles south of Cedar Grove."

"So she ran away from Grundy to the woods of Tallabusha. She didn't get very far, did she."

"We're dealing with a meth head here, Jake. That's why she ran off from her husband and two boys. She couldn't shake it."

"She came to the right place, Willie Mitchell. It's everywhere out in these woods. Redneck chefs cooking up meth by the boat loads. It's bad."

"Burr and Deputy Tyler said they were going to step up their search for her. Tyler's heading it up. You ever heard any of your new friends talk about him? Ronnie Tyler. Used to be a city cop."

"Never heard the name mentioned. Course these dumbasses out here have nicknames for every cop or deputy they're familiar with."

"You haven't run into this Gianelli woman?"

"Pretty sure I haven't, but I need to take a closer look at her picture. I'll see if her flyer is at Kip's Korner, which is like an information clearinghouse for the deadenders living out in these woods."

"Nice trailer," I said.

"How'd you find it?"

I told him about my trip to the local newspaper and my call to the elderly lady who rented to him. I also mentioned that I left the Eleanor Bernstein card on my second recon of his trailer.

"Now that I have your burner number, and you've got mine, let's don't make any more trips out here, okay? Too risky."

"No problem. But I had to tell you about Lynda Gianelli. If you find her, there'll be a trail leading to the shooter."

"I'm on it. This is huge."

"Turns out your gut instinct was right about them being local."

"I never had a doubt. I've been here long enough to have become part of this community of losers. I'll start snooping around about Mrs. Gianelli. I guarantee you Q-Man knows her if she's still here."

"I think she is, Jake. From what I've learned about her, she's got no place else to go."

"She's not one of the regulars working the sex for meth exchange. I think I would have come across her."

"She's getting the meth from someone," I said.

"Hey," Jake said, "what's Eleanor Bernstein doing these days?"

"She's an Assistant U.S. Attorney in the Oxford office. I've run into her a few times."

"And her Asian girl friend?"

"They share a condo somewhere in town. The girl friend still works in Jackson, I think. Not sure."

"Good for her. Everybody needs somebody to love."

"How about you?"

"Not since Kitty. Plenty of sex on demand out here and all over the world these days, but in my situation...."

"I know," I said. "Stay in touch."

I got back in bed, which was a mistake. I was wide awake and saddened at the thought of the loneliness inherent in Jake's life. As long as he was working "with the government" or in the woods of Tallabusha posing as James Agee, there was no opportunity for intimacy.

Intimacy could get Jake killed.

CHAPTER THIRTY-EIGHT

I don't know how or when, but eventually I fell asleep after Jake's call. I woke up at eight, and hustled to get ready for my first fighting tutorial at Brass Tactical. Before I got in bed the night before, I had gone online to the two websites Darwin had recommended. The first showed dozens of fights, some on the streets, some in bars. The video clips were obviously made by phone cameras and all participants were amateurs. Most fighters were drunk.

I realized quickly what Darwin had told me the day before is true—real fighting is nothing like what is shown in movies or television, and it's nothing like professional boxing or mixed martial arts matches. It's survival of the fittest and the most aggressive. Another thing I learned on the first site—sucker punches may not be gentlemanly or fair, but they sure work. Several of the clips showed two men face to face, jawing and threatening. All of a sudden, one of the two takes the initiative and coldcocks the other without warning. Some of the sucker punches knocked the opponent out—fight over. Other sucker punchers stunned the other fighter badly with the first blow. The sucker puncher then pummeled the other guy with additional hits and kicks when the other went down. Some of the sucker punches were delivered when one of the two turned to walk away from the confrontation.

The other website was professionally produced and showed two well-trained instructors demonstrating simple street fighting techniques on each other. They pulled their punches and kicks, but the message was still clear—use every bone and muscle at your disposal to overcome the threat. Forget about the Marquis of Queensbury rules.

I put on my running gear and took off, checking my watch to make sure I had enough time to make my ten o'clock with Darwin Brass. I went through my drills and calisthenics when I got back, quickly showered, and headed for my lesson at Brass Tactical.

I almost laughed when I walked into the small gym. Darwin was wearing thick pads everywhere on his body. He looked like the

Michelin Man on steroids. He gestured for me to join him on the thick rubber mat.

"Hit me," he said through the small opening in the pads around his face.

"How do you want me to hit you?"

Darwin smashed the side of my head with his heavily padded fist, knocking me sideways. I staggered but managed to stay on my feet.

"Any way you want to," he said.

I cupped my right hand and hit him on the ear.

"Good," he said, right before he hit me with his other padded fist. This time he knocked me to my knees. I was grateful for the soft rubber pad.

"Get up," he yelled. "Never go to the ground. If you're knocked down, get up as fast as you can. The ground is your enemy. Your opponent will kick the shit out of you, and it will hurt really bad."

I popped up, ready for the next strike. Darwin took two steps back, and removed his head pads first, then took off his arm, leg, and torso pads.

"I'll put the pads back on after we go other some things. You okay?"

I rubbed the side of my head and said yes.

"What we're talking about today," Darwin said, "is the most primitive part of our brain. Some call it the reptile brain, others say frog brain. It controls our involuntary muscles—our heart beating, our breathing, internal organ functions—things we don't have to think about. But more importantly for you and me today, the reptile brain controls our survival instincts, our flight-or-fight responses, our anger, our body's responses that are automatic. It also is the source of our instinct most responsible for keeping us alive—fear."

"Right," I said.

"And with the fear your reptile brain produces, comes the adrenaline dump that helps save you or, if not controlled, can cause your death."

I was fascinated with what Darwin Brass was telling me. I had never heard these words, nor ever given a thought to being in the situations he was describing.

"When your reptile brain kicks in, fine motor skills go out the window. You have to rely on gross motor skills, the big muscles. Adrenaline can cause slow reactions, tunnel vision, and confusion. One way to control it is to breathe. Take deep, slow breaths if you can.

"If you are in a fight situation, forget about boxing punches or karate chops or anything else. If you watched the videos on the first site I gave you, you can see that real fights don't involve technique. Unless you train for it every day, your primitive brain relies on gross motor skills like this."

Darwin drew closer to me and raised his open hand, pointing to the heel of his palm.

"This is your most effective weapon," he said. "Use it against your opponent's nose, chin, ears, or throat. You can deliver a crushing blow with it and you don't risk breaking your hand. You can also cup your open hand and slap the son-of-a-bitch or cuff his ears. You can bust an eardrum with a cupped open hand."

I pantomimed hitting Darwin in the chin with the heel of my palm.

"Rule number one: action always beats reaction. No matter how good your reflexes, you won't be able to block a punch. It looks easy on T.V., but it's hard to do. So, you strike first. Sucker punches get a bad rap, but in a street confrontation, they work. Like you saw on those videos, nine times out of ten the guy who throws the first punch and lands it will win."

I nodded.

"Number two: the head is the best target. From the ear through the jawline to the chin is your target area. A head blow shakes the brain and stuns your opponent.

"Next thing. Your knees, elbows, and feet, especially if you're wearing boots, are very effective weapons that don't require much skill. If you're in close quarters, knee or kick the other guy in the groin or the knee. Knock him on the ground, and while he's there, kick him in the head or the gut."

I winced at the thought.

"Oh, you don't think that's fighting fair. I can guarantee you the other guy will do it to you. That's another thing. If you go down, get up immediately. Again, the ground is not your friend. You are at your most vulnerable and he will be kicking you. His blood will be up, and he will try to kill you any way he can. You cannot be squeamish about doing the same to him. Either he dies or you die. Which would you prefer?"

I was far beyond second thoughts about my fight training. I wasn't sure I had the guts or the killer instinct for this kind of fighting. My last fight was in college, and there's wasn't much to it, mostly pushing, shoving, grunting, and headlocks until a frat brother broke it up. What Darwin Brass was saying was foreign to me. I wasn't sure I could do it, even to save my life.

"I see that look on your face, Willie Mitchell. You think you're too gentlemanly to get down and dirty like I'm talking about. That's fine if you just stay in polite society. But if you put yourself out among the great unwashed and come up against someone dead set on killing you, you either shoot him, cut him, or use these gross motor skill techniques we're going to practice. If you don't, you're going to be pushing up daisies."

"I understand," I said, but my heart wasn't in it.

"Before we start getting physical, two more things. If your head is jammed against any part of your opponent, bite the crap out of him. Biting hurts like hell and it shows him you'll do anything. And don't just bite, try to rip his skin and muscle off with your teeth. Go Mike Tyson on his ears.

"And this is the last thing I'll say. Carry a sharp knife. Not from the kitchen and not a Swiss Army knife. Buy you a combat knife and keep the edge sharp. A knife is more effective in close quarters than a gun. You'd be amazed at how easy it is to slash through meat, cartilage, and arteries. If you've ever been cut, you know how painful it is. Disabling, really. And if your opponent has a knife and you don't, haul ass. You can't block a slashing knife and come out with anything but huge slices in your arms and hands."

Darwin looked at me, deadly serious.

"I don't know what you have planned, or where you're going, but if you are putting yourself in danger, you're going to need all these skills. If you don't have some ability with these techniques, you'll get killed. Now, let's get some water and take a break, then I'll put the pads back on for some close contact fighting."

He disappeared out the door, leaving me alone on the soft rubber mat. I walked over to the heavy bag hanging from a ceiling beam. I pushed it, feeling its heft. When it swung back to me, I rammed the heel of my palm into it. The bag was more solid than I thought. I pushed it and hit it again, this time as hard as I could. It didn't hurt my hand, and I could see how it would disable someone if I hit him in the windpipe or nose.

I pushed it again, and hit the heavy bag with the heel of my left palm, which was much weaker than my right. I hit it with my left palm again and again, until I felt like I was using the most power as I could generate.

Darwin returned and strapped on his pads.

"You ready to fight, Alice?" he said.

CHAPTER THIRTY-NINE

It was Friday, the last day of November, four weeks from the Saturday night El Ray went missing. I was worn out from no sleep the night before, waiting for Jake's call. The tough late morning workout with Darwin Brass took the rest of my energy. I dropped off for a moment Friday afternoon at my desk in my office, took a fifteen-minute power nap on the couch, and called Detective Burke to ask him if he could stop by the condo later. He said he'd stop about four-thirty or five.

I had a couple of hours before my meeting with Burke. I called Robbie Cedars at the crime lab. He said the package from Kentucky had not arrived, but UPS delivered late on Friday, sometimes long after five. I hated to impose on Robbie, but did it anyway.

"If this weren't important," I said, "I would never ask you this. If it does come in tonight, do you think you could get it analyzed over the weekend?"

"Our weekend staffing is minimal, Willie Mitchell, and the contract workers who work weekends, I wouldn't trust them to handle this unless I supervised them very closely." He paused for several seconds, increasing my anxiety. "Only for you would I do this. I'll check the deliveries first thing tomorrow morning. If it's there, I'll pull a couple of techs and we'll get started on the processes. Maybe we can have something Monday."

"Thank you, Robbie. When this is over, I'm taking you to lunch and explaining what this is all about. All I can say right now is it's more important to me personally than anything I've ever asked you to do."

"Let's hope it comes in tonight."

I breathed a sigh of relief and called Aunt Bee. She was in a meeting but called me back within fifteen minutes. I asked her if the NCAA's Jeffrey Blanchard had been making any more waves in the athletic department.

"Not since our meeting Wednesday," she said. "I think you put the fear of God in him."

"Not hardly, Clare. He's the type of guy who's not easily intimi-dated. He likes to throw his weight around, make threats."

"In my entire tenure here in Oxford, this El Ray situation and the NCAA has caused me the most emotional turmoil."

"Just try not to think about it," I said, "because there's nothing you can do to remedy it. And remember, don't talk to him without me."

"No worries there, Willie Mitchell."

"Do you know if Sam Raymond is still around?"

"I have not heard anything else about him since our meeting."

"Would you do me a favor?" I asked.

"If I can."

"Would you ask the A.D. if Reggie Barnes has come back to work? He's been under the weather and I thought I might want to talk to him again. But, don't mention that I asked you to do this for me."

"I'll find out and let you know," she said. "Probably send you a text."

"Okay, thanks," I said and ended the call.

I made a quick run to Kroger with a list to stock up on the same things I've been buying since I took over grocery shopping duty after Susan's death—bananas, apples, oranges, salad stuff, Triscuits, Fritos, Blue Bell ice cream in the small cups, vanilla wafers, jelly beans, Raisin Bran, Quaker Oats Squares, raw peanuts to roast in the oven, two percent milk, sharp cheddar cheese, cottage cheese, one ribeye steak, ground chuck hamburger meat, Dave's *Killer* Bread, Hellman's, Heinz ketchup, a case of Heineken in bottles, eggs, bacon, and grits. I know it's *declassé* to eat the same things over and over, but that's the way I've done it since the BP. It's not intentional, but I don't give much thought to eating. Right after her murder, depression took away my appetite. I get hungry now, but I cannot bring myself to waste mental capital at the grocery store deciding what to buy. I grill a steak and hamburgers once a week or so, and eat salads, fruits, and cereal the rest of the time. It's not elegant, living and eating like I do now, but it's simple and good for weight control.

Detective Burke arrived close to five. I pulled the two Heineken bottles I had put in the freezer and gave him one.

"Cheers," he said. "Anything new?"

I told him about my fighting tutorial at Brass Tactical. After laughing at my characterization of Darwin's instructions and our sparring, Burke said Darwin was spot on about the nature of fighting in the real world.

"I've seen my share and been in a few," he said. "It's mostly grabbing and grunting and missed punches. The guy who gets put on the floor first loses nine out of ten times. Also, if you're not willing to fight 'dirty' you're going to lose. The best opening in a bar fight is to hit them when they're not expecting it. It's by far the best strategy."

I took a long pull on my beer and brought up the first of several things I wanted Burke to look into.

"Seeing Deputy Tyler on the trail camera going into Sammy's on a Tuesday afternoon before the place opened was very odd, the more I thought about it. He didn't spend much time in there, so it probably wasn't a social call. Why was he there? And what's the deal with the bag?"

"Sammy's Place probably doesn't smell all that great in the daytime," Burke said. "I've been wondering about Tyler's visit, too."

Without naming the banker Russell Friedman as the source, I told him what Jimmy Gray found out about Ronnie Tyler's first marriage—the beatings, the jealous rages. I could tell Burke was surprised.

"That's not the Ronnie Tyler I've dealt with," he said. "Of course, all my dealings with him have been professional, asking for help or information on one of our cases with a Tallabusha connection. He follows through on what he says he'll do, which is rare, in my experience dealing with law enforcement at this level. I don't know anything about his personal life."

"It's also rare that a wife beater gets rehabilitated," I said. "If the marriage breaks up because of abuse by the husband, when the husband gets into a new relationship, it's the same paradigm, another woman to abuse."

"Yeah. It's strange. I've seen women divorce alcoholics or abusive husbands then get right into a new relationship with another drinker or abuser. Damnedest thing."

"A lot of those women had drunk or abusive fathers," I said. "It's what they're accustomed to, as if that's the way it's supposed to be." I paused. "Do you think you could nose around about Ronnie Tyler, see what you can find out about his personal situation?"

"I can try. That's a pretty close-knit group over there in that Sheriff's office, though."

"Well, just do what you can do, and be really discreet. Tyler's supposed to be heading up the search for Lynda Gianelli, so I don't want to get crossways with him."

"You think she's still there in Tallabusha?"

"I hope so. I think finding her's my best shot at solving Susan's murder."

I retrieved two more Heinekens from the fridge.

"You checked the trail camera again?" I asked.

"I'm going out there early in the morning, right after daybreak," Burke said. "We'll see what kind of week Sammy's had."

"You know, Sammy's Place is where Reese Conklin says she picked up El Ray and dropped him off that Saturday night. Based on your prior relationship with her and everything we know about Reese, we've been assuming that's true. And Sammy's is where his Toyota was found the next morning. Plus, it's only about ten minutes from the ravine where El Ray's body was found the following week."

"You're saying we need to focus on Sammy's as the *locus in quo*."

I raised my beer to Detective Burke.

"Impressive, David. Maybe not the scene of the actual crime, but a scene highly relevant to the crime, and I don't know the Latin for that."

"I had a criminal procedure professor in law school who used *locus in quo* in almost every class discussion."

"Don't use the term when you're dealing with Sheriff Burr or his deputies. They'll think you're talking about ravenous insects."

"No kidding. How 'bout if I hang out at Sammy's Place and try to get Sammy talking. He likes to run his mouth to let you know he's a big shot."

"It's worth a try. I mean, Sammy's parking lot is where El Ray spent some of his last remaining minutes on this earth. Maybe we ought to pay more attention to what goes on out there."

"He only serves domestic products," Burke said and held up his bottle.

"But you'll be on the Tallabusha line, only ten miles from Reese's house. You could drop in on her. Maybe get lucky."

"Not interested in Reese in that way anymore," he said. "I'm like that dog having sex with a skunk. I've had about all that fun I want."

CHAPTER FORTY

I woke up early Saturday morning, dressed for cold weather, and ran three miles at my fastest pace since the BP. Back at the condo, I did my calisthenics, stretching, and strength exercises. By eight o'clock, I had showered and dressed. Drinking coffee and scanning the news online, I realized I felt better and stronger than I had in years. I was sore in places, but it was a good kind of sore, a by-product of getting back into shape and learning to fight with muscles I didn't know I had.

My cell phone buzzed. I recognized the voice.

"Am I waking you up, Willie Mitchell?" Sheriff Burr said.

"No, sir, Sheriff. I've been up a while. Already worked out."

"Good for you. I got news on the Gianelli woman."

"Good or bad?" I asked.

"I guess it depends. Bad for her, that's for sure. She's dead."

I didn't know what to ask first: when, where, or how. Sheriff Burr filled the dead air.

"We got a call about three this morning. Dispatched patrol units to the back of the Gianelli place which adjoins a gravel road. They found her Expedition burned up, still on fire. She was in it, all crispy."

"Do you have any idea what happened?"

"We ain't moved the body yet. Coroner wasn't at home. We're still tracking him down. I've got my crime scene people out there, including Deputy Tyler, who was heading up the search for her. He's telling me his first impression is she killed herself."

"I'd like to come see," I said, suppressing my urge to point out to Burr that self-immolation is only common among religious zealots and other fanatics, and meth addiction did not count as a radical cause.

"Come on. I'll meet you out there in about forty-five minutes."

He gave me directions. I called Jimmy Gray, who had spent Friday night in Oxford with Martha at their place. He was at the Oxford branch bank.

"I want to go," he said. "I'll be at your condo in five."

"All right, but hurry. We'll go in my truck. It's in a remote area off a gravel road on the back of the Gianelli farm. Bring boots."

"I'll be damned," he said. "On my way."

I was already in jeans and a long-sleeved knit shirt, so I took off my sneakers and put on my duck boots. I stuck a K-cup in the Keurig and opened the back door and garage door while it brewed. I poured it into a Styrofoam cup, brewed another one for Jimmy, put our coffees in my F-150's cup holders and backed out of the garage to wait for Jimmy. He pulled into the common drive and I gestured for him to park in my garage.

"What else do you know?" he asked as he blew on his coffee.

I told him everything the Sheriff said.

"Something's not right about this," he said as I headed west on Six.

"My thoughts exactly," I said. "Three days after I told them the woman on the flyer was the driver at the BP, she ends up dead."

"Giving those Tallabusha dumbasses the benefit of the doubt," Jimmy said, "maybe she got word they were looking for her hot and heavy and decided to end it all."

"That's possible," I said, "but she's known for a year there were flyers all over North Mississippi with her face and her mother's phone number to call. People have been looking for her since December. Why kill herself now just because she's been reminded of that fact?"

"And burning yourself up ain't exactly the easiest way to go. She's a dope fiend, so she should have been able overdose herself on Oxycodone or Fentanyl and take the painless way out of this vale of tears."

I called Detective Burke to let him know about Lynda Gianelli. It didn't have anything to do with his El Ray case, but I had been talking to him about it and wanted him to know. He thanked me and asked me to let him know what we found at the scene.

I followed the Sheriff's directions and drove deep into the Tallabusha woods, finally reaching the road leading to the back of the Gianelli place. I slowed when I came upon law enforcement and emergency vehicles lining both sides of the gravel road, including two small fire trucks with "South Tallabusha Volunteer Fire District No. 1" printed on their doors.

I passed the rear entrance to the farm and caught a glimpse of the smoking SUV. I parked and Jimmy and I walked back on the gravel road and through the cattle gap into the small pasture. Black Brahmas grazed in the distance, oblivious to the buzz of the humans gathered around the Expedition.

I introduced Jimmy Gray to Sheriff Burr.

"A damned mess is what this is," Burr said with disgust, then spit on the ground. "Drugs, that's what this is all about."

"What do you mean?" I said.

"She was a dopehead, strung out on whatever. Her mother said that's why she abandoned her family. Goddamned drugs. It's all out in these woods."

I nodded and walked closer to the vehicle. The windows had shattered from the heat, spewing glass everywhere, and the tires had exploded and burned off their rims. The grass around the Ford was scorched black and brown, and water from the fire trucks had created a sodden, muddy mess around the SUV, with dozens of deep footprints on both sides where scores of emergency workers, police personnel, and citizen gawkers had walked up to see the blackened corpse of Lynda Gianelli Guthrie.

"So much for preserving the crime scene," I whispered to Jimmy Gray. "I guess two more sets of boot prints won't make any difference."

We stood outside the driver's door and stared at the charred remains. The body's mouth gaped open. The skin had burned away, baring her teeth, leaving a cadaver appearing to be screaming silently in the throes of a painful death. A metal gas can whose red and yellow paint had burned away lay on its side on a metal frame and springs, what was left of the passenger seat.

I watched Deputy Ronnie Tyler through the scorched hole where the passenger window used to be. He left a group of about a dozen men in uniforms gathered under an old hackberry tree, and walked toward Jimmy and me. I tapped Jimmy on the arm and gestured for him to come with me to talk to Deputy Tyler.

"Bad as I've seen," Tyler said to us after I introduced Jimmy to him. "I know you noticed all the footprints in the mud around the SUV. Lot of that was done before I got here. The volunteer firemen don't know crime scene protocol, and the truck was still partly on fire when they got here, so they pumped a good bit of water on it."

"Who called this in?" I asked.

"Someone who said they drove by on the gravel road and saw a car on fire. Said where it was but wouldn't give their name. Phone number's no good to i.d. the witness, either. Everyone out in these woods uses pre-paid phones."

"Burners," I said and Tyler nodded. "Man or woman?"

"A man called it in," Tyler said, "according to the dispatcher. I haven't listened to the tape yet. I've been out here since we got word. When I turned on to the gravel road, I could see the glow of the fire at least a mile away."

"How do you know it's Lynda Gianelli?"

"We got the VIN off the frame and asked the state troopers to run it. Came back as originally purchased by a Delbert Guthrie of Grundy. I called Mrs. Gianelli in Grundy early this morning. Woke her up. I was as gentle as I could, but when I told her the SUV in question had been purchased by Delbert Guthrie, she started bawling. When she could talk, she told me Delbert Guthrie was her son-in-law Tim Guthrie's father, who had transferred the title to Tim after he and Lynda got married. VIN is more reliable than the license plate around these parts because these dopeheads switch license plates like they're trading baseball cards. I guess they think it fools us."

"So you know it's the vehicle Lynda Gianelli left home in," I said. "I don't guess there's any way to identify the body except through dental records."

"Pretty much. All her clothing and personal items burned up. Her extremities, too. Mrs. Gianelli gave me the name of their family dentist. I've sent a man to Grundy to get Lynda's dental X-rays so the coroner can compare them to the teeth on this body for a positive i.d."

"Lots of meth users lose their teeth," I said.

"Right. But if this is Lynda, she's got plenty enough teeth left to make a comparison. The coroner uses a local dentist to study the X-rays and compare them to the victim's teeth."

"What's your best guess?" I asked Deputy Tyler.

"From the size of what's left of the body, I'd say it's a woman. And since this is the Ford Expedition Lynda Gianelli ran away in, and this is the same type vehicle you saw her driving that day at the BP, I'd say it's her."

I nodded. Hard to disagree with Tyler's logic.

"The Sheriff said on the phone your office thinks it's a suicide. Pretty tough way to go."

"Probably is self-inflicted," Tyler said. "And it wouldn't be the first doper to burn themselves up out here. I think this woman didn't want her body to be identified and cause her family any more embarrassment."

"I don't know, Deputy Tyler," Jimmy said. "I ain't no policeman or deputy, but seems like a gun or an intentional overdose would be a lot less painful way to go."

"I'd agree with you, but we had a woman do the same kind of

thing two years ago. She survived somehow. Second thoughts, I guess. I talked to her afterwards and she said she didn't want anyone to know it was her. She left the gas can in her vehicle, too. Said she took a whole bottle of pills and wet the front seat with gas, waited for the dope to make her pass out while she held a lighted candle of some kind. But I guess she wasn't under all the way because the fire woke her ass up with the pain and she jumped out of her car while it was still burning."

I nodded as though I agreed, but what Tyler said was a crock.

"You need a complete toxicology work up to see if you're theory is correct," I said as the Sheriff walked up. "You might be right. You know, Deputy Tyler, once the body is removed by the coroner, y'all ought to ship the entire vehicle to the state crime lab."

"What the hell for?" Sheriff Burr said loudly as he joined us. "That'd be a waste of time and money. Crime lab will bill me for it."

"Deputy Tyler might be right about his suicide theory, based on the previous case he handled. But if this body is confirmed to be Lynda Gianelli, she might have been murdered. The crime lab could help you figure that out."

"Who gives a rats ass?" Burr said. "One more dopehead ends up dead, ain't a loss to anyone in my county. She wasn't even from here."

A man in a firefighter outfit called out to the Sheriff. He gave the burned-out Expedition a dismissive wave and walked over to the hackberry tree to see what his voter wanted. I looked over at Ronnie Tyler, who rolled his eyes as if he agreed with everything I said, and was apologizing for his ignorant boss.

I started walking away with Jimmy, back to the gravel road, just as the coroner's van pulled into the pasture. The coroner stepped out and shook hands with the men gathered under the hackberry.

"They're his voters, too," I said quietly to Jimmy. "Most elected coroners in North Mississippi aren't medical doctors. They contract with a forensic pathologist to do their autopsies." I paused. "Let's get out of here."

"First time I've ever been around a burned corpse," Jimmy said as we walked on the gravel road back to my truck. "Smells like brisket."

CHAPTER FORTY-ONE

The smell of burned metal, rubber, and flesh clung to me, reminding me of the screaming corpse. I stripped in my laundry room and threw my clothes into the washing machine. I stepped into the shower to wash off the stench. When I closed my eyes shampooing my hair, I saw Lynda Gianelli's macabre, grinning remains, a new image added to my pantheon of murder victims accumulated over twenty-four-year career as a prosecutor. During those years, I saw plenty of murder and suicides victims *in situ* and later in the morgue.

Lynda Gianelli's death was no suicide.

Deputy's Tyler's theory was a stretch, to say the least. From my dealings with the Sheriff's department in Tallabusha, Tyler seemed to be smarter than his fellow detectives and his boss, Sheriff Burr. Why would he jump to the suicide conclusion so readily? It made me question his motives, not his intellect. The more I learned about Deputy Tyler, the less I trusted him or his judgment, especially after I called Detective Burke to tell him about what Jimmy Gray and I saw at the Gianelli farm.

"I've never seen a suicide by fire," he said. "And I think that would be the least plausible explanation for her death. Let me tell you what I saw while you were at the farm."

Earlier that morning, David had driven the department's camo-painted jeep into the woods across the road from Sammy's Place to check the trail camera again.

"Guess who showed up at Sammy's at 1:34 yesterday afternoon?"

"Deputy Tyler," I said.

"You got it. This time, he had something in his hand, coming and going. I think it's the same kind of bag he carried on his other visit. Picture wasn't clear enough for me to be absolutely positive."

"He shows up at the same time of day on Tuesday and Friday," I said. "He's picking up or delivering something."

"Tyler's a bag man," Burke said. "Literally."

"Now you've got better intel to use to draw Sammy out. We need to find out more on Tyler, too. What's he picking up at Sammy's?"

"I'm planning on going to have a few at Sammy's tonight. Want to come?"

"No, thanks," I said. "You're more likely to get him to say something without me there."

"And he doesn't serve Heineken."

"That, too. Call me tomorrow with a report."

My fingers crossed, I called Robbie Cedars's direct line at the crime lab.

"Tell me some good news, Robbie," I said.

"I'd like to have lunch somewhere that serves a really good grilled steak," Robbie said, "one that's charred on the outside and very pink inside."

Exhibiting a rare modicum of maturity, I suppressed the gallows humor that popped into my head. *I did not say to Robbie*: "Charred on the outside and pink inside would be like the body I had just seen in the remote methamphetamine forests of Tallabusha."

"You're on," I said to Robbie. "UPS finally came through?"

"Your package was in last evening's delivery. I grabbed my best fingerprint guy before he left yesterday. He lifted several good prints off the beer can. We're processing for DNA right now, but that will take longer to know how successful we'll be. DNA data systems are works in progress, so your guy might not even be in the database."

"If you're trying to build the suspense, you're succeeding."

"I ran the fingerprints through the state AFIS," he said, referring to Mississippi's version of the Automated Federal Identification System. "Got an immediate hit. The owner of those prints is a fellow from your old neck of the woods, James Lee Payne. You ever heard of him?"

I was glad I was sitting down. Q-Man, Quintavius Jackson, was James Lee Payne. Payne grew up in Sunshine, reared by his grandmother, Lucretia Payne. I convicted him in 2009 of attempted murder and possession of crack cocaine with the intent to distribute in Sunshine. The last I had heard of James Lee, he was serving fifteen years in Parchman.

"I know who James Lee Payne is, Robbie. I sent him to Parchman."

"Well, he must be out because he was drinking beer out of this can you sent me."

"I can take it from here," I said. "I want you to know how much I appreciate your doing this for me, Robbie. I'll fill you in on all the details the next time I see you."

I took a deep breath. James Lee Payne was one of my failures. His grandmother Lucretia was best friends with Ina, my family's longtime housekeeper in Sunshine. Ina worked for my parents when they were older, then for Susan and me, helping to raise Jake and Scott. Ina was gruff and businesslike. She and her husband John worked hard their entire lives, but their children were nothing like them. I had helped several of them out of jams, mostly financial, but some had occasional brushes with law enforcement. Ruby, Ina's wayward drug-using daughter, was allegedly trying to stay straight, chauffeuring Ina as needed around Sunshine in Susan's Lexus, title of which Jimmy Gray had completed transferring to Ina only three weeks earlier.

Eleven years ago, Ina had escorted Lucretia Payne into my office in the Yaloquena courthouse to plead for mercy for her "child," James Lee Payne. I was familiar with the charges, because he had almost taken out one of Yaloquena Sheriff Lee Jones's deputies during a drug and gun bust. I knew James Lee well, having coached him in Little League baseball when he was part of Scott's nine-and ten-year-old team. James Lee was a good baseball player. He was smart, and even at his tender age, a master manipulator. He once tried to convince me that the reason he was thrown out at home was because my teenaged third base coach had signaled him on to score as he rounded third. James Lee was persuasive, even though my third base coach said he didn't, and even though I saw, with my own eyes, the coach giving James Lee the signal to stop at third.

James Lee was the victim of his absent parents' failure to care about the child they brought into the world. His mother was seventeen when James Lee was born. After a couple of months of parenting, rearing James Lee turned out to be just too much trouble. She turned over the responsibility to Lucretia, who was too old at the time to deal with a child. James Lee's father joined the army and left town. As far as I know, he had never laid eyes on his son. It was a pattern I saw all too often in my home town, where over eighty percent of children were born out of wedlock with few of the biological fathers even acknowledging, much less supporting or rearing, the children they sired.

James Lee quit playing summer baseball a year later, but I continued to see him on occasion. He always struck up a conversation. He also never failed to try work a con on me in our casual visits, which disappointed me. I know we had him in juvenile court several times. The first time, I asked the juvenile officer bring James Lee into my office for a sit down. James Lee was very sorry for what he had done and promised he would never do it again. His next trip to juvenile court was for burglary, which was a serious upgrade from his previous offense of stealing a bicycle. I talked to him again in my office. James Lee had matured considerably since our previous "come to Jesus" conference. He was older, bigger, and a much more polished grifter. If he ran afoul of the law as a minor again, I was not aware of it.

My next encounter with James Lee was serious. At age nineteen, James Lee was a major distributor of crack cocaine in Sunshine for a regional drug lord in Clarksdale. James Lee lived alone in a rent-subsidized unit in a small apartment complex on the outskirts of Sunshine financed by a division of the U.S. Agriculture Department known then as Farmer's Home Administration. I never found out how James Lee qualified for government housing as a single nineteen-year-old, but it was a government operation, so I figured James Lee conned his way around the regulators in charge.

In the wee hours one morning, James Lee got into an argument in his apartment with his boss from Clarksdale, who ended up in the Sunshine Hospital emergency room with a bullet hole in his shoulder. A neighbor in an adjoining apartment called 911. Two of Sheriff Lee Jones's deputies showed up at James Lee's apartment. He denied anything had happened, and refused to let the officers search his place. While one deputy went outside to call his supervisor, James Lee offered a large wad of $100 bills to the remaining deputy, which led to a physical altercation and James Lee getting the drop on the deputy. James Lee tied up the deputy, then engaged in a standoff with a squad of deputies, refusing to come out until the following morning, when his grandmother Lucretia Payne talked to him through the door and escorted him down the steps to be arrested.

The Clarksdale drug lord had no explanation for the bullet hole in his shoulder, and told the deputies he had never heard of James Lee Payne. Sheriff Lee Jones, citing the large cache of crack cocaine, money, and guns found in a search of the nineteen-year-old's apartment and his assault on his deputy, wanted the book thrown at James Lee. I assured Ina and Lucretia during their visit to my office that I would do what I could, but the combination of drugs and guns required a substantial time in prison. There was just no way around it. James Lee's public defender, Eleanor Bernstein, and I came to an agreement to recommend to Judge Zelda Williams that he plead to two felonies and receive fifteen years. The Department of Corrections insisted his time be served in Parchman, the most punitive environment in the Mississippi system.

I lost track of James Lee Payne after the sentencing.

After digesting the fingerprint news, I called my friend Sheriff Lee Jones in Sunshine to ask if he would use his contacts to find out what kind of prisoner James Lee had been. Late Saturday afternoon, Lee called me back. His sources told him James Lee was a model prisoner, getting his GED and taking some community college courses while at Parchman. He taught reading and math to hundreds of other prisoners in his final three years inside. Because of his good behavior, James Lee was released after seven years and his parole time was abbreviated. Sheriff Jones said he talked to James Lee's P.O. who said James Lee completed his supervision and moved away from Yaloquena County three to four years ago. They had no information on his current whereabouts. But I did.

James Lee Payne, a.k.a. Quintavius "Q-Man" Jackson, was now living large, deep in the sparsely populated woods of southern Tallabusha County, running a rural criminal empire with my oldest son Jake, a.k.a. James "A.G." Agee, as his newest, and apparently closest, advisor.

CHAPTER FORTY-TWO

Worst case scenarios romped unchecked through my brain as darkness fell that Saturday night. First and foremost, I was worried that Q-Man might know "A.G" was really Jake Banks because he played on younger brother Scott's baseball team when they were kids. Advancing this hypothesis in my mind, Q-Man was "keeping his enemy close" by conning Jake into thinking he had worked his way inside Q-Man's organization.

On reflection, I decided that Jake, especially with his current physical appearance, looked nothing like the tow-headed nine-or-ten-year-old Scott. It would be almost impossible, I concluded, for Q-Man to make the connection. On the other hand, Q-Man would recognize me immediately, because except for a smattering of gray hair and a few well-earned wrinkles, I looked the same. All the more reason for me to stay out of Tallabusha County.

I sent Jake a text from my burner after I got off the phone with Robbie: "Call me asap. Mr. Pinckney." Pinckney was Jake's little-known middle name, and if Jake's phone fell into the wrong hands, the text might be explained as a wrong number. Might be.

I answered my regular phone, hoping Jake called it by mistake.

"Hello," I said, trying to hide the urgency I felt.

"Is this District Attorney Willie Mitchell Banks?"

"Former D.A.," I said.

"This is Richard Conklin. We met in my office a week or so ago, maybe two. Do you have time to talk?"

"Yes, sir, Mr. Conklin. What can I do for you?"

"I'm sorry to handle this on the phone, because it's delicate, but I'm still swamped wrangling with contractors in Texas trying to get new stores opened. I'll be on this non-stop for a least a week."

"That's all right. What's up?"

"It's Reese. Something's going on with her. I was hoping you'd find time to talk to her." He paused. "In person, not on the phone."

"Okay. Tell me what you're concerned about."

"Well, I know people think I'm an oddball. And they're right. I've been this way all my life. All I really like doing is working. I'm worth a fortune by small town standards but I have no interest in spending money or traveling for pleasure or doing other things that normal people my age do."

"That's your prerogative. You shouldn't apologize for it."

"I'm not, I'm just trying to explain why I'm so awkward at everything in life except business. I think it's a kind of...."

"Obsession?"

"Oh, it's all of that. But what I was trying to say is I'm not autistic like the guy in *Rainman,* but I'm not normal, either. All I know how to do is work and make money, and that's all I want to do. I'm good at it, but I'm not able emotionally to enjoy the fruits of my work."

"If you're happy working all the time, that's what you should do."

"And I do. But about Reese, I know people think I'm a rich old man with a beautiful young wife half his age who cuckolds him all the time. They're right. But I'm okay with Reese's activities because I love her. I'm seventy years old, and Reese is the first woman I have ever had feelings for. I love waking up with her next to me. She makes me coffee and breakfast. She's with me whenever I want her to be, no questions, no excuses. Her activities away from me—I put them out of my mind, never give them a second thought. I know that sounds very strange, but I have come to accept the fact that I am not like other people, never have been."

"What has you concerned now about Reese? Why do you want me to visit with her?"

There was silence on his end for several seconds.

"She's had an injury. I noticed her grimacing when she bent to get the skillet out of the cabinet under the stove. I asked her what was wrong, and she said nothing, she was fine. When she sat at the breakfast table with me, I noticed a discoloration around her left eye. She had covered it with makeup, but I could still see it."

"You think someone has been physically abusive to her?"

"I do. She would never admit it to me, and I would never ask her. But I'm worried that her activities have brought her into contact with someone who has mistreated her. I don't want her hurt again."

"Text me her contact information and I'll call her to set up a meeting."

"Just you, Willie Mitchell. She wouldn't be comfortable talking about it with Detective Burke around for reasons I think you know."

"Very well. You're sure she doesn't have girlfriends, a support group, that she could confide in?"

"Reese is an unusual woman. She doesn't have women friends, none that are close, anyway. She has plenty of acquaintances. She's like me in that respect. I have no close friends, just acquaintances I deal with in business. She has no support from family or friends. She's really an island unto herself."

"Send me her number and I'll call her tomorrow."

"I don't expect you to do this for free, Willie Mitchell. I know you're a lawyer and your time and knowledge are worth plenty."

"No, Mr. Conklin. I have a client I'm working for. Talking to Reese again is well within the parameters of my investigation."

"Thank you very much, Willie Mitchell. Don't feel like you need to report back to me unless you feel she's in danger. I hope you can get her to open up about it. She's very honest, a straight shooter. She's never lied to me. Given her activities, that may ring hollow to you. But our relationship is 'don't ask, don't tell' about those things."

I hung up and thought about something my mother used to tell me from time to time. She had it needlepointed and hung on the wall in her bathroom.

"You never know," her saying went, "what's cooking in someone else's pot."

CHAPTER FORTY-THREE

Jake finally called a little before midnight, rousing me from a half-sleep. I had begun re-reading *Lost City of the Monkey God* in bed, trying to stay awake, but after twenty minutes, the book dropped onto my face. I fluffed my pillow and tried to continue reading, but dozed off and on until my cell phone buzzed.

"Mr. Pinckney?" Jake said. "Haven't thought about the awful middle name you and Mom hung on me for quite a while."

"Family name from your mother's side. Wasn't my idea, but Pinckney name has a lot of history, especially in the Carolinas. Anyway, let me tell you...."

"I can't talk right now."

"This is important. Really important."

"Things are just getting rolling over here. These people are nocturnal. They don't get cranked up until about now. They'll run out of gas when the sun comes up and go back in their holes. Some of the places they live in out here make my little trailer seem like the Ritz."

"Jeez. What a life."

"How about the abandoned farm at seven in the morning. I'll be getting off work about then."

I chuckled, but I guess Jake's looking at what he was doing as a mission, the kind of "work" he did for David Dunne's Domestic Operations Group, was a healthy way for him to view his self-imposed redneck doper assignment.

"I'll be there. Same routine?"

"Yep."

I turned off the light, but was too jazzed to get right back to sleep. I picked up *Lost City* and resumed reading about sand flies, *fer de lances,* lidar, and the ancient lost cities of the Mosquitians in eastern Honduras.

I woke up at five-thirty, showered and dressed, which took all of fifteen minutes. I cooked myself a breakfast of bacon, toast, and eggs and grits, not so much out of hunger, but more to pass the time. At six-fifteen, I raised the garage door and headed west to CR 402.

Jake's little Nissan zoomed around me and turned into the well-hidden drive. He opened the gate. It was the first time I had seen the place in daylight. In the early morning sun, I was taken with the beauty of the farm, with its rustic home built on its steepest ridge. Might be a nice place to own, I thought. Thirty minutes from Oxford but remote. I decided that when all this was over, I might to some title work, check out the ownership, and try to buy it.

I glanced over the pond as I drove on the levee, noticing the unusual number of migratory mallards and teals peacefully floating. By this time of year, the ducks had usually headed further south on their annual travels. Past the water, the road inclined to the house, where I stopped and enjoyed the three-hundred-sixty degree panorama of the old farmstead from atop the hill. Beautiful place.

"Pretty, huh?" Jake said, walking to the porch with a cup of steaming convenience store coffee.

"Nice and isolated," I said. "Hard to believe the people don't come out and enjoy it. You have any idea who owns it?"

"None at all. Tell me your news."

I studied Jake a moment. His hair was longer and dirtier than when I last saw him in daylight, which was at the Tallabusha courthouse. He was thin, his cheeks sunken further than when we met on Sardis dam.

"You getting enough to eat, Jake? You don't look healthy."

"I've got to look like a doper, Willie Mitchell. And I think I've got it about right. None of the deadenders out in those Tallabusha woods look healthy."

"Two things," I said. "I told you Friday night when you called, or I guess it was about one-thirty yesterday morning, about the woman on the flyer, Lynda Gianelli, being the driver of the Expedition at the BP."

"Right. Her flyer's still on the wall at Kip's Corner. I looked at the woman's picture yesterday. I've been out in those woods for going on six months now, and I have never seen her or her SUV."

"I saw her yesterday morning."

"You what?" Jake said. "Where?"

"I should say I saw what was left of her. Sheriff Burr called me."

I related everything I remembered about the scene on the back of Paw-Paw and Mee-Maw Gianelli's place; the charred corpse in the driver's seat of the burned out Expedition; the number of law enforcement and civilians at the scene tromping on potential evidence; the "good riddance" comments of Sheriff Burr; and Deputy Tyler's suicide theory involving opioid pills, the gas can, and some mystical source of ignition.

"That's no suicide," Jake said. "What's that deputy smoking?"

"Have you ever seen or heard of this deputy Ronnie Tyler?"

"No. But like I told you, they give everyone a moniker, initials or something in the drug community I'm part of now. I'm sure the locals have a name for Deputy Tyler. I just don't know what it is."

"Anyway, Tyler said he headed up the search for Lynda after she abandoned her home in Grundy back in December of last year. And when I gave the Sheriff and Tyler the information about Lynda and the Expedition I had gotten from her mother, Burr told Tyler to start up the search again."

"And a few days later she's dead."

"Yeah. Some coincidence, huh?"

"You think the Sheriff or Tyler were involved somehow?"

"I don't know. But here's the thing. If Lynda Gianelli was still in Tallabusha after the BP murders, the shooter probably was too."

"I've kept the description you gave of the shooter in the front of my brain, and I may have seen him and didn't know it. But, Willie Mitchell, there's dozens of light-skinned black dopers out in those woods who fit the same description—lean, ragged jeans, an unkempt short Afro."

"This one would have to be a cut above the rest. It took some nerve to do that shooting. He's no ordinary reprobate. If Q-Man rules the roost in his drug domain, I guarantee he knows the shooter."

"Q-Man knows everyone connected with his inland empire. He's very sharp at reading people."

"I've known Q-Man since he was nine-years-old," I said. "His name is James Lee Payne and he grew up in Sunshine, reared by Lucretia Payne, one of Ina's best friends."

When Jake calmed down from his initial shock, I told him about Robbie Cedars's fingerprint search after finally receiving delivery from UPS. I went through with Jake everything I knew about James Lee, including my dealings with him as a nine-year-old baseball player, juvenile offender, and as a *bona fide* nineteen-year-old criminal peddling crack and guns out of Farmer's Home housing in Sunshine. I filled Jake in on James Lee's exemplary conduct in prison, teaching other inmates, earning him early release.

"I can see him as a good teacher," Jake said. "He's smart."

"The thing I want to stress to you is how manipulative James Lee is. He was a con artist of sorts in Little League, a natural born manipulator even at that young age. And something else. He was on Scott's nine-and ten-year-old team, the one I coached."

"Small world, Willie Mitchell," he said. "We've both spent a good bit of time with this sociopath. What are the odds?"

"You think there's any way Q-Man has put it all together? I mean you and Scott. Is there any way he's shining you on and knows your identity?"

Jake thought a moment. The sun had risen above the horizon while we were on the porch, making Jake look even more drawn, haggard. I worried about his drug use and its toll on his perception of what was going on around him. I knew from my D.A. years how stressful undercover work was for law officers, how some of them never returned to the normalcy they enjoyed before their immersion into the drug underworld.

"I sent him to Parchman," I said. "He will recognize me on sight. Might have some payback in mind involving you."

"No way he associates me with you or Scott," Jake said. "I never reached out to Q-Man and went out of my way to lay low, to let the deadenders come to me. I told you about April, the girl I met at Kip's the first month I was here. She spread the word about me, even though I made sure she knew I was a serious loner and wanted to stay that way. She asked me several times what I was hiding from, but I brushed her off. About a month in, I saw April at Kip's again, and she said Q-Man wanted to meet me. I told her I didn't want to meet with anyone.

"It wasn't until his third outreach that I was introduced to Q-Man. And I played hard to get even after that. He sent me a complimentary box of assorted drugs, I guess like a Welcome Wagon gesture. That's when we began to hang out. There's no way he connects me with Scott."

I was satisfied Jake was right, and breathed a quiet sigh of relief.

"Will you know the shooter if you see him again?" Jake asked.

"Absolutely. Especially if I see him walking. People have a way of walking that's unique to them. He was a loper, his center mass moving slightly up and down with each step. I've pictured him a million times walking slowly, loping past me in those flip-flops wearing a red windbreaker on that warm summer day at the Varner exit to hide his semi-automatic pistol."

"You cannot be seen by Q-Man," Jake said. "You're the only eyewitness, but it's going to be very risky to set up an i.d. situation that's safe for you."

"You know more how to do this than I do, but can you nose around about Lynda Gianelli's death and find out who she hung out with? I mean without raising suspicion."

"I'll be careful, Willie Mitchell. It's a relatively small community of probably no more than fifteen hundred people, ranging in age from sixteen to forty-five, and Kip's Korner is like a clearinghouse for scoop on who's doing whom, what drugs are in plentiful or short supply, and drug bust rumors.

"After you saw me get bonded out of jail, when Q-Man brought me back to the woods, everyone I ran into out there knew I had been arrested and what I was charged with. There's a real 'us against them' camaraderie out there."

Jake pulled his phone from his pocket and checked the time.

"Time for me to be getting back. The Tallabusha vampires have turned in or passed out by now and won't be stirring until well after noon. I need to get some sleep and think about where we go from here."

"I'll do the same," I said. "Though I'll be in more comfortable surroundings."

"With this news, maybe I won't have to live in the woods much longer."

"I pray you're right," I said.

"That's something I haven't done since Mother died," Jake said. "Kitty and Susan taken from us by two-bit sociopathic gangsters. Even if there is a God, I'm not sure praying does any good."

"There is a God," I said. "He just doesn't pay much attention to what goes on down here."

CHAPTER FORTY-FOUR

Back on CR 402, I drove south toward Highway 6. After closing the farm gate, Jake zoomed around me on the winding county road, hurrying back to Tallabusha. I was much closer to Cedar Grove than Oxford, so I pulled over when I got to the highway and called Reese Conklin on the cell number her husband had shared with me.

"This is Willie Mitchell Banks, Mrs. Conklin," I said when she answered. "I hope I didn't wake you."

"Oh, no. I fixed Richard's breakfast and he left for work an hour ago."

"I'm not far from Cedar Grove right now, and I'm wondering if it would be convenient for me to drop in and talk with you for a minute."

She was silent.

"I'm sorry to bother you on a Sunday morning, but your husband called me about suppertime yesterday and asked me to contact you. He sent me your number. He's worried about you."

"He is?" she said, her voice catching. "Did he say why?"

"Yes. And he asked me to talk to you in person, not on the phone."

More silence.

"All right," she finally said. "You know where I live. When can you be here?"

"Twenty minutes."

"I look a mess, Mr. Banks, so you'll have to forgive me. I'll fix you a cup of coffee when you get here." She paused. "Are you alone?"

"Call me Willie Mitchell, please. And yes, I'm by myself."

"All right, Willie Mitchell," she said, resignation in her voice.

Twenty minutes later, I pulled into the circular drive and parked at the front door of the Conklin mansion. Reese opened it before I could knock.

"Thank you for seeing me, Reese," I said.

She nodded, embarrassed. Reese was not nearly as open and gregarious as on our last visit. The confidence and verve I saw in

Reese during our first interview was gone. She was more reserved, more like an admonished child than the strong, independent woman she evinced before.

"Do you mind if we sit in the kitchen?" she asked.

"Not at all. Lead the way."

She did, walking in a demure manner this time, not sashaying like she did on our first meeting. I sat at the kitchen table, which had been wiped clean of any breakfast she had served an hour or so ago to Richard. There were no dishes in the sink or on the counter. The kitchen was neat as a pin. She placed a K-cup in the Keurig, continuing to stare at the cup while it filled. When she turned to place the mug in front of me on the table, I looked closely at her left eye, which did show signs of dark bruising covered by makeup. She handed me a cloth napkin, which I intentionally let drop to the floor. I watched her as she picked it up. She kept her back awkwardly straight, being more careful than necessary.

"Is your rib broken or just bruised," I asked when she handed me another napkin and sat down. "Have you been to a doctor?"

"No," she said, and turned her face away.

"Richard told me he believes someone has hurt you. Is it true?"

"I cannot believe this," she said through watery eyes.

"Don't be upset with Richard. He's very concerned that you've been hurt by someone, and he says he doesn't have the emotional equipment to talk to you about it. It's part of his personality he describes as an odd inability to connect with others, which has led him to devote his life to his business. He says he loves you, that you're the first woman he has ever felt that way about."

The dam broke, and Reese began to cry. Large tears streaked her cheeks. She wiped her eyes and buried her pretty face in her hands.

"I feel so trashy," she said between sobs. "Because that's what I am—white trash from Greenville." More crying and sobbing. "I grew up poor, jealous of the girls who lived in the big houses on Washington Street who wouldn't give me the time of day." She inhaled deeply and wiped her eyes. "It's no excuse for the way I act. And I do love Richard, and he loves me. I know it's hard to understand."

I said nothing. Reese was doing fine on her own. I sipped my coffee and waited for her.

"I *have* been to a doctor. He took x-rays. My ribs are bruised, not broken. He said they will be painful for a couple of weeks and will heal on their own. I didn't tell him about my eye and he didn't ask. It looks bad but doesn't hurt anymore."

"Who hit you?" I asked.

"It doesn't matter. I'm not filing any complaint or pressing charges."

"You shouldn't let him get away with it. He'll hurt someone else."

"Oh, he has, believe me. I knew about his problem before we went out."

"But you still saw him. How long have you been getting together?"

"Probably three or four months, off and on."

"You call him to set up your dates?"

"I did at first. Then he began to call me. Wanted to see me when it suited him, which was way more than I was interested in. But he was persistent."

"When did he hurt you?"

"Last Sunday afternoon at my condo. Richard was working, as usual."

"Where did y'all get together over the four-month relationship?"

"Mostly at my place in Oxford. Sometimes he parks on Highway Six and I pick him up at the truck stop where you turn off to go the back way to Taylor. It's usually dark by the time I drop him back off."

"Are you going to see him again?"

"No," she said. "Never. He got really possessive, started checking up on me. Calling me all the time. Acting really jealous, like I was his property."

"Has he stopped calling since this happened?"

"Yes. After he hit me, I told him I was going to report him to his boss, who Richard knows. Richard could get him fired with one call, and he knew it."

"So, you're not afraid of this happening again?"

"Not from him."

"Has it ever happened before, I mean with another guy?"

"There have been times I was kind of scared by someone I was with."

"Maybe this is a wake-up call."

"I've been home every night since it happened."

"Does he know where you live?"

"Yes."

"Are you afraid he might show up here while you're alone?"

"I told him if he did I would shoot him. And he knows I can handle a gun. We've gone shooting out in the woods once. I hit more paper targets with my little Walther automatic than he did with his pistol. But he's more afraid of losing his job than anything."

"I think you should file a police report. Just in case."

"I can't do that, Willie Mitchell. People already make fun of Richard because of the way I behave. This would make them ridicule him more."

"I'm not going to mention it to anyone, Reese. But you should tell Richard when he gets home tonight, or when you fix him breakfast in the morning. He's going to be sympathetic, I know from our conversation. Maybe this will draw him out emotionally. It's worth a shot. If you don't, I'll have to. He wanted me to report back to him."

She thought a moment. "All right," she said. "I'll tell him."

"I'll be calling him Tuesday to make sure you do. If you don't, I'm going to tell him everything we've talked about today."

"I promise I will."

I stood to leave. She walked me to the front door and hugged me.

"Thank you, Willie Mitchell."

I opened the door but before I got to my truck, she called out.

"Have y'all figured out what happened to El Ray?"

"Not yet," I said, "but we're getting close."

"I hope you do, because he didn't deserve what happened."

I drove away, saddened by Reese Conklin. She was beautiful and smart with unlimited access to money. Her low self-esteem had been imprinted in her as a young girl. Trying to boost it by seeing one man after another was not going to raise it. It would do the opposite. I hoped the beating from Mr. X would cause her to change. Not sure it would.

Pulling onto Highway 6, I had a good idea how to find out the identity of Mr. X if he had ever been arrested for abuse before, though his identity would probably be "apropos of nothin'," to use Sheryl Crowe's words.

CHAPTER FORTY-FIVE

I returned to the condo from the Conklin home about ten Sunday morning. I put on my workout gear and ran three fast miles, then two more at an easier pace. I did my strength and mobility exercises, grabbed my Glock, and drove to Brass Tactical. Darwin Brass had texted me saying he would be at his place around noon Sunday.

The entrance door was unlocked. Two younger men were exercising separately in the gym. I worked out hard on the heavy bag, practicing my palm heel punches. I was gaining more confidence in my left, which had a long way to go, but was improving. I practiced frontal kicks to the bag, heeding Darwin's warning that a spin kick was less effective than a frontal kick because it was hard to pull off successfully in close combat without years of practice.

Darwin donned his pads and we sparred for twenty minutes, which took more out of me than all the running and exercises I had already done. Close contact fighting and grappling takes a lot of energy. I understood now why Darwin had said that most bar and street fights last less than five minutes, and long, drawn-out bouts only existed in the movies.

I thanked Darwin, dried off and rested a while before tackling the outdoor shooting range. My arms were tired, so I figured the shooting would be a good test of my ability to handle the Glock with muscle fatigue. I went through a hundred rounds from different positions and stances, and was not as accurate as normal, which I should have expected.

I left Brass Tactical and thought about stopping at Walmart to replenish my ammo supply, but decided to wait until later after I cleaned up and napped. Back home, I showered and made a sandwich with bacon left over from breakfast, but the nap I planned was derailed by an article in the statewide Jackson paper.

Jeffrey Blanchard and his NCAA thugs had issued a press release to announce that investigators from the enforcement division were still in Oxford and elsewhere in Mississippi looking into claims that El Ray or someone on his behalf had received money and other impermissible benefits from Ole Miss. Blanchard was quoted saying "...we've received information from reliable sources about unauthorized benefits and have interviewed other Ole Miss recruits concerning their knowledge of the enticements allegedly offered and received. The enforcement staff has recommended offering immunity to recruits who ultimately signed with other schools in exchange for their testimony."

There it was. The offer of immunity to recruits who chose to attend rival schools would be providing hearsay and innuendo, no real evidence. Their new coaches were no doubt suggesting that their new recruits tell everything and more about what they "heard" about Ole Miss's practices. What better way to undermine an archrival than to allow eighteen-year-olds from competing schools to pile on with "what they heard" had taken place. I thought of Jeffrey Blanchard confidently boasting in the meeting with Sam Raymond and Aunt Bee that his division was not bound by evidentiary rules of criminal or civil law.

The press release ended with a paragraph about El Ray's homicide that occurred "near Ole Miss" while on an "allegedly unauthorized" visit to Oxford and its environs. The implication was clear—but for Ole Miss's illegal inducements, El Ray would not have been in or around Oxford in November and would still be alive.

While my blood was up, I called David Burke to bring him up to speed on my discussions with Reese and Richard Conklin in the previous twenty-four hours. David did not seem surprised at the abuse, given her *modus operandi*. She had unfortunately hooked up with the wrong kind of guy.

"She said most of her trysts took place at her condo at the golf course."

"Her love nest," David said.

"This is my question. You were with her at her condo a couple of times. Do you think you could get in there to print some surfaces?"

"You're talking about a warrantless entrance?"

"You said she left before you and asked you to lock the door. I imagine some of her guys are not as careful as you and forget to lock up."

"I guess that's possible. I'd have to check the door to make sure."

David was getting the message, warming to the idea.

"And I'd want to check every surface I might have touched when I was there," David added, "because it's likely some other fellow recently in the condo for the same reason might have left prints in the same places."

"Time is of the essence," I said. "Whoever cleans the place for her may destroy any prints, so we need to get in before they do. It may already be too late, but we can try."

"Even if we get lucky and lift some fingerprints, unless her guest has a record the prints won't do any good."

"I know it's a long shot, but if the guy got rough with Reese, he's probably done it before. Maybe he's been arrested on an assault charge. And I can get the prints analyzed off the books."

"Is this the way you operated when you were District Attorney?" Burke asked. "If it was, I can see how you got so many convictions."

"Not hardly," I said, "but there's not much harm in this. Richard Conklin asked me to look into what happened to his wife. So, we've got tacit approval from the co-owner of the condo, which is probably marital property."

"The condo's in her name."

"Purchased with money he earned," I said. "Think about it. What's the worst can happen? We probably won't find any usable prints. Even if we do, they might not be in the system. It's a long shot, but if Reese were a former 'friend' of mine, I'd want to find out who hit her."

"Let me call our best print man. If he's available, we ought to get in there tonight before any cleaning service."

"Now, you're talking," I said. "If Reese is wrong about the guy no longer being a threat, we might be saving her from another beating, or worse."

"I'll call you tomorrow," Detective Burke said.

I was not only recommending, but actually planning a warrantless search. It was another step down the rabbit hole. Operating outside the law was becoming more palatable.

I was bone-tired, but I dragged myself to my F-150 and drove to Walmart to buy some bullets. I hoped shopping there late on a Sunday afternoon might be less stressful than wading through the hordes of overweight shoppers I had encountered at Walmart in the past. It was an experience that always depressed me, leaving me walking to my car, channeling Haley Joel Osment in *The Sixth Sense*, muttering "I see fat people."

I arrived at the gun sales department, where there was only one other Walmart shopper. It was none other than Sammy Kerry. We spotted each other at the same time.

"How are you, Sammy?" I said, extending my hand.

"Well, look what the cat done drug up," he said with a grin, while giving me a bone-crunching grip, which I had grown to expect from Tallabushans.

"Why aren't you working today?" I asked. "I'd figure Sunday afternoons to be prime time at Sammy's Place."

"Eloise opens up for me on Sundays at two and works until six or seven, or whenever her drinking starts interfering with her making change for the customers. She don't steal, which is more than I can say for most people I've let behind the counter."

"She's the lady sitting at the end of the bar when Detective Burke and I were in there a few weeks ago."

"That's right. Jawing with your big banker buddy Jimmy Gray."

I nodded. Sammy didn't miss much.

"You do much shooting?"

"Naw," he said. "Just enough to stay handy with my pistol. You?"

"I shoot some at the local range. I've sent so many people to the pen I figure I need to keep my skill at a decent level, just in case."

Sammy released a loud, honking laugh. "That's a good one, Mr. D.A."

The Walmart clerk finally showed up behind the counter. Sammy paid cash for three boxes of Remington .40 caliber bullets and a box of shotgun shells and stepped away from the counter, lingering while I placed my order.

"Any progress on the El Ray case?" he asked quietly.

"Not much. Fighting the NCAA where I can. Still pretty much a mystery what happened to El Ray."

"I figure it was something personal," he said. "That kind of injury came from someone he knew. You got to be real close to stab somebody under their arm like that."

"Agreed," I said as I gave the clerk my credit card. "You got any ideas?"

"Me?" he said. "I'm just an old bartender at a run-down road house. What would I know?"

"A lot more than most, I'd guess," I said, working him. "You seem like a pretty smart, well-connected guy who knows a lot more about everything than you let on. I know how to read people, Sammy. You got a quick mind, and a quick wit."

"Why, thank you, Mr. D.A.," he said, pleased to hear confirmation of something he already knew. "That's high praise coming from you."

"Let me ask you something, Sammy," I said. "You know your clientele out at your place. Is it possible some of your customers who might not be as open-minded as you might have taken offense to El Ray being out there that night?"

"I ain't saying they like someone like him being there, but these days and times, hassling a nigger's about the last thing anyone of my customers would do. They know the press and the law will eat 'em alive if they get wind of it, and most of my customers don't want no trouble. People like us, Mr. D.A., we've been beaten down by the media and national politicians. We all 'deplorables' out there at my place and we mainly just want to be left alone."

"Say hello to Sheriff Burr for me next time you see him," I said.

"Aw, you'll see him before I do. He's probably busy with that woman who burned herself up yesterday morning. You know she'd been missing for almost a year, they say, before she wound up dead."

"I know. Flyers out and everything."

There was a look Sammy gave me. He knew I was probing. There was no way I would be able to get him to slip up and say something helpful. I certainly wasn't going to ask him why Deputy Ronnie Tyler showed up at his place at the same time, one-thirty in the afternoon, on two days the week before. He and Tyler and maybe Burr had something going on out there, but I wouldn't learn about it from Sammy Kerry.

Back home, I channel surfed while I ate a salad. I then made a peanut butter and jelly sandwich on lightly toasted bread, one of the most underrated gastronomic delights of the Twentieth Century.

I trudged upstairs after a while and fell asleep, hoping to dream about the amazing Mosquitian empire that existed a thousand years ago in Honduras, rather than the murders of Susan Woodford Banks and Elston Raymond. Not likely, though.

CHAPTER FORTY-SIX

I pulled up the Jackson paper online as I sipped my coffee the next morning at seven. On the front page above the fold was a grainy reproduction of the Lynda Gianelli flyer, and a long article about her gruesome death in rural Tallabusha. A photo of the burned-out Expedition taken after the body was removed appeared on page two along with the remainder of the article.

Sheriff Burr was quoted extensively, bemoaning the tragic impact of the trafficking of illegal drugs on the people of Tallabusha County. He failed to mention that almost all of the crystal methamphetamine being consumed was home grown in labs out in his own county, labs whose production could be diminished with a modest effort on the Sheriff's part.

The Sheriff went into detail about the previous attempted self-immolation by another woman interrupted by her failure to self-administer enough opiates to keep her unconscious during the ordeal. In his wisdom, Burr opined that these unfortunate young ladies chose to be consumed by fire to cover up their identity and avoid further embarrassment to their families.

There were no quotes in the article from Deputy Ronnie Tyler, and no mention of his restarting the search for Lynda Gianelli just days earlier. The article cited the Cedar Grove paper as a source, so I assumed the Cedar Grove paper had run the sensational piece on Saturday, which was probably forwarded to the Jackson paper by an area stringer.

I hoped the publicity from the Cedar Grove paper would percolate through the woods of south Tallabusha County. Jake had mentioned he had seen a copy of the paper in Kip's Korner. If word spread about her grisly death, it would be easier for Jake to ask questions about Lynda Gianelli without raising suspicions. I put the thought out of my mind, reminding myself that Jake knew a lot more about what he was doing than I ever would. He would know how to handle it.

I picked up my buzzing cell phone. It was Detective Burke.

"News?" I asked.

"I'm on my way to you. Want to open the garage door?"

Five minutes later I let him in the back door. He walked straight to the kitchen and laid on the counter five celluloid sheets of fingerprints his technician had removed from the bedroom and living room of Reese's condo at the Oxford Country Club.

"We struck gold," Detective Burke said. "My guy dusted and came up with these five sets of what he thinks are adult male fingerprints. He took photographs of them in place with his hi-res camera then lifted and preserved them on these adhesive sheets. I asked him how old they appeared and he said there was no way to tell when they were made."

"Reese needs a new cleaning service," I said. "You should have called me as soon as you found them."

"It was in the wee hours, and I thought it better to wait until this morning. I know how you older guys need your sleep."

Burke grinned and gave me a fist bump.

"Did y'all clean the place up?" I asked.

"Spic and span. Didn't get out of there until about two-thirty. And I made sure I locked the door, unlike the previous guy," Burke said with a wink.

"Any of these prints yours?" I asked.

"I doubt it. It's been a while since I was there. What's next?"

"I'm driving these to Robbie Cedars at the crime lab to run them."

"I can do that," Burke said.

"No. Robbie's sticking his neck out for me. I'm going to put these in his hands personally and wait for the results. I don't want a repeat of UPS."

I told David briefly about my running into Sammy Kerry at Walmart and voiced my suspicion that he was involved in something more than running a honky-tonk. Burke left after I assured him I would let him know something about the prints as soon as Robbie ran them. I collected the print sheets in an accordion folder, grabbed my coat and headed south toward Jackson. The drive seemed to take forever.

Finally, I arrived at the crime lab and told the receptionist who I was and that Robbie Cedars was expecting me. I had called Robbie on the way down to tell him what I needed. He said, "Come on," after I told him I was only an hour out from Pearl. Robbie came out to the waiting area to escort me back to his work area. I gave him the folder. He glanced quickly at the five sheets.

"Fairly good quality," he said pointing to a small sitting room and kitchen in the corner of the lab. "Let me get to work on these."

I knew the odds were long. It was unlikely that the prints would be identified in the AFIS state database, but I had a hunch, deep in my gut, that something would come of the search. Maybe I was just being hopeful.

At about one in the afternoon, Robbie joined me in the small kitchen.

"Before I forget," I said, "have you gotten the results back on the DNA analysis of the marijuana roach that I submitted with the beer can?"

"Not yet," he said, "but I got a hit on one of the five sets of the prints you brought me this morning."

"One out of the five has a criminal record?"

"No. None of the five matched known prints in the AFIS criminal database. I struck out there."

"How'd you identify the one set?"

"I wasn't sure exactly why you were trying to identify whoever made these five sets of prints, so I ran them through a non-criminal database the state compiles of non-criminals who get fingerprinted for jobs, licenses, and the like. There are a lot of those folks out there, more than you suspect. All of law enforcement, for example, and that's many thousands of people in Mississippi right there."

He placed one celluloid sheet on the small table in front of me.

"These prints were left by a law officer. One Ronald J. Tyler, a deputy sheriff in Tallabusha County. Is this relevant to what you're working on?"

"Yes," I managed to blurt, overcoming the distracting effect of the chill bumps popping up on my arms and the nape of my neck. "Very helpful, Robbie. You're up to two steak dinners now. I really appreciate your doing this for me."

"What do you want me to do with these?" he asked, holding the sheets.

"Could you put all five back in the accordion folder and let me take them back with me? And would you print out the results of the i.d. search on the one set that hit and tape the printout to the celluloid sheet?" I paused. "And I'll get out of your hair. I'd like to promise you I won't be asking for any more personal favors like this, but you never know."

"Long as it's for the cause of justice and getting to the truth," Robbie said, "you can count on my help, Willie Mitchell."

Driving north on I-55 back to Oxford, I thought of the implications of Deputy Ronnie Tyler being one of Reese's "friends."

Jimmy Gray had found out from his Cedar Grove banker friend that Ronnie physically abused his wife, causing their divorce. The banker said Ronnie's extreme jealousy led to the beatings.

Reese had admitted to me in her kitchen the day before that her Mr. X, who gave her the bruised ribs and black eye, had been in her condo for sex on many occasions, including Sunday the week before. Reese's description of her Mr. X as possessive, controlling, and jealous fit Ronnie Tyler's personal history to a tee. Reese also said she picked him up on Highway 6 at a furniture store between Cedar Grove and Oxford. Reese had been seeing the abusive Mr. X for three or four months. That made September the likely month of the beginning of her relationship with Mr. X.

Reese had also admitted she hooked up with El Ray the first time after a home game in September. If Deputy Tyler learned about her seeing El Ray during the same time period she was seeing him, given his history, I was sure that wouldn't sit too well with Tyler. I thought through the possibility for ten more minutes and called Detective Burke.

"I'm on my way back from the crime lab," I said.

"Robbie find anything?"

"Deputy Sheriff Ronnie Tyler's fingerprints."

After a long pause, Burke said, "You are shitting me."

"Nope. Tyler is in a non-criminal database of people who have to be fingerprinted for work in Mississippi."

"Well, I'll be damned. And Tyler's a jealous lover, we know from Jimmy Gray's banker friend. And the kind of guy he is, the fact that El Ray was an African-American kid just made it worse."

"That's right," I said. "Reese was doing both Ronnie Tyler and El Ray during football season."

"Tyler's the mystery guy who gave her the beating last week."

"That's what I figure. She threatened Tyler with getting Richard Conklin to lean on Sheriff Burr, get him to fire the bastard."

"Sorry I was wrong about Tyler being a good guy."

"You think he's strong enough to carry El Ray to the ravine?"

"I don't know," Burke said. "What's our next move?"

"Looks like Ronnie Tyler might be in the middle of the El Ray murder. Whoever picked up El Ray at Sammy's probably killed him. And we know from your trail camera that Deputy Tyler has some kind of business with Sammy Kerry at about one-thirty in the afternoon a couple of days a week."

"Wednesday and Friday."

"Why don't we plan on being in the woods close to your camera on Wednesday and drop in on Deputy Tyler and Sammy when Tyler shows up?"

"It's a plan, all right. But I'm not sure it's a good one. Tyler'll be armed, probably Sammy, too."

"I didn't suggest we get into a shootout with them," I said. "I think we just ask them what they're doing. Besides, you carry a gun. I'll bring mine."

"We should have backup. I can talk to the chief."

"Let's just keep this between you and me for now," I said. "I might be blowing the significance of this new evidence out of proportion."

"I don't think so, Willie Mitchell. I think we're well on the way to solving the murder of Elston Raymond."

"Hope you're right," I said. "Two more things, David. Can you check in on Reggie Barnes, see how he's doing? Maybe try to bring him around to talking about El Ray and Reese. Just see where it goes."

"Okay. You said two."

"I'll be back in Oxford around four, I hope. See if you can contact Reese and set up a time this evening when we can talk to her. I want her to know we've identified her Mr. X."

"Will do. Call me when you get close."

I tossed my personal phone on the seat and grabbed my prepaid from the console. I sent a text to Jake's burner.

"Call me, please. Mr. Pinckney."

Chapter Forty-Seven

I pulled into the OPD parking lot and walked into the station with my accordion folder. The receptionist waved me through to the hallway leading to David's office. He locked the folder in a small safe on the floor behind his desk, a safe he assured me only he could access.

"We don't want to lose these prints," I said. "Did you see Reggie?"

"At his house," Burke said. "I'll fill you in on the way."

I was happy to sink into the soft leather passenger seat of Detective Burke's Tahoe. After five hours on the road to the crime lab and back, I was glad to be riding instead of driving.

"Reggie's still in bad shape emotionally," Burke said. "Lana says she's never seen him like this."

"Has he been back to the Manning Center since I talked to him at his house?"

"No. Lana says he stays in bed most of the day. I asked her if she had talked to Coach Goodson and she changed the subject. I imagine the Head Coach is putting pressure on him to get back to work. This is prime time for recruiting and Reggie's not in the game."

"What did he tell you is his problem?"

"Something vague about not feeling right. I think he's really depressed. I can't blame him. He's gone from being on the top of the college football world with El Ray's commitment back to being on the bottom. El Ray was the lynchpin to Ole Miss having their best recruiting class in history. Now they're scrambling to salvage the other players who committed because of El Ray."

"I know it's tough," I said, "but Reggie ought to be at work. Goodson is not the type to put up with it much longer."

"That's what Lana thinks, too."

Twenty minutes later we parked on the circular drive in front of the Conklin mansion. The weak December sun had sunk below the western horizon, and we were losing the light. As usual, she opened the door before we knocked.

"Come in," Reese said. "Let's sit in the kitchen."

She seemed more like her old, confident self than the Reese I had spoken to at her husband's request just thirty-six hours earlier, but she didn't offer us coffee or water. It was a pretty good indicator that she wanted the interview to be as brief as possible. Reese wore tight-fitting skinny jeans and a long-sleeved knit turtleneck sweater. No cleavage this time.

"You feeling better?" I asked as we sat around the kitchen table.

"My ribs are not as painful," she said with a big smile.

"Had Deputy Ronnie Tyler ever hit you before?" I said.

"Uh...," Reese stammered.

"We know he's the jealous, abusive type you were seeing this past fall at the same time you were seeing El Ray."

She took a deep breath and exhaled slowly. Reese's will to deny what I said seemed to dissipate with her expiration.

"No," she said. "He never hit me before."

"Did he tell you to stop seeing El Ray?" Detective Burke asked.

"He didn't like it," she said, "and raised his voice a couple of times. I told him it was none of his business. He wouldn't tell me how he found out."

"He's a pretty good detective," Burke said. "I've worked with him."

"What caused him to hit you last Sunday?" I asked.

"I told him I didn't want to see him anymore."

"Have you talked to him since he hit you?" David asked.

"Once, but it really wasn't a discussion. I told him if he ever contacted me again I would get Richard to make Sheriff Burr fire him. I also said if he showed up unannounced at my house or my condo I would shoot him."

"Did you tell your husband about Tyler like I asked?" I said.

"This morning at breakfast. He knew some man I was seeing had hit me, but he didn't have the details. Richard still doesn't know it was Ronnie. He told me he didn't want to know, he just didn't want me being hurt."

Tears filled Reese's eyes. She grabbed a napkin and dabbed her eyes.

"He was so sweet about it," she said. "He said he loved me and only wanted me to be happy." She paused. "He deserves better than me."

"I think he appreciates you more than you know, even with your shortcomings," I said. "He told me you're the first woman he's ever had feelings for in seventy years. He knows you're not perfect, but neither is he."

Having Reese's secrets out in the open around the breakfast table seemed to have reduced her anxiety. I decided to probe deeper.

"Does Ronnie Tyler know Sammy Kerry?" I asked.

"I'm sure he does," she said. "How well I don't know."

"Has Tyler ever mentioned to you that Sammy might be selling more at his honky-tonk than Bud Light?" I asked, climbing out on a limb I wasn't sure would help or hurt my investigation. I figured it was time to shake things up.

"What do you mean?" she asked.

"Methamphetamines," Burke said, following my lead.

"I don't know anything about that stuff," she said. "I hear there's all kind of drug heads cooking it out in the county in the woods, but that's all I know. Ronnie never said anything about it."

"And you don't know how El Ray got meth in his system?" I said.

"I've never used the stuff, and El Ray never used it around me," she said, "and that's all I know to tell you about that. We never even discussed it."

I looked over at Burke to see if he had anything else. He shook his head slightly, so I stood up to leave.

"Let's keep this discussion to ourselves," I said to Reese.

"Don't worry," she said. "I don't want anyone else to know."

She walked us out and opened the front door. There wasn't anything else to say except good-bye, which Detective Burke and I did, thanking her for her cooperation.

Back in the Tahoe on the way to Oxford, it was full dark.

"Shortcomings," David said. "I thought that was a gentlemanly way of putting it."

"No sense in being ugly about her personal life."

"Did you give some thought to asking her about Tyler's visits to Sammy's Place, exactly what he was delivering or picking up in that bag?"

"No. I doubt she knows about whatever business Tyler and Sammy have going on out there. I didn't want to take the chance that she might actually still be talking to Tyler. If she mentioned it to him, it might get him to thinking about how we knew about his trips to Sammy's."

"I think that's the right play," Burke said. "I don't want Ronnie Tyler putting a bullet through my trail camera. You still intend to wait for Tyler out there at Sammy's day after tomorrow?"

"Sure do," I said. "Time to get Deputy Ronnie Tyler's activities with Sammy out in the open. What do you think?"

"I think he's going to be surprised when we walk out of those woods."

CHAPTER FORTY-EIGHT

Back at home in Oxford, I was beat. I showered and read the Wall Street Journal online, channel surfed for twenty minutes without success, and tried not to worry about Jake. When I could stand it no longer, I sent him another text: "Call immediately for important words from your provider."

Time crept along. I lay on the couch reading about the lost civilization of the Mosquitians again, but could not concentrate. I grabbed a legal pad and started toying with different scenarios connecting Deputy Tyler with El Ray's murder. He had motive and opportunity, the classic elements of any murder investigation. I jotted down questions like, "Does Burr know about Tyler's activities with Reese? With Sammy Kerry?" My hopes of stimulating my brain evanesced when I realized I was tapping my pen on the written question, but thinking about Jake.

I turned in with little hope of sleeping, but dozed off, waking every hour or so to check my phone for a response. No call from Jake. I made it through the night somehow and took off for a fast three miles through campus, then slowed the pace for the last mile back to the condo. I went through my exercise regimen and at eight I called Darwin Brass to see if he could spar with me a bit before his morning sessions began. He said okay, and I asked him to look for me at the indoor shooting range when he arrived at Brass Tactical.

I shot for twenty minutes from different positions and distances, and was putting my Glock back in its case when Darwin stuck his head in and whistled, gesturing for me to join him in the gym.

"I want you to hit me," I said, "like you mean it. And then let me hit you. No pads today. Let's simulate a real fight."

"Somebody piss you off already this morning?" he asked smiling.

"I want to see what it feels like to take a punch, and find out if I can muster the balls to hit someone in the face with the heel of my palm."

We faced off. I knew I was outclassed. Darwin could easily kill me if he wanted. I was pretty sure he could modulate the force he used to sting me rather than break my jaw. We circled each other, then he lunged to my left and hit me with the cupped palm of his trailing hand on the side of my jaw. I was late seeing it coming, and was jarred by the punch, which I knew he pulled.

I shook it off and circled Darwin, faked a left slap and struck him hard with the heel of my right hand under his chin.

"Shit," he said, rubbing his jaw.

"I don't want to make you mad," I said.

"No problem, Willie Mitchell. It was a pretty stout blow. What do we do now? I'd kind of like to return the favor."

I gestured for him to come on. He spun around and kicked me in the left hip, knocking me to the ground. Darwin pinned me face down and after a moment, let me up. Adrenaline was pumping through me, and I felt little pain. He let me hit him again, this time with the heel of my left hand, a punch in which I had growing confidence. Darwin backed off and held up both hands, palms out.

"We probably ought to stop this, because it's liable to get serious if you hit me like that again."

"Okay," I said. "I guess I can fight if I have to."

"Just who are you planning to take on in your first professional fight?"

"No one. Checking out my nerves and my backbone."

"Remember," he said before he walked away. "You hit him first."

Back home, I showered and dressed. I broke down the Glock and cleaned it while watching the markets roller coaster on CNBC, refilling the magazines with .45 caliber bullets. I spent the rest of the afternoon pacing in between calls to Detective Burke about our plan to surprise Ronnie Tyler at Sammy's the next day. No word from Jake. At nine o'clock, I sent another text asking Jake to "call his provider."

After a long night of tossing, turning, and checking my phone, I dragged myself out of bed and did my conditioning. By mid-morning I was wound tight, waiting for Burke to pick me up. I gobbled down a chicken sandwich, and mercifully received a text from Detective Burke that he was at my garage door. I grabbed my gun case and the small plastic cooler I had filled with ice, water bottles, and two additional chicken sandwiches, just in case.

I walked out the back door with my gear and touched the panel on the wall to open the garage door. When the door was fully open, I saw Burke in the driver's seat of the OPD camo Jeep, and Jimmy Gray riding shotgun.

"I don't think this is a good idea," I said to Jimmy when I climbed in the back seat. "We don't know what these people are up to."

"Jimmy flagged me down this morning when I drove through the Square past his bank. I told him what we were doing and insisted on joining us."

"Come on, Willie Mitchell," Jimmy said, patting the stainless steel case on his lap. "You two can't have all the fun."

Burke drove us on county roads I had never ridden on before, and after forty minutes, he pulled off the road and onto an old, overgrown logging road.

"We're about a half-mile south of Sammy's," he said. "This is the way I've come in to set up and check the trail camera. No one's spotted me yet."

It was a bumpy ride. I noticed broken branches hanging limply from pines growing close to the trail.

"From earlier trips," Burke said quietly. "Hold on."

The Jeep lurched left and splashed muddy water against the bushes and trees lining the trail.

"Hog hole, I think," Burke said. "How we doing?"

"Don't worry about the mule," Jimmy said to him, "just load the wagon."

Detective Burke pointed to a big oak about two hundred feet ahead.

"That's us," he said.

When we arrived at the base of the tree, David turned the Jeep around and backed up so that it was partially hidden by the massive trunk. We exited the Jeep.

"Sammy's is that way," Burke said pointing. "When we get to the top of that ridge, we can see Sammy's parking lot and front door."

He gestured for us to follow him. We walked through the pines and oaks, dodging a couple of places thick with briars. In moments, we crouched as we neared the top of the ridge and could see Sammy's Place. There were no vehicles in the parking lot and no signs of life in the building.

"He opens at two," Burke said, "but Sammy usually gets here about one-fifteen and parks around back. We've got about an hour to wait. I suggest we hunker down here with our gear, making sure we're not visible from across the road. If Tyler shows up, we can be over there in two minutes. Make sure your phones are off and anything else that might make a noise."

The woods were quiet, only the sounds of birds singing and the occasional rush of a car passing by on the road between us and Sammy's. Right on time, we saw a red Chevrolet pick up drive through the parking lot and disappear around the back of the building."

"That's Sammy's truck," Burke whispered. "Let's get ready."

He pulled his automatic pistol from the holster on his hip while Jimmy and I silently opened our gun cases. I stuck my Glock in the back of my waist under the black bubble jacket I had on and checked the two extra magazines in my pockets. Jimmy did the same with his gigantic Desert Eagle, though with his waist size, I didn't know how he did it. Burke whispered for us to stay put while he edged further up the ridge. Ten minutes later, he whispered.

"It's Tyler," he said. "On my signal."

A few seconds later, Burke waved us on. I chambered a round and so did Jimmy. We topped the ridge and walked steadily through the woods until we crossed the road and leaned against Tyler's car.

"Let's wait here for Tyler to come out," Burke said.

Five minutes later, Deputy Ronnie Tyler came out the front door with a bag in his hand. He didn't notice us until he was down the steps and on the gravel.

"Gentlemen," Tyler said, trying to smile. "How'd you get here?"

"We were out walking for exercise," I said. "Fancy meeting you."

"I've got to be at the courthouse at two," he said.

"This place is not on your way," Burke said. "What's in the bag?"

"Nothing, really," Tyler said.

"Could I see?" Burke said.

"I don't think so," Sammy Kerry said from the rickety front porch, staring down at the three of us. "The deputy's got to be on his way."

His words carried some authority, as did the black twelve gauge shotgun with a pistol grip Sammy held at his side, the business end pointed down, but definitely in our direction.

"No cause to be alarmed, Sammy," I said.

"Aw, I ain't upset, Mr. D.A.," Sammy said. "This old Mossberg in my hand keeps me calm. You boys are carrying. I saw you adjusting your pea shooters in your britches when you crossed the road. And Detective Burke's got his in that handy little holster on his waist. Now, my way of thinking, when three armed full-grown men approach my business establishment and accost a sworn deputy of the law in my parking lot, I've got every right to defend myself, the deputy, and my property from whatever harm you're planning on rainin' down on us."

"We certainly don't want any trouble," Burke said. "We just want to see what Ronnie has in that bag."

"You care to show 'em?" Sammy said to Tyler.

"I'm late as it is," Tyler said, walking around me to get in his car.

"Well, there's your answer. Let the deputy get on about his business now, fellows. You three stay where you are and we'll chat a while."

Tyler threw gravel as he spun out and took off.

"You boys want a beer?" Sammy said, pointing the Mossberg near my feet. "I'm opening up in a bit. First one's on the house."

"Not me," Jimmy said. "I'm trying to cut back."

"Good for you," Sammy said with a threatening grin.

We stood there for five minutes. It seemed like an hour. Sammy backed through his front door, still cradling the shotgun. He closed the door behind him. We heard the door's deadbolt slam into place.

"I thought that went well," I said as we headed back to the Jeep through the woods."

"If I was you," Jimmy told Burke, "I'd take my camera out that tree now."

CHAPTER FORTY-NINE

Jimmy Gray and I put our pistols back in their cases as Detective Burke shinnied up the tree trunk using a linesman's strap until he could grab the first limb. He stepped from branch to branch, removed the camera, and dropped it for me to catch. He hung from the lowest branch and dropped the remaining ten feet onto the soft ground.

"If I did that you'd have to dig me out with a backhoe," Jimmy Gray said.

We piled into the Jeep and drove slowly out of the woods, keeping an eye out for others who might be intent on finishing what Sammy started. David pulled onto the country road and headed south, away from Sammy's.

"I don't want to drive by Sammy's Place again today," Burke said.

"Good thinking," I said from the back seat. "Tyler's long gone now. Gotten rid of whatever was in that canvas bank bag."

"It was cash, or meth, or both," Burke said. "No doubt in my mind."

"Someone told me in Sunshine," Jimmy said from the front passenger seat, "and I ain't saying who, that he heard Sammy's Place is definitely a place to score some meth."

"Let's assume Tyler's a bag man," I said, "either picking up cash and meth or bringing cash to Sammy's. El Ray's last known location was Sammy's parking lot. He had meth in his system. He was with Reese earlier in the night. Reese has been involved with Ronnie Tyler, who is involved, we think, in the meth trade for someone else or on his own account."

"Ronnie's not management material," Burke said. "He's working for someone else. Probably Sheriff Burr."

"What's our next step?" Jimmy Gray said. "Call in the FBI?"

"And tell them what?" I said. "The evidence left with Tyler. Sammy's in that honky-tonk right now flushing or burning anything that could link him to the drugs or the money. All we have to go on is suspicious activity."

"Maybe y'all can talk the Conklin woman into filing battery charges against Ronnie Tyler for beating her," Jimmy said. "Put the squeeze on him."

"Those are state charges," I said. "They'd have to be tried in state criminal court in Cedar Grove, in the same courthouse as Sheriff Burr's office."

"No way the case against him would go anywhere in Cedar Grove," Detective Burke said. "And what I know about Reese, she's not going to be talked into filing charges."

"I agree," I said. "She's contrite right now, and dead set against doing anything more to add to Richard's humiliation. A public airing of her dirty laundry with Tyler would do just that."

"You boys are on the right track on El Ray," Jimmy said. "The way I see it, Reese was screwing Tyler and getting meth from him to share with El Ray to pump up the sexual excitement between them. I don't know why they'd need to make the sex more intense, as hot as she looks and eighteen-year-old El Ray likely to have the sex drive of a bull moose, but let's say that's how it happened. Then Tyler finds out Reese is playing around with El Ray, gets insanely jealous and somehow waits for El Ray at Sammy's, drives him off and kills him then dumps him in the ravine. It's the oldest motive in the book. Biblical."

"I don't think Ronnie Tyler's strong enough to force El Ray into a car," Burke said. "Or to carry him to that ravine."

"Tyler's got a gun, ain't he?" Jimmy said. "And El Ray's not armed. A forty-five's a pretty good equalizer."

"But El Ray wasn't shot or beaten," I said. "He was stabbed under his arm with something other than a knife."

"Tyler's a detective," Burke said. "He'd know not to use his own pistol."

"How about reporting all this to Sheriff Burr," Jimmy said. "Lay it all out. If Burr's not involved in Tyler's drug selling, then he ought to take an interest."

"Burr's in up to his eyeballs," Burke said.

"I've considered telling Burr about our suspicions," I said. "But it's going to end up just like our heads-on confrontation with Tyler and Sammy this afternoon. Nothing's going to come of it. If Burr is in on the drug dealing with Tyler, he's going to protect him out of self-preservation. If Burr is not in on it, he's going to protect his deputy anyway to cover his own political backside. Sheriff Burr is the big dog in Tallabusha County politics and power. Either way, he's not moving against Tyler in a public way. There's no upside for him."

"And to those people over there," Burke said, "we're smartass outsiders trying to tell them how to run their business. We won't get anywhere."

"Well, you boys are in the law enforcement business," Jimmy said. "I'm just a little old country banker, trying to make a nickel. You two come up with a plan, and me and my Desert Eagle will back you a hundred percent."

We crested the final hill to Oxford and saw the Wellsgate lake on the left and car dealers' row on the right. I glanced at my personal phone, then my burner. No message from Jake. No call. Something was wrong, I could feel it. Not sure what I could do about it without putting him in more danger.

"Damn," Jimmy said, checking his calls. "Ruby called me, Willie Mitchell. I hope to God she hasn't wrecked Ina's Lexus."

"She probably just needs to borrow some money," I said.

"I'm driving back to Sunshine this afternoon," Jimmy Gray said. "I'll run Ruby down tonight and find out what she wants. If it ain't important, I won't bother you with it, partner."

I nodded to Jimmy, but was barely listening. My mind was about forty miles away, focusing on a crummy little trailer off a country road where Jake had been living, searching for Susan's killer for almost six months.

I resolved to let Detective Burke work on solving El Ray's murder without me for a while.

I was going to find Jake.

CHAPTER FIFTY

I learned during astronomy class in college that if I looked indirectly, rather than right at a small star, especially in the dimmer constellations, I could actually visualize the tiny star better. That may sound implausible, but in my experience, sometimes an indirect approach works in problem solving, too. If I fiddle with the tangential issues, or toy with work-arounds or non-linear solutions, rather than thinking, "how do I solve X + Y = Z," the answer comes to me laterally, sometimes in fragments.

That's kind of what happened after Detective Burke dropped me off at my condo after the cluster-you-know-what at Sammy's Place. I didn't say anything to Burke or Jimmy about my prioritizing Jake's situation. Burke didn't know anything about Jake. Jimmy would want to help, and I would adamantly refuse to let him. It was my mission, and mine alone. I just didn't quite know how to go about it just yet.

I sent a new text to Jake around four that afternoon, and one more at ten when I went to bed. I endured another restless night of shallow sleep, checking my phone every hour. At five in the morning, I gave up and walked downstairs for my first K-cup.

That's when Jake's comments about April Wolff popped into my brain—sideways. I had not thought of April Wolff since Jake described her to me on our first visit on the Sardis Lake dam two weeks earlier.

"Like the animal, with an extra f," she explained to Jake. She was the twenty-year-old blonde who introduced herself to Jake in Kip's Korner in the first week of his life in the Tallabusha woods. She was his welcoming hostess who hung out and showed him the ropes. I wasn't sure what else she did with Jake, but I had a pretty good idea. Talk about southern hospitality.

Jake told me she identified some of the players, including the outlaw James Lee Payne of Sunshine, a.k.a. Q-Man. Jake didn't think it possible that Q-Man could connect Jake to nine-year-old towhead Scott Banks and their little league coach. Jake was probably right, but I still worried about it.

Jake said April was uneducated, but relatively intelligent and insightful, given her upbringing. He said she seemed to have her own particular sense of right and wrong. April's mother was deep into the sex-for-drugs lifestyle of the Tallabusha woods when April was born, and checked out permanently when April was ten, leaving her in the clutches of the mother's drugged-out sister and her child-molesting live-in boyfriend.

I sat at my desk sipping coffee and Googled Kip's Korner Tallabusha County, MS and was astounded when the Kip's Korner website popped up. A picture of the store's exterior graced the home page, making the hole-in-the-wall country convenience store appear quaintly retro, much more chic than it was in real life. I entered the site, noting the "Contact Us" number to call. There were photographs of the interior, and "selfies" of patrons posted on the "Our Friends And Customers" page of the site. I studied the photographs—millennials of all races and shapes hamming it up for their self-portraits, but no attractive twenty-year-old blonde named April.

When I saw the "Message Board" page I knew what I was going to do.

I fiddled with the wording of the message I was going to post on the board to April, grinding for the right words and tone, and using my burner number for the reply. This is what appeared on the Kip's Korner website at six-thirty that morning when I hit send: *Anyone knowing the whereabouts of APRIL WOLFF, approximately 20 years of age, please contact the undersigned at 662-807-0703 regarding possible inheritance. RON J. DeLOUCHE, Estate Administrator.*

It was a long shot, but I hoped it would give me the opportunity to meet April and size her up to see if she could be trusted to help me find Jake.

I put on my running gear and was about to take off on a three-miler when my phone rang. Jimmy Gray wanted me to open the garage door. I hit the remote and unlocked the back door. Ten seconds later, Jimmy blustered in, tossing an envelope on my kitchen counter.

"What's that?" I asked.

"An envelope addressed to you. Taped to your garage door. You ain't going to believe what I'm about to tell you about Ruby."

"What's she done now? Is Ina all right?"

"It ain't that. I saw her about seven last night. Drove over to Ina's house to pick up what Ruby asked me to give to you."

Jimmy reached into his overcoat pocket and pulled out a black electronic device slightly bigger than a matchbox. He put it in my hand.

"What is this?" I asked.

"That's a Spy Tec GPS Tracker, state of the art. Our bank has a repo contractor who uses them."

"What does this have to do with Ruby?"

"She had Susan's Lexus detailed for her mama, and her detail man pulled this out from under the driver's side rear wheel well. The man told Ruby what it was. Ruby asked me if Mrs. Susan had been catting around on you and you were keeping track of her."

I sat down and studied the small device.

"Someone put a tracking device on your Lexus when Susan was still driving it," Jimmy said. "Ruby said she didn't know anything about this thing, but figured it was yours and wanted you to have it back."

I jumped up and grabbed my best flashlight from a kitchen drawer, walked into my garage and turned on the light. I lay on my back on the cold concrete and looked under my truck, starting with the frame surrounding my truck's rear passenger wheel well. I shined the light on every surface, scooting around on my back, but saw nothing. I was about to move on to the next wheel when my light reflected off something. I moved the light closer.

"You see anything?" Jimmy said standing in my back door.

It was a device of some kind, configured slightly differently than the tracking device Jimmy handed me. I slid out from under the truck, opened my red plastic tool kit case, and retrieved a screwdriver. Back under, I gently pried the small box from the metal frame. While still on my back, I held it out for Jimmy to see.

"This is a different model," he said, "but it's a Spy Tec GPS tracker. Probably a newer model than the one off the Lexus."

We walked back into the house.

"Someone was tracking Susan," Jimmy said. "And you, too. Who would do a thing like that?"

"I don't know," I said, but the answer was percolating in my brain.

"I got to get to the bank," he said. "Hold on to these. I'm going to check with my repo man and see if there's any way to trace these back to the buyers. We're getting to the bottom of this."

I felt the skin in my scalp tightening when Jimmy closed the back door. I was beginning to understand.

I glanced at the envelope Jimmy tossed on the kitchen counter. He said it was taped to my garage door. I picked it up. "D.A. Banks," was printed in thick black ink. I grabbed my sharpest knife and sliced open the flap, careful not to disturb the note inside.

But it wasn't a note. It was a faded newspaper photograph on yellowed newsprint showing a Little League baseball team. The caption read: "Coach Willie Mitchell Banks and Nine-and-Ten Kubota Tractor Team."

I remembered the picture. In it, I stood proudly behind the players, hands on my hips, elbows akimbo. Kneeling on the first row was Scott Banks. I looked at the other boys on the team, trying to pick out James Lee Payne. There were three other black kids on the team. I recognized each of them in the photo. James Lee was not in the picture.

Then it came to me. James Lee failed to show for a number of team events, not games, but picture day, registration day, and some practices. He wasn't there the day this photo was taken.

I went into my office and sat down, the two GPS trackers and the Little League photograph on the desk before me. I picked up the tracker that had been under my truck. The little black box was how Q-Man knew I was in Natchez, and enabled him or his men to steal my 1911 Springfield out of my desk and substitute the Raven Saturday night special.

Just to mess with me.

I shook my head, realizing Q-Man and his people were tracking me when I drove my F-150 to do recon in Tallabusha the first time. Because of the GPS device, Q-man knew I drove past Jake's trailer, turned around, and drove past it again. I had ignored Jake's insistence that I stay out of Tallabusha. My scouting trip to the trailer confirmed what Q-Man already knew—James Agee, "A.G.," was Jake Banks, son of Willie Mitchell and brother of Scott. The detective work I was so proud of, finding the rental ad for Jake's trailer, getting the address from the elderly lady owner, and my checking out Jake's trailer may have cost my oldest son his life.

James Lee Payne had orchestrated Susan's murder, and maybe Jake's. The Little League team photograph was an invitation for me to come see him in his Tallabusha *demimonde*.

It was an offer I couldn't refuse.

CHAPTER FIFTY-ONE

After Jimmy Gray left for the bank, I sat in my office making notes to myself, trying to control the conflicting emotions raging inside me.

Susan Woodfork Banks, who never hurt a soul in her life, was dead because I sent James Lee Payne, a.k.a. "Q-Man", to Parchman for seven years. Susan's murder was payback. I was supposed to be killed that day, too.

James Lee's crime spree in Sunshine involved multiple guns, drugs, mounds of cash, a bullet hole in an accomplice, and a tense standoff with Sheriff Lee Jones's deputies. He deserved more time than I agreed to, but obviously, he didn't think so.

Jake said from the beginning that Susan's killers were locals. He was right. Lynda Gianelli and the shooter weren't "interstate bandits" from out of state. They were living in Tallabusha and following orders. Sheriff Burr was wrong about that, just as he was wrong in describing Susan's murder as random, and wrong about Lynda Gianelli's death being a suicide. James Lee Payne had the GPS tracker planted on Susan's Lexus. Lynda and the shooter in the Expedition knew exactly where Susan and I had been in Louisiana for her father's funeral. They tracked our return trip, and probably followed us on I-55 that day in June, waiting for the right opportunity. They found it at the Varner exit BP station.

Solving the mystery of Susan's death did nothing to mitigate my fear that Q-Man may have already killed Jake. I had to suppress my anxiety and outrage, though, in order to plan my mission to rescue Jake on the chance he was still alive, or to go after James Lee Payne if Jake was already dead. I had no time to grieve or worry. I had to get to Tallabusha. And, as much as I hated to involve him in the law-breaking I was planning to do, I needed Jimmy's help.

After I called him at the Oxford branch, he was back in my condo in ten minutes. I described for him each step James Lee had taken to exact his revenge against me and my family.

"I need you to swap vehicles with me," I said. "And I want you to have your repo man reinstall the GPS tracker on my truck."

"You don't want them to know we found the tracker," Jimmy said.

"That's right. You drive my truck. Let them think I'm going about my business as usual."

"You can't go over there by yourself," Jimmy said. "You don't know your way around, don't know the players. Sheriff Burr and Tyler and probably the rest of the deputies ain't gonna be on your side in this."

"That's why we can't tell them. And we have to keep Burke in the dark, too. Only you and I will know what I'm doing." I put my hand on the big man's shoulder. "And Jimmy, you've got to let me go in alone. I need you to help me from the outside. It's the only chance we have to rescue Jake, if that's even still possible."

"This is a bad plan," he said.

I showed him the message I posted on Kip's Korner's website, and filled him in on all the details I knew about April Wolff.

"You don't know this girl," he said. "She's just as likely to turn you in to Q-Man and get you killed, too."

"I don't have time to decide if I can trust her," I said, raising my voice. "I've got to rely on Jake's judgment."

I took a deep breath.

"Look, Jimmy. James Lee Payne had Susan killed. Wanted me dead at the BP, too. He's holding Jake or already killed him. If he takes me out, so be it, but I'm not going to make it easy for him. We can't get the Sheriff involved, and there's no time to bring any other agency up to speed. Besides, if James Lee got wind of law enforcement looking for him, that would be the end of Jake for sure. This girl, April..., I've got to take the chance."

I held up the Little League clipping.

"Q-Man wants *me*, Jimmy. That's why he had this taped to my door. I just pray he's keeping Jake alive to get me over on his turf."

I ticked off what I needed Jimmy Gray to do.

"I'm on it," he said on his way out the back door.

I made notes of the gear I was going to need, and began the process of gathering it when my cell phone rang. It was Detective Burke.

"You come up with a Plan B yet on Ronnie Tyler?" he asked.

"No. Still thinking. You?"

"No. Trying to get over our Keystone Cops routine yesterday."

"Nobody got hurt. We'll think of something," I said.

"Did you see the article in the Jackson paper this morning on the preliminary autopsy results of that woman who was burned up over in Tallabusha last weekend?"

"The Gianelli woman?" I said. "No. What did it say?"

"She was still alive when the SUV was burning. They found smoke in her lungs."

"Damn," I said. "Bad way to go."

"But it also said she had a toxic level of opiates in her body, more than enough to kill her. She might have been still breathing, but the pathologist said she was probably not conscious at the time of the fire and didn't feel a thing."

"Good news for her mother," I said. "Maybe she didn't suffer."

"I'm going to talk to our narcotics detectives to find out how much they know about the drug trade over there in Tallabusha. Maybe we'll get lucky."

"All right," I said and ended the call.

Jimmy Gray pulled into my garage in his Silverado and showed me the two cases of water bottles, food, and ammunition he had stashed in the cab.

"And here's a backup for you," he said, pulling a new-looking, very compact automatic pistol from under the Silverado's front seat. "It's the new Sig Sauer P365, chambered in nine-millimeter. I got you plenty of ammo for it, and added a couple of boxes of .45 caliber rounds for your Glock. You can carry this little Sig in your front pocket. Got night vision goggles and skull cap stuffed under the passenger seat inside a black Swiss Gear backpack. Couple of tiny flashlights you can carry in your pockets, too. The stack of cash you asked for is in an envelope under the Sig. There's a box of Nitrile gloves so you won't leave your prints all over the place. They're tougher and don't rip like latex. What about clothes?" he asked. "It's going to be cold out there."

"Already got my cold weather clothing and boots, plus long johns, gloves, hats. I don't know how long I'll be living in your Silverado."

"I put in toilet paper and paper towels, a first aid kit, a Schrade tactical knife. It's sharp as hell, so be careful. See this little safety? You have to disengage it. When you see the red, it's live."

"What about your Escalade?"

"It's on its way from Sunshine. They'll drop it off here for you in less than an hour. I've got the GPS tracker from your truck in my pocket. I'll drive it down to the bank. Repo man will be there before noon and put it back under the rear wheel well where you found it. What else?"

I felt my burner phone vibrating in my pocket. I checked the number. It wasn't Jake.

"Yes," I answered.

"Is this Mr. DeLouche?" a young woman's voice asked.

"It is," I said and pointed at my monitor for Jimmy to know it was a response to the note I had left on the Kip's Korner message board.

"This is April Wolff," she said.

"Well, Ms Wolff, I'm certainly glad you called. You saw my note on Kip's message board, I take it."

"Yes, sir. A friend called me this morning and I went online and read it. Have I inherited something?"

"I didn't have an address for you, just information that you lived in southern Tallabusha County near this store, Kip's Korner. I apologize for the unorthodox way I've located you."

"As long as it worked," she said. "Who did I inherit from?"

"It appears from a distant relative of yours in Vidalia, Louisiana, right across the river from Natchez. A Mrs. Yvonne Frederickson."

"I've never heard that name."

"She was a spinster with no children, and you are listed as a collateral heir inheriting through your late mother, who was Mrs. Frederickson's third cousin, once removed."

"Do I need to do something?" she asked.

"I am in Vicksburg and can be in your area in an hour or two. I will need to see some identification to verify your identity. There's an affidavit you'll need to sign to request your possible inheritance. It's a legal matter, so I hope you understand that this process will take some time."

"How much do I get?"

"It's hard to say at this time, but I think you'll find it's a tidy sum."

"I hope it's enough to move away from here," she said.

"I'm going to remove the notice I posted on Kip's message board, so be sure to write down my number. And I would caution you not to share this information with anyone at this time. This is your private business, and there are some unscrupulous people in this world, some of whom may want to ask you for money."

"Believe me, Mr. DeLouche, I know that. People will steal you blind out here if they know you have anything."

"Is there an office plaza or shopping center in your vicinity where we can meet? We will need some privacy."

"Nothin' out here but woods," she said.

"What if I meet you at Kip's Korner at three o'clock this afternoon, and we can drive to somewhere else for our discussion. A coffee shop, perhaps?"

"I live in a trailer a few miles from Kip's. We could go there. It's nothing fancy, but I try to keep it clean. And I got coffee."

"If you have an address, I can put it into my phone and follow directions to your trailer."

"Uh...," she said, thinking.

"Perhaps it would be better to meet at Kip's first, maybe in the parking lot if it has one, and if you're comfortable I'm who I say I am, then we can proceed to your home. It will be entirely up to you."

"Oh, I believe you, Mr. DeLouche. I've been praying for you, or something like you, to happen to me. I never thought it would."

"I'm happy for you. Is this number that appears on my phone a good contact for you? I'd like to text you when I get close and we can meet at Kip's around three this afternoon."

"Yes, sir."

I ended the call and leaned back in my chair.

"I take back what I said. You a pretty decent liar after all, Willie Mitchell."

"I've been a lawyer a long time, Jimmy. Comes with the territory."

I went upstairs to change into a dark suit I hadn't worn in two years, a white shirt and red tie. I combed my hair straight back and slicked it down with some kind of gel I found in Susan's shelves in the bathroom. I searched for and found a pair of glasses Susan had found for me to attend a Halloween costume party two years before as Stephen Colbert. The frames were real but not the lenses. I rejoined Jimmy downstairs.

"Good to meet you, Mr. DeLouche," Jimmy said.

"What do you think?" I asked.

"I think we better pray hard that this bull shit is going to work."

"Already have," I said.

CHAPTER FIFTY-TWO

I texted April Wolff when I was twenty minutes from Kip's Korner. It was a pretty day, bright sunshine, but chilly. Driving the county road bordered by a dense forest of pine and hardwoods, I marveled at how peaceful it seemed out in these woods, and how appearances can deceive. The day was the seventy-seventh anniversary of Pearl Harbor. I hoped for a more favorable outcome.

I pulled into Kip's parking lot right on time, and saw a slightly built blonde waiting on the concrete walk in front of the store. It had to be April.

I waved at her and lowered my window. She walked over and extended her small hand through the window. I shook it with a big smile.

"Miss Wolff, I presume?" I said.

"Yes, sir, Mr. DeLouche."

"Why don't we sit here a minute and talk," I said.

She walked quickly around the front of the Escalade and hopped into the front seat. She looked into the back of the SUV.

"This is so big," she said. "I've seen these but never been in one. What exactly is it?"

I pointed to the silver script on the dash that read: "Cadillac Escalade."

"It's really nice."

"Did you bring your identification?" I asked.

She gave me her driver's license which I studied and pretended to compare with the contents of the dummy legal file I had assembled and labeled "Estate of Yvonne Frederickson" in bold for her to see. I noticed April was 5'2" and weighed 105 pounds, and was born twenty years ago.

"Everything seems to be in order," I said. "I failed to mention that I will also need to take a photograph of your birth certificate. Did you by any chance bring it with you?"

"No, sir," she said. "I have it at my trailer if you want to go there now."

"Very well," I said. "Do you want me to follow your vehicle?"

"I don't have a car. I'll just point out the way. Head in that direction," she said pointing to the road heading south.

I followed her directions and in less than five minutes turned into an unpaved driveway and stopped in front of a trailer that was larger than Jake's. It seemed less sturdy, however, because of the rust spots spreading along the metal exterior near the steel frame on which the "home" rested.

"Your yard is neatly kept, Miss Wolff," I said.

"I hate clutter and trash. Before my Aunt Shirley left she signed the mobile home over and deeded the one-acre it sits on to me, too. All I have to do is make sure the taxes are paid every year, which isn't much."

"How long ago was that?"

"Three or four years," she said.

"But you were a minor then," I said. "Was there a guardian or custodian appointed to accept the transfer on your behalf?"

"I don't know. We just went to this notary in a little house on the other side of Kip's Korner. Aunt Shirley and I signed papers and the notary stamped it and said he would take them to the courthouse to register them. Shirley's boyfriend was already working on a rig in North Dakota and sent money for her to join him, and I guess she used part of it to deed it all over. I have a copy of the land deed and the bill of sale for the trailer if you want to see them inside."

"Let's go in," I said.

She bounced out of the Escalade and up the metal steps to the front door. I followed slowly behind her after making sure the small Sig Sauer in my front pocket was hidden by my coat, but ready to fire. She flipped on a light and I looked around. There was no one inside, and the place was too small to hide anyone of any size. The door opened into the "living room" which was a sitting area with chairs, a couch, and a television. On one end was a small kitchen and eating area. On the other a metal or composite wall and door, which I assumed led to the bedroom and bath. I sat so I could see the bedroom door and the front entrance as well.

"Let me get my birth certificate," she said.

April entered the bedroom door, leaving it open. I heard the sound of papers rustling. I slipped the Sig from my pants pocket into my inside coat pocket and continued to grip it. If someone besides April came through the open door, I was ready. In less than a minute, she rejoined me.

"Very good," I said, taking a photograph with my personal phone. "You'd be surprised how many people don't know where their birth certificate is."

"A place for everything," she said. "It saves time hunting for stuff if you put everything back. Can I get you some coffee or water or something?"

"No," I said, looking around. "You do keep it very neat in here."

"I wasn't due to clean for a couple of days, but I went ahead and did it today after we talked. I didn't want you to think I was a slob. What paper do I sign for my inheritance?"

"On second thought, I would like a small glass of water."

She hopped up before the words were out of my mouth. As she turned on the faucet, I mentioned I had read about the young lady who died in a car fire out in the county this past weekend.

"Did you know her?" I asked.

"This is well water," she said giving me the glass. "It may have a stronger taste than you're used to. I don't use any softener."

"It's fine," I said after a sip. "I read the lady's name but don't recall it."

"Lynda Gianelli," April said. "She was a friend of mine."

"Oh, I'm sorry for bringing it up. What an awful way to pass."

"The Sheriff said she did it herself, but I don't believe it." She looked around as if to make sure we were alone and whispered. "People get murdered out here in these woods and nobody does anything about it."

"Our paper in Vicksburg carries statewide news," I said, "and I try to keep up. There was another awful murder in this county over by the interstate last summer. Lady was killed in a convenience store for no reason. The clerk, also. And I believe the husband was shot, too, but he survived."

"I remember that," April said. "Like I said, this place is dangerous."

"Why do you think your friend, the Gianelli lady, didn't commit suicide?"

"Because I knew her, that's why. She was really hooked on meth, but she was trying to quit. She missed her two boys something awful. She used to sit right where you are and cry about leaving her kids. The paper said she was full of downers, Oxycodone or something, enough to kill her even if she hadn't burned up. I think someone made her take them, or tricked her into it. Just a week ago she told me she was going to clean herself up and leave this awful place. And she meant it."

"Why would someone want to kill her?" I asked.

"When Lynda partied hard, I mean, when she was drinking or used a lot of meth, she did a lot of talking. And she's seen some bad things out here, I know for a fact. I think someone was worried she was going to say something she shouldn't, and that's why they killed her and burned her up. To keep her quiet."

"I'm sorry to keep talking about this, Miss Wolff, but the subject fascinates me. I guess I'm a frustrated criminal lawyer. All I do is estates."

"I got plenty of time," she said, "and it's kind of nice to talk to someone intelligent for a change. Most of the people I hang out with, it's like they have brain damage."

"Could be the drugs. I hope you avoid them."

"I like coke and weed, and that's about it. Nothing that's addictive." She sat up. "I hope that doesn't disqualify me from my inheritance. I don't know anything about law. And, Mr. DeLouche, I've almost quit doing the coke. I do like to smoke pot, though. Better for me than beer or whiskey."

"How do you get around?"

"I get rides. I can walk to Kip's from here, cut through the woods. There's always someone there who'll take me somewhere."

"Do you have to pay them?" I asked.

"Sometimes," she said. "Not usually."

"Do you think there's a chance the law will catch up to whoever killed your friend Lynda?"

She hesitated.

"Mr. DeLouche," she said, "it's the Tallabusha County Sheriff's office the ones saying she killed herself, which I know cannot be true." She paused. "Please don't tell anyone what I just said."

"I won't," I said. "Could I have another glass of water?"

I was stalling. My next few questions would let the cat out of the bag. I hoped Jake's judgment about April Wolff was correct. His life depended on it.

Michael Henry

CHAPTER FIFTY-THREE

"Miss Wolff," I said when she gave me the water, "if you were able to help get justice for Lynda Gianelli and punish the people responsible for her murder, would you do it?"

She studied me a moment.

"Why are you asking me that?" she said quietly. "You're not a lawyer. I haven't inherited anything, have I?"

I took a deep breath and relaxed, sinking deeper into the chair. So did April. She wasn't angry. She seemed calm, resigned to hear the real story of what I wanted from her. Her preternatural serenity in the face of my deception surprised me, especially in light of her feral upbringing. I had the sense that she was accustomed to men lying to her to get an advantage, that misrepresentations and lies were commonplace to her, even expected, in her everyday existence. Her low expectations for humankind made me sad.

"I am a lawyer. I'm not a policeman. I used to be District Attorney in Sunshine, over in Yaloquena County. For twenty-four years. My name is Willie Mitchell Banks."

"I've never been to Sunshine," she said. "What should I call you?"

"Call me Willie Mitchell. May I call you April?"

"You can if you tell me why you're really here."

"My wife Susan was the woman killed at the BP station at the Varner exit last June. We were married for thirty-eight years. I was shot that day, too, but I survived."

"Oh, my God. I am so sorry. That was you?"

"I saw Lynda Gianelli drive her Expedition into the station that day, and watched as a young, light-skinned black man wearing a red windbreaker and raggedy jeans stroll into the store and kill the clerk and Susan. I tried to shoot him when he left but missed. He shot me right here."

I pointed to the scar on my forehead.

"Did the man have on flip-flops?" she asked.

"Yes. Who was he?"

- 242 -

"I don't know his real name. Everyone calls him Flip-Flop, because that's all he ever wears, even on a cold day like today. He's just a couple of years older than me. He's a bad guy."

"Did Lynda tell you about the shooting?"

"I was partying with her one night a few weeks ago and I heard her telling this other girl. I told Lynda to stop talking about it but she was so high, she just waved me off. Running your mouth around here can get you killed. I believe that's what happened to her."

"Do you remember meeting James Agee last summer? He lives in a trailer off the road to Cedar Grove, north of here."

"Everybody calls him A.G. I met him when he first moved into his trailer. He's on the run from something. I see him around almost every day, at Kip's or on the roads. He's tight with Q-Man now. How do you know him?"

"He's my son. When's the last time you saw him?"

"Your son?" she said. "Why'd he move out here in these God-forsaken woods? He must have gotten in some kind of trouble." She thought a second. "I know I saw him last Saturday afternoon at Kip's. Haven't seen him since."

"He moved here last summer to find out who killed his mother," I said. "He's kind of a special investigator." We sat in silence for several moments. "I'm here trying to find him. I believe he's in danger if he's still alive. His real name is Jake. Will you help me, April?"

"I'm not sure what I can do to help, Willie Mitchell."

"You can educate me on who the players are, where they live. You're part of this community and I'm not. I don't know who to talk to or where to go."

"It's really dangerous, what you're talking about doing. I mean like murder dangerous. They won't think twice about making you disappear. And the law in this county is in on it."

I reached into my coat and pulled out a stack of fifty one-hundred-dollar bills. I placed them on the plastic coffee table between us.

"I don't expect you to help me for free." I pushed the cash toward her. "I lied about saying you inherited some money to get you to meet with me. But I have plenty more where this five thousand dollars came from. Even if you decide not to help me, I'm leaving this cash with you. It's yours."

I picked up the money and put it in her hands.

"You say you want to leave here," I said. "Jake told me you were a good person. Sharp, too, he said. He thought you deserved a better life. After spending this time with you, I agree. If you help me, I promise I'll pay to move you somewhere, go to school, have a nice apartment, and a car. I'm desperate to find my son. This is a way out of here for you. You can start over."

She took a deep breath and thumbed the bills.

"I've never seen this much money in my whole life," she said. "I can keep this? You mean that?"

"No matter what. Consider it part of your inheritance."

April was more than attractive. No makeup, worn out clothes, hair uncombed, but she was pretty, a natural. Like Jake, I didn't know how, but she also seemed to have developed a moral compass out in the Tallabusha woods, a modern Gehenna populated with trashy, cutthroat people of all races and stripes. April Wolf may well have been modern proof of Seventeenth Century British playwright John Dryden's concept of the "noble savage," a primitive unsullied by the corruption of society, proving the innate goodness of man. After seeing the havoc humans wreak on each other on a regular basis in twenty-four years as District Attorney, the "innate goodness of man" seemed like a fairy tale to me.

"Have you ever been to New York City, Willie Mitchell?"

"I have. Many times."

"Those buildings and all those lights and people—what's it like?"

"I like Oxford better," I said. "But if you and Jake and I come out of this alive, I'll send you to New York, and any other place you want. And April, I don't want anything else from you. I promise. Just your help."

"Q-Man is the boss man out here, Willie Mitchell. And Flip-Flop? He does whatever dirty work Q-Man tells him to do."

"Do you think they killed Lynda?"

"I do," she said. "And your wife."

CHAPTER FIFTY-FOUR

April was a storehouse of information. She told me in lurid detail what life in the sex-for-drugs world in the Tallabusha woods was like. For walking around money, her peers manipulated and abused every federal and state program meant to provide help to the unfortunate. She told me of food stamp scams, Social Security disability hustles, welfare frauds and other schemes delivering money every month to the drugheads around her, which they invested in meth, crack, Oxy, heroin, and any other illicit drug finding its way to the woods.

"I went to the Job Center several times right after I turned eighteen," she said, "but bad things happened to me over there, so I stopped going."

She admitted she had used some of the scams to get more money from the government than she was supposed to, but stopped after she turned twenty, because it made her feel guilty. She knew it wasn't right.

"And when I was a little girl, I watched my Mama have sex with these men out here for drugs. She would swap the drugs for cash or other drugs. She thought I was too little to know what was going on, but I did. I just never said anything about it. When I was fifteen I started doing the same thing, but then I stopped. It made me feel dirty, and I didn't want to turn out like my Mama."

I retrieved a county map from the Escalade, and April marked where her trailer was, Kip's Korner, Jake's trailer, Q-Man's house and land, the Job Center, and a dozen other spots where other dopers congregated or lived.

I opened the trailer door at about five-thirty. I was dark outside, time for me to return to Oxford to swap the Escalade for Jimmy's Silverado with all the gear we had loaded that morning. Time to get rid of the smarmy lawyer persona Ron J. DeLouche, too.

"I have to drive back to Oxford now, April. I've got a truck there loaded with things I think I'll need out here. Will you be all right?"

"Sure. But can I go? I've only been there a couple of times."

"If you want to," I said. "It'll be suppertime when we get there. We won't have a lot of time, but we can stop by any fast food place you want and order food and eat it on the way back over here."

"I love pizza, but you have to go all the way to Cedar Grove to pick it up. They don't deliver out here. I guess they got tired of people robbing them."

"Pizza it is," I said. "Let's go."

She clutched the stack of cash and looked around the trailer, looking for a safe place to hide it.

"You can bring it with you if you want," I said. "Or stick it in a can and bury it outside. It's yours now."

"Just to be safe," she said, stuffing it down her pants. "I'm ready."

Either April was oblivious to the danger she was putting herself in by helping me, or she knew the risk and was willing to face it in order to escape from Tallabusha. Riding east toward Oxford, she was excited, asking me questions I would have expected from a child.

"How did Lynda avoid being discovered for a year by deputies who were looking for her?" I asked when she stopped to catch her breath. "And her Expedition she drove to the BP, seems like law enforcement would have come across it. It was still registered in her husband's name."

"Nobody from the Sheriff's office came out our way looking for her. I would have known if they did. There were a few flyers about her at Kip's Korner at first, but no one pays much attention to those. Lots of people out in these woods don't want to be found. They don't believe in telling on each other, either. The law is everyone's enemy around Kip's."

"And her SUV? Did she drive it?"

"Not much. Then after the murders at the BP, I never saw it again. She and Flip-Flop must have kept it hidden in the woods somewhere."

"Were she and Flip-Flop living together?"

"No way," she laughed. "She got meth from him, that's it. I don't think Flip-Flop is interested in sex. I guess he gets off by hurting people. He used to beat up Lynda for nothing, or so she told me." She paused. "Tell me again why Q-Man has it in for your family."

I told her the saga of James Lee Payne.

"I never thought Quintavius was a real name," she said. "Who would name a kid something like that?"

"You afraid of him?" I asked. "I mean Q-Man."

"Most definitely, Willie Mitchell. Most definitely. Flip-Flop, too."

I parked in my garage and led April inside the condo. She wandered around while I gathered things and loaded the Silverado.

"This place is really nice," she said. "Did your wife live here?"

"Until she was killed."

I went upstairs and ditched my lawyer suit, showered, and dressed in long johns and insulated camo coveralls. When I walked downstairs, April was looking at photographs of Susan and me on the walls.

"Your wife was a pretty lady," April said. "Could I ask you a favor?"

"Anything," I said.

"Could I take a shower in your bathroom, the one you just used? And if you still have any of your wife's clothes, could I...,"

"Absolutely," I said, "but we have to hurry."

I led her upstairs and showed her how the shower worked, where the towels, soap, and shampoo were. I asked what kind of clothes she wanted and she said jeans and tops. I turned on the shower, closed the bathroom door, and went through Susan's closet and drawers.

I stopped for a moment. I had avoided her closet since her death. Susan's scent permeated her clothing and overwhelmed me with grief and loss. I longed to hold her, smell her hair, whisper in her ear. But those days were gone. I cleared my throat and got busy, quashing the memory of Susan each sweater, jacket, and camisole brought back.

I laid out several sets of jeans and long-sleeve tops, sweaters, jackets, underwear, coats, and sneakers. I grabbed Susan's make-up travel bag, tossed it on the bed. I had long fussed at myself for not cleaning out Susan's stuff and giving it to Goodwill or The Salvation Army, but walking down the steps to my kitchen, I was glad I had not.

Thirty minutes later, April joined me in the kitchen. I was sipping on a cup of coffee.

"Wow," I said. "You look beautiful, April."

"You think so?" she said, her face lighting up. "No one's ever said that to me, Willie Mitchell."

"It's true. You are very pretty." I smiled at her. "Everything fit okay?"

"Not exactly. Your wife was tall. But the things I'm wearing come pretty close. And the clothes are all so nice, not cheap and third-hand, like mine."

"And you found the makeup, I see."

She had done her eyes, used lipstick and a bit of rouge. Tastefully.

"Why don't you take that bag of makeup with you?" I said. "And if I live through this you can come back here later on and take everything of Susan's that you want. I was going to give it to charities, but I'd rather you have it all. If you know a seamstress, some of the clothes can be made to fit."

"I feel like Cinderella," she said as her eyes filled with tears.

"We should go," I said. "You have your money?"

She nodded vigorously. We drove the Silverado to Jackson Avenue, picked up a pizza in a drive-through, and headed west on Highway Six. April had eaten two pieces before I finished one. I called Jimmy Gray on my burner, gave him a status report and April's number, just in case he could not reach me. Forty minutes later, I turned into the driveway to her trailer.

"You should park in back," she said, and directed me to drive around the trailer to a barely visible trail through dense undergrowth.

I inched the Silverado through the brush, briars and branches scratching against the finish, producing an ear-piercing, high-pitched metallic scraping, like fingernails on a chalk board. I stopped in a small clearing beyond the foliage.

"They can't see your truck from the main road back here," she said, "and if you have to, you can drive out this way to a dirt road."

"Is this part of your one acre?" I asked.

"My aunt told me it was the day she signed the deed at the notary."

"It's ten o'clock," I said. "You think it's safe to drive around?"

"Let's wait for an hour inside," she said. "People don't start moving around until between eleven and midnight."

I sat in the "living room" while April walked into her bedroom and closed the door. I experienced a momentary, frightening thought. What if she were conning me? What if she were sending a text in her bedroom to Q-Man or Flip-Flop telling them to come get me?

"I hid my money," April said when she came out the door, "in a really good place."

She seemed so guileless I felt guilty doubting her *bona fides*. I went over the county map with her again, trying to orient myself. At eleven-fifteen, we climbed back into the Silverado, drove out the back way to the gravel road, and then to Kip's, stopping at the intersection of the two county roads. There were only two vehicles at the store.

"It's still early," she said. "Let's drive by A.G.'s trailer, then I'll show you where Q-Man stays. He claims it's heir property, where he says his grandmother used to live."

"Heir property" was a term I had not heard in a while. It meant land owned many decades ago by a long-deceased individual or couple for whom no estate proceeding was opened to place the children or heirs in possession. After a couple of generations, there might be scores of descendants who inherited an interest by law, but which ownership had never been recognized by a legal transfer proceeding. "Heir property" was a title-examiner's worst nightmare—dozens of heirs spread across the country with addresses unknown.

We drove slowly by Jake's rented trailer, which was barely visible because of the inky darkness. There were no lights on, inside or out. His Nissan truck was gone.

"Now Q-Man's place," I said and followed April's directions.

"It's huge, like ten acres," she said as we approached Q-Man's. "There's a main house, a barn that's falling down, and an old smokehouse. I've been in the smokehouse a few times, never the main house or barn." She giggled. "Q-Man says his ancestors called it a smokehouse because that's where they smoked weed. That's what I did when I was in there."

"Where does Flip-Flop live?"

"In one of these buildings, I think," she said. "I don't know of him having any other place. Q-Man likes to keep him close for security, I guess."

"What's Flip-Flop like? You've talked to him?"

"He doesn't talk. I mean, if everyone's sitting around or hanging in a vacant lot, he just mostly listens. And sometimes he'll walk right past you without saying a word or even looking at you. Weird. But people tell me he'll do anything Q-Man asks, like he's his servant or something." She paused. "They also say he'll kill anybody Q-Man asks him to without a second thought. Like he doesn't have a conscience."

"Q-Man has guns, I'm sure. You ever seen him with one?"

"A pistol, but I don't know anything about guns. They say he gets all his guns from Clarksdale and Cleveland."

I pulled onto the shoulder a few hundred yards past Q-Man's and took another giant leap of faith.

"I know you don't have a car," I said, "but do you know how to drive?"

"I drive all the time. Other people's cars or trucks. But I can't operate a stick shift where you change gears."

"I'm going to get out here. Drive back to your trailer, park the truck behind it. Wait for my call."

"What are you going to do?" she asked.

"Some sightseeing," I said.

CHAPTER FIFTY-FIVE

I turned one of the tiny Fenix flashlights Jimmy had given me and walked into the woods, pointing the Fenix at the ground.

A hundred feet in, I put on the Nitrile gloves and removed the night vision goggles from my black Swiss Eagle backpack. I had practiced using the NVGs briefly at the condo, but not nearly enough. I struggled getting the skull cap on correctly and making the goggles snug around my eyes. I took one last look at the map April annotated for me, turned off the Fenix light, and flipped on the NVGs.

I walked through the woods for fifteen minutes toward Q-Man's place. When his house came into view, I stopped at the edge of the trees and undergrowth, about fifty yards away. Lights were on inside the house, distorting the NVG image, flooding it with glaring brightness from the small windows. I checked my Glock in the holster at my waist, the compact Sig, and the Schrade knife in the coverall pouch at my chest. I felt my pockets to make sure the extra magazines for both guns were there. It was time to see if James Lee Payne, a.k.a. Q-Man, was home.

I continued to use the NVGs until I was fifty feet behind Q-Man's house. I stopped, stuck the skull cap and goggles in my backpack, and waited for my eyes to adjust. After a few minutes, I crept closer, my heart pounding so loud I hoped no one could hear it.

There were two vehicles in front of the house. One was an older model Camaro, the same make and model as the Camaro that picked up Jake at the courthouse after his arraignment three weeks earlier. The other was a small, dark Nissan truck, which was probably Jake's. I wasn't sure the Camaro or the truck were actually black because the feeble light from the front windows of the house barely penetrated the dense darkness enveloping the place.

I moved quietly to a side window and looked inside the house. Sitting at a rickety wooden table under an overhead light dangling from a cord in the ceiling were James Lee Payne and a young, light-skinned black man with a short, unruly afro, wearing tattered jeans, flip-flops, and of all things, the same red windbreaker he wore that day in June at the BP.

I felt rage building inside me and began the adrenaline control protocol I learned from Darwin Brass, taking deep, slow breaths. I pictured myself in a hammock on a porch looking out over a white sand beach and the Gulf of Mexico. A warm breeze washed over me as waves broke gently on the shore. The idyll was brief, however, because the delicate sounds were replaced by a growing roar inside my head, more like the sound of giant breakers crashing into the sand rather than gently lapping. I continued taking deep breaths and trying to meditate until the roar subsided and my fingers ceased trembling.

Back on task, I watched through the window. James Lee was staring at his phone screen. There were three empty beer bottles on the table in front of Flip-Flop next to a gun that looked like a shorter version of an AK-47 but with no stock and a large banana-shaped magazine. I had seen an ex-military-looking guy shooting one like it at the outdoor range at Brass Tactical. Darwin told me it was a "Draco" and was currently the weapon of choice for gang-bangers and gangsta-rappers in Memphis, Chicago, and East St. Louis.

The Draco was a lot more firepower than my Glock and Sig combined, so it was important to avoid a shoot-out with Flip-Flop and James Lee unless I could get the drop on them. Strategy and tactics were going to be key in my confronting the two killers, which was a disturbing realization for me because I was winging it. I had no idea what I was going to do next.

I continued to watch James Lee through the window. I didn't hear his phone ring, but it must have vibrated because he picked it up and began talking. I couldn't understand a word. Flip-Flop continued to sit impassively, sipping his beer. James Lee ended the call and said something to Flip-Flop, who picked up the Draco and cradled it in his lap.

I hit the ground immediately when I heard the sound of an engine, then saw the lights of a vehicle approach the front of the house. I scooted behind an old, spherical butane tank between me and the two vehicles parked in front. Lying on my stomach, I watched the vehicle stop next to the Nissan truck. The driver exited, carrying a flimsy plastic grocery bag.

"I'll be damned," I whispered under my breath as I recognized Deputy Sheriff Ronnie Tyler walk from his detective's sedan through the front door into the house. I stood and peered through the window again. Tyler sat down, and dumped cash on the table from the grocery bag. James Lee used both arms to gather the cash to himself, as if raking in winnings from a major pot at a casino poker table.

Flip-Flop left the table and returned with two beer bottles, placing one in front of Deputy Tyler, who took a long pull on his before resting it on the table. James Lee Payne, a.k.a. Q-Man, and Deputy Tyler carried on a lively conversation which I could not hear. It must have been entertaining, because both men were smiling and laughing as they spoke. Flip-Flop sat stone-faced. He seemed oblivious to the conversation.

After ten more minutes of chatter between Q-Man and the deputy, Tyler turned his bottle up, took a final swig, and stood to leave. He wadded the empty plastic grocery bag and tossed it on the table, bid them good bye, and walked out the front door.

As soon as Tyler stepped through the front door, I watched Flip-Flop walk quickly after Tyler, the Draco in hand. I scooted around the propane tank and lay flat to watch Flip-Flop unleash a burst of gunfire into Tyler's back as the deputy stood at his car door.

Tyler landed face down in the dirt. Though Tyler was most certainly already dead, Flip-Flop calmly walked over, aimed the muzzle two feet from his victim, and fired a quick burst into the back of Tyler's head.

I moved back to my vantage point outside the window, and saw Flip-Flop return his Draco to the table inside, sit down and take a drink of his beer. It was as if he had returned from bidding Tyler a fond farewell instead of pumping him full of high-velocity lead.

Two thoughts popped into my head. First, Deputy Ronnie Tyler had beaten his last woman. Second, I felt pretty sure I was not in Kansas anymore.

Chapter Fifty-Six

I put my NVGs on and walked slowly away from the house. When I reached the cover of the woods, I called April.

"Come get me, April. Same place you dropped me off."

"On my way, Willie Mitchell," she said.

Ten minutes later, she pulled onto the shoulder. I ran out of the woods and jumped into the passenger seat, tossing my backpack onto the floor.

"Drive to the turn off into Q-Man's place," I barked.

"Okay," she said and gunned the Silverado, throwing gravel and dirt behind us.

"Whoa," I said. "Pull over. I'll drive."

"That's the first time I scratched out," she said apologetically.

I grabbed the backpack off the floor and put on the skull cap and NVGs. I turned off the Silverado's headlights and flipped on the NVG switch. I guided the Silverado slowly toward Q-Man's driveway.

"You're like a spy or something," April said. "Those things see in the dark? Do they really work?"

"Yeah," I said. "Buckle up."

When we were a hundred yards from the turnoff to Q-Man's place, the dark Nissan truck barreled out of the drive, fishtailed on the country road, and took off north. I floored the accelerator to catch up.

"Where's he going?" I asked April. "What's on this road?"

"Run down houses and trailers. Who's driving Jake's truck?"

"I don't know."

We hit a straight stretch that ended in a sharp turn, almost ninety degrees west. I recognized the turn from my earlier trips to Tallabusha.

"Jake's trailer is somewhere around here," I said.

"About a fourth of a mile," April said. "On the left."

The Nissan's brake lights flashed in front of me. I slowed to keep pace. The brake lights flashed again, and the Nissan jerked left, pulling off the road. I realized the truck had turned into the driveway to Jake's trailer.

5 STAR

I stopped on the road when I got to Jake's drive. I watched the trailer door close and a light come on inside. I jammed the gear shift in park, and ripped the NVGs off my head.

"Drive to your trailer and wait to hear from me," I said to April.

"But, why...?"

"Now!" I demanded in a frantic whisper. "Now!"

I jumped out of the Silverado and raced toward the trailer door. I pulled my Glock from its holster as I ran. I stopped at the door and tested the knob. It wasn't locked. Darwin Brass's words about sucker punches in bar fights flashed in my brain—whoever acts first wins.

My ears roared. I took one deep breath, exhaled, and burst into the trailer.

Flip-Flop stood over Jake's inert body on the floor, holding a syringe, its needle pointed to the ceiling. I pointed my Glock at Flip-Flop.

"Get away from him," I growled.

Flip-Flop stared at me, his face blank. He didn't seem surprised or scared. He looked like he didn't give a damn about me, what I ordered him to do, or about Jake. He jammed the needle into Jake's arm. I shot him twice in the torso. What Darwin Brass called a "double tap."

Flip-Flop fell back, leaving the syringe dangling from Jake's arm. I pulled it out and held it up to the light. The plunger was still extended. The deadly fluid in the barrel, whatever it was, was still there, and not in Jake's veins.

Thank God.

I called April. She was on the road to her trailer, less than a half a mile from me.

"Turn around and get back here," I yelled into my phone. "Hurry."

I knelt by Jake and felt for a pulse. It was there, but weak. I pulled the duct tape from his mouth and removed the damp, wadded cloth jammed inside. I bent low, my ear to his nostrils and mouth and almost cried when I sensed Jake taking a deep, deep breath. He was alive.

I heard the Silverado engine and jumped up to open the door. In the glare of its headlights, I yelled at April.

"Clear the passenger seat! I'm bringing him out."

I fumbled to remove the Schrade knife from my coverall bib, but my hands had a life of their own. I stopped for a moment and took several deep breaths, willing my body's "fight-or-flight" response to stand down and let me get on with taking care of my boy.

I opened the knife and carefully cut the rope and duct tape from Jake's wrists and ankles, extended his right arm, ducked under it, and hoisted him onto my right shoulder, all in one motion. I must have still been wired with adrenaline, because lifting Jake was smooth, requiring only a modest effort. I appeared at the door in the bright headlights with Jake on my shoulder. April hopped out of the truck, wide-eyed.

"Is he all right?"

"I don't know. Open the passenger door."

I dropped Jake onto the passenger seat as gently as I could, and strapped him in with the seatbelt. I checked his pulse and his breathing again. He was alive, but weak.

"Listen to me," I said to April, grabbing her by the arms, my face inches from hers. "Do you really want to leave these woods and never come back?"

"More than anything," she said.

"Then here's what you have to do."

I entered an address on her phone's map app. The destination and route popped up. I took a minute to go over it with her.

"Drive to your trailer, get your money and whatever else you want to take with you. Not clothes, but anything you can't do without, because you're never going to see your trailer again."

She nodded.

"What are you going to do?" she asked.

"I'm going to follow you in Jake's truck, but I've got to do something first, then I'll drive to the same place you are."

"What do I do when I get there?"

"I'm going to call a doctor friend of mine. I'm going to give him your phone number and tell him what's going on with Jake. He'll call and meet you at the address I put in your phone. Drive carefully. Jake needs medical care and doesn't need to end up in a ditch on the road."

"I will," she said. "I promise."

I looked in the Nissan truck ignition to make sure the keys were there. I jumped in and started the engine, then ran back over to April, who was putting the Silverado in reverse to back out.

"Take care of him, April. I'll see you in a bit."

CHAPTER FIFTY-SEVEN

I drove the Nissan truck back to Q-Man's with the headlights on. There was no need for stealth this time. I glanced at the time. 2:45 a.m. I slowed to turn into Q-Man's unpaved driveway and drove to the house like I thought Flip-Flop would if he were returning to report to his boss.

I neared the house and saw Deputy Tyler's official Sheriff's vehicle was gone. So was Tyler's body. Q-Man's Camaro was the only car in front of the house.

I turned off the Nissan, readied my Glock, and walked to the door. No need to burst in this time. I opened the door quietly and went inside. The light dangling above the table was still on, but Q-Man wasn't in his chair. The Draco rested on the table, along with a deck of playing cards, and the empty beer bottles. I knew it was an inanimate object unable to kill without human guidance, but the Draco still seemed menacing. I had seen what it did to Deputy Ronnie Tyler's body. I felt threatened by its mere presence.

I heard a toilet flush and turned to see a door open.

"Take care of that loose end?" Q-Man said before he looked up.

"Pretty much," I said. "Why don't you have a seat, James Lee."

The surprise on his face turned into a wide grin.

"Well, look who's here. I didn't expect you so soon, Mr. D.A."

"That's surprising, James Lee, because I got your invitation. The Little League clipping you were thoughtful enough to send. I also want to thank you for the two GPS trackers you gave my wife and me." I paused. "By the way, your buddy is not coming back."

"Who you talking about?" he said.

"Flip-Flop."

"That fool? I don't know what that boy's up to half the time." He smiled. "You want a beer or something?"

Keeping my Glock on him, I picked up the Draco, took a step toward the open front door, and tossed it outside.

"I want you to walk over to the table, James Lee. Slowly. Hands on top of your head with fingers interlocked. Like you did when they used to roust you at Parchman."

"Ain't you heard? I was a model prisoner. A wise and caring teacher, and an advisor to many. They hated to see me leave."

"I'm sure," I said.

I patted him down with my left hand. I wasn't sure exactly how to do it, so I mimicked the cops on Blue Bloods and Law & Order. I may have been a bit too personal in my execution, but I made damn sure he wasn't carrying a weapon.

"Sit down," I said after checking his chair and glancing under the table for a hidden gun. "Keep your palms down flat on the table."

I sat across from him, the butt of my Glock resting on the table, the business end pointed at his sternum.

"What did you do with Deputy Tyler's body?"

"Lots of people coming and going out here all hours of night and day, Mr. D.A. I can't keep up with everything."

"How did it work? Your deal with Tyler and the Sheriff?"

"Wha'chu talking 'bout?"

"Sammy selling meth out of his honky-tonk, Deputy Tyler picking up the money twice a week, coming back here to split it with you."

"Don't know anything about that Deputy Tyler's business," he said. "I left Parchman to get a fresh start, get back to my Tallabusha County roots, my family property. Like the way you feel about that big cotton farm in Sunshine your daddy left you. Land is a part of our heritage, you and me."

I wasn't going to get a straight answer out of James Lee.

"Just tell me why you did it," I said. "You did seven years in Parchman. Everyone else in the Sunshine courthouse, Judge Williams, Sheriff Lee Jones and his deputies, they all wanted you to serve a lot more time than I agreed to. When they busted you after the standoff at your Farmer's Home apartment, they found a bunch of cash, schedule two drugs, and enough guns to do a lot of harm. I'm the one kept you from doing twenty years in Parchman."

"Yeah? So you say."

"You know it's true. You're a smart guy, James Lee. You could have made something of yourself. Instead you killed my wife. She used to bring drinks and cookies for the team after our games. You knew her, knew she was a good person. Why did you have to kill her?"